Dead In Iraq

Eve Ottenberg

Plain View Press
P. O. 42255
Austin, TX 78704

plainviewpress.net
sb@plainviewpress.net
1-512-441-2452

ISBN: 978-0-911051-54-4
Library of Congress Number: 2008936012

Cover Image by Adrienne Ottenberg.

Fast Forward

The shell hit thirty yards away, and Animal went down immediately. He had been standing by his Humvee, waving to a small Iraqi child across the road, to whom he had just given a few hard candies, a bit sticky from the heat but still decently wrapped. He did not have his helmet on, and that, he realized at once, had been a mistake, because before he knew it, blood clouded his eyes, filled his mouth and throat, was all over his face, his hands, his chest, every part of him it seemed, but worst of all his head. He spat out a mouthful of blood so he wouldn't choke – he still had that much presence of mind – but then in no time it was gurgling in his throat again, filling his mouth, warm and salty, his twenty-three-year-old life's blood. Things did not get dark, they were dark from the instant he was hit. He did hear someone screaming, "Medic! Medic!" and thought it sounded like Edgar Ortiz. Maybe Edgar got hit too? Animal could not seem to focus on this question. He was beginning to dream about his mother, about home in Anne Arundel County, Maryland. It was summer and he and his friends had gone to the pool. He was just ready to dive in when he heard Edgar's voice, right in his ear, "you're going to make it, buddy. The medic's here. Hang on, Animal." The water in the pool gleamed aqua; overhead leafy trees, the kind he had not seen in months, swayed in a warm breeze. Harry, in the deck chair next to him, was bragging that he was the Halo champ of the county. "No way," Animal contradicted and gave him a friendly shove on the shoulder. Overhead strange and beautiful white birds had begun to appear. "Funny," Animal mused. "I never saw them around here before." One flew down and lit on the back of the chair in front of him, settled its snowy white wings and cooed at him.

He strained to hear it, but Harry talked too loudly, bragging that he had beaten every level many times, that no one could match his score, and then, every few seconds there was the loud, panicky voice of Edgar Ortiz, "hold on, Animal. You ain't goin nowhere. Hold on." He was aware that somehow someone assisted him in his next attempt to clear his mouth and throat of blood. Without help, he would have choked. "He's gonna lose that leg," Animal heard and then, "he'll be lucky if that's all he loses. Hey Animal, wake up! Stay awake!" Then he was back at the pool with his friends, the eight of them, laughing and joking, the strange white birds, whose cooing he had such difficulty making out, the warm breeze, the oneiric moment – but was it a dream? No, he really did see Harry and Kevin and the low-hanging branch of the tulip locust, in whose shade they found refuge from the June sun. Across the pool, in the lifeguard's seat, sat Anna, with whom he was still in love, but she didn't care, and so he had stopped life-guarding, so he would not have to see her so much. She had her whistle in her mouth, and her curls flashed gold in the sun. It rang out shrilly. She had ordered a rambunctious ten-year-old to stop dunking his pal in the sparkling water, the water that glittered like jewels beneath the sapphire sky, surrounded by flowers, tiger lilies mostly, the daffodils having gone by, and those gorgeous white birds everywhere. The place was paradise, even if Anna did not love him. He knew there was no place better, no place of more beauty or happiness; why, he wondered, had he ever left?

A hand wiped the blood out of his eyes, but he still could not see the ground, the dusty, sandy dirt he was laying on, the tire of his damaged vehicle or the medic's worried expression as he worked. Vaguely Animal knew all these things were there, *had* to be there, but he kept slipping back to the pool, he chose it, he preferred it – who wouldn't, who wouldn't prefer suburban splendor to this, to the dirt and chaos that was Iraq in 2004? He wanted to forget Baghdad and his forward operating base and his comrades and his gear and his ready-to-eat meals. He had never much liked this Middle Eastern megacity; he came from a quieter place, one that was sleepy and peaceful, where people did not kill each other, did not abduct their neighbors, torture and kill them and throw their mutilated bodies into roadside ditches. He wanted to return to the gentle greenness of Crofton, of what he had read was now called exurbia. That was all that he wanted – his parents, their small colonial house, his younger brother, his friends from high school, his job in web design, weekends at the pool and now, he realized with an ache of longing and sadness, he would never see any of it again, never get back there. It had all been a dreadful mistake. He saw it now, what he had had and how he never should have left it.

"The water," he gurgled, trying to describe the pool to Edgar, how the water flashed in the late spring sun.

"He wants water," Edgar told the medic, who simply shook his head grimly and kept working. Animal tried to grasp Edgar's hand. His aim was to pull him closer, to whisper about the wonders of his suburban home, to convey, somehow, its unique goodness, to let someone know how much he loved it before he lost it forever. But Edgar misunderstood. He pressed his hand back, saying, "I'm glad we agree, Animal. You're not giving up."

But Animal already had. He was back in Maryland, in the TV room of his parents' house, watching the tube in shock and horror as the World Trade Towers, filled with people, crumbled into nothing. All eight of them, himself and his friends, crowded into the small room, not noticing the heat, their eyes riveted on the screen. "Somebody's got to do something," Harry said, and the room filled with strange, lovely white birds.

"He's gone," the medic said. "There's nothing more I can do."

One

Dorian Lenthican, aka Animal, let the screen door at the back of the house slam shut. He shoved the inside door to, flipped on the air-conditioning to counter the thick humidity that made the house feel like a steam bath, then raced up the stairs to the television room. Both his parents were at work and his little brother was in school, ninth grade, so his hurried footfalls filled the empty, two-story house. It was September 11, 2001, and he had left work early because of the attack. He grabbed the remote, and the picture came on. First one tower smoking, then the plane crashing into the other, then the images of one tower crumbling into dust, then the other. Animal punched Harry's number into his cell phone.

"Harry, you seeing this?"

"Nothing else, man. Nothing else all day."

"Get over here. And call the guys."

Animal returned to staring at the television. In the back of his mind he saw Harry Sullivan dialing Kevin, then Patel, Goodman, Luis, Jones – as they called Donald – and Paul. They were all twenty years old, had been in the same graduating class in high school, and none, except Luis Ignacio, were in the military. Chandra Patel and Paul Lirano were in college. Everybody else just worked. Most lived at home, contributed to the cost of groceries and had slid from the rhythms of school into those of their jobs, still hanging out with each other, enjoying the occasional wild party, but mostly keeping to the sleepy suburban pace they had grown up with. Nothing more exciting than the discovery of snake-heads in a local pond had ever happened in Crofton, Maryland, and these children of the middle-class basically liked it that way. Harry, Animal and Chandra were, in Mrs. Lenthican's phrase, "huge, hulking things." The others were not small, either. When the entire group gathered in the upstairs sitting room to play Doom, there was scarcely room to cross your legs.

Animal shoved the video-game equipment under the TV cart to make more space for his anticipated visitors. He was not sure why he had summoned everyone, but the impulse seemed right, and Harry's ready assent confirmed it. They had to view this atrocity together, look into each other's faces and find there some clue or perhaps even the entire answer as to what they should do. Because above all, something had to

be done. Of that he was sure. Whoever had perpetrated this horror had
to be found and had to pay, and he, Animal, was ready to go looking
for him, whoever he was, wherever he was. He was certain his friends
would agree on that much, that they could not just sit idly by. On his way
home, driving along Route 50, he had seen some men on an overpass,
waving an American flag. That, Animal believed, was not enough. They
could wave flags later, after they had seen the corpses of the criminals
who had caused planes full of people to fly into buildings full of people.
As Luis said, when he called Animal on his cell, "they did this to
Americans. What did we ever do to them?"

Slowly day turned to twilight. Animal's mother, who hated air-
conditioning, went around the house opening windows and turning
on fans. His friends trickled in. Outside late season fireflies lit the
sultry gloom, and rabbits hopped across the weedless lawn. A morning
dove cooed in a branch, swaying in the crepuscular breeze, by the
television room window. For what seemed like the twentieth time, the
little assembly of young men watched one of the towers crumble. Then
came some footage of people jumping to their deaths – young men like
themselves, middle-aged women like their mothers; the images of these
people stranded high above the concrete pavement, desperate to escape
the roaring inferno behind them, with no help anywhere in sight, caused
Kevin to grind his teeth and pound his fist on a chair. The other seven
watched speechless, until a red-eyed Mrs. Lenthican came in, a wad of
tissues in one hand and a pitcher of lemonade in the other. Her cousin,
who worked at the Pentagon, had been killed in the attack. Animal never
thought much about Uncle Felix. When he was little, sandy haired Felix
had been a source of candies, trinkets and toys. He was a yearly presence
at Thanksgiving dinner, and the Lenthicans often visited him in Virginia
between Christmas and New Year's. They had shared a house at Bethany
Beach with him for a few summers, but that was long ago. More recently
the relationship had grown somewhat distant. It was now only Animal's
mother who kept in contact, but she did so faithfully, visiting him every
couple of months on a weekend afternoon, schmoozing over coffee
and pie and gossiping about the rest of the family. Now he was dead,
incinerated by the burning fuselage of a passenger jet. Animal took the
pitcher of lemonade and filled Styrofoam cups for all his friends. He
did it quietly. His mother did not like them getting rowdy, and at that
moment he did not want to upset her. Besides, anything other than a
silent, horrified shock was the last thing anybody was capable of. What

they all wanted was clarity, the ability to think precisely and accurately about what had occurred and what they should do about it.

Animal, towering over his mother, tried to comfort her by putting an arm around her shoulder. "They don't know for sure, yet, about Felix," he said. "You shouldn't jump to the worst conclusion."

Isabelle Lenthican wiped a tear. "One of his coworkers called Annie. He told her. He was sure about Felix." There came the sound of one strangled sob, then Isabelle blew her nose. "I'm going back downstairs to sit with your father. He's pretty stunned about Felix and doesn't have the heart to watch the news in the kitchen."

The seven young guests sipped their lemonade grimly. Another picture of the doomed, stranded high on the walls of one of the World Trade towers, flashed on the screen.

"Couldn't they have gotten helicopters?" Sherwin Goodman asked, "or something, to rescue those people on the window ledges? And what about everybody trapped on the floors above where the plane crashed – couldn't they have rescued them off the roof with helicopters?"

No one said a word. At length Luis spoke up: "Well, I guess I'll be shipping out to the Middle East pretty soon."

"I'll be there with you," Harry said. "I'm enlisting first thing tomorrow."

Chandra nodded approvingly. "Business administration may have to wait." Chandra had long been regarded as one of the brains in the group. If he was considering leaving college for war, then they all had to take it that much more seriously.

"War," Luis said, and pointed to the image of one of the towers collapsing. "That's what that means."

They watched the news far into the night. Various politicians had their moments before the cameras. Intelligence experts, newsmen, firemen, ordinary people in the street – all made their appearance and expressed their opinions. Finally very late, there were only Animal and Jones, who yawned and reminded his host that they both had work in the morning. Animal walked through the darkened house with his friend, the rooms and halls filled with the dense, shadowed breath of slumber. Fans whirred and night breezes gently tossed the curtains through open windows. This was his home. Animal loved it. At that moment, more than anything else he did not want to leave, but he already knew in his heart, as surely as he knew what they meant to him, the three sleepers whose dreams and somnolent shiftings and turnings so transformed the house, knew that he was going to war.

Jones paused on the darkened threshold. "You'll be signing up I guess."

"Looks like it."

"But maybe…" He paused, his pale, freckled skin and red hair glowing luminously from a nearby streetlamp. "Maybe it's not really war stuff. I mean, from everything we saw, it's clear that it wasn't another country that attacked us. It was this gang, they think. This criminal gang."

"Some country has to be behind it."

"You think?"

Animal nodded. "But if you're not sure, don't enlist."

"Oh, I never thought I'd say this, but I may very well enlist." The pale forehead wrinkled in worry again. "I'm just not sure about using the army to go after a gang."

"You heard Chandra. We'll be bombing Afghanistan before you know it."

Jones sighed and looked off into the darkness, his pale gaze no longer accessible to his friend. "I just hope they get it right."

"They? Who?"

His blue eyes shifted back to Animal. "The ones in charge of dropping the bombs." With that he turned and walked away, quickly vanishing in the night.

As he lay in the dark, thinking about all the people who had perished that day and his resolution to enlist because of them, Animal recalled that he had promised his mother that he would apply to college this fall. He had made good money at his computer job and had saved thriftily. Unlike Harry, who had been amassing credits at the community college while he worked, Animal had taken his time entirely away from school. Isabelle had urged him to apply to the University of Maryland, to the Baltimore, College Park or Towson campus and to Frostburg State, and finally, that, summer, he had felt ready to face school again. Never a star student, Animal had been a good athlete, but not good enough to make up for mediocre grades.

One friend of his, Mathew from the football team, had gone to the University of Pennsylvania. Animal had been awed by this acceptance into the Ivy League and could never seem to match up Mathew the stellar student with Mathew the party boy who excelled at sports and dated a cheerleader. They had not kept in touch. Mathew moved in a different world now, breathed the rarified air of an elite institution. Animal felt certain that the mass murder that morning would not lead Mathew to enlist. And then he was ashamed of the assumption. It seemed cynical and cheap. Who knew? Mathew was a corporate finance major. He might have worked in the World Trade center that summer. He might have been killed or maybe people he knew had been. Perhaps at that very moment Mathew lay in his bed thinking that corporate finance would wait while he joined the marines. Perhaps they would meet again in basic training, the easy-going camaraderie would revive, the years in the Ivy League would not stand between them, they would play Doom in their spare time, or maybe Myth, if they had access to a computer. Mathew, Animal remembered, loved Myth, had played it in high school over the internet with computer nerds in Finland and a househusband in Germany, who had to pause the game periodically when he went somewhere to pick up his kids.

What did Mathew think about the day's events? What would he do? Animal could not get these questions out of his mind as he lay in the shadows, faint moonlight silvering the bedside window frame and fainter starlight visible in the heavens. A gentle fragrance from late blooming flowers in his mother's garden wafted in on the night breeze, freighted with more questions, not just about Mathew but about people like him, the people who ran things, politics, the government, the universities, the military. What did they think? What would they do? He thought of red-headed, freckle-faced Jones with his doubts, his questions, his possibilities that those in charge might just get it wrong. How like Jones to view things that way; but what if those people did, if today's terrible events set even more in motion? What then? Animal could not imagine.

Over the next few weeks Animal found himself more and more attached to home and more and more reluctant to enlist. He had taken to helping his little brother Sandy with his world studies homework, the one subject in which Animal had, for some reason unaccountable to himself, excelled. After all, he had no particular interest in history, but somehow it all made sense to him, and he had a good memory for it. All this came back as he quizzed Sandy or helped him with his papers. Unfortunately, he could not assist with math or biology, having barely passed those subjects. Throughout his entire high school career, he had never gotten above a C in math, something all his teachers professed not to understand, insisting that he somehow exhibited aptitude for it.

How they divined this mysterious aptitude, he never knew. His English teachers claimed the same thing. But not his Spanish instructors, no. There the agreement had been unanimous. Animal had not a trace of talent for foreign languages. He had no ear, no memory for vocabulary, could not get the hang of another language's grammar and syntax. He was lucky they did not flunk him outright, but somehow they pitied him, gave him extra work to bring up his grades, and he got through. "Average or below average," he told Sandy. "That's what I am. But you've got the knack for all these subjects. What happened, Ma?" He demanded of Isabelle, with mock irritation as she passed by the table where he helped Sandy study. "How'd you produce this bright light here, after a dim bulb like me?"

"You were good at history," his mother remarked.

"I was an oaf then, and I'm an oaf now."

"I don't think an oaf could do such a good job of clarifying the social systems of ancient Egypt and Mesopotamia," Sandy objected.

"Mesopotamia was my favorite," Animal mused.

"Maybe someday you'll go there, see the ruins," Isabelle said.

"Maybe someday."

When he finished with Sandy, he took a beer out back onto the patio. The humidity enveloped him like a warm, damp blanket, but he didn't mind. He had grown up in Maryland and was used to mid-Atlantic summers and early fall. He sprawled in a lounge chair. It was dusk, and the fireflies had come out, lighting the gloom with little, cheerful flashes of yellow. Rabbits hopped in the bushes, and across the way something, most likely a raccoon, clawed and rattled the neighbors' old-fashioned metal garbage cans. Suddenly, out of nowhere, an enormous deer bounded across the back yard. "You're going the wrong way," Animal addressed it. "That's the highway. You'll get hit. The park's back there."

Isabelle came out with a glass of red wine. "You're not an oaf," she said.

"Don't worry. I was just fooling," he sipped his beer. "My self-esteem's just fine."

"I don't like it. You joke like that about yourself a lot."

"It's just that, a joke."

They sat in the twilight and talked about work. Isabelle was an assistant in a doctor's office and always had some shocking tale of accident or illness. To Animal, Dr. Shoreton and Dr. Bolano, both internists, were practically family. He had heard about their doings since elementary school. Currently they were considering changing their practice from internal medicine to gastroenterology, taking new doctors on board, accepting no new internal medicine patients and so forth. What Isabelle only rarely mentioned was how much time she spent at the office thinking about her sons, and when she did mention this topic, it was a prelude to a serious discussion about some worry of hers.

"I was thinking about you today, Dorian."

He almost replied that she shouldn't waste her time thus, but stopped himself, considering that any such self-deprecation would make her anxious, would lead to an anatomization of his feelings about himself and would add to her conviction that in some profound way, her son was not happy.

"I thought we should start requesting college applications. It was very wise of you to get those teacher recommendations last year, but we should start the application process early. Writing those essays takes time."

What she really wanted to know but did not ask, was, he saw, which school would he want to attend most – one where he could live at home and commute or one elsewhere in the state. And then, of even more concern, was his passing remark on the morning of September 12, that he might enlist. She had been so quiet on that topic that at first he wondered if she had heard him. But then one evening, when his parents thought he had gone out, he had heard them discussing it.

"If he wants to join the military, we can't stop him," his father said. "He's twenty, Isabelle. You have to let go a little."

"Yes, but there's also going to be a war. He'll get killed."

"How can you say that like it's a certainty?"

"I just feel it."

"He's a serious kid. He wants to do what's right, and you have to let him."

He had slipped softly out of the house. No one had mentioned the military in weeks. Now his mother sat on the patio with him in the gathering darkness, in her jeans and T-shirt, drinking wine and waiting for him to say that yes, he would apply to college, that he would not go to some dry, dusty, hot Middle Eastern country to be shot or blown up by a suicide bomber, that he was still seriously considering living at home and commuting to school, that she and his father and Sandy meant more to him than anything, that he would stay with them, not risk his life, not be changed into a killer, a soldier, forever scarred by the terrible things he had seen and done, that nothing meant more than the time with his family, in his hometown, with his friends, these sultry evening amid fireflies and crickets, every sound, everything in view old and familiar and speaking the peaceful word "home."

"I don't know what I'm going to do, Mom."

"Oh."

"But I'll get on it. I'll request the applications this week." He did not want to brush her off, nor did he want to lie, so he said no more about it, told her, instead, that Anna had agreed to go out to dinner with him Friday night. This puzzled her, so he quickly explained that now they were just friends and, as such, could go out for a meal in all innocence, with no expectation on his part that anything other than friendship would ever come of it.

Then she said something that made him regret choosing this topic: "You never know."

"But I do. It's over, Mom. She's got somebody else."

His mother shook her head in disagreement or disbelief, her salt and pepper hair, down to her shoulders, rippling in the moonlight. She said no more on the subject, but he knew that she clung, almost fiercely, to the idea of him and Anna, knew how much she liked and approved of the girl, how much she had hoped they would stay together.

Animal sighed and drank his beer. Suddenly, out of nowhere, a very light rain started up. Isabelle let out a little shriek and darted under the awning over the back door. But her son did not move. The water pattered down, its touch delicate and refreshing, and it released wonderful odors from the ground, the scent of wet plants and damp earth, of spring, even though it was late September.

"Dorian, get out of the wet!"

"I like it, Ma. It means," he teased, "I can skip a shower tonight."

"Not if you don't want to offend everyone at work tomorrow. You need soap, my boy." She retreated into the kitchen, from which a yellow rectangle of light stretched out the window to the patio. Rain grew stronger and rattled the grill's cover. The fireflies had disappeared. Animal threw his head back and opened his mouth. He wanted to stay there all night, had no desire even to go out with his friends, just wanted his back yard, warm and watery, with the leaves rustling in the rain, the puddle forming by the door step, Sandy's skate board dripping under the window and later, ancient Mesopotamia in the family room, conversation with his father, a video game, his mother's hand on his shoulder as she reminded him that he had to get up in the morning, leftover pizza in the fridge and the inviting familiarity of the bed he had slept in his entire life. "I guess I'm just a homebody," he said to the rain.

The next night he biked with Kevin and Sherwin to the gym. They lifted weights and ran on the treadmill for an hour and a half, then showered and biked to the sub shop. Sherwin had an idea for a start-up, some kind of online magazine, the esoteric niche of which Animal could make neither heads nor tails of. But he wanted to be encouraging, so he just kept mumbling "sweet," "terrific," "awesome," as Sherwin rambled on about the investors it would attract and the market it would serve.

"Did you catch any of that?" Kevin asked, when Sherwin went to the restroom.

"Uh, not exactly."

"Me neither, but I think I'm roped into it."

"I'd say so."

"You too."

"Un-hunh. I gathered that as well."

"Just so long as we don't have to put up any money –"

"'Cause if we do, I'm gone."

"Deal."

They biked back to the trim little townhouse where Kevin lived with his mother. Monica Dawn worked for a publishing company and traveled the region, setting up book fairs at elementary schools. It was hard work, and she always looked tired, but she adored Kevin and never complained, even when she was trying to sleep, while her son and his friends roared and hollered over the progress of their video games. She always made them feel at home. She never had a cross word about a four a.m. arrival or a midnight pizza run. Kevin joked that she wanted him never to leave, to live there with her for the rest of his life. They all knew it was true.

Somehow Animal, on a trip to the fridge, encountered her alone at the kitchen table. "Who had this terrible idea to enlist?" She blurted out. Animal averred that he thought it had been Harry. Elbow on the table, she leaned her head in her hand and gazed up at him. Only then, pausing to glance into her face, did he realize how exhausted she looked. Her beringed eyes, her pallor made her look much older than fifty. "Are you enlisting?"

"I don't know, Mrs. Dawn. I'm having a hard time with it. And my mother really doesn't want me to."

"No kidding."

"I don't like to cross her," he went on, "but this is so big. After what happened, I really feel like I should just *do* something."

"Like run out and get yourself killed."

"That's not a guarantee."

"But it sure increases the odds over what is it, web design?"

"Yeah. That's my job. But what happened on September 11, I can't just walk away from. It's too horrible. It cries out, like in the Bible, the blood crying out to God."

"They are criminals, who did that. Criminals. And the police catch criminals. Not the army. This whole rush to enlist is a big mistake. I wish you wouldn't do it. I wish you'd tell Kevin not to do it."

"I'm sorry, Mrs. Dawn."

"Of course you are. You're a good person, and you want to do what's right, but what you don't see is that something like the military, it's bigger than you. It's huge, it's impersonal. And a war, somewhere in a part of the world where people hate us? Dorian, you might as well paste a bull's eye on your back and take a walk among fanatical Muslims," she paused and gnawed on her fist. "This can't lead to anything good, just a lot of dead, young Americans, caught up in a frenzy, not thinking straight, trying to do the right thing. Oh God, I have such a bad feeling about this."

Animal patted her on the shoulder.

"And our leaders," she went on, "they're just not up to the job. If they were, September 11 never would have happened."

"They may not be," he said, "but *we* are."

She cast him a woeful, worried glance. "You have a responsibility to your family not to do anything rash, anything misguided."

"Have you said this to Kevin?"

"Twenty times a day."

"You might want to let up."

"If you think that would be more effective, I will." She ran her fingers through her thick dark hair, which, Animal observed, was two-toned, gray at the roots. "The world is yours," she said softly. "You're at the age. If you go to college, find a decent career, you, Kevin, your friends, you won't be breaking your backs at fifty like me. You have everything before you. You haven't made any big mistakes. True, you're getting started on college a little late, but that's okay. Kevin wants to go to UMBC. He might even live on campus. Pre-law, that's what he wants. To be a big defense lawyer, stand up for the little guy, or the environment. Where he got this, I don't know, certainly not in high school, when he almost flunked out in tenth grade. But he pulled himself together the last two years, got decent marks. For what – so he can go die in a desert?"

She paused to sip her herbal tea. "I look at him now and I see a cloud over him, the shadow of death."

"Don't you think that's maybe a bit, uh, melodramatic, Mrs. Dawn?"

"I hope so," she sighed. "We've been so close, ever since he was born. If anything ever happened to him...I just don't know."

There came a deafening war whoop from the basement, as Kevin beat Sherwin at F zero X. He thundered up the stairs. "You're looking at the new champ," he hollered.

"Aw that's just a racing game," Animal said. "Who cares about that?"

"You did when I beat your ass twenty minutes ago."

"Kevin!"

"Sorry Mom."

Sherwin trudged forlornly up the steps, muttering something about winning some and losing some, hearing which Kevin began hopping around in a sort of victory dance, even tried to pull his mother out of her chair, but she remained resolutely glued to it. At length Animal observed that he had to rise early for work the next day, that he had a big project and had to be sharp.

"Wuss. You just don't want to get beat again," Kevin teased. They started shoving each other, a mock brawl, until Monica intervened with a reminder that Kevin too needed his sleep.

Outside, Animal glanced up at the billions of stars. It was a clear night, and they spangled the black heavens, making him feel small and insignificant in the vastnesses of time and space at which they hinted. "Little planet earth," he murmured, and a sudden wave of emotion, attachment to his home, his family and friends, Monica Dawn, to Central Maryland with its sticky hot summers and short but unexpectedly cold winters, with its small houses, cape cods and colonials, its townhouses on cul de sacs, the nearby highway that led to Annapolis and others that led to Baltimore or Washington D.C., its lawns, trees, maples, tulip locusts, evergreens – the hemlock on the corner of his street in whose cool shadows he hid as a child playing hide and seek – this wave of feeling crashed over him, and he wondered how he would ever extricate himself and did he want to, and what would the army be like?

He swung onto his bike, Sherwin behind him, and they glided through darkness, through the somnolent development that stretched out for many, many acres around them. Everyone slept, dreaming of commutes on Route 50 or the Beltway, of their just past vacations on the Delaware shore on in overcrowded Ocean City, Maryland, of their children back in school or their work or their bills, or maybe they dreamt about dying, as he had been doing recently, about people incinerated on planes and in buildings, about people jumping from sixty stories and vaporized on the ground into a pink mist. He had seen little identity pictures of the victims in the newspaper, little black and white rectangles that floated through his sleep along with dreams of his own death, by drowning or bullets or falling off a high building. Lately he had begun waking up thinking, "I just died," and the memory of water in his nostrils or his body hurtling through air would be right there with him, but not at all a source of panic. He was never in a sweat about it. On the contrary, in his dreams he accepted it as inevitable and with a kind of curiosity, night after night, sleep, dream, die, wake. In one dream that had recurred several times, he stood in a flimsy beach house too close to the shore. The waves got bigger, became mammoth, rocked the house, but he did not flee. Instead he stood at a second-story window and watched the water rise, until eventually, it swept over him, filled his lungs, and his eyes flew open, but he would not at first recognize his warm bed in the shadowed, slumberous house. He would be puzzled about why he wasn't dead and what had happened to all that ocean water. On he pedaled, down sleeping streets, wondering if the houses, full of dreams, contained one whose dreams resembled his.

At the edge of the development, by the deserted main road, Animal and Sherwin parted, each going in the opposite direction. Animal coasted along, waiting for his turn-off, and finally swung into a web of quiet suburban lanes that stretched around him for miles. Huge, hulking old trees shaded the streets with their dark masses piled high, indistinguishable from the night sky above. Here and there street lamps cast weak circles of light, oases of visibility, where Animal paused now and then to get his bearings. Not that he really needed to – he had bicycled these lanes since he was four years old – but he liked the inviting feeling of the light, as if, long ago, someone had considered this moment, him coming home late, and had wanted to light the way, so that his journey would not entirely be through shadows.

At one such light, he paused to look at the Alden's house, a mansion by any standard, but older, built fifty years ago, and quite different from the mega-houses then in vogue. It was in the Tudor style, with lots of stone and pointed gables and a vast garden where, in spring and summer Mrs. Alden and sometimes her investment banker husband could be seen, pulling up weeds. When Animal was about ten, he used to engage them in conversation, and once Mrs. Alden had cut an armful of gladiolas, purple, orange, vermilion, for him to take home to his mother. That had been some trick, riding his bike home while balancing an enormous sheaf of gladiolas. After that, he always politely declined the offer of blossoms.

He pedaled on, down streets dark and silent except for the whoosh of rubber bicycle tires on asphalt, past house after house asleep in the shadows, until he came to the swim club. He turned in there, rode across the empty parking lot, circled idly under the street lamp, then approached the wire fence. Through it he made out the muffled shapes of tables and chairs, the long low shed that served as locker rooms for women and men, the other low building that housed the office and snack bar. He discerned the rough shape of picnic tables past the empty pool and, looming over it, at regular intervals, the gleaming poles of the high lifeguards' seats, where he and Anna used to face each other across an expanse of water that their feelings for each other shrank to nothing, for four years, starting in tenth grade. As he gazed at the nocturnal, abandoned scene, it all rushed back so vividly that he caught his breath and grabbed the fence. It seemed he saw her, legs crossed, pale and beautiful, lounging in the sun once again.

She held a can of Coke and smiled up at him as he stood, dripping and laughing and toweling off, beside her lounge chair. They had just finished eleventh grade, and summer stretched before them, a succession of afternoons like this one, just like the previous summer, just like the next summer and on, in Animal's mind, indefinitely. He saw no reason for it to change, and Anna, he thought, was happy with it too. At least she was then. She rested her Coke can on the grass and began slathering on more sunblock, something she had to do often, or her pale skin would burn. She moved forward, and he sat behind her, to apply the lotion to her back.

"So the movie tonight sounds good?" He asked.

"Sure, after I help Leonard pack." Leonard, her older brother, had been home for a few weeks from Penn State. He was a hopeless slob.

His room even outdid Animal's – all the clothing on the floor, plates with old food everywhere, papers strewn about, money scattered hither and yon. Mrs. Reilly refused to pick up after him, saying that he was grown man and had better learn how to keep his own room. So now, before he moved into a dorm in Washington D.C., provided for federal government summer interns, he was desperate to straighten things up and pack. So he had offered to pay Anna twenty dollars if she got the room looking normal. Anna, thrifty and sharp, always on the lookout for a bargain, had taken him up on it at once. But she did so holding her nose and confiding to Animal that the room "beat the Augean stables." The worst part, she explained, was that Leonard had bad allergies, and he left his used Kleenex everywhere, so she had taken to wearing latex gloves. Animal had volunteered to help her, and this, for some reason, put Leonard to shame.

"Aw geez Ann, you didn't have to drag in your boyfriend," he moaned, the first time he caught sight of Animal sifting through the debris.

"Yes I did," she snapped, "and be glad I'm not making you pay him, too."

They had spent several late afternoons sorting through Leonard's junk; Leonard, whom Animal had always envied for his closeness to Anna, now swung into view, his extensive sci-fi collection, his computer games, the papers for his classes in government, his major, which Animal picked up from the floor, scanned and rescued from the trash – all clarified his character, helped Animal get to know him, so that he now looked forward to their passing pleasantries as an opportunity to get Leonard's opinion on Asimov's *Foundation* series, of Clinton's welfare overhaul or how often he beat Starcraft. He discovered that he liked Leonard, in a way that was very similar to how he had found out about Anna, piece by piece, one small bit of information at a time, until, all at once, he realized he had a complete picture before him, a picture that had begun to fascinate him, one from which, in Anna's case, he could not look away.

"So he's ready to go finally," Animal queried, still rubbing sunblock into her shoulders.

"Finally. I'll miss him. But he said we should come down to D.C. on the weekends. His friends know all the good, cheap places to eat."

"I didn't think there were any."

"Me neither. I always come home from D.C. hungry."

"Cheapskate."

"Well, I'm not about to drop twenty dollars for a sandwich and a beverage. I might as well stay here and go to Starbucks, save five dollars."

"That place is so overpriced. Too bad their coffee's so good."

They sat, palavering aimlessly about this or that, Animal continuing to rub her back, long after the sunblock excuse could even remotely be cited. Their friends milled around the pool. The sun beamed down from an azure sky, dotted by an occasional silver or white cloud, and Animal, surveying this, and how the orange of the tiger lilies floated in the green garden and set off the gold of Anna's hair, the yellow and white lilies off to one side, the rosy toddlers in bathing suits, gorging on pizza and ice cream at the snack bar, the rose bushes blooming by the fence – it made Animal think of Faust, which Anna had forced him to read, and of Faust's fateful cry, "stay this moment." That was what he wanted, for it never to end, for it not to pass into the next and so on until he reached the end of his mortality, but for it to stay, here, now, bright flowers, laughing children, painfully beautiful Anna, forever.

Anna was a reader, an A plus English student who did not hesitate to recommend books to her less literate boyfriend. But Animal did not object. All the books she put before him had great merit – he could see that. And some, like *Faust*, had scenes that came to him in moments of epiphany, when he connected some powerful feeling with some literary remark, some quote or descriptive poetic passage. This was new to him. When he and Anna had started going out in tenth grade, all he read was Tom Clancy; he had read everything by that author and was, in fact, at loose ends in terms of reading matter when he asked Anna for a date. She had accepted, and that evening, after a movie, had lent him a copy of *Crime and Punishment*.

She kept him busy with an unending series of classics: *War and Peace*, *Our Mutual Friend*, *Little Dorrit*, *Lost Illusions*, until he adapted and learned to say that he was still reading a book long after he had finished. She was an admirer of nineteenth-century social realism, she told him, and he would smile patiently as she launched into a litany of this form's virtues over those of modernism. Her English teachers submitted her essays for state and national prizes, which she won, and she fully intended, on the strength of her English excellence, to attend the University of Maryland at College Park.

Unfortunately she was not an even scholar – her grades in other courses did not match up. She scraped by in math and barely escaped a

D in chemistry, managing, by volunteering to do extra work, to bring that grade up to a low C minus. She fretted over what such a spotty record would look like to an admissions committee. Animal tried to comfort her, pointing out her vast literary superiority to anyone else in the school and arguing that if, in her admissions essay, she stated her intention to major in comparative literature, the committee would overlook her science and math grades. But Anna, like his mother, was a worrier. By her senior year, she had almost convinced herself to give up on the university and simply set her sights on community college. Animal, from the best motives but in the end to his own serious detriment, bolstered her confidence, told her she was too good for anything but a four-year university, tried to talk her into "following her dream," and ultimately prevailed.

Anna, in turn, encouraged him to think of a future as a history professor, or, if that was too onerous, or in Animal's words, "highly improbable," a high school history teacher. He played along with this fantasy to humor her, without ever perceiving how pivotal it was to her plans with him. But he had no intention of teaching in a college, high school or day care center, as he put it to Harry, who agreed that teaching was simply too unpleasant. It was bad enough sitting in class, learning, "can you imagine actually standing up there and doling the stuff out, yelling at kids like us for talking or the special ed kids for cutting up? Yikes. I go kinda cold all over just thinking about it." So did Animal, whose most ardent wish was that when he graduated high school, his formal education would end, forever. He liked football, he liked history, but that was it. No day was happier for him than the one on which he removed his cap and gown and entered the job market.

When he had accepted the volume of *Crime and Punishment* that cool autumn night in the beginning of tenth grade, outside the movie theater, he had no idea of what he was getting into. All he knew as he gazed into Anna's crystal blue eyes was that he had somehow wangled a date with the most beautiful cheerleader, well, ex-cheerleader – she had quit to concentrate on her grades – on the team. He gazed at her mop of blond curls, her long athletic legs, delicate hands and remarkable cheekbones and wondered how he had managed it. Would he read it? Of course he would read it. He would have said yes to reading the Encyclopedia Britannica if she had asked, or to changing his career goals from computer troubleshooter to rocket scientist. He would have taken up Chinese or quit the football team. But fortunately she did not ask these things; her demands were moderate, and he slipped, all too happily, into fulfilling them and, without knowing it, into a four-year, serious relationship, his first and hers, and one that they both, by the end of eleventh grade, assumed would end in marriage.

What he had realized early on and tried to ignore, as it was a source of exquisite anxiety, was that he needed her more than she needed him. "Animal," she had said at that moment, "you got your nickname from the way you play football. But I like Dorian better. I'm going to call you Dorian." He had not dared argue; there was something, just an elusive hint in her tone of a take-it-or-leave-it attitude, which, in the instant he detected it, became in his mind a nagging, little, half-real threat. Take it or leave it translated somehow, in some deep subterranean layer of anxiety that he had never felt before to "my way or the highway," or "I can take you or leave you." He did not know what prompted the fear, but once articulated in his mind, it was most tenacious. It led him into a little thicket of lies, about his ambitions, about being a history teacher, about college, in all of which she delighted – oh, how her blue eyes would sparkle as she made plans for his future and then, the moment he was alone in his own, poster-filled room again, his lazy, easy-go-lucky nature reasserted itself, a nature he knew he would not be able to remake in the image she had for him and his hopes for their future became ashes.

Overall, however, things went so well for them that Animal was able for the most part to smother this unexpected fear, to drown it at the source, the spring of his emotions, and, over time to forget about it. He and Anna got on so well. They discussed her beloved books, went to movies, studied together, and she even came to his games, which, considering what it had meant to her to quit cheerleading, was no small thing. And then, senior year, at the biggest game of the season, the cheerleaders came out and there was one extra, tall, lithe, with a mop of gold curls. She had done it for Animal, got the coach to let her participate just that once, and this gesture so overcame him that he nearly lost his concentration and fumbled. But he quickly pulled himself together and went on to make the winning play. "I did it for you, because you were there," he told Anna afterward.

It was the same with the books. He read them, at first anyway, because it so obviously meant so much to her. "But what do you think of Svidrigailov?" She had asked, as he labored through *Crime and Punishment*. To her the characters were so vivid, they were like real people. She talked about them as if they existed, and thus, in her vibrant enthusiasm for them, seemed to reaffirm something he caught the hint of when he read about them and that he thought of as their eternal life, eternal but sporadic, existing only, at any given time, in the mind of their readers. She was more interested in Clenham or Lucien de Rubempré than she was in her schoolmates. And now, with Animal, she had someone she could share these literary creations with, discuss their doings, pick apart their flaws and strengths. She became so animated that it infected him, that it would cause him to stay up late, just to see what Vautrin would do next. But he began to get bogged down with *The Bethrothed*, and when Anna lent him her well-thumbed copy of *Les Miserables*, he was dismayed to hear her commenting: "after you see what a masterpiece this is, you should compare it to *Remembrance of Things Past*, then tell me what you think of proto-modernism."

"*Remembrance of Things Past*," he murmured meekly, "isn't that the one you told me was several thousand pages long?"

She nodded. "It's a tour de force, of course, as you'll see –"

Inwardly he groaned.

"But you can't avoid the inescapable conclusion that modernism is a decline, a falling off from something far greater, in no way an improvement in the history of literature."

"No, no, of course not," he muttered and tucked *Les Miserables*, gigantic tome that it was, woefully under his arm.

At times like this she awed him. Her enthusiasm for these literary characters and the intelligence from which it sprang were admirable and utterly alien. He believed she would make a formidable professor of comparative literature, one who presented papers, published essays, taught, reviewed books. She would go to literary conferences in Italy, her opinion on texts would be sought by other experts. She would achieve no small renown. All this he envisioned and with it the little prickling of anxiety about where he would fit in this picture sprang back to life. For clearly, such an eminence as she would become could have no mere computer repair man as a husband.

Most of the time though, such unseemly worries were not felt. Animal spent his weekends with his girlfriend and his weeknights with his friends – when they all should have been doing homework, they were whooping and hollering over video games. All the guys just assumed he would marry Anna some time after graduation.

"Marry her while she's young and beautiful, but don't have kids until later," Luis advised. "She'll lose her figure and never get it back. Look what happened to my older sister Nathalie." Indeed Nathalie was a byword – a former prom queen and Miss Maryland contestant, she had started her family before the age of twenty and had lost her looks by gaining an enormous amount of weight. Luis did not care how fat she became, he still adored her, but he had a clear-eyed assessment of what an extra hundred pounds meant for her, namely a straying husband, health issues and, as he succinctly put it to Animal, "her self-esteem's in the toilet." To which Animal replied, "well, none of ours is exactly sky high."

What he did not mention, however, was his certainty that Anna would never let herself go. She would be a two-child mother, max, he believed, and she would never lose sight of her waistline or her career. She had too much common sense and was too stubborn. "She's full of brains," as his mother said, "and she knows how to use them. Look how she snagged you." To which Animal would reply with an embarrassed and disbelieving "geez Ma," and then, joking, "it wasn't her brains, it was her looks." They would laugh, but they both knew that Anna had discerned in her boyfriend something good and reliable, trustworthy, faithful, serious, and she had set about making sure that it was securely hers.

Every day in June, July and August, they would sit on a lounge chair at the swim club and slather sun-block on each other. "I am determined not to burn," Anna would say, surveying her pale, freckled arms and legs, and in this, as in almost everything, except math and science, her determination paid off. She tanned a little, but never turned pink. Animal, on the other hand, browned. His thatch of blond hair was bleached even lighter by the sun, and he chuckled at Anna's summer nickname for him, "surfer-boy." Several times she came out to Bethany Beach with the Lenthicans, and while he never exactly lived up to his nickname, he got her hooked, as he was, on the boogie board. They would spend hours, riding the ocean waves, or lying in the sand, or sitting under the beach umbrella with Isabelle, Tom and Sandy, eating chicken salad sandwiches and drinking ice tea. "Middle-class paradise," Sherwin Goodman had said when Animal described it. "That's what it is, and I love it."

"What about ten kids?" Animal asked teasingly, as he and Anna, holding hands, strolled down the beach at the water's edge, the pale green ocean foaming and swirling up to their bare, sandy feet.

"You're out of your mind," she smiled, and then, with a hand to her forehead to shield her eyes, gazed out at the horizon. "Look, dolphins. Very sensible animals, one child at a time." A pod of the magnificent creatures leapt and flashed silver and black in the waves.

"Maybe not ten. Maybe three or four."

"Think college tuition."

Animal thought about it as a wave splashed up his leg and drenched his khaki shorts. "Maybe only two," he sighed. "Maybe you're right."

"I always am," she grinned and then raced him to the jetty, where they then spent a half an hour inspecting mussel shells, seaweed, barnacles and the occasional stray crab, something he had been doing his entire life, as long as he could remember, every summer, and something that never bored him.

At times he and his friends would drive out to the Chesapeake, where Animal had started collecting fossils when he was four. There were far fewer now, but still the occasional shark's tooth, iron gray, hard as stone and still sharp after millions of years, or prehistoric whale vertebrae might turn up. The water was dirtier here than the Atlantic, greasy sometimes, and a power plant loomed huge and ugly on the cliffs, but that did not stop him from wading in, if he saw some form that might be a fossil on the water's bottom. He, Harry and Kevin might spend hours on the scummy shore, turning over slimy pieces of driftwood, poking through rotted debris, eating their tuna sandwiches on whole wheat, their trail mix, their yogurt and Gatorade. It was always healthful potluck, seeing what Mrs. Sullivan had packed for their lunch.

"We're grown up, we can do it ourselves," Harry would insist.

"Nonsense. If I let you, it'd be pork rinds, chips and Slurpees from the Seven-Eleven, with Hostess cupcakes for dessert. No way, young man," Mrs. Sullivan brushed him off. "I'll pack your lunch, thank you very much." Harry's mother had been a hippie as a teenager, and the only vestige from those wild years was what Harry and his friends regarded as an unaccountable attachment to organic food. Harry always had snacks like sunflower seeds or flax wafers with his lunch. And he was well known to the entire high school cafeteria staff, because his mother had notoriously complained to the county about fat in their school food. She had further failed to ingratiate herself with the administration and students – and embarrassed her son – by starting a school-wide, parental campaign to improve the nutritional value of items sold in the vending machines. There were to be no more chips, honey buns, pop tarts, Milky Ways and sodas, no. There were to be trail mix, nuts and yogurt-covered raisins. "Good goin,' Sullivan," was a gripe Harry heard every time he approached one of the new, improved vending machines, as some teenaged boy looked in vain for a candy bar and pounded the Plexiglas in frustration.

But time passed and Animal and company forgot their Reese's Pieces and their Starbursts. They grew accustomed to sitting on a log by the edge of the turbidly brown Chesapeake and munching on dried fruit and nuts.

"Look," Animal shouted, pointing at a rusted metal cylinder, half-submerged in the bay, "part of the power plant."

"A fossil-to-be, in twenty thousand years," Kevin mumbled, his mouth full of food.

"It's metal, you idiot," Animal guzzled his blue Gatorade. "It won't last twenty years, no less twenty thousand."

"Don't look now, but there's a red salamander by your foot," Harry informed him.

"Can you eat those?" Kevin asked.

"Good God, Kevin," Harry blurted out in exasperation. "Can't you ever think about something else?"

"Yum," Animal said, watching the little red amphibian race from his foot back under the log, "toss it in a pan, with a little butter and garlic. Oh boy, I can hardly wait. Can you eat it – what kind of question is that?"

"If we discovered a woolly mammoth," Harry continued, "trusty old Kevin Dawn's first question would be, how we gonna fit it in the oven? Then he'd dibs the rib eye. Geez, if we found a dinosaur –"

"Enough," Kevin belched. "I'm not the only one who thinks about food."

"Yeah, but you're the only one who thinks about it all the time – " Harry began.

"And who regards the wonderful world of wildlife as the answer to the question, what's for my next meal?" Animal finished.

"Aw, I just wondered."

"Keep wondering. But not out loud."

They had a friend, a stocky, dark-haired fellow named Bradley, who was three years older and who, upon graduation, had joined the army. Bradley was a fanatical fossil collector, with friends, professional paleontologists and geologists, at the Smithsonian, who were glad to look over his finds and assess them and to do the same for Animal and his buddies. To Animal's immense pride, one of his prehistoric shark's teeth had made it into a Natural History Museum display. On many occasions Bradley accompanied them to the little, secluded strip of Chesapeake shore.

"It's been combed over real good," he said once, his hands on his hips, despite the taut dog leash in one of them, as he surveyed the beach and his Labrador strained for freedom. "Frankly Animal, I'm amazed you find anything here anymore." Bradley unleashed his huge dog, and the canine took off down the beach after some gulls.

"I got a new place I go," Bradley went on, "not far from Andrews Air Force Base."

Harry and Kevin crowded around. Animal worked to control his excitement. He knew Bradley frequented other, better fossil sites, but until then, the older fellow had never brought up the topic in an inviting way.

"I'm going over there tomorrow. If you're interested, I'll tell you where to meet me."

The three of them talked eagerly, all at once, but fell silent when Bradley launched into his description of the vast shallow sea that had, eons ago, submerged Maryland and of the deposits of marine life that could be unearthed, if only one knew where to dig. "I'm telling you, this is my best site. One of my friends got a trilobite."

"No way!" Animal exclaimed.

"Yup. Not one of the first trilobites, but they dated it, and let me tell you, that fossil was *old*."

Animal, Harry and Kevin stared at each other.

"We'll be there," Animal said. "Of course. Just tell us what to bring."

"All your gear," Bradley said. "All of it."

The next day they assembled with their picks and their shovels in an open yellow field off the highway, not far from an office park. Even at nine a.m., the sun was brutal, so Bradley and Animal wore pith helmets. The other two had baseball caps. Mrs. Sullivan had packed a politically correct lunch, and they snacked on unsalted nuts when they were not digging. Bradley was always strangely competitive about finds. There was no bad feeling in it, but it was unmistakable, and mixed with his superstitious fear of bad luck, of somebody somehow jinxing him, this made him a somewhat prickly companion. One had to be careful about him; so for the most part, they worked silently and understated their jubilation when they came across anything good. They had been working for an hour when Animal unearthed a layer of rock encrusted with fossils, flora and fauna that got Bradley so excited he visibly held his breath while dusting it off. He exhaled, stood up straight, put his hands on his hips. "This goes to the Smithsonian," he said, "with a little plaque – uncovered by Dorian Lenthican." He rubbed his hands happily. "Of course if you want to give credit to your three friends, you can do that too. After all, by finding this, you have, in the great scheme of things, limited what we'll be able to turn up today."

Behind Bradley's back, Harry whirled his forefinger round and round, pointing at his head and mouthed the word, "cuckoo." Animal suppressed a laugh. "Of course everyone gets credit," he said. "It was a group effort."

After this glorious find, Animal and his friends were very eager to get back to the site, though they never would have dreamt of going without Bradley and, more specifically, an invitation from Bradley. The stocky young man had proprietary rights, as it were, of which, although he never spelled them out, his younger friends were quite aware. To go without him, as Harry accidentally suggested one hot August afternoon, would "violate the paleontologist's code of conduct," Animal said.

"The what?" Harry stared at his friend in disbelief.

"You heard me."

"But we're not even paleontologists. We're amateurs. We don't even have a code."

"Yes we do. Besides it would be rude. And can you imagine how suspicious it would make Bradley? Why, he's already, already –"

"Psycho?"

"Superstitious enough."

"That's the understatement of the year. The last time I found a shark's tooth, he told me that from the cosmic, get this, karmic, perspective, that had been his find, and as a result, he wouldn't be able to find anything for the rest of the day. When he did, he dismissed it as a fluke."

They went only with Bradley.

At this site, Animal unearthed a trove of fossils, prizes he would spread out on the picnic table in the back yard to dust off and spruce up. Sandy and Anna were always agog and would lurk on the edges of his activity, asking questions.

"Paleontology – that's a kind of history," Anna offered one afternoon. But Animal avoided the painful and worrisome topic of his ambitions, or, rather, lack of them.

"This shell," he pointed to a broken bit of fossil he had just cleaned. "A good guess is it's over one hundred million years old. But the experts at the Smithsonian will fix the date exactly. And this," he held up a rounded bit of gray stone, "an ancient sea urchin, not all that different from the ones seen today, like the one you stepped on Sandy, at Sanibel Island."

"Gee Animal. Can I have one of these teeth? To put on my shelf in my room?" Sandy had a treasure shelf above his desk, which he kept neat and orderly. On it were shells, stones, odd souvenirs from vacations in Florida and upper New York State and several trinkets from the nearby NASA Goddard Space Flight Center gift shop. Sandy had a NASA T-shirt from that shop that he wore as often as he possibly could. "I got it at NASA in Greenbelt," he would tell his admiring friends, who never tired of his descriptions of the tour and the gift shop and many of whom talked their parents into similar visits and purchases. Quite a few boys in Sandy's class had NASA T-shirts.

"It's *the* thing," he told Isabelle, when she demanded that he don a different shirt. "I have to wear it."

Animal gave him a fossilized tooth and vertebra, and then demonstrated, with a little brush, how to clean them. A warm, dry breeze rustled the stand of bamboo behind them, taking the edge off the August heat. Though it was not humid that day, Animal was shirtless and barefoot, in khaki shorts only, and so was Sandy. Anna wore a tank top and shorts and had put on her glasses to inspect the items on the table. The sun blazed down on them from a cloudless sky, and a sheen of perspiration glistened on Anna's forehead.

"Better get the sun-block," Animal half joked. She was, he teased her, "sun-block obsessed."

Anna nodded, went to the back door and then into the house. The screen door slammed shut. Sandy glanced at him. "When you gonna tell her?"

"Tell her what, nosy?"

"Tell her you're going to be a computer guy?"

His eyes met those of his younger brother, periwinkle, like his, and he was surprised to see, mirrored there, his own sadness and worry. "I don't know," Animal mumbled.

"She won't like it. She has high expectations."

"Let's not talk about it."

Sandy's glance shifted away, as if he had glimpsed what Anna would regard as some future failure and was considering it. Then he delivered his young, preteen verdict. "If she doesn't like it, it doesn't matter. Don't beat yourself up."

Animal reached over and roughly tousled his younger brother's blond hair. "Think you're pretty smart for a twelve year old."

"Yeah," Sandy grinned. "I do."

"You're right. Here – start brushing this Pleistocene clam shell."

Anna returned with the sun-block, and after applying it to Animal, Sandy and herself, sat down and joined in the brushing and washing. It was a hot afternoon, but the crickets still chirped in the grass, an animal rummaged in the ramshackle shed buried deep in the bamboo and the deadly nightshade, which Isabelle had given up trying to extirpate, bloomed deep purple on the wire fence that separated the Lenthican's from the neighbor's yard. That was Mrs. Oldam, an aged and befuddled widow, who so feared ghosts that she turned out the lights and went to bed at seven o'clock on Halloween. It was she who, for some incomprehensible reason, had planted the deadly nightshade, bane of the Lenthican boys' childhood, when every time they approached the overgrown fence, Isabelle would fly out the back door screaming, "don't touch the purple flowers. Don't even get near them..." So thoroughly had they been indoctrinated with the terrors of the fence that even now, toddler years long gone, they would not dream of approaching it.

Cardinals bickered and flashed scarlet in the dogwood tree, and Isabelle came out with a pitcher of lemonade, screen door slamming, sandals flapping loudly as she approached to set it on a corner of the picnic table. She then decamped to the vegetable patch and commenced weeding.

"I'm sure the Smithsonian would pay you to do this kind of work," Anna quietly ventured.

Animal looked up, right into the level beam of Sandy's blue-eyed gaze, sharp and contemplative at the same time.

"Let's not worry about that," Animal replied gruffly, and then, showing her the bit of rock he was working on, "here – see those lines, that's the skeleton of a small marine life form."

"Maybe an eel?" Sandy asked.

"Something very like an eel." Animal replied.

Harry and Chandra dropped by, ensconced themselves in the shade of the umbrella on the patio, and kibitzed.

"Brush the big piece of rock."

"Don't waste your time on those little bits."

"Rinse it, Sandy."

"Hey," Animal called across the yard. "You wanna help or just give instructions?"

"Giving instructions is my forte," Harry said.

"So I've noticed," Animal grunted.

"Harry, Chandra, you could help me in the garden," Isabelle called out, sitting cross-legged by the tomato plants, tossing weeds into her compost pile.

"Sorry, Mrs. Lenthican, it's against my religion. You see my mother," Harry began.

"Edie, yes?"

"Well, she had a vegetable garden, but then she consulted some organic guru who works at Whole Foods, and he told her he would never eat anything that grew in the soil of suburban Maryland."

"Oh, for God's sake, why not?"

"Too much lead. All those years the cars had no lead emission standards – he said it poisoned the ground and gets in the vegetables. He won't even touch the soil."

Isabelle pushed back a wisp of gray hair, streaking her sweaty forehead with a brown smudge of dirt. "You tell Edie not to listen to this quack," she said. "If it's true in Maryland, it's true everywhere, even the produce in the supermarket would have lead in it. When gas had lead in it, it affected all cars – everywhere. So all the soil, in all the states, would have lead."

Harry chomped on his gum. "I'm just telling you what the health food aficionados believe."

"Well, ignore it and come weed these zucchinis, which are all, by the way, over a foot long. I'll let you take one home to Edie."

"For the reasons aforementioned," Harry popped on his gum, "I have to decline your offer of zucchini. However, I'll help you pull up some weeds."

"Not me," Chandra muttered. "I'm stayin' in the shade."

The afternoon passed hot and sunny, the breeze carrying a faint fragrance from Mrs. Oldam's garden. The raccoon – Chandra had ascertained it was a raccoon – rattled in the rotted shed, and sparrows fluttered noisily about the edge of the vegetable patch. Suddenly Harry loomed over the picnic table, shirtless, sweaty and soil-streaked, holding an enormous, bright green stalk of polk.

"Get it away," Sandy urged. "I'm allergic."

"That's one monster weed," Animal averred. "Proof of my mother's sporadic attention to her vegetable garden."

"What say you to a trip to the swim club?" Harry asked. "I'm melting."

"It's our day off," Anna explained. "We go there all the time. Give us a break."

"In a word, no," Harry chomped on his gum. "I won't go alone."

"It's rather hot," Chandra commented from the safety of the umbrella shade.

"Tropical," Animal put in.

"Cave, cave," Harry chanted at Anna.

"Oh all right," she relented. "I never win around here."

Later that evening the same group assembled in the backyard, as Animal and his father grilled burgers and hot dogs on the patio. Paul Lirano stopped by and, "don't mind if I do," scarfed down two cheeseburgers. Paul's father owned a small chain of computer repair stores in the area and had offered Animal a summer job, declined, however, as life-guarding afforded more opportunities to spend time with Anna. Fireflies lit the gloaming here and there, especially over by the bamboo and picnic table, now cleared of fossils. Neighborhood cats padded through the grass and one growled aggressively, crouching beneath the marigolds – planted to repel aphids – in the vegetable patch. High above the house bats dived and circled in the dusk. Their wings made a muted whirring. A few stars came out. Tom Lenthican held forth for a few minutes on the dot-com boom, then lapsed into pointing out the now visibly twinkling constellations. Chandra complained about mosquitoes, Harry indulged in some alarmist talk about West Nile disease, and soon the moon hove into view.

Two

They dug out by Andrews' Air Force Base. The sun, a roaring furnace in the sky, caused them to pause every five minutes or so, slurp Gatorade or Perrier and complain about their lot in life. Harry was most vociferous on this subject. His four-year-old cousin Benjie, love-child of a wayward aunt, lived with his family and had a big birthday bash, scheduled for tomorrow. Mrs. Sullivan had commandeered Harry's entire morning: he was to manage a house full of screaming, over-excited, four year olds, hyped up on cake and ice cream, and he could think of no excuse to get out of it.

"I'll help," Bradley volunteered. "In fact, I'll do the entire job."

Harry put down his shovel. "Seriously?"

"Seriously. I'm great with kids." Bradley turned his back to continue scraping at a ledge of sandstone. "They love me."

"I'm glad someone does," Harry muttered almost inaudibly.

"Say what?" Bradley asked.

"Nothing. Just swallowing. So they love you."

"Yep. You'll see."

Harry saw. Indeed he had never seen anything quite like it in his life. The next day Bradley arrived at the Sullivan house dressed as a chicken. It was quite the professional get-up, and the four year olds went wild. They mobbed the chicken, chased the chicken around the backyard, pelted the chicken with food, and went for piggy-back rides on the chicken. Bradley squawked, quite unconvincingly, Harry thought, but the children entertained none of Harry's doubts. They squawked back, crowded around and competed with each other to do what Bradley called "the chicken walk." As Harry stood on the back deck and watched the enormous chicken, with a line of ten screaming, pushing four year olds trailing behind, his mother Edie Sullivan came up next to him.

"Who is this Bradley?" She asked, staring at the antics in the yard.

"Just some lunatic I knew from high school. He's in the army now."

"Well then, you stay out of the military."

"Don't worry."

"I don't want you coming home dressed up as a turkey."

"Ha!"

"If you did, your father would probably eat you for dinner. You know he eats everything in sight, especially if it has wings. I'll probably have to protect this Bradley idiot from him."

"Do the chicken walk, squawk, squawk," Bradley roared and flapped his wings.

"Good God, I need a drink," Edie said and headed for the back door.

Later that afternoon, Animal dropped by. "Who's the chicken with the kids in the family room?" He asked.

"Bradley," Harry replied sourly. "We tried to get him to take off the costume two hours ago, but he refused."

"Let him keep it on. It's an improvement."

"But he's very demanding, says the get-up's hot. We have to keep the air on full blast. That's why it's frigid in here. And we have to keep him supplied with a steady stream of ice tea and lemonade, but that makes him have to go. He's holding it, because a trip to the bathroom would require getting out of the costume, and Mr. Chicken can't do that, oh no."

"Holding it?"

"Yeah. He's quite heroic and doesn't hesitate, the minute anyone over the age of four comes by, to go on at great length about it."

"Geez, how peculiar."

"Frankly, another word comes to mind, but I'll keep it to myself."

"You do that Harry," Edie waltzed by, waving a glass of red wine. "Your pal Bradley may be the biggest fruitcake on the mid-Atlantic coast, but you gotta hand it to him, he's kept the little monsters occupied all afternoon."

"He made me do the chicken walk."

"Oh sweetie, there are worse things in life."

"That's what you think. Thank God Animal wasn't here to witness my humiliation."

"Well, you'd both better hide or you're liable to be witnessing each other's humiliation. I was just in the family room and Mr. Chicken's lickin' to do another walk."

Harry grabbed Animal by the arm and pulled him to the front door. "We're going to your car," he explained. "We're gonna sit there. If he catches sight of us, we drive off."

"You can't leave, Harry," Edie, on the front porch, called down the steps after them. "I'll need you to manage the kids if Mr. Chicken decides to call it quits."

Harry and Animal spent an hour in the Toyota with the air conditioning on full blast, then quietly drove away to the ice cream parlor. When they finally returned, Edie was fuming. "He made me do the Chicken Dance, Harry Sullivan. That's what your friend Mr. Chicken did. I felt like a world-class idiot."

"Has he left?" Harry whispered, holding up crossed fingers.

"No, he hasn't left. He has no intention of leaving, now or ever. Nor does he have any intention of going to the bathroom, though he won't hesitate to discuss his urinary agony in interminable detail. Honestly Harry, you can really pick 'em."

"He's a great amateur paleontologist."

"He's a nutcase."

"Well," Animal said, returning to the Sullivans, having peeked into the family room, "the kids don't seem to mind."

Edie rolled her eyes. "I need a Valium."

"Mom, I thought you didn't take those anymore."

"Well today's a special day. Mr. Chicken has driven me to booze and drugs. Go ahead, call the DEA, see if I care." She stalked off to the kitchen.

"I guess you gotta tell Bradley it's time to go," Harry said.

"Me?" Animal asked. "I don't even live here."

"True. But he's your friend, technically."

"Technically."

"You should tell him it's time to remove the costume, use the facilities and depart."

"The kids aren't going to like this."

"They have no vote. They're underage. Besides, they're leaving soon. Their parents are late. I'll be in here phoning them, reminding them it's time to come collect their progeny."

"Benjie will hate me."

"I'll have to live with that. Get going."

Animal stood in the doorway of the family room. Before him, seated on an overstuffed ottoman was Mr. Chicken, holding court, ten little boys transfixed by him, their shining, expectant faces beaming up at Mr. Chicken as they sat, criss-cross apple-sauce on the carpet, their hands in their armpits as they flapped their wings and chanted "squawk, squawk." The huge brown chicken head with the yellow beak, red comb on top and red dewlap, the brown wings flapping, the long, elaborate plumage from the rear of the costume made Animal realize that it really was more of a rooster than a hen. But, figuring that such a correction would not be welcome, he merely waved at Bradley, who ignored him.

"Bradley!" He shouted. The room fell silent.

"There is no Bradley," Bradley said, "only Mr. Chicken."

"Okay, fine. Kids, Mr. Chicken has to go. It's also time for you to head home. So let's give Mr. Chicken a big round of applause and come into the next room to get your goodie bags." The doorbell rang. "There's someone's mom right now."

"Squawk, squawk, squawk," the kids flapped their elbows as they trooped into the next room.

"Boy do I hafta go," Bradley groaned.

"Don't tell me about it," Animal snapped. "The bathroom's right over there."

Mr. Chicken lumbered to the door.

"Oh, I think you're going to have to get out of your costume."

"I know that," Bradley snapped back. "Gimme a hand."

"Who are you?" Edie demanded, when Bradley came out of the bathroom.

"I'm Mr. Chicken."

"Oh, well, you look ordinary enough."

"I beg your pardon?"

"Never mind. Thanks for keeping the little tykes occupied."

"My pleasure. Do you have any more parties coming up for Benjie and his friends?"

Edie took a gulp of wine. "You think I'm a masochist?"

Bradley ignored that remark. "I'd just love to help out."

"I'm sure you would," Edie turned to look at Animal and rolled her eyes. "But unfortunately, I don't think Mr. Chicken's services –"

"Oh, not as Mr. Chicken. That's done."

"Of course."

"As Mr. Duckie."

"Mr. Duckie."

"Yes. Quack, quack. But I do it much better than that. You see, I have a quacker."

"Of course. What could be more...more normal? How could I have failed to assume you would have a quacker?"

"And webbed feet, and a green back. It's a mallard, you see. Oh, it's a great costume."

"Yes, well," Edie coughed and cast a sidelong glance at Animal, a glance that said "I don't believe this," much better than if she had uttered the words, "I'm afraid Mr. Duck,"

"Duckie."

"Duckie, will not have the opportunity to entertain here. You see we are going on a long trip."

"Really? Harry never mentioned. Where to?"

"Nepal. For a long time."

"So Harry won't be digging for fossils?"

"I'm staying behind," Harry put in. "To go to school and take care of the house."

"How exciting," Bradley burbled. "I would love to go to Nepal."

"Well, if you'll excuse me now," Edie edged away. "I have to go pack."

Later, after Bradley had departed, she collared her son in the kitchen. "Don't you ever bring that raving lunatic back here. Mr. Duckie! Mr. Chicken! What next – Porky the Pig?"

"Calm down Ma, he's harmless," Harry shook free of his mother, "just a little eccentric."

Edie narrowed her eyes. "And what does he wear when you go digging?"

"Khakis and a pith helmet. He's really just a regular guy, who likes to, to...dress up as barnyard fowl...to entertain kids."

Later, in the Toyota, on the way to the sub shop, Animal said: "Your mom got a strange impression of Bradley. After all, he's almost a professional paleontologist." Animal admired many things about Bradley, especially his skill at finding and unearthing fossils. His eccentricities were, in the bigger scheme of things, unimportant. The man had an interest, something that had started as a mere hobby but become a passion, one that could infect other people, a passion for a kind of knowledge that had no immediate use, no purpose other than the satisfaction of knowing, the contemplation of new pieces in the evolutionary puzzle, a passion that made strangers in the cool, high-ceilinged museum say, "ah, will you look at that? To think things like that lived in Maryland, two hundred million years ago." He wanted to transcend time, Bradley did, to collapse the millennia between himself and a pattern gently etched in a bit of rock in his hand, to feel the feathery fern as it swayed in breezes eons ago, to put together a complete picture of it now as it was then –that's how Animal understood him, because Bradley's enthusiasm had infected him, his desire for knowledge about ancient swamps, oceans and the creatures that dwelt in their murky depths had become Animal's, and they stood together, in the long dark corridors of prehistoric time, with the centuries whistling by, and the little flame of their desire to know illuminating an occasional plant or animal, long extinct, whose traces only rarely or never had been seen before, whose life they imagined and thus rescued from the obscurity and dust of the ages.

Harry was still making fun of Bradley, albeit gently, but Animal would have no part in it. They settled into a booth, already occupied by Chandra and Luis, and ordered twelve-inch subs, with meatballs, cheese and marinara sauce. Harry ordered a whole wheat sub, explaining apologetically, as he always did, that what had begun as his mother's health food indoctrination had now become a matter of taste. He preferred whole wheat. At this, Luis, as always, guffawed in disbelief, and took a few moments out from the history of outrageous and idiotic high points of tech class that he and Chandra had been reviewing to razz Harry about his mother, the ex-hippie.

"That's the one bad thing about going into senior year," Harry reverted to the previous subject, "no more tech ed."

"Yeah, remember your contests with Jones and Luis to see who could make their stool spin the most complete circles when Mr. Nagoulsalaam's back was turned?" Chandra chuckled. "Jones was the champ."

"Nagoulsalaam," Harry meditated, "Now there's someone who's really from outer space. Remember his cell phone conversations about his car repairs when we were welding? Those poor guys on the other end couldn't understand a word he said, between our noise and his accent. His accent was so thick, half the time I had no idea what he was telling us to do."

"Or his arguments with the veterinarian about his cockatiels?" Luis grinned. "Those had to be some of the weirdest damn discussions I ever heard: 'No, no, nothing but birdseed. No lettuce, it causes avian indigestion," Luis mimicked his teacher's south Asian accent.

"Nagoulsalaam never really got it," Harry went on. "It's like the world is one vast mystery to him." Which was why Harry had gone out of his way not to make his befuddled teacher's life miserable. He had never spun on his lab stool, never chucked spitballs, because Nagoulsalaam had been at sea, a man with great mechanical ability, at home most with machines, lost in the alien expanse of American culture. He had been in the United States for a decade, he had a good job, he was respected, but he would never fit in; Harry sensed it so strongly it was palpable, every time those misty, vaguely bewildered dark eyes peered at him through lenses as thick as the bottoms of old Coca Cola bottles. And his own reaction, something akin to pity, startled him, for Harry was not known to go easy on a teacher just because of some weakness. On the contrary, such flaws produced an irresistible mocking and, he shamefacedly had to admit, predatory reaction in him, as his regular attendance in after-school detention attested. He simply could not take the pretense; and his teachers were, in his view, for the most part, pretentious and pompous beyond endurance. But not Nagoulsalaam; he was just odd, baffled and at loose ends, struggling to make himself understood in a cripplingly thick accent, with ideas and assumptions about people and behavior that came straight out of another world. No, Harry could never bring himself to mock him or tease him or play a practical joke. He would have felt like a heel.

Luis was telling a story of one of Nagoulsalaam's particularly out-of-it moments, so Harry let his thoughts wander, to Bradley, to his mother, to his meatball sub, and his friends noted it quizzically, as they always did when this happened, when they joined in, making fun of the tech ed teacher, and Harry, usually right in there with the best of them, imitating other teachers' annoying mannerisms or self-important turns of phrase, would quietly, when Nagoulsalaam was the butt of jokes, zone out.

"Remember the day he brought one of his birds to school, in a cage?" Luis asked.

"And it escaped?" Chandra guffawed. "I thought we were going to have to get the men in the white coats."

"He really went bananas," Animal slurped on his marinara sauce.

"They're worth a lot of money, those birds," Harry said.

"But they're not worth jumping up and down on a table top, nearly killing yourself, screaming in Hindi or whatever he speaks and causing an entire class of sixteen year olds to stampede into the hall," Luis replied. "If I recall correctly, Guiles almost had a fit." Guiles was an epileptic, whose disability was easily brought on by stress or commotion.

"Guiles *did* have a fit," Animal slurped, "Next period, in Sanchez's Spanish Two class."

"Well that indubitably had more to do with Sanchez, who we know is a raving lunatic, than with Nagoulsalaam, who's just peculiar," Luis corrected himself and then went on to detail the criminal charges against Sanchez, brought by the Humane Society and the police for keeping a house full of neglected Dobermans and pit-bulls. "And then there was the time he assaulted Dr. Managan, the department chair, over a container of bottled water. Whereupon Luis performed a rendition of Sanchez's thickly accented English: "if you ever touch my water again, you disgusting pig, I will whip your fat ass."

Chandra and Animal howled and slapped the table.

"I saw it! I saw it!" Harry cried. "He went for his throat."

"The guy's bonkers," Luis continued, "certifiable. Assaults a colleague, but does he get fired? No. Gets hauled up on charges by the Humane Society. It's a scandal in the papers – do they even put him on administrative leave? No. They continue to subject us, the students, to his obvious insanity. Nobody cares about you, if you go to public school. Dr. Ramirez got a petition to get rid of the guy. The entire department signed it. Nothing, zip. Then Sanchez goes and slaps a student on a field trip. Dr. Ramirez threatens to go to the county, says the parents of the kid, Albert Delgado, are considering suing. What do they do? Five days leave, after which the fruitcake's back teaching his class. No wonder Guiles had a fit. *I* almost had a fit, every time I passed him in the hall, and I'm not even epileptic, nor do I have to sit through his class. Thank God I'm fluent in Spanish and placed out of it."

Harry had had Mr. Sanchez for Spanish One and nearly flunked the course, not because he did not do his work, but because he and Sanchez had formed an immediate, mutual and immutable animosity, in which they were bound like a wrestling grip, from the moment Harry walked into the classroom in late August until the last day in June. All the students agreed that Mr. Sanchez was out of his mind to begin with, but also that Harry had noticeably worsened his condition. For his part, after the initial classes in which he assessed the fact that his teacher was mad, Harry had made manful efforts not to provoke him – it not being fair, as he said to Animal, to play games with a mental defective. But this reserve was to no avail. Mr. Sanchez believed he discerned in Harry and implacable opponent and treated him as such. Harry responded with stony silence, but was unable to conceal the occasional flash of hilarity in his eyes, when Mr. Sanchez pulled one of his wilder stunts. Somehow, Mr. Sanchez always caught those flashes; or if Harry, thinking his back was safely turned, rolled his eyes in disbelief, Mr. Sanchez could tell by the suppressed laughter of those in Harry's vicinity that he was the butt of some comical facial expression. Every time this happened, Harry got detention either for "disrespect" or "disruption." One day he got triple detention – three days in a row; that was for being unable to suppress his laughter during a long, very long and rambling speech by Mr. Sanchez that, Harry later told Animal, could have been entitled, "Fidel's plot to take over the world." Mr. Sanchez larded this lecture with many a reference to the sinister plotters, whom he referred to as "the gun control cabal, who want to take away our means of self-defense, prevent us from purchasing machine guns and steam roll us into detention camps. But I, Jorge Sanchez, have outwitted them. In my house are many, many Uzis; when Fidel comes, I will be waiting for him."

"You do that, Jorge," Sherwin had muttered under his breath, and Harry had been unable to control himself. A strange gargling sound that everyone immediately identified as strangled laughter emanated from his throat. Mr. Sanchez turned purple with rage, sentenced him to triple detention, and launched into a ferocious invective on those who mocked and belittled the danger of the communist threat. This second speech made many references to Fidel's close ties to the Soviet Union.

Sherwin raised his hand. "Uh, Mr. Sanchez, I don't think it's the Soviet Union anymore. They're not communist. It's Russia."

"Don't you believe it!" Sanchez shrieked. "The KGB still runs that country, always has and always will. They and Fidel have been after me for many years."

"God help them," Sherwin muttered.

Dr. Ramirez poked his head in the door. "What's going on here? I heard yelling."

"The students fail to appreciate the threat posed to our freedom by that totalitarian dictator who goes by the name Fidel."

"Oh. What other name would he go by?" Dr. Ramirez asked.

"Many, many. He is a great deceiver."

"What has this got to do with the past tense or the vocabulary on a European vacation?"

"Petty concerns," Mr. Sanchez waved an arm, dismissing Spanish grammar and vocabulary with one gesture. "You think your average Cuban is free to take a European vacation?"

Dr. Ramirez scowled.

"You think Fidel would let me live free for one instant if I set foot back in my native land?"

"I'm not sure *we* should let you live free," Sherwin muttered. "Where are the men with the straight jackets?"

"You will return to teaching the past tense," Dr. Ramirez roared. "While Dr. Managan is on leave, *I* am the acting chair. And if these students cannot pass a test on the past tense by the end of next week, you will be back in Miami, running your insane, underground anti-Castro group and barred from teaching in Anne Arundel County ever again!"

Mr. Sanchez glared back at Dr. Ramirez through narrow, paranoid eyes, his gaze and expression indicating that he believed that there, incarnate before him, stood one of the detestable Fidel's many minions. But he said nothing. He had still more than a shred of healthy self-preservation.

"All right señor," and he bowed his head in mock deference. "The past tense it is."

"And better stay," Dr. Ramirez snapped and slammed the door.

"Harry Sullivan, you will remain after class."

"But I have chemistry."

"Too bad. It was your provocation that caused the shouting and led to this unfortunate directive from *Mister* Ramirez. I would not be surprised to learn that you are a supporter of the unholy one."

"The who?"

"Who have we been discussing for the last half hour?" Mr. Sanchez shrieked. "He is tall, Cuban, bearded and a dictator."

"Oh."

"And he wears a funny little cap."

"Got it."

"Ahh, so now you deign to acknowledge him." And thus it continued until the bell rang, by which time, mercifully, Mr. Sanchez had forgotten about keeping Harry after class.

Harry and Luis did not see eye to eye on Mr. Sanchez. Luis wanted him fired, the sooner the better. Harry believed some form of mandatory psychotherapy was the answer. He stated the view that if fired, Mr. Sanchez would eventually become a wild-eyed, homeless bum and that therefore, he ought to be required to get help, if he wanted to keep his job. "Let him work at the Humane Society," Luis said. "At least the dogs and cats won't have to understand what he's ranting about."

"Sounds like cruelty to animals, to me," Chandra said.

"What about cruelty to people?" Luis demanded.

"You just don't like him 'cause he's prejudiced against El Salvadorans," Chandra averred.

"That would be accurate," Luis replied, "plus he's a loon and a gun nut, and dangerous and vindictive – need I go on?"

"Look," Harry began, "the guy has his defects –"

"The understatement of the year."

"But he is a qualified Spanish teacher."

"I could teach it better," Luis said. "At least I'd teach the language, not my crackpot political conspiracy theories. But that's not for me. I'm going into the air force."

"And if there's a war, you could get killed," Animal remarked.

"War? What war? The worst thing that happens is I wind up in the Balkans. Nope, the air force will pay for my engineering education, and if I have to do a little peace-keeping on the way, so be it."

"You could wind up having to kill people," Harry said. "That's one of the things my mom said was so horrible about Vietnam, all those vets with their gruesome experiences. It warped their minds."

Luis chomped down savagely on his sub. "It's almost the millennium," he began.

"There was Yugoslavia," Animal added.

"I'm not going to be killing anybody."

They ate in silence for a while, Chandra and Animal ordering second subs, Harry silently turning over his thoughts about Mr. Sanchez, everything about whom, he concluded yet again, was unappealing. He agreed with Dr. Ramirez's desperation to get rid of him. He saw that Luis loathed him, and there was reason in that too. Yet he felt certain that the one thing Mr. Sanchez needed and that would change him dramatically, namely psychiatric help, had so far not been available. Maybe, he thought whimsically, someone should spike his Perrier with meds. Or maybe Luis was right, and Harry's mother, despite her often sarcastic exterior, had raised someone who, underneath, was just another bleeding heart liberal, like her.

"Don't brood about it," Luis interrupted his thoughts. "Mr. Sanchez would screw you over in a minute. He hasn't got a compassionate bone in his body."

"You're telepathic?" Harry asked with a laugh.

"I know when you're wasting your time."

Later, as they stood in the strip mall, in the dark, inhaling the odors of traffic and thinking about work the next day, the brevity of summer and what being seniors would be like, Harry turned it over in his mind, one last time. "You're right," he said to Luis with no further explanation, because none was needed.

"I know I am," Luis replied, unlocking the door to his battered Nissan Sentra. "I knew it the first time I laid eyes on the guy."

The next morning was Monday, steamy and hot, a typical August day in Maryland, where the humidity filled the air like a sauna and everyone hid from it in air-conditioned rooms or cars. Harry rode to work in his Toyota, the radio blasting. He passed strip malls and idled in congested traffic and did so with a vision before his mind's eye of the entire Baltimore/D. C. metro area, clogged with vehicles on sizzling asphalt, surrounded by car dealerships, fast food restaurants and supermarkets as far as the eye could see, some areas upscale, others blighted with vacancies, boarded-up windows and check cashing joints, but everywhere the ubiquitous suburban sprawl.

Harry worked at Best Buy. He intended to become store manager one day, not too long after graduation. For the moment, he worked on the floor, selling mini-fridges and televisions, and sometimes he helped with the loading in back. He had promised Edie that he would take classes at the community college after his senior year, but he was determined to earn as much as possible to contribute to the future cost of a four-year university. After all, he had two younger brothers and Benji, and his father worked for the Parks Department, a stable position but not one that left, in Mr. Sullivan's words, "a lot of economic wiggle room." Edie worked part-time at the garden center, advising customers to purchase the organic vegetable seeds and carefully holding her tongue about the poisons lurking in the red, clayey Maryland earth. The house was paid off, so were the cars; there was some retirement money, but almost nothing for college.

Harry liked the different rhythms of the two kinds of work. He enjoyed scouting the floor for customers, greeting strangers, introducing them to various products, describing the sundry facets of different appliances, demonstrating how they worked. He never pushed, never engaged in a hard sell, saw no need to, since his customers almost always did buy something. Besides, to him there was something unseemly in pitching a product too aggressively. It ruined the interaction with the person who was making a decision, who wanted honest advice. So Harry did not hesitate to point out the flaws and drawbacks of some items and reaped a reward in gratitude, and, he saw over time, customer loyalty. "I don't know what you're doing, Sullivan," the manager remarked. "But I like the way your customers keep coming back."

He approached the physical labor of storing the boxes from the trucks with a similar optimism, but a completely different enjoyment. Lifting, stacking, rolling, unloading – the rhythm of the work emptied his mind of worry, of stray thoughts, of the continuous ironic mental commentary on his surroundings. Whole mornings could pass with him thus engaged and at the end, when he took off to go to Subway for lunch, he would realize that not one verbalization, not one thought had clouded his mind; instead he had been thinking visually, surveying picture after picture of memories that, for one reason or another, concerned him. It was a relaxing, associative process and led him to request work in the stockroom. The manager joked that he was crazy.

"I could manage this store," he thought one day, as he stepped out the back to go buy lunch. "I could manage it with both arms tied behind my back." He planned to achieve that goal, then use his credentials to get into the communications industry. Harry read everything he could on this field, in the business sections of newspapers, magazines and online. Someday, he told Animal, everyone, even children would have cell phones that would be tiny and have computer functions. They were the wave of the future, the wave, already of the present, just growing bigger and bigger. People would do their banking on them or buy plane tickets or get medical diagnoses. There would also be video phones. They would be invaluable. Everyone would have to have them. He, Harry, would not wait for anything, would not even let college slow him down. "So you want to be a communications czar," Animal grinned. "Dream on." And Harry did. He took out his cell phone, a long black Nokia. "You're going to change the world," he addressed it.

"Out of you freakin' mind, Sullivan," one of his co-workers commented, passing him on the way back to the stockroom.

"Don't you listen to them" he addressed his phone. "We know what you're capable of."

One evening over dinner, just out of the shower, his light brown hair freshly washed, his cut-offs and T-shirt recently laundered – by him, of course, since Edie had taught all her boys to do their own wash – he felt so clean and presentable that his confidence suddenly soared and he disclosed his plans.

"So you want to be a communications mogul," Edie said, inspecting her salad.

"Not a bad gig," his father, James Sullivan, munched on his broccoli, "if you can get it."

"You know there's a funny-looking herb in my salad."

"That herb has antennae," said Harry's brother Jonathan.

"I thought I washed this lettuce."

"Even without washing," munch, munch on the broccoli, "there shouldn't be bugs in it. Better complain to the supermarket. Next thing you know there'll be bugs in the broccoli." James paused, speared a large floret on his fork and examined it. "Nope, no bugs here."

"Did anyone hear me?" Harry asked.

"You wanted more steak?" Edie asked. "Or was it water? I hope everyone appreciates my new water filtration system. It gets rid of all sorts of nasty chemicals polluting our tap water."

"Mother," Harry tried to interrupt.

"And, we don't have to participate in the bottled water craze, the biggest scam since cable television. I hate it when there's something you get free, like tap water and broadcast TV and then some corporate creep decides to set up a system whereby you have to pay for it."

"Sounds like what Harry here wants to do with cable TV on your cell phone," munch, munch.

"I never said that. I said some day you'd be able to get TV on your cell phone."

"But you won't charge extra for it," Edie said. "Go ahead, make millions in the cable business if that's what you want, just don't expect you mother to approve if you start charging for things that used to be free."

"It's not the cable business."

"You know," James raised a forkful of brown rice, "we never got cable."

Harry put his head in his hands. "I think I knew that, Dad."

"Your mother here, Edie –"

"I know who she is."

"Yes, well of course you do. She's against cable," munch, munch on the rice. "Something to do with being allergic to paying for TV when it used to be free. It all used to be free – did you know that?"

Harry rolled his eyes.

"I won't have you working for a cable company," Edie said. "I'm against that, against the whole idea."

"I never said anything about cable," Harry clarified.

"Good," James was cutting his steak now. "Because I'd never hear the end of it from your mother if you did. Edie - steak's tough."

"That's because there are no hormones or antibiotics. It's completely range free steak. Costs a fortune."

"But it's tough."

"Don't complain about it. Eat it. At least you're not being poisoned by some recombinant something or other developed by Monsanto or somebody or other –"

"Could you be a little more specific?" Jonathan demanded. "I think this conversation's kind of vague."

"What's a mogul?" Benjie asked.

"A muckety muck," Edie explained. "That's what Harry wants to be."

"I'll play in the mud with you, Harry," Benjie offered. "If Aunt Edie'll let me."

"I was talking about cell phones," Harry said in despair.

"Edie won't let you take your cell phone in the mud," Benji warned him. "I'm sure about that."

"What's this about cell phones, dear?" Edie asked. "You said something?"

"Can't imagine how you could hook your cell phone up to the cable," munch, munch on the broccoli again, "even if we did get cable. You'll have to give that idea the old heave ho, Harry."

"I wasn't talking about hooking my cell phone up to the cable," Harry cried in exasperation.

"Good," Edie was now inspecting every leaf of lettuce in the salad bowl, "because I'm against that."

"She always has been," munch, munch.

"As I've now heard, three times," Harry said, "and that's not counting all the other times, thousands of them –"

"Now, now, don't criticize your mother. Steak's damn tough."

"Eat it and be quiet," Edie advised.

"Everybody repeats themselves from time to time, you know," James was chewing vigorously. He looked most unhappy. "Like leather," he said.

"It's good for you."

"Not for my teeth."

"For the rest of you. You don't need your teeth."

"Won't have any, if we keep eating steak like this."

"Well then, it won't be an issue, will it?"

"You'll feed me something else?" James sounded hopeful.

"Tofu."

"Not tofu. Lose my teeth to your lousy free range steak as tough as leather just so you can starve me on a diet of tofu?"

"Tofu's good for you."

"But it tastes like putty."

"That's irrelevant."

"Harry, be very careful, when you get married, about your future wife's culinary views. It's no understatement to say that your very life may depend on it. Who you marry is more important than this mogul business."

"I like the mud," said Benjie.

"They're not talking about mud, moron," thus Billy, Harry's eight-year-old brother.

"Well if you're so smart, what on the face of the earth are they talking about?" Jonathan demanded.

"Nothing on the face of the earth."

"You lost me, son," chew, chew. "Maybe I could have chicken, instead of tofu?"

"Something underground," Billy explained. "Cable TV. The wires go underground."

"This conversation is too unfocused," Edie said. "I need a drink."

James clapped his hands and rubbed them in eager anticipation. "A Heineken for me."

"No Heineken."

"What? No Heineken? Then a Molson."

"No. No Molson either. No beer. Only wine, red wine."

"But I like beer."

"Wine's better for you. People who drink it live longer."

"Why would I want to live longer with no beer, no teeth and a diet of tofu?"

"Next thing you'll be saying is 'just kill me now.' "

"Just kill me now."

"Well, we have again reached that point that we reach at every family dinner, every night," Harry said, "where Dad begs for a swift bullet to the head."

"Sounds better than tofu."

"I definitely need a drink," Edie said, pulling the cork out of the wine bottle.

"So what's this with being a cable king?" Jonathan asked Harry.

"I never said –" Harry exploded.

"Calm down. I was just trying to make conversation, before Mom accuses us all of being barbarians."

"That comes later," Billy said.

"How do you know?" Edie snapped.

"You haven't had your wine yet."

She glared at Billy, then filled a glass for herself and one for her husband, who scowled in disgust.

"You know I'm not going to drink it. In ten minutes you'll drink it to keep it from going to waste." He turned to Harry. "Just one beer. That's all I ask."

"Don't look at me. I don't do the shopping."

"The doctor said you need to lose a little weight," Edie sipped on her wine. "You're not going to, drinking beer."

"But I sure as shooting am, once you get rid of my teeth and start feeding me tofu. Then I'll starve to death. So you might as well –"

"Just shoot me now," Benjie and Billy chanted in unison.

Harry decided to try out his idea on the guys, thinking that perhaps they would be a little more receptive.

"Sounds like a shitty idea to me," said Jones. "If you can't beat 'em, join the corporate hotshots who are globalizing the world, off-shoring jobs and generally eliminating middle-class life as we know it. Join the plutocracy, yah-hoo!"

"Thanks for looking on the upside of my plans, as always," Harry grumbled.

"What did you expect him to say?" Chandra demanded. "You know Donald here always sticks up for the little guy and generally thinks that the little guy's world is coming to an end. Surely you didn't expect encouragement?"

"A little sympathy would have been nice."

"Be a labor organizer," Jones said. "Then you'll get my sympathy. You expect praise for wanting to rise through the ranks of AT&T? Firing opponents, issuing rafts of pink slips, depriving workers of pay raises and hitting on secretaries?"

"Who's hitting on secretaries?" Harry cried.

"By the time you're done, I won't even shake your hand."

"I thought it was only war criminals like Henry Kissinger whose hand you wouldn't shake."

"Well, if you have been at that Georgetown lecture, would you have shaken Kissinger's hand afterward?" Jones' blue eyes were blazing.

"Kissinger? What's Kissinger got to do with this? I'm talking about my career."

"Your career as a corporate toady, who dreams of one day having the livelihood of thousands at his merest whim."

"Not everybody has a dad who's a Teamster. Not everybody has an in with a union."

"I'd try to get in one even if my family wasn't. It's a matter of priorities and values. I just think this whole dream of some corporate communications empire is for the birds. Come on Harry, your dad works for the Parks Department. You could do a lot worse than a job in county government, and you might actually do some good, too."

Harry sighed. "What do you think, Chandra?"

"Business and finance," Jones put in. "That's what he thinks."

"I'm not saying a word," Chandra replied blandly. "I know when my opinions will be treated as apostasy."

It was Saturday, they were seated on deck chairs at the pool, and Sherwin came by, resplendent in a new, bright blue pair of swim trunks. "What's up?" He asked.

"Harry here dreams of taking over AT&T," Jones said sourly, "Jacking up all our phone rates and making a bundle."

"Harry, I'm surprised at you," Sherwin began, seating himself and pouring a cup of soda. "I thought you were facing life after high school with the same intentions I have – life at home as an unemployed eccentric."

In frustration, Harry ran his fingers through his hair. "If I do that I'll be an unemployed psychotic. You have no idea how disorganized, desultory, meandering life is in my house."

"Then do something worthwhile with yourself," Jones said.

"I'm not complaining. I love my family. But I just can't get them to listen to me."

"And you're having better luck with your friends?" Chandra asked.

"I think cell phones are the future," Harry said and immediately felt like an idiot.

"They've been the future for years," Sherwin replied, "and lots of other people have already cashed in on them. You're better off trying to make manager at Best Buy than pining over cell phones." He guzzled his soda. "Hey, haven't we had this conversation before?"

"Yeah knucklehead, last weekend," Jones put in. "Verbatim."

"And the weekend before," Chandra added, "Unless I'm very much mistaken."

"You're the Brahmin," Harry said, "so you're entitled to act superior. But I don't see where Mr. Teamster booster Jones gets to ride his high horse, when he repeats the same spiel about labor organizing and war criminals not just for a few weekends, but nonstop for the past three years of high school."

"Don't forget middle school," Jones added. "I wouldn't want anyone to think I'm not consistent."

Chandra rolled his eyes. "No worry there."

"So you think I'm too late," Harry concluded glumly.

"Way too late," Sherwin said.

"Even for banking by cell phone?"

"Even for teleporting by cell phone."

Harry decided that perhaps he needed female advice, that a girl might listen more attentively to his ideas and help him sort them out. The trouble was – who? He had broken up with Jennifer in the beginning of eleventh grade, and it had not been amicable. He knew for a fact that she no longer referred to Harry by his name but as "that big jerk" or "the idiot." Word of this had reached him from several corners, but he had not allowed it to ruffle his generally serene view that all was right with the world. Now, however, he wished he was on speaking terms with Jen. She was, in her way, sensible and, after a fashion, down to earth, and her affection for him had manifested itself with so many plans for his future that he often found himself wondering why he had broken up with her.

"She wanted you to perform in a ballet for dance class in Phys. Ed., that's why," Animal reminded him whenever he asked the question.

"Oh right. I forgot."

"You objected to the leotard. *I* objected to the leotard. I said if you so much as put it on, I would never be seen in your company again. So did Chandra, Sherwin, Luis, Jones, Kevin and Paul. It was unanimous."

Jennifer had been stubborn and had taken great umbrage at his refusal to don the aforementioned garment. Thus commenced the hostilities that ultimately doomed the relationship. Harry had tried to make it up to her with offers of dates to football games, but these were not to Jen's taste. She had an artistic streak and could spend entire weekends in D. C. or Baltimore at art museums. Thither Harry had accompanied her on many occasions and had there plumbed depths of boredom he had previously never dreamed existed. Ennui so overcame him on one occasion at the Walters that he literally wept.

"Harry, what's wrong?" Jennifer asked in alarm. "There's a tear on your cheek."

"Allergies."

"But it's October."

"Must be the paint in the pictures."

"Aren't they gorgeous? This Corot's a classic."

"I can see that."

"Wonderful. Let's go upstairs. There's another exhibit we haven't been to."

"Aargh."

"What?"

"Just clearing my throat."

Jennifer could wander down the airy, high-ceilinged corridors for hours, commenting on this picture and that. She loved the galleries, and it had never occurred to her that Harry was less than fascinated. Often he would sit on a bench in the middle of a room and study her long red hair and nearly perfect figure. When she approached him, blue eyes glistening with enthusiasm over some piece of statuary, he would almost believe his own act, that he had been moved by it too, that it was the nonpareil of its sort, and so forth. Only later would he settle down and remember that it had been her eyes and face that so affected him, not some object d'art.

"Another weekend at the National Gallery, eh?" Jones would razz him at Friday football practice. "Lucky you."

"It's not so bad," Harry would whimper.

"Neither is strychnine."

Harry would jog away.

"You might want to consider that," Jones would call after him. "Suicide's always an option."

Jennifer did not like Jones. She considered him a boor. When Harry refused to wear the leotard, she crossed her arms, tapped her foot and said, "this is Donald's idea."

"And Animal's and Luis' and mine."

"I don't know about your friends, Harry."

"They're just ordinary guys."

"Ordinary vulgarians."

"That's not fair."

"Well, look at Donald. He considers all of the arts part of some upper-class conspiracy. What's his idea of a viable contemporary art form? The Simpsons."

"That doesn't make him a vulgarian. It's not like he reads nudie magazines or *The National Enquirer*. He likes Dilbert."

"He's low-brow."

"Maybe."

"It was his idea for you to refuse to participate in this ballet."

"She's a harpie," Jones replied when these complaints were reported to him. "A very good-looking harpie. And a snob. She thinks we're plebs. I've actually heard her use that term."

The dispute over the leotard lasted one week. At the end of that week, Jennifer returned some books Harry had given her, and he reciprocated.

"I notice she kept the jewelry," Animal said.

"She's very practical," Harry replied.

So he could not consult with Jennifer about the future of cell phones. On second thought, it seemed unlikely that she would have warmed to the idea anyway, given her conviction that Harry should make his way in the world either as a writer of post-modernist fiction or the member of an itinerant troupe of performance artists.

"Post-modernist fiction!" Luis exclaimed. "Sheesh. I thought you said she was down-to-earth."

"She is," Jones added sourly, "if you consider the upper troposphere down-to-earth."

"And practical," Luis went on. "You said she was practical."

"She's very practical about money," Harry ventured.

"Yeah, she's a cheapskate, like Anna. Never spends a dime of her own," Luis chomped down savagely on his meatball sub, "runs through yours like it's water. You two sure can pick 'em."

"I like the itinerant performance artist idea," Jones slurped on his soda. "You could be a mime, spend the rest of your life performing at elementary schools."

"Now there's a thought," Harry replied dourly.

"While she marries some professor of literature," Jones went on, "or a hot shot investment banker. I think she's showing you the door. What girl in her right mind wants her boyfriend to have a career as a performance artist?"

"She'll definitely show me the door if I don't wear that leotard."

"Opportunity is knocking. Take it while you can," Jones went on rather acidly. "Hundreds of beaming, upturned kindergarten faces await the display of your talents."

Luis threw the stub of his sandwich down on his plate. "I don't believe you put up with this. You tell that pretentious art lover you have no intention of putting on a leotard, now or ever. She has to take you for what you are."

"Now there's a winning argument," Jones rather sarcastically averred.

"I could say I sprained my ankle."

Jones rolled his eyes.

"Chicken," Luis accused.

"I don't want to lose her."

"Why not? If my girlfriend told me to do ballet or write the next *Ulysses*, I wouldn't wait to lose her. She'd see the back of me so fast she wouldn't have time to think about it. Performance artists. Now I've heard everything."

No, Jennifer would not have had much interest in the future permutations of cell phones and the relevant markets, unless, of course, he stressed his belief that there was lots of money in it. That might snag her attention. She was, after all, as Harry knew first hand, quite practical, though she had her other side, which might require him to donate a portion of his expected fortune to the National Endowment for the Arts.

His thoughts turned to Anna, more flexible than Jen, not given to ultimatums about leotards, more understanding of those whose aspirations differed from hers. True, she had a one-track mind when it came to her own future, and a professorship in comparative literature was at the end of it, but she was open to other possibilities, witness her latest plan for Animal, namely, a career in the federal government, specifically the FDA. Why or how she had chosen the FDA, neither Harry, nor Animal, nor anyone else had the slightest idea, given Animal's complete lack of interest in the regulation of food and drugs. A friend of her father's worked at the FDA – perhaps that was where she got the notion. She had taken to emailing articles that had anything, the remotest connection to the FDA, to Animal, had in fact inundated him with this literature. He was desperate to get her to stop, but Harry thought this bizarre idée fixe on Anna's part vastly superior to the thought of composing a post-modernist masterpiece or performance art. It showed a link, tenuous, no doubt, but a link nonetheless to the reality of her boyfriend's prospects. Animal might indeed someday be able to get a federal job, and such jobs paid well and offered security. The idea of the FDA showed that Anna was thinking realistically about what he could and might like to do. Perhaps she might have some advice for Harry.

"Cell phones? Who in their right mind would see a future in cell phones?" Anna demanded, sitting right up in her lounge chair at the pool. She had on a visor and sunglasses and was slathering sun-block on her pale, freckled, perfect legs.

"Some day people might do their banking on cell phones."

"And people might live on Alpha Centauri."

"It's a star, not a planet."

"That's exactly what I meant."

"So you don't think I should consider a career in communications."

"Definitely not. You should go to culinary school."

Harry looked perturbed. To encourage him, she elaborated: "I see you as a chef at a five-star restaurant."

"But I can't cook a hot dog."

"Then you better get crackin.' There's an excellent culinary school in Baltimore."

Jones ambled by. "What's cookin.' "

"Harry," Anna said. "He's thinking of becoming a chef."

Jones looked surprised. "I didn't know you could cook."

"I thought it was cell phones," Sherwin, seated a few chairs away, added his two cents, "correct me if I'm wrong, but cell phones don't have much to do with cookery."

"He's ditched that idea about cell phones," Anna clarified.

"Maybe he can get a job at the FDA," Jones grinned, "with Animal, sautéing the vittles his buddy regulates."

Anna decided to ignore this. "He's going to the culinary school in Baltimore."

Harry's jaw dropped open. Observing this, a wicked gleam flashed in Jones' eyes. "Why don't I just give you a lift over there," he grinned again at Harry, "we'll sign you up today."

"It's Sunday, you moron," Sherwin delicately corrected him.

"It's the thought that counts," Anna simpered. "Maybe Donald –" Jones winced at this and indeed any use of his first name, "will drive you over tomorrow."

"I've got my own car," Harry grumbled.

"Maybe Donald – Donald, you know you have a tic. That's the second time your shoulders have sort of tightened up in the past few seconds. Maybe Donald,"

Donald winced.

"There you go again. You should see a doctor. There may be something medicine could do for you."

"I doubt it," Sherwin snickered.

"Well, maybe Donald, my, I find that tic of yours quite distracting."

"You were saying?" Jones asked between clenched teeth.

"Maybe you should consider culinary school too. You might make an excellent chef."

"Yeah," Jones said, "and pigs might fly out my butt."

"Excuse me?" Anna sat up.

"Ignore him," Sherwin placated. "It's his low self-esteem. Donald," he paused to beam at a wincing Jones, "Donald doesn't think he can do anything that's not mechanical."

"Well, it is precisely Donald's – oh, that tic – mechanical abilities that made me think he would make a first-rate chef. He so likes to use his hands. The things he's done in Mr. Nagoolsalaam's class are legendary."

Sherwin, turning purple as he strangled on the hilarious recollection of Jones' Tech. Ed. pranks, gasped, then said, "yes, that's the perfect word – legendary – for Donald's...Donald's activities in poor Mr. Nagoolsalaam's class."

"Yes poor Mr. Nagoolsalaam. Rather a lost soul," Anna simpered again.

"Rather an imbecile," Jones remarked.

"What's this got to do with cell phones?" Harry demanded.

"Oh," Anna airily waved a hand, "we disposed of that."

"It's cooking school for you," Jones snickered.

"And you, Donald. My goodness. Get a sound medical opinion about that tic."

"Some people don't listen," Harry began.

"And some people have obsessions about futures in industries that have already been snatched up by everybody else," Sherwin said. "I won't mention any names."

"Maybe you could combine cell phones and cuisine," Jones beamed at Harry.

"I've got it!" Anna smacked her forehead with the palm of her hand, as if the thought that had just flickered behind it were sheer genius. "Harry could be a personal chef to the CEO of Verizon."

Sherwin's eyes crossed.

Jones' eyes glittered, and he rubbed his hands. "How *do* you come up with these things?"

"Don't ask," Harry said sourly. "I'm sure she amazes herself."

"I do," Anna said. "Sometimes I really do."

In the end, Harry gave up his search for advice. He was, he concluded, the only one who cared about the future of cell phones and his role in it. Even if this aspiration was utterly ridiculous, and in the complete solitude of those moments when he fixed his eyes on himself ten years hence, he sometimes had to admit that it very well might not happen, but even if it was absurd, it was his; he had found it himself, alone; no guidance counselor had suggested it, it belonged to him, it endowed every instant with value. Sometimes, walking from his car parked in the lot to work, passing shoppers and other clerks he knew, he would wonder how they got through the day, what each second could be worth without the certainty of technological advance and their future role in it. This vision of his career made everything humdrum come alive. It was why he got up in the morning, it pulled him through his tedious chores, it enriched everything, this knowledge that he was on a path to a different world, the image of which had come to him one night as he drifted off to sleep. He saw a giant metallic wheel, many times bigger than the space station, huge, filled with people at computerized tasks, an entire world, one of billions, spinning slowly through space, dotting its dark vastness, its many galaxies, with the advanced technology of human life. This vision came to him at the oddest moments, and though he knew it owed something to the sci fi he read and the futuristic movies he watched, he cherished it and kept it to himself. For in one of the millions of little windows on that giant, spinning, computerized wheel, he had seen his own face, in a moment of rest, taking a break from work that he loved, reveling in being a part, a small cog in the gigantic human enterprise. Of course he knew very well that his real future, even if he succeeded in the communications industry, would look very different, but he kept this image before his mind's eye, and because of it, preposterous new uses for cell phones kept springing up in his brain and growing into bizarre, enormous shapes, like the elephant zucchini in

Mrs. Lenthican's vegetable patch – how they got so strange and big, no one could say.

"So you've finally given up on cell phones," Animal remarked one afternoon before football practice.

"What makes you say that?"

"A tall, good-looking blonde, who claims you're going to cooking school."

Harry lunged at Animal, who stepped quickly out of the way.

"That is the last time," Harry said, making a vigorous semicircle with his hand, index finger extended so that it finished pointing to the ground, "the *last* time," he gestured again, "I ever ask Anna about anything. She is a dingbat."

"Watch it, Harry."

"A dingbat. You know that, don't you?"

Animal backed off and sighed. "She can be a little flaky."

"Personal chef to the CEO of Verizon? I'm interested in new uses for cell phones. That does not include eating them. By the way, how's your career at the FDA coming along?"

Sudden unhappiness flickered across Animal's face, flickered and vanished. "It's not such a wild idea, you know."

"It's wacked out."

"I could be in IT for the federal government."

"That's not what she has in mind. I think something with the title 'director' in it has captivated Anna. I notice cooking school is not on the agenda for her future husband."

In subdued silence they strolled out of the locker room, then jogged onto the field. It was a gorgeous September afternoon, warm, dry, only a few silver and mauve clouds scudding across an otherwise clear blue sky. "So I guess you haven't given it up," Animal said after a moment.

Harry shook his head. "But I've abandoned talking about it. The only person who even came close to giving me the time of day on the subject was Luis."

"So did I."

"And you," Harry conceded. Luis and Animal both had good minds for electronics and had seen at once the possibilities Harry was reaching for. "Luis thought some of the features I'd come up with, like banking by cell phone, might go over well in poor countries, where cheap cell phones could make up for lack of infrastructure and development. He thinks I should get a job in a small cell phone company, work my way up, get in on the research on shared computer and cell technology, then pitch my idea about marketing it in Central or South America."

"Or for that you could start your own company. Chandra could do the financial setup for you."

They started warming up, sprinted off around the track. "Maybe you should take a few business classes at the community college, while you work?"

"My idea exactly," Harry replied. Optimism surged through him; he felt it pulsing in his legs, arms and neck. Out in the depths and blackness of space, huge silver wheels, filled with people, working, relaxing, living, rotated away. Harry was in one, turned away from his computer for just a moment to gaze out at the stars. "I want to be part of the future," he explained and somehow there, on the track with Animal, did not feel like a dope for saying it.

"I know," Animal replied seriously. "That's what we all want, and we will be."

After practice Harry visited Luis, who had been taking a late afternoon siesta when he arrived. They went out on the back deck, so huge it dwarfed the Ignacio's little rambler. They discussed computers, software engineering, cell phones, satellite technology and Luis' theory that this new technology could enable third world countries to skip the disastrous phase of the industrial revolution and morph right into development in the next century. "Maybe everybody doesn't have to repeat the same steps in history," he said. "Maybe there really is another way. I remember our house in El Salvador. It was a shack really, with a dirt floor. I left at age five, and after growing up here, I concluded that people should not have to live that way, nor should their only way out be life in the type of factories that fill up China. There's got to be another model for development. I believe that. I believe that is the real, true future."

They talked as dusk came on, and fireflies came out. A morning dove cooed in the gently swaying boughs above them. Then Luis began rambling about the air force, the engineering skills he would acquire and what he would do later, in civilian life, how he would join up with Harry perhaps and how they would help bring a higher standard of living to certain parts of Latin America. "This is what I want to do," Harry thought, sitting in the twilight, calm in the certainty that he could achieve his goals, delighted at having them taken so seriously. But then later, a group of murderous fanatics flew crowded planes into crowded buildings, and everything changed.

Three

Sherwin Goodman's father was an accountant and his mother a homemaker. They lived in the toniest neighborhood in Crofton, in a large white house, filled, twice a day, morning and night, with Jacob Goodman's vociferous complaints about his commute to the nonprofit he worked at in D. C. Sherwin's older brothers were both lawyers in the district, one a do-good and one a corporate attorney. Bertram earned pots of money and lived in wealthy Potomac. Harvey's more modest income as a poverty lawyer had permitted him to buy a house in a borderline, gentrified section of Southeast. Sherwin's mother Stella was terrified of this vicinage and had been unable to bring herself, in the two years he had lived there, to set foot in it. Jacob and Sherwin, however, visited regularly. It was there that Jacob first encountered Sherwin's theory of "the younger brother of two over-achieving lawyers," and how said sibling need not achieve anything, even a bachelor's degree.

"Do you realize our son, Sherwin," Jacob bellowed upon setting foot inside his enormous house.

"Yes, I know his name," Stella said.

"Did I say you didn't?"

"You picked it, not me. I liked Hugo."

"If he had been named Hugo, he would have been pummeled, every day on the playground."

"I bet Hugo Black wasn't pummeled every day on the playground."

"Did I just commute an hour and a half from Washington D. C. to hear piffle about Hugo Black?"

"Piffle?"

"Do you know what traffic was like on the Beltway?"

"Yes I do. You tell me every day."

"Do you realize that Sherwin does not intend to go to college?"

"Maybe he could have used a little pummeling on the playground."

"You're not stunned, shocked and appalled?"

"No. He told me last year."

"He intends to sponge off me, with a little hiking in Greenland on the side."

"Greenland? He told me Western Maryland."

"Well, he modified his plans."

"Take off your tie, it's too tight."

"It is not."

"Then why is your face purple?"

"Because I'm staring at the prospect of supporting a very odd, aimless, goofy, do-nothing lie-abed for the next twenty-five years."

"I tell you, if we had named him Hugo, none of this would have happened."

"You coddle him."

"He's the baby. Harvey and Betram picked on him."

Sherwin came in from the car.

"You!" Jacob pointed a finger at his youngest son. The gray hair stood out in angry tufts around Jacob's otherwise bald pate.

"My name is Sherwin."

"It should have been Hugo."

"*You* are going to college!" Jacob shouted, and his finger shook.

"We'll see about that," Sherwin said. "What's for dinner?"

"Your favorite," Stella said.

"What about my favorite?" Jacob asked.

"Nobody likes that. We're all sick of roasted chicken."

"Black bean quesadillas?" Sherwin asked brightly.

Stella nodded and gave her son an adoring look.

"I'm sick of black bean quesadillas," Jacob said. "They give me gas. I want something else."

"There's a vegetable stir fry."

"I'm sick of that too. I'd like something different," Jacob said. "Something that's not Mexican or Chinese. Something like Oysters Rockefeller. That's what I'm waiting for."

"You've got a long wait," Stella informed him.

"How long?"

"Kingdom come. I don't do oysters. You know that."

"Then surprise me."

"All right. When Sherwin graduates, he's going to live at home, pursue his interests and maybe take a class or two at that fancy cooking school in Bethesda."

Jacob, purple again, began to sputter.

"But there's an upside for you."

"I can hardly wait."

"*I* will take cooking classes with him. As a result you will finally get food that's neither Mexican nor Chinese."

"Thank God."

"It will be Thai."

Jacob slumped into a chair, put his head in his hands and exclaimed, "I'm on the fish oil express."

"Yes, I have decided to master Thai cuisine."

Though well into middle age, Stella's slim figure and platinum blond hair often misled strangers into the assumption that she was in her late thirties. She applied more creams and potions to her skin than her husband could count, and often, on a search for dental floss in Stella's bathroom, he would find himself agog at the rows and rows of bottles, jars and tubes of sundry elixirs, all guaranteed to keep his wife looking young. The odd thing was, they worked. At office events or official get-togethers of any sort, Jacob's colleagues all assumed he had a much younger trophy wife. Jacob greatly appreciated such flattering assumptions but would have been happy to tolerate a few wrinkles in exchange for an occasional fillet mignon. Unfortunately for him, Stella had befriended Edie Sullivan, and he bitterly rued the day. Fillet mignon, bad for his arteries and full of alien hormones, was off the menu forever. Omega-three fish oil pills, various extracts, antioxidants and more vitamins than he could count, greeted him on his plate each morning. "You'd think I'm an invalid," he would grumble, swallowing them down.

"You will be if you don't take that E and licopene," Stella warned.

Sherwin, far more open-minded about these many panaceas, approached each new one with curiosity. He would raise the newest gelcap up to his glasses for inspection, run a hand through his straight black hair and take a stab at it: "green tea extract?"

"Nope," his mother corrected. "Beta carotene."

"Says here in the newspaper too much beta carotene's associated with an increase in lung cancer," Jacob dourly read aloud. "Great. I haven't smoked in thirty years, but my wife's going to kill me with lung cancer."

"Don't believe everything you read in the *Post*."

"It's my Bible," he shot back, looking over the tops of his glasses and the top of his paper at his wife, fashionably attired in a designer top and capris at seven a.m., "that and *The New York Times*. I almost went into journalism, you know."

"How could I not?" Sherwin asked, placing the gelcap in his pajama pocket. "You've told me every morning of my life for the past seventeen years."

"Who did that study?" Stella demanded.

"The NIH. And I don't think you're going to be able to impugn the credibility of the NIH."

"Hmmph."

"Score one for Jacob Goodman," Sherwin's father addressed him. "I'm *not* taking the beta carotene."

Sherwin loved the rhythm of summer, of part-time, well-paid employment at Starbucks, of hours spent lounging in front of his computer, the latest Apple model, planning his online startup magazine for computer geeks, reading sci fi on the living room couch, napping in what his mother called his "mind-bogglingly messy" room, hanging out with his friends at the pool, dining with them at the sub shop, cruising around the sleepy suburbs in their beat-up Toyotas or Nissans or his own impeccable Audi, or dropping in to play video games far into the night. He intended to extend this round of activity and, he had to admit, inactivity, permanently, after high school. He liked stories of computer tycoons who had started out running little business in their garages.

"Yes, but they had *inventions*," Jacob protested.

"I will too, eventually."

"Get an MBA."

"Maybe later."

"That means never."

"Bingo."

He expected the paternal harassment to last several months. Then, Jacob would become bored with a situation he could not alter and stop complaining.

"Don't be too sure," Stella warned him. "He's been driving on the Beltway for over twenty years and he still kvetchs about it morning and night, like clockwork. Regular complaining is his strong suit. Look at the meal situation. It's obvious he's not going to get roast chicken. We haven't had it in over a year. I got so sick of roast chicken, the sight of it made me want to throw up. I calculated he was eating a small farm's worth of chickens every year. By now it should be crystal clear – no more roast chicken. But every meal, the same lament about the same missing chicken. This MBA business could go on for quite a while."

Stella was on her son's side. She wanted him to be happy. She considered him easygoing, atypical and completely lacking in ambition. He would eventually find his way, she believed, but it would be harmful to try to cram him into a mold. That would just lead to psychological

problems or perhaps a nervous breakdown, which had happened to her
beloved uncle Eugene when his parents insisted that he take over their
toy manufacturing business in New Jersey instead of becoming an artist
in Greenwich Village. She empathized with Sherwin, because she herself
had seized the opportunity to leap out of the job market by marrying
Jacob upon graduation from the University of Delaware, where she
had majored in fashion and business. One visit from a real live Seventh
Avenue designer to a class in that subject had convinced her of the
unbeatable allure of being a housewife. She had no desire to swim in a
sea of sharks. And since a fashion career would have required a move to
Manhattan, Jacob, allergic to New York, was only too happy to oblige.

"Bertram has become one of those sharks you were so eager to
escape," Sherwin said at one point.

"He makes a little money."

"Mom, he started out at one hundred thousand dollars per year,
fresh out of AU law school. I can't even imagine what he makes now."

"You know you can," Stella diverted the discussion into pleasanter
channels. "Imagination is your strong suit."

And so it was. Given any situation, Sherwin had a remarkable
ability vividly to picture all possible outcomes. He had had it since
babyhood. It was evident when he learned, at nine months, to speak;
because he had not merely spoken a few words, no, he had emitted whole
paragraphs, discourses on whatever happened in his immediate vicinity,
whatever that led him to imagine. With a shock, Stella realized that
she had given birth to an exceptional child. It was a shock, because she
judged herself and her two older sons to be average, and her husband
to be slightly above average. She had rather liked this assessment, liked
considering herself just the same as anybody else, and now, here was this
extraordinary baby, not yet able to walk, sitting in his playpen, describing
his rattles, their shapes, sizes, colors and the things you could do with
them. For instance, his mommy could use them to stir soup.

"Why would I use a rattle to stir soup?" She had asked the precocious
infant.

"This end looks like a spoon. Of course you could use it to stir soup."

"Of course? Where did you learn 'of course'?"

"From you, Bertie, Harvey and Daddy. Of course."

Stella had not known what to do. She felt she should do something,
enroll him in some class for special children or take him to some expert,
but really she was flummoxed. So was Jacob. "Finally, some brains in the

family," was all he would say, and that was not helpful. She consulted her dear uncle Eugene, who journeyed down to Maryland, had an hour's chat with the loquacious infant and delivered a most emphatic edict: do nothing. Let the child do exactly as he pleased and never pressure him. "But won't he be bored in school?"

"Out of his mind," Eugene replied, smiling blandly.

"But then maybe a special school. Maybe the Jewish Community Center has something."

"Not the JCC. Never the JCC."

Stella did not know what her uncle had against the JCC and decided not to ask. "Maybe he needs a psychologist. There could be something wrong. All this talking, and these imaginings, and he's only nine months old! He could have a brain tumor."

Eugene looked at her like she was a cracked pot, then, in a most patronizing manner, repeated his advice, namely, to let the boy be, let him pursue whatever interests he developed and not pressure him in any particular direction. So she had followed this advice, mainly for lack of a better idea, but her youngest son's genius never seemed to flower. He was an average student, interested mainly in computers and video games and singularly unambitious. Most of all he wanted to be accepted as perfectly ordinary by his friends, who did, but who also appreciated his vivid imagination.

"Ask Sherwin," Luis would say, if someone wanted a solution to a problem. "He'll think of all the possibilities and then some."

Aside from this recent ambition to spend the rest of his life vegetating, there had been only one other worry for Sherwin's parents. That had occurred in middle school: shyness. It lasted for Sherwin's entire seventh grade year and then vanished. During that year, he would flee encounters with new people. He stopped inviting his friends over. At family events in Delaware or New Jersey, he would take his gameboy, find and empty room and have nothing to do with anybody. He cowered at the approach of strangers. Alarmed, Stella had consulted a psychologist, but found him unctuous and overbearing, so she gave that up. Then eighth grade came, and Sherwin was back to normal, happy-go-lucky, aimless. It had been a phase.

She had been delighted when he acquiesced in the cooking classes plan. It meant he enjoyed her company, did not merely tolerate her as his mother, because she was fairly certain he had no great interest in cuisine. This new-found confidence about her appeal as a friend led Stella to

be even more lenient about her son's paucity of future plans. If she
benefited by getting to spend more time with him, so be it. He clearly did
not mind maternal company.

"You don't care about him not going to college, because he'll be
home with you," Jacob accused. "You're turning him into a mama's boy."

"Very few of his friends are going directly to college."

"Directly, yes. But they'll go eventually. Ask them and they don't say
'never'."

"When they all do, I'm sure some of the appeal of sleeping 'til noon
and lounging around all day will wear off."

But she was not at all sure of this. She would find Sherwin barefoot,
in a T-shirt and cut-offs, whipping up an omelet for breakfast at one p.m.
and chide him about rising so late – to which he would reply that he
was practicing for the rest of his life. No more high school would mean
no more early rising – ever. She decided against reporting these chats to
Jacob.

Most obnoxious about Sherwin's plans or lack of them was Bertram,
who would sojourn over to the family manse on weekends, sit by the
pool in the back yard, while Sherwin was out at the swim club with
friends and work Jacob up into a frenzy of paternal umbrage.

"Well who do you think's going to be supporting him for the next
couple of decades?" Betram asked. "Not me."

"Me? Me!" Jacob roared in a fury.

"That's why I'm not having kids," Bertram elaborated, sipping his ice
tea. "I do not want to be a sucker."

Jacob, thoroughly empurpled, sputtered in speechless fury.

"Well thank you for helping your father enjoy his weekend," Stella
said. "And for making things so much easier for your younger brother."

"I'm here to oblige," Bertram beamed his oleaginous, professional
attorney's smile upon her, as Stella vowed to catch a few flies and put
them in his soup.

"What do you expect, Mom?" Harvey demanded. "Bertram's got a
chip of dry ice where he should have a heart. To make matters worse,
he spends every hour of every day in the company of cold, competitive,
calculating, corporate lawyers."

"Do you think you could add some alliteration to that?" Stella asked.

Harvey smiled, then frowned. "The guy's a prick. I hate to admit it.
He's my own brother, but he has the conscience of a gnat, the heart of
an ice cube and the soul of a shark. And that's probably unfair to sharks.

His idea of fun is seeing to it that billionaires get tax cuts or that gigantic corporations get to merge into mega-corporations, lay off thousands and not get sued for anticompetitive practices or price fixing."

"You're saying I raised a monster."

"Nah. You were fine. He did this all on his own."

"Won't you come out back to the pool?"

"And ruin my afternoon sitting with him? I'll stay right here in the dining room, thank you very much."

"But someone needs to protect your father. Look." They both gazed out the picture window, past the peonies and petunias to the pool, where Jacob, having leapt up from his lounge chair, was now pacing and gesticulating wildly in what was quite obviously a rage.

Harvey punched a few numbers on his cell phone. "Hi Sherwin. Come home late tonight. Bertie's got Dad all worked up again over your future plans."

Stella brought the coffee pot in and sat with Harvey, who did not seem to care that Sherwin lacked all ambition. "At least he won't be making the world worse," Harvey said. "Unlike his oldest brother." They watched as Jacob paced and ran his fingers through his tufts of gray hair. "I'm not going to let him do this to his father," Stella said at length and went to the next room, opened the sliding glass doors and stepped out on the path that led through the flower garden, between two huge, blue-blooming hydrangeas to the pool.

"What have you two been doing?" She asked innocently.

Jacob sputtered incoherently.

"Oh dear," she looked Bertram in the eyes. "I do hope you haven't upset him. He has a blood pressure problem."

Betram was surprised.

"Yes, that came out at his last check-up."

The smallest hint of contrition flickered in her oldest son's dark eyes.

"Now you go, Bertie, and get the pills on the kitchen counter by the sink and bring them out here. You wouldn't want to give your father a stroke."

Bertram rose and rather sheepishly made his way back to the house.

"Jacob Goodman," she began. Her husband sat down meekly on a lounge chair. "I do not believe you have allowed that sneaky, mean-spirited rat of an oldest child of yours to manipulate you –"

"I don't believe you talk about our son this way."

"I talk like this because he *is* our son, and we know him better than anybody. You know I would never tolerate it if someone outside the family described him that way."

"Good. Important things first."

By the time Bertram reappeared with the blood pressure pills, Stella had managed to soothe her husband. She rose, took Bertram by the elbow and led him over to the diving board. "You will never mention your brother Sherwin to your father again."

"Oh, Mom –"

"Because if you do, it will kill him. And then I will kill you."

"Stop joking."

Stella glared at him.

"All right," Bertram raised both hands and his shoulders, conceding the point. "I won't discuss my lazy, sponging, no good little brother, who you baby."

Stella's eyes flashed, and her son took a step away from her. "Say what you like to me, Bertie. But when you're around Jacob or Sherwin, you just keep it to yourself. Or else."

Thenceforth, Bertram avoided the subject. He had, however, an odd, condescending sniffle, which became, in Sherwin's presence, rather pronounced.

"You know mom, I think Bertie has allergies," Sherwin remarked.

"I hope so."

"You do?"

"Suffering builds character. And Bertie could use a little."

Summer rolled into fall, and Sherwin made no college applications.

"So what schools are you applying to?" Jacob asked Luis, who had dropped by to visit one balmy, late September afternoon.

"I'm not."

Jacob looked pleased. "What'll you be doing?"

"The air force."

"Well, well...Stella," Jacob hollered from the front hall into the kitchen. Stella emerged into the doorway with an apron over her designer jeans and top. She was cooking pad Thai.

"Luis here is going into the air force."

"How nice."

"Maybe Sherwin should consider the military."

"Maybe he should."

Luis suppressed a chuckle.

"It's not that far-fetched," Jacob persisted, "for Sherwin, I mean."

"Luis," Stella said, "you tell him."

"Ah, Mr. Goodman, I really don't think, short of a national emergency, that the military is for Sherwin."

Jacob looked dejected.

"It's just not for some people."

"Sherwin is one of those," Stella elucidated, "for whom it's not." Sherwin ambled in.

"So you're not joining the air force," Jacob addressed him sourly.

"Who me? Oh no. That's Luis. He's the one wants to do that."

"What about the marines?" Jacob asked. Sherwin shook his head. "Or the army? Or the navy? Or the coast guard?"

"I know what the five services are, Dad."

"How about the national guard?"

Stella came forward, grasped Jacob under the arm and propelled him into the kitchen. "Taste my latest creation," she said.

"Do I have to?"

Sherwin and Luis opened the glass sliding doors and stepped out into the garden. They sat at a table under an umbrella by the pool, and Stella brought them ice tea. Luis looked around at the trees, whose leafy branches swayed softly above them, at the flowers, the aqua water before him, a little stone wall at the edge of the property with ivy growing on it and a small fish pond that Stella had put in over there and sighed that he could fully understand Sherwin's wish not to leave home. Sherwin explained that he simply did not know what to do, that he had imagined every choice and every possible outcome, and nothing seemed right. "I'm like the piece that doesn't fit anywhere in the jigsaw puzzle."

"It's no big deal. You'll figure it out." Luis drank his ice tea, then quietly averred that Sherwin could do anything, if he put his mind to it. What he did not elaborate was his conviction that within their group of eight friends, Sherwin was the one who would do something exceptional. Oh, Chandra was a possibility too, there would be no keeping him back. But Chandra would excel at something practical, like business; with Sherwin, it would be something different. Not that Luis didn't have high hopes for himself, he did, but he knew something unusual when he saw it, and he had been seeing it in his friend Sherwin since the eighth grade.

For his part, Sherwin was always a tiny bit embarrassed by this confidence Luis had in him. He felt so at sea, so overwhelmed by the welter of possibilities before him, that he failed to see how he deserved the certainty so implicit in Luis' casual "something will happen, then you'll know." How could Luis be positive that Sherwin would not just flounder for the rest of his life? Luis, who had already decided upon an engineering career, who had plans, with Harry, for fantastic inventions to ameliorate the lives of millions in Central America. What could he possibly believe Sherwin would do that could be of any benefit to anyone, even to Sherwin himself? Whence this belief in Sherwin's destiny? For that's what it was, unspoken between them, that Sherwin would do something of exceptional worth, that all his lounging and late-rising and lying abed was preparation, the chrysalis stage, from which something astonishing would without question emerge. Except that Sherwin did question it. In his paralysis at the array of choices before him, he recognized a condition that had afflicted him for years and that could continue to do so, perhaps for the rest of his life. Yes, it was more than likely that he would live until old age as someone who had always been promising, who, as a child, had tested off the charts, but who had been utterly unable to make up his mind what to do with himself. There was no end to his quandary, nowhere in sight.

Luis, however, did not, apparently, see his predicament that way. Maybe this was part of the unaccountable closeness Sherwin felt to him, a closeness he could not generally explain, other than to point to its obvious causes – that Luis never treated him like an oddball, that Luis had such an obvious affection for Sherwin's parents, admiration for his home, respect for Harvey, for his work as a poverty lawyer, for the fact that he could have made hundreds of thousands of dollars a year but chose instead something selfless, so much less remunerative and the subdued awe that Luis reserved for what Sherwin regarded as his own rather questionable intelligence. These were the obvious reasons. Less visible and, if mentioned, something Luis would dismiss, was Luis' eminently practical mind and rock solid common sense. Only once had Sherwin alluded to these virtues, and Luis had been so embarrassed that he never did so again. But they were always there, so different from any mental strengths that Sherwin possessed that they drew him, reassured him, made him believe that perhaps his friend's faith in him was not misplaced. After all, if such a down-to-earth pragmatist as Luis considered it unmistakable that Sherwin would find his way, what was there to worry about?

With Luis, Sherwin became meditative about his prospects. He would contemplate Outward Bound, being dropped in the wilderness of an island off the North Carolina coast and having to survive for a week, as he had read about in a brochure. He would be taught how to make fires, how to find food, how to set up a temporary shelter. Or he would consider getting an internship at the National Institutes of Health, then, after a year, he would apply to college after all, major in biology and search for the cure for diseases that ravaged Africa – malaria, sleeping sickness or AIDS. Luis became especially enthusiastic about this scenario, and they could ramble on about it for an entire evening, out by the pool.

"What's this about biological research?" Stella asked. She had come out with portions of pad Thai for each of them and more ice tea. "You have to go to college for that, unless I'm mistaken."

"Maryland's biology department is not bad at all," Luis said.

"The question is, what kind of research do they produce?" Sherwin asked.

Stella looked from one boy to the other, as if she did not believe her ears.

"You can look into that on the internet," Luis slurped his ice tea.

"I've heard Hopkins is good in bio too."

Stella's hand, clutching the pitcher of ice tea, trembled ever so slightly.

"Hopkins is great," slurp, slurp, "and you're lucky – you could probably afford it."

"Could we?" Sherwin asked his mother.

"Oh," she shrugged as if it were the most natural thing in the world, "of course we could afford it. A drop in the bucket."

"You got to go online," more slurping, "see what all the concentrations are, look up the professors, find out who's famous for what. Are there any Nobel laureates? Who published what research and in what journals. Then for the area you're interested in, pathology –"

Stella nearly dropped the pitcher of ice tea.

"Pathology research," Sherwin corrected.

"You've got to see who's done what work on what diseases. Do the same thing on the NIH website."

"NIH," Stella repeated, and as Luis explained that Sherwin was considering an internship there, her mouth formed a little, surprised "o." As Luis went on to clarify that her son intended to search for cures for tropical diseases, which would require joint NIH/Johns Hopkins research, publishing papers, travel to Africa and a PhD, her eyebrows rose, and her eyes rounded. At that magical set of initials – PhD – Stella tottered, ever so slightly, but caught herself in her Jimmy Choo slingbacks, murmured, "why don't I just leave the pitcher here on the table. I don't want to disturb your discussion," and tottered back into the house.

"Jacob!" She shrieked. "We need to invite Luis over more often."

"I beg your pardon," Jacob put down his *New York Times* and pressed his head against the back of the leather wingback armchair, "but I believe that's Sherwin's bailiwick."

"Maybe for dinner. This weekend," she screeched breathlessly, as she hurried into the living room.

"Maybe not. Unless you haven't noticed, Sherwin prefers dining at that sub shop with his friends to a meal of Thai noodles and dumplings drowned in fish oil here at home."

"Fish oil's good for you."

"And frankly I can't blame him. Now if you'd said we should *accompany* Sherwin and Luis to the sub shop, you might have received a more sympathetic hearing from me." Jacob folded his paper, and misty longing clouded his eyes, which gazed unfocused at the abstract, yellow and orange painting over the mantelpiece. "I wouldn't mind a twelve-inch meat ball sub myself, right now."

"Luis has talked Sherwin into college."

Jacob snapped right to, sat up, folded the paper again and threw it on the floor. "Sit down, sit down, Stella. You're shaking."

"Stella sat in the armchair across from him.

"What college?"

"Johns Hopkins."

A look of utter amazement crept over Jacob's face.

"That's not all," Stella went on breathlessly. "They were discussing a major in biological research. Pathology! Pathology, Jacob!" Jacob leapt up, grabbed Stella and began waltzing her around the living room. "So what about my idea," Stella went on. "Luis comes over for dinner."

Jacob stopped. "That'll be the last we ever see of him. No. Like I said: we'll go, with them, to the sub shop."

Stella looked skeptical. Then she said brightly: "you know where a major in biology leads." They beamed at each other, clasped hands and said in unison: "medical school."

Stella wanted to offer the two boys dumplings, but Jacob talked her out of that and into ordering a large pizza with all the toppings.

"What's the occasion?" Luis asked, as Stella brought forth the pizza box, and set it on the table by the pool.

"Yeah, how'd we get out of the dumplings?" Sherwin wanted to know and then, upon opening the box, "and what happened to half the pizza?"

"Your father got to it first," Stella said sourly, " but don't worry, it's a large. There will be plenty."

She returned to the house, to the dining room, where Jacob had taken up his post at the window with his binoculars. "They're eating," he reported, and he chomped down on a slice of pizza. "But I'm no good at lip reading when a person's mouth is full of pizza. It just looks like glob, glob, glob. Maybe if I move over here."

"No, no, then you'll be visible. Where you are is good. The angle, the bushes conceal you."

"I think Luis just said 'Johns Hopkins.'"

"Are you sure he didn't say 'pass the pizza?' Looks like Sherwin just passed him a slice."

"Hey, who's got the binoculars?"

The Goodmans stood in the gathering gloom and watched their son and his friend devour the pizza. Not once did Jacob observe the words 'medical school' on either young man's lips. "But this is not a setback, Stella. I may simply have missed it. We need to strategize."

"First," she said, holding an index finger up in front of her husband's face.

"Get that away from the binoculars," he said.

She did so. "First: never push. We never mention medical school. We stick to what he knows we know."

"Which is? Wait a minute, Luis is gesturing. Biology! I saw it, Stell. He said biology."

"Which is," she continued, "biological research, college, maybe Johns Hopkins and pathology. Write all that down, Jacob, because you'll forget and mention medical school and then all bets are off." Jacob rested the binoculars on a sideboard, got a crumpled piece of paper and a pen out of his pocket and began writing. "What next?"

"Next, we don't mention college for the year after high school. We return to this notion of an internship at NIH."

"Good, good," Jacob said, scribbling.

"I'll contact the internship coordinator at the school. She'll arrange it."

"You're a genius, Stella."

"Then, as he gets interested in the research, next fall – because he can start part-time this spring – then he applies to colleges. Nothing too far away."

"How far is that?"

"He can live on campus."

"Well, that's a concession."

"I'd like to see him on weekends."

"So I guess Harvard is out."

"So are all the Ivy Leagues. Besides he doesn't have the grades."

"Got it," Jacob scribbled: "fifty-mile radius. No Ivy Leagues."

"Can you remember this?"

"Well, if I can't I can look at my notes."

"That would be rather odd, wouldn't it? You're in the middle of a conversation with Sherwin about his future and you suddenly start reading from notes?"

"I'll say I have to go to the bathroom. Read up there and come back."

"Now we have a plan."

"Pass me the binoculars."

Meanwhile Sherwin had no idea of his parents' dreams for him. "What's with the binoculars?" He asked one afternoon.

"Your father's taken up bird watching."

"In the evenings? From the dining room? I only ever find them here, at night."

"There's a very rare bird that hops around in that maple," Stella pointed out the window. "It comes out only at night."

"Really? What's it called?"

"The Hopkins Boobie."

"The Hopkins Boobie? Never heard of that. What a strange name."

"It's only found within a fifty-mile radius of Crofton."

"Indigenous?"

"No. Invasive."

"Like the snakeheads."

Yes, Stella conceded, like the snakeheads.

"Where's it from?"

Stella tossed her mane of platinum blond hair. "What am I, the Hopkins Boobie expert?"

"You seem to be. You don't know where it came from?"

"Eastern Europe. Minsk, to be exact."

"Minsk. Isn't that where your family's from?"

"Yes and part of your father's."

"What a coincidence."

"Yes indeed. Well, now you know why your father's so interested in it."

That evening Sherwin ambled into the living room. Jacob had completely disappeared behind the *Times* in his high, wingback armchair.

"Now I know what you're doing with those binoculars."

The newspaper went down to Jacob's lap. "You do?"

"You're watching the Hopkins Boobie."

"That's an odd way to put it."

"That's what Mom said. You've taken up bird watching."

"Oh," Jacob raised the paper again.

"I'd never heard of the Hopkins Boobie before."

"That's because it's so rare."

"From Minsk, Mom says."

"A very intelligent bird and much underrated."

"How did it get here?"

"On a boat."

"Why is it called Hopkins, I mean, isn't that kind of English, for an Eastern European invasive species?"

"Short for Hopinski."

Sherwin scratched his head. "You've got to be pulling my leg."

"That's what everybody said about the snakeheads. Now look, they've fanned out from Crofton. Soon they'll be everywhere. The guy who first identified them looks like a genius. Someday that's maybe all Crofton will be famous for – snakeheads and the Hopkins Boobie. Something to think about."

Luis could not praise Sherwin's parents enough. He thought Stella looked like a fashion model, and she was so understanding and fair-minded, treated everyone equally, for all her wealth. She had not a trace of social snobbery. He also had boundless respect for Jacob's work at a healthcare nonprofit, where he obviously earned a bundle but could, just as clearly, have earned much more at a major accounting firm or corporation. He liked the way they spent their spare time reading instead of watching television, was curious about the fact that they appeared to observe no religion whatsoever and approved of Stella's culinary eclecticism, her eagerness to find out about cuisines from various corners of the earth. "They're so *different*," he told Sherwin one late afternoon, when twilight was coming on out by the pool "And they've always been so welcoming, but lately, I gotta say, they really roll out the red carpet for me."

"Yeah," Sherwin guzzled a container of Gatorade, "I noticed that too."

Stella appeared in a dark tan Coco Chanel outfit with chocolate colored trim. She was carrying an oversized bag of Chinese takeout.

"I thought you boys might like some food, while you sit out here and...talk."

"What else might we do?" Sherwin demanded.

"Well, you might swim, I guess."

"Have we ever?"

"Talking's better."

"Thanks Mom."

"If you need anything, anything at all, just give me a holler," Stella backed away, then turned toward the house through the garden.

"See what I mean?" Luis asked.

"They must have decided you're a good influence," Sherwin chuckled. "That's it."

"Well I am, of course," Luis said, opening the food and passing his friend a paper plate and plastic utensils. "She gave us enough food for an army," he exclaimed. "Look, eight big boxes."

"That's my mother," Sherwin said. "It's a miracle I'm not a six-hundred pound wonder."

"At least you're not on a diet of health food, like poor Harry. Geez, it's a miracle he hasn't starved to death."

"Are they talking?" Stella, entering the darkened dining room, demanded in a whisper.

"No, they're eating," Jacob replied sourly, also in a whisper, as he stared through his high-powered binoculars at the poolside meal.

"Why aren't they talking?"

"Because you emptied the entire kitchen of Szechuan Palace, since they hadn't eaten in twenty minutes and gave them enough food to fill a cargo jet. That's why. And stop whispering."

"You're whispering."

"That's because you are."

"Well, if they're not talking, I don't know what we're doing here. You can't read their lips, if all they're doing is chewing."

"I'm getting hungry."

"I made fish. Don't look so disappointed. Yes, it's Thai."

"That does it," Jacob put down the binoculars and headed for the next room.

'Where are you going?"

"Out there, with them. Why should they be the only ones to get a decent meal tonight?"

Sherwin made many reciprocal visits to the Ignacio's tiny, three-bedroom rambler as well. Luis' two younger brothers shared a room, and his sister Elena, only a year younger than Luis, had a tiny bedroom to herself. The parents' room was always immaculate. It looked to Sherwin as if no one lived there. The polished dressers never had a drawer open. The double bed, neat as a pin, looked as if no one ever sat on it, no less slept in it. Not a speck marred the wall-to-wall carpet. Luis slept either on a roll-out bed in the living room or a cot in the basement, which, Mrs. Ignacio would often explain in her broken English, was under construction by her husband, a contractor. The renovations were almost completely finished. As soon as Cesar Ignacio put on the finishing touches and cleaned up, there would be a family room, a laundry room, a bathroom and a private bedroom for Luis, all ready for use. "It'll be done just in time for me to join the air force," Luis joked. "So guess who'll get it? Nathalie, her husband and two kids will move in. You wait and see." The family room already showed signs of use by Cesar and his buddies, as well as Nathalie's children.

"No, no. No Nathalie," Sandra Ignacio would exclaim. "I work ten hours a day at the dry cleaners. I can't have two babies in the house. Is too much."

Sandra looked much older than her thirty-nine years. When her hair turned prematurely gray, she dyed it. When she lost a bottom tooth, she had it replaced. But two of them still had partial gold caps, and crow's feet had appeared at the corners of her eyes. Most telling of all were the deep, dark circles under her eyes. She had consulted Nathalie, once the family's beauty expert, who had directed her to the appropriate cosmetics, but even with make-up, she looked worn out. She cooked continuously and always handed Sherwin a plate of tamales on his way to the back deck with Luis.

"My parents and Miqueas and Rafael go in the pickup. Elena and I get Nathalie and her family in the minivan," Luis explained how they all crammed into two vehicles to go to church every Saturday and Sunday morning. No one would be seen in Luis' battered Nissan, so that was left behind. Lately, now that Elena had her driver's license, Luis had been accorded, in his words, a reprieve. He was permitted to sleep in Saturday mornings, which he did with such gusto that often when they returned from church, he still had not arisen. He found late rising so appealing that when he arranged summer hours with Paul Lirano's father, he snagged the late shift – eleven a.m. 'til closing. His father had just about completed the bedroom renovation downstairs, so, to keep from being awakened early, Luis slept there. "Now I see what you've been raving about," Luis told Sherwin. "Getting up before seven really is for the birds. I don't know how I'm going to readjust to school."

They would sit on the enormous back deck, under the blue and white umbrella, drinking orangina that Sandra brought to them in iced glasses on a tray. "This is the life," Luis would say, looking out over the back lawn and into the back yards of his neighbors.

Only once had he opened up about where they lived before moving to Anne Arundel County. It was an apartment in another county, Prince Georges,' in a neighborhood called Langley Park that was filled with poor African Americans and immigrants – African, Central American, Indian, Asian. They had lived there until Luis was in eighth grade, sharing the three-bedroom apartment with another family. Originally they had shared it with two other families. With no mattresses, they had slept on newspapers laid out on the floor. Sandra sold flowers on the street corner, and her husband was a day laborer. In those years, elementary school and middle school, Luis had loved nothing better than sitting in the classroom, listening to the teacher. It was so quiet, everyone had their own little space, a desk and a chair, and there was so much less chaos. He was a star student, soft-spoken, obedient and appreciated by all of his teachers. By fourth grade he had grasped that this thing called school, this system with its clear punishments and rewards, with its ever-present rules, might be a way into a better world, a world with mattresses and pillows, sidewalks that did not smell of urine and were not covered with litter, a world where he could have a large, sunny room to himself. Even when he was older, with a much clearer picture of what he would wrest from the world for himself, the longing for a large sunny room, just for him, remained. It was at the top of his list. He had hoped, when his parents became legal aliens and had saved enough to purchase their little house, that his dream might come true. But no, he was the oldest boy and thus deemed most capable of sacrifice. He slept in the living room. And at last, when it looked like he would get his own room, it was to be in the basement, with little or no sun. "I guess I'll have to wait 'til after the air force," he told Sherwin, "to get that room." He sighed and gazed appreciatively at all the little, green backyards laid out in view before them. "But you can bet, when I'm done, and I've paid all my dues, that's the first thing I'll get – a big, quiet, sun-filled room, just for me."

Luis found it uniquely peaceful and soothing to sit on that back deck, to have a little, unsullied bit of green to look at, to watch the neighbor's cat prowl in the shade along the wire fence, mesmerized by the ubiquitous rabbits safely on the other side. Or he would gaze over Elena's vegetable patch and flower garden, where she would often weed and water in the late afternoon, after the heat of the day had passed. Like Luis she was quiet and kept to a small group of friends. She read a lot, did her gardening and, as always, looked after her younger brothers. She had practically raised them – Sandra had been so busy working. But she did not complain, preferring housework and home childcare to sallying forth in search of paid employment. She had very long brown hair that she tied up under a floppy hat when she gardened and an attractive face, paler than her brothers,' with high cheekbones and slightly slanted eyes, a face that exuded a strange mixture of shyness and self-possession, the face of someone who listened quietly to everything said to her, remembered it and turned it over thoughtfully in her mind later. To Sherwin, it was an extraordinary face, and he, like Jones and Chandra, found himself oddly subdued in her presence, awkward and full of wonderings about what she was thinking. To Sherwin it was a prize to win a smile from her, not because he harbored any romantic feelings, but because she had baffled his usually unstoppable imagination. Jones and Chandra felt the same way, and Luis, the protective older brother, knew they had no designs on her whatsoever when they said that there was something marvelous about Elena.

"Elena rocks," Jones summed it up.

"She'll go to an Ivy League school," Chandra added. "You'll see I'm right."

"From Chandra," Luis chuckled later to Sherwin, "that is the highest possible praise."

They drank their orangina and watched Elena toss weeds into a pile.

"I notice he didn't say Harvard," Sherwin commented.

"Oh well, you know," Luis grinned, "that's reserved for Chandra alone." He leaned forward, placed his drink on the table and called to Elena: "mariposas."

Indeed white butterflies, seemingly from nowhere, fluttered through the garden. It was a joke between Luis and Elena that they followed her everywhere. "She is the mariposa queen," Luis explained to Sherwin, who laughed and replied: "it fits. One more incongruity about Elena. Why am I not surprised?"

"Here we are in the lap of luxury, eh?" Luis asked. He gazed around at the splendors of suburbia and wondered, as he sometimes did, why he had chosen the rigors of the air force, when he could continue after graduation to work for Mr. Lirano, making good money, sleeping late, watching Elena garden on weekends in the late afternoon, maybe eventually going into contracting with his father. At moments like that he felt no urge to make something of himself, no need to master the intricacies of engineering, no desire to pilot a fighter plane. He could just drift through high summer like several of his friends, Animal and Harry for instance, chat with Elena about the great Latin American writers whose novels she read in Spanish, tinker with computers, with his Nissan, plunge into the water at the swim club or the Goodmans,' when it became too hot – but somehow when his thoughts reached winter, they became ambitious again. The idea of sleeping late in December lacked appeal, and there would be no long warm twilights to lounge in on the back deck; from December, his mind's eye gazed down the years into more advanced adulthood, and he remembered Aesop's fable about the grasshopper and the ant, read to him by his fourth-grade teacher, never forgotten, and knew he had better be an ant and make up his mind to it once and for all. He could not afford to meander like Sherwin, for whom he harbored no resentment of this luxury that he himself could not afford. Besides, there was something exceptional about Sherwin, something that might take a long time and many false starts to develop, something that, Luis felt reasonably sure, he himself did not have nor need to worry about nurturing.

His parents wanted him to work with his father. Though he never would have dreamt of even hinting that for him this would be a dead end, they saw it, and both were resigned to the military. Nathalie supported him, and so did her husband, but not Elena. When he first told the family, at dinner, she had become very quiet and stopped eating. Later she had knocked on the bathroom door, while he was brushing his teeth.

"What will you do if you have to shoot someone?" she asked, opening the door.

"That won't happen."

"It's the military. What if?"

"Then I guess I'll do it."

"I don't think so," she said. "I think you'll get shot instead."

He stopped brushing, his dark brown eyes fastened on her lighter hazel ones. He was almost angry, and if it had been anyone else, would have been, very, and insulted, but it was Elena, and she was not trying to provoke him or demean him or even argue. She was telling him the truth as she saw it. He turned and spat in the sink. "Then I guess that will be that."

"And what do you think will happen to us?"

He hung up the toothbrush, leaned over the sink with each hand on a side of it. She had made him feel horrible.

She stood there a moment longer, in her long, white, cotton nightgown with her long light brown hair and waited for the reply he was determined not to give. At last she spoke for him: "nothing would ever make us whole again." He did not look at her, he continued staring at the sink, at the water running down the drain. When he finally glanced up, the white nightgown, the light brown hair were gone, and the door to her tiny room was shut against him.

For weeks she was distant; their usual closeness, ability to finish each other's sentences, know each other's thoughts – all that had ruptured. She did not smile at him when he came home from work, sometimes did not even look up from her book or whatever kid's show she was watching with Miqueas. When they were alone together, out back, he relaxing under the umbrella, she in the vegetable patch, she weeded so savagely that sometimes he thought she imagined it was him that she was uprooting from his misguided ambitions, his dreadful dream for the future. "That is what I think of you going into the air force," she seemed to say, as she wrenched some vine out of the ground and tossed it onto the compost heap. She lost all reason about it, pulling so vigorously that one late afternoon he noticed her hands were bloody. He got the gardening gloves and offered them to her. But she pushed back a strand of brown hair, leaving a reddish brown smudge on her forehead and said: "what's a little blood, eh?"

He retreated to the umbrella, telling himself that if it were anyone else he would not tolerate this assault on his manhood for an instant. And it was true. Had it been Nathalie's husband, Mauricio, for example, he would have socked him in the jaw and for a while, soothed the strange, mixed up, hurt emotions that swirled around inside him by imagining that it *was* the faithless Mauricio who disapproved of his plans, who condescended to him, who told him things about himself he had no right to utter, and he would salve his wounds by imagining himself pummeling the bastard. But it was no good. Mauricio thought the air force was a dandy idea, had even winked at Luis and said, "maybe I'll join you," hinting at an intimacy that did not exist, as if Luis shared his brother-in-law's feeling that his marriage unfairly confined him.

Elena's silence continued to bother him, and he could not bring himself to mention it to anyone. Conveniently, no one seemed to notice. Or perhaps his parents had, understood the cause and avoided the topic. But it was too personal to discuss. It went to the core of who he was and who his sister was, to his vague sense that because she was right about most things, she might also be right about this, and to his despair about his prospects if he didn't take the educational opportunities the military afforded. And then there was his patriotism – he knew it was flashy, and he knew Elena had long disapproved. She objected to most kinds of show, but especially something that could so easily be misinterpreted and abused. When her history class studied the 1960s in ninth grade, she had learned the word "jingoistic," and she did not hesitate to use it. Though she had never applied it to him, Luis felt her censure on certain topics, felt that word, lurking not so far back in her mind and wondered if she might be right.

"What's with Elena?" Jones asked one afternoon.

"Nothing," Luis replied. It was beastly hot, even with cold drinks under the umbrella, but that did not stop Elena, on her hands and knees in the garden, unprotected from the blazing sun, from ferociously ripping up weeds right and left.

"Usually she talks to you," Jones observed. "And usually she's reasonable about the weather."

Suddenly Luis could not wait another second to unburden himself of his embarrassing and painful predicament." She's angry at me about the air force."

Jones eyed him coolly. "She's right," he said after a moment.

"You think I don't have doubts?" Luis exploded, relieved at last to have someone he could yell at. "You think I'm some kind of nitwit incapable of second thoughts, unaware of possible drawbacks?"

"Nobody said that."

"It's implied, as if I'm some kind of jingoistic moron, gung ho for every war –"

"Well, people who volunteer to be soldiers often are."

"People who volunteer to be soldiers often don't have a lot of other choices."

"Not you. You could put yourself through the state university, you know that."

Luis knew a losing argument when he saw one, so he tried another approach. "Maybe I have feelings about my country that you don't."

"If that includes volunteering to kill foreigners in imperialistic wars, well, maybe you do."

"Imperialistic!" Luis pushed his glass of orangina away in disgust. "That's just cant."

Jones shrugged. "Maybe. But I'd rather spout cant than further the aims of the military industrial complex with my body and brains. Some things are so bad they reduce you to cant. There's no other way to respond to them."

"I respectfully disagree."

Jones sipped his drink. His blue-eyed gaze flickered over to the garden. "How long's this been going on?" He asked.

"Weeks," Luis said. "You don't know her. She could keep it up all year."

"I guess respectful disagreement doesn't cut it with Elena."

"You could say that," Luis replied sourly.

Jones rose and ambled over to the garden. "What you doin' there?" He asked.

"What's it look like?" Elena asked.

"Weeding, I guess."

"Pulling out the garbage."

"Kinda hot."

"The heat makes me feel better."

"And your hands are bleeding."

"That makes me feel better too."

Jones nodded pensively. "You won't join us for some orangina?"

"Luis wouldn't like what I have to say to him."

"We could all just sit – quietly."

"Maybe you could. Maybe I can't."

Jones ambled back to the umbrella.

"It's hopeless," Luis said.

"You may be right," Jones replied, eyeing him coolly again. "If you won't change your mind for her, I doubt you'll do it for anybody."

"That's not what I meant."

Once Jones knew about this dispute, word got around.

"Wow," Sherwin exclaimed one hot afternoon, when the same scene – Elena in the garden, Luis on the deck – repeated itself. "She's really giving you the cold shoulder. So that's what it's like to have a sister."

"Quite an advertisement," Luis grumbled.

"It is. My brother Bertie wouldn't care if I joined the air force or strapped explosives on my chest and became a suicide bomber."

"I hope you're not equating the two, because that would be –"

"No, no. Elena just really cares about you. I've never seen anything like it."

Luis liked this view; it took the edge off his sister's silence and was balm to his wounded pride. Of course he had known it all along, because he knew Elena, knew that nothing minor could ever come between them, and thus her reaction told him again how important his decision was, how large it loomed in his family's little world, how serious it was and how much he meant to her. He could not stay angry with Elena, especially when it was what she saw as a threat to his welfare that had turned her away. Sherwin was amazed that she was so uncompromising, but Luis was not. He knew her depth, understood that she had seen clear into a future without him, seen herself, her parents, the boys made miserable by his absence, seen herself years hence with nothing but a memory of a muscular, dark-haired young man, steady, intelligent, whose great common sense had failed him, her brother, in an air force uniform.

"She sees only the worst possibilities," Luis explained.

"She needn't. There's no war. And it doesn't look like there'll be any."

"I would have said so too, before her reaction. But Elena has a sixth sense about things, especially things in the family, things that are very important to her."

"Then don't join," Sherwin said simply.

"And if I go on like that, she'll have me afraid to cross the street. You can't let someone else's fears do that to you, become your own. It's crippling." Luis paused, thinking how his decision to enlist would benefit his family and at the same time enable him to "give back," as he thought of it, to repay what he regarded as a debt to a country that had enabled him to go from a shack with dirt floors and open sewage in the street, from a bed on newspapers spread out on the hard floor of an overcrowded apartment, in a neighborhood where derelicts huddled in rags on the corners of dusty highways and women who spoke no English except the words "flowers for sale" approached cars at streetlights to support their young children – to go from all that to the marvel of where he was now. He believed in that debt and chose, stubbornly, he wasn't sure why, to ignore what he knew without asking Elena would say about it, namely, that it could be repaid in other ways. And there were other things she might say, like that many Americans, born well-off, had just as much of a debt, but did not feel it. He could hear her criticisms bombinating in his brain, told himself that they stung like hornets, but they did not. They swarmed, fluttered, filled his mind with possibilities other than his decision, just like the white butterflies that at that instant drifted through the garden toward Elena.

"Lot's of people go in the military," Sherwin said.

"Lots," Luis agreed.

"There's Ronald Johnson, who just graduated. Remember? From Nagoulsalaam's class."

"There's Ronald Johnson."

"And there's Miguel Salamanca."

"And there's Miguel."

"Miguel Salamanca's an idiot," Elena said, passing by the umbrella on her way to the back door. "If you told him to jump off the Washington Monument because he'd be able to fly, he would do it."

Luis looked up. These were the first words that could even remotely be taken as having come from her to him in over a month.

"Well, forget Miguel," said Sherwin.

"Forget Miguel," Luis repeated.

"There's Randy Tyrone," Sherwin went on.

"There's Randy."

"Randy Tyrone is a first class nitwit, who flunked geometry twice," Elena snapped.

"Forget Randy," said Sherwin.

"Forget Randy," said Luis.

"What are you? The echo?" Elena demanded.

"Well, somebody got out of bed on the wrong side today," Luis said.

"Somebody may never get out of bed on the right side, ever again," Elena snapped again.

The door slammed shut.

"Sheesh," Sherwin said.

"Oh brother," Luis breathed and slunk down in his chair, as if hoping that somehow he would be less visible and thus less of a target for her wrath, when Elena returned to the garden.

Thus began the next phase of Elena's anger at her brother. Mostly she continued to ignore him, but on this vast glacial surface of her silence were occasional outcroppings of something else, the random furious retort that hinted at volcanic churnings deep, deep under the surface. But Luis did not mind this new development, because it meant that at least, from time to time, his sister would communicate with him. It also meant things could change, that he would not be frozen out on the ice forever. Best of all, he believed that basically it meant that he had won, that he could go forward with his plans and that she would eventually accept them. She would never like them, or agree with him, and she might very well harass him mercilessly, but their relationship would continue, would no longer be suspended in arctic air.

"There's nothing worse than the silent treatment," he told Sherwin one Saturday afternoon at the gym.

"I wouldn't know," Sherwin replied. "No one in my family ever shuts up." He stopped lifting weights and turned his head to look at Luis, similarly prone, sweating, his arms, neck and jaw muscles working furiously. "Maybe I should suggest it; it might be an improvement."

Luis put down the weights. "It's the second time she's done it to me. Last time, we were little kids. I was nine, she was eight. She's got some determination. Back then she didn't speak to me for seven weeks."

"What did you do?"

Luis turned his head and looked at Sherwin. Sweat glistened on his forehead and temples. "I ate a Reese's pieces that belonged to her."

"Geez."

"I never did that again." He turned his head back, started lifting again. "But at least," he groaned, "back then, there was an easy solution once I swallowed my pride." He put the weights down, panting. "Namely, saving my pennies and buying her a replacement Reese's pieces."

"I guess there are no replacement Reese's pieces in sight this time."

"I guess not," he said dourly.

They showered, dressed and walked out to Sherwin's silver Audi in the parking lot. Luis loved that car and had resolved that one day, when he was a successful software engineer, he would own one. It would go well with his other car, a BMW, and his large house with his wife and kids and the large house next door that he would buy for his parents and whatever other family members lived with them. The house would have many rooms, but there would be one, large, sunny, quiet, that belonged to Luis alone.

"Don't forget the Jacuzzis," Sherwin joked. "And the beach house on the Outer Banks."

"You joke because you've already got it."

"Our beach house is in considerably less tony Rehobeth, Delaware. And no one in my family besides Bertie would be caught dead in a Jacuzzi. My mother considers that conspicuous consumption, or, if you catch her after a drink or two, parvenu."

"Your mother, Mrs. Goodman, who I've never yet seen in a less than high three figures designer outfit?"

Sherwin shrugged, parked the car in a spot outside the sub shop and said: "She's quirky. But if I decided to join the air force, it would not be the silent treatment, oh no. Boy, I'd never hear the end of it."

Luis chuckled, and they both sat for a moment, contemplating the reactions of mothers and sisters to what they regarded as, in some way, a uniquely male decision. Not that women didn't join the military, they knew they did, but not the women in their families. No, their female relatives all had what could only be called a pacifist streak.

"And maybe they're right," Jones said, chomping on his sub in one hand, while he snatched away his soda from Chandra with the other. "Maybe they're the ones with the brains in your families."

"But not yours," Luis said. "The one with the brains in your family–"

"That would be me," Jones said, "And you won't find me signing on to the massive death wish promoted by the state and corporate interests that run this plutocracy we live in. Not now, not ever. And yes, we've had this conversation before."

Four

Later that evening, Donald Jones, who insisted on being addressed
only by his last name, made his way to his father's Ford pickup outside
the sub shop in the dusty little strip mall parking lot. He had a bit of
a drive ahead of him – over to Baltimore in fact, to fetch his father,
Clarence, who was putting in some overtime at the fast freight company
where he had worked for nearly a decade, since retiring from long
distance trucking. Jones' mother, Jessie, who had a low level managerial
job at a nursing home out by the airport, was away for the weekend at
Bethany Beach with his younger sister. She had the other car. His older
brother, who also worked at the fast freight company, refused to set foot
there on weekends. Besides, he kept his own rather wild hours and stayed
out, carousing with his friends and girlfriend who knew where – in short,
his car was unavailable. Hence the deal with Donald – drive his father to
work, pick him up and get to use the car all day Saturday. Jones popped
his Bob Dylan classics into the CD player and sang along to "Masters
of War," as the pickup bounced along suburban lanes and back roads,
somewhat in need of repair, he noticed. With this in mind, he resolved
to come home by a different route. His father entertained a rather odd
view on the department of transportation, an idée fixe, actually, and pot
holes always summoned verbalizations thereof, or what started as mere
vocalizations, a grunt here, a sarcastic comment there, and then, before
you knew it, a full-blown rant.

Clarence sat behind his gray metal desk with the slab of glass on
top, in his cramped little office filled with beat-up old file cabinets and
posters of big rigs. He and his son were mirror images of each other,
he just looked older. He still had most of his red hair, and his blue eyes
were as sharp as Donald's. He had the same medium height, squared-off
physique too, and lots of freckles. He had been a shop steward for his
union for many years and when the freight company finally decided to
pull this thorn out of its side with a promotion to low level management,
he refused. They rewarded him with a closet-sized office anyway, in the
hopes that that would buy him off. His immediate supervisor referred
to him as "the bulldog" or in tipsy moments as "that relentless fuck,"
but despite overt and frequent hostilities, they got on. Most of the crew
was African American or Hispanic, though Clarence was not the only
white, and he filed grievances regularly. He was well known within the

union hierarchy as a squeaky wheel. His grievances received prompt attention. He had been an officer in the union for many years, but now contented himself with being a mere shop steward, though he still received invitations to important confabs and some of the older officers and organizers continued to consult him. A life-long Democrat, he could go on at great length about the treachery of the Reagan Dems in the 1980s. Clinton was too conservative for him, but, he argued, far better than any Republican alternative. He often held forth at the dinner table for the duration of the entire meal on the duplicity of the Republicans who called themselves conservatives but ran up huge deficits, while a moderate Democrat like Clinton had, in a few years, turned up a wonderful surplus that would soon be available to work miracles through social spending. "How's that for irony?" He would demand of his silently chewing family, and when his second son would point out that those deficits were due in large part to unnecessary defense spending, Clarence would be off and running again, on his favorite bête noir, the defense industry.

Unfortunately, on the way back, they hit a pothole. "Those lousy bums in the DOT," Clarence said. "They can arrange to block off two lanes of the interstate for construction during rush hour and back traffic up for fifteen miles and twenty hours, but can they fix a single pothole? What about the one on our street? You could fit a compact car in it. It's been there over a year. I've called and written letters. Nada!"

"Maybe you shouldn't write so many letters."

"And now the geniuses in the DOT have decided to repave parts of Route 50. Route 50 doesn't need repaving. Their heads need repaving. And I said so."

"I hope not in writing."

"In writing and on their goddamned voice mail. You try calling that department. All you get is machines putting you on hold. Twenty years I been trying to get a person on the phone there about the street lights, ever since I went to Fort Worth."

Years before, Clarence had driven a tractor-trailer through the Dallas-Ft. Worth metro area and been very impressed with the sanity brought by modern technology to the business of the timing of traffic lights. "Everywhere else in the country," he said to Donald, "street lights are timed. One turns green, and a few seconds later the one at the next corner turns green. Not here. The Einsteins in our department of highways and transportation think it's better to have one turn green and the next one turn red. Makes for better congestion."

They hit another pothole.

"Jesus Christ, they're idiots!" Clarence exploded. "Before it's over, Donald, I'm gonna sue."

"Don't sue, Dad."

"They're drivin' me to it. Stop the truck."

Donald pulled over. Clarence stepped out and inspected the tires. "No damage this time," he said, getting back in and slamming the door. "I guess we got lucky."

"You can say that again," Donald grumbled. "Anything to stave off a lawsuit."

"You know what I read in the papers," Clarence went on, furious now, jabbing a forefinger in the air in front of him. "They've decided to sic our brilliant traffic planners from the state of Maryland on those poor bums in the Balkans." He glared at his son, as if to say, "what do you make of that?"

"They sent them over with the military, to win friends and influence people. I guess they figured they did such a great job of screwing things up here—after all, the Baltimore/D.C. metro area is the third most traffic congested in the nation—that they'd send them over to Kosovo and set civilization back a few centuries over there too."

"Uh, Dad, have you eaten dinner?"

"What do I care about dinner?"

"Well, I thought we might get you some takeout somewhere."

"Those morons at the DOT have stolen my appetite." Clarence paused and ran his fingers through his sparse red hair and then spoke with suppressed fury. "Donald, do you know how many hours, days, weeks of my life I've spent stopped at red traffic lights?"

"Not this again."

"Those imbeciles with their faulty timers have robbed me of years. Those lousy Maryland transportation 'planners,'" and he raised two fingers to make quote marks, "have been as bad as smoking. What did I quit smoking for?" He hollered. "So I could waste my life at red lights?"

They hit another pothole.

"Great God in heaven!" Clarence yelled. "Can't those idiots do anything right?" After another inspection of the tires, Clarence commenced humming. "I bet you don't know why I'm humming," he said after a moment.

"I do."

"I'm humming to keep myself calm."

"You've told me at least once a day for the past fifteen years."

"I'm not going to let those nitwits ruin my life."

"Keep humming, Dad."

"I am. That's what I'm doing."

At Jones' insistence they stopped at Szechuan Palace, so his father could eat dinner.

"Boy, this place gives you big servings," Clarence said, admiring a huge platter of Buddhist delight. "Do you mind?" He asked, scooping half the contents onto his plate.

"Go ahead, knock yourself out."

"You know, Donald,"

Jones winced.

"Stop wincing, Donald."

Another wince.

"I'm gonna take you to a doctor, if you keep that up."

"Our insurance won't cover it."

"Goddamned insurance companies," Clarence crunched on his broccoli, "all they do is deny your coverage. That's what those lousy bums train those poor, underpaid clerks and adjusters to do – deny, deny, deny. We need universal, government-backed health care."

"You're preaching to the choir, Dad."

"Like I started to say—just because I'm a little, how would you say, *focused* on certain things,"

"Focused?"

"Yeah, like on traffic congestion, just because I'm a little focused on that –"

Jones rolled his eyes, but his father, scrutinizing his plate of vegetables did not discern this ocular response.

"Doesn't mean you should be sarcastic with me about my views on health care or my vegetables."

Jones made a T with both hands. "Time out," he said. "Your vegetables?"

"Yeah," crunch, crunch, "you said, 'knock yourself out.'"

"We're a little sensitive this evening, aren't we?"

"What's with the royal we? I don't see any royalty in here."

"I just meant I'm not interested in any food right now."

"Why not? Those bastards at the DOT stole your appetite too?"

When they left, Clarence had a doggie bag and, as always, could not resist razzing the cashier about the absence of unions in Chinese restaurants.

"Maybe we hire you, and you unionize us, Mr. Jones."

"I'd overdose on MSG, my first week on the job," Clarence said, then out by the truck, "you drive son. I'm digesting and thinking."

"Uh-oh."

"You know," Clarence reminisced, "I spent decades on the road, and I saw a lot of things,"

"Please let this not be what I think it is."

"But the strangest thing I ever saw was when the frigging Maryland transportation planners decided to 'fix' that light down at Powder Mill Road near Beltsville."

Donald groaned, but his father barreled on. "I swear to you, you'd think space aliens designed the signals at that interchange. First one turns green. Then red. Then another one turns green. Then they're all red. By then traffic waiting to turn left is backed up to the next intersection. Then the green arrow comes on, for five seconds. Then, with no yellow, it goes straight to flashing red, and one of the other lights turns green. Then they're all red, and the arrow's still flashing –"

"Then one starts flashing yellow."

"Then it goes back to red. Kosovo. Those poor people in Kosovo will never know what hit them, once they get Maryland's space age traffic designers fixing up their roads."

"Maybe the traffic planners will like it so much over there, they won't come back."

"I'm trying not to get my hopes up."

"Me too. But if they didn't come back, I wouldn't have to hear about them anymore." Jones drove on in silence, thinking about his job Monday at "Designer Works," where he moved heavy boxes all day long. It was excruciatingly boring, but the pay – ten dollars an hour under the table – was irresistible. His father, he figured, was mulling the many injuries that the transportation planners had perpetrated upon him and, doubtless, formulating the numerous epistles he intended to fire off in response. In this silence, pregnant with a sense of injury and of fatigue from heavy lifting, Jones turned the pickup onto their block, a little street of what realtors called "cozy Cape Cods," with silver maples overhanging, azalea bushes, hedges, gardens of hosta and tiger lilies all gone by and all muffled in night shadow, and a large pothole. Enjoying the quiet, he was careful to avoid this pit and the eruption of invective that crashing into it would provoke. He parked in their short driveway. "One of these days I'll put a garage in," his father said, as Jones turned the ignition off and evening silence descended upon them. His father had been threatening to install a garage for over a decade, so Jones paid this remark no mind.

"I smell Kentucky Fried Chicken. Your brother Everett's here," Clarence said. Sure enough, the roar of hilarity, a rumble that signified many guests, emanated from the basement.

"Uh-oh," Jones muttered.

"Go get me a piece."

"Get it yourself."

"I don't like to interrupt."

"You think I do? Every time he brings his friends, I have to cadge a piece of chicken for you."

"You have to what? What's that word? I'm not asking you to do anything illegal."

"Cadge. Finagle. Swipe. Filch."

"Stop complaining and go get it. A drumstick. Make that two."

"You just ate."

"My appetite came back. I just finished composing a letter in my head. Wanna hear it?"

"No. I'll get the drumsticks."

"He can't have any, so get lost," Everett said, upon descrying his younger brother on the stairs.

"What am I supposed to say?"

"Say we ate it all."

"I heard that," Clarence's voice bellowed from the top of the stairs.

In disgust, Everett held the bucket out for his brother. "Two?" He exclaimed as Donald picked around for the second drumstick. "You don't have to touch every piece."

"Then why don't you take it up to him yourself, and let *him* touch every piece?"

Everett had nothing to say to that, so Jones extracted the second drumstick and returned upstairs. "You could use a plate," he said, watching his father devour the first drumstick as he stood in the kitchen. "It's a wonderful invention, keeps crumbs off the floor, provides a place, other than the bare counter, on which to lay the chicken bone."

Clarence ate the second leg in a flash. "You sound like your mother."
Then he licked his very greasy fingers and ran them under water in the
sink. "I've been thinking," he began.

"God forbid."

"Something you could help me with."

"I don't like the sound of this."

"Get your camera, tomorrow, and take pictures of that pothole on
our street."

"I'm busy."

Clarence's eyebrows went up. "All day?"

"From morning 'til night."

"It doesn't have to be tomorrow."

"It will be never."

"You don't have to be so final about it."

"Yes I do. I remember all too well our trips around the county,
snapping pictures of potholes, when I was in middle school."

"Maybe I overdid it. But it's been a long time."

"Not long enough."

"Well maybe I'll get Everett to do it."

"And maybe you'll grow wings and fly to the moon. Maybe Everett
– ha! Now *that* I'll take pictures of."

"Ye of little faith."

"As I recall, when I was in middle school, Everett always managed to
wriggle out of these excursions. He never went once."

Clarence poured himself a glass of grape juice, returned to the living
room and popped a tape, "Rocky III," into the VCR. He fast forwarded
to his favorite part, and as one of the theme songs, "Eye of the Tiger,"
came on, he began to sing along.

"You know you've only seen this thirty times," Jones remarked sourly,
seating himself at the computer in the corner.

"It's the e—y—e...of the tiger," Clarence sang.

Jones turned away in disgust. "He played Rambo, you know."

"I know," Clarence was tapping his foot now and humming.

"A horrible piece of reactionary propaganda, if ever there was one."

"I know," tap, tap. Clarence stopped humming. "But he's a working
class hero for these Rocky movies."

"Some hero."

"You know, where your mother and I grew up in West Virginia was very poor, and life was hard. The mines were no picnic for our parents, or for her older brother Teddy, who lost his leg, you know."

"Of course I know."

"No need to snap," Clarence guzzled his grape juice. "Every day I wake up and go to work I think, 'at least I'm not in the mines.' I got away, Donald. I escaped. But sometimes I feel guilty thinking about everyone else who didn't."

"They didn't have to stay there."

"You have no idea what it's like. How hard it is to leave, how many people try and go straight to...to nothing. That's why they stay. There's not a lot of choice."

Jones gazed at his father's slightly grizzled face, entranced now by a fight scene and felt, for the umpteenth time, a mystery to his character, to how its parts all fit together, his eccentricities, his little obsessions, his rabid hatred for the owning, corporate classes, his tenacity that had enabled him to start anew, a life away from the mines, but his utter lack of interest in rising through the ranks to become management. He could have; he had the drive, strength and brains to have gone high up, but it was as if he had drawn a line – "so far and no farther." He escaped the miner's life, but he had no intention of making a race for the top. Escape, work, suburban comfort – that was enough for him. That notion of what was enough had something to do with his self-respect, with his sense of decency, that he would never do anything or become the sort of person, a grabby sort, or someone who fired people, someone of whom he would be ashamed. Above all, he did not want to feel shame for anything he did. He did not want to be a louse or ever forget the dignity of his fellow man. "You've got to be able to look yourself in the mirror in the morning," he loved to say to his sons and daughter. And Jones often found himself looking and wondering, "but what am I searching for?" The answer that gradually came was that he was looking for some trace of his father, some purer lineaments, in which the oddities were smoothed away, of Clarence's great decency. He thought, as he grew older, that there was a resemblance, that he saw some of his father's humility, though the crankiness was ineradicable. But then, Jones thought anyone who wasn't climbing over other people to get to the top *was* marginalized in this society, became, of necessity, a crank. It was simply too peculiar not to take, take, take.

"How about we go to Annapolis tomorrow," Jones suggested, in despair at the sight of Rocky pummeling an opponent for the millionth time. "I'll take you to that off-beat video rental shop. We'll get some classics."

"You mean Italian films?"

"Yes, about the communist resistance in World War II."

"I can't watch those. I get too worked up. My father was wounded at Anzio."

"I know, Dad."

"And my uncle was killed in the Normandy landing. But of course you know that too."

"Of course."

"Every generation in my family has been in a war," Clarence said. "Including me. But I was the only veteran to join an anti-war group."

"Vietnam was different."

"Not as different as you think. They say now they have smart bombs and can fight clean wars. Don't you believe it, not for a second. It's still little people getting blown to bits. That's what it is – average people torn into lots of bloody pieces. There's nothing romantic or heroic about war."

"I didn't say there was."

"But lots of idiots think there is. Bombing Yugoslavia! What next? Get me a beer, will you, Donny?"

Jones rummaged through the fridge, crammed as always, with leftovers. There was vegetable casserole with green beans poking out of yellow, congealed oil. He snagged a few of those and wolfed them down. Then he poked through a salad Jessie had saved and munched on that. There was a tray of deviled eggs, which he sampled along with a few white-chocolate chip cookies in a Tupperware container – his sister's latest baking effort.

"Bring me some of those deviled eggs you're eating," Clarence called. "And Janie's cookies."

"How did you know I was eating them?" Jones asked, bringing the open bottle of ice cold Heineken and the food on a plate to his father.

"I'm not the only one around here who's predictable."

Everett emerged from the basement stairwell. "Not Rocky again."

"All Rocky, all the time," Jones said sourly.

"I'm getting a beer."

"You can't have it," Clarence said.

"You took my chicken."

"You're underage."

"I'm twenty three."

"Emotionally you're about thirteen."

"Hogwash."

"Don't touch my beer."

"Then I'll take the Scotch downstairs."

"One beer. That's it. That's the limit. Don't you dare touch my Scotch. I'll wring your neck if I find so much as a drop missing."

"You've been saying that since I turned twenty one."

"One of these days, Everett –"

"You sound like Ralph Kramden."

"You never came with me to photograph the potholes," Clarence said, sitting up and pointing a finger at his eldest son.

"Do I look suicidal? Do I look like a moron?"

"Tomorrow we're going to take Donny's camera and photograph that crater down the street."

"Tomorrow I'm going to Las Vegas."

Clarence glared at Everett through narrowed eyes: "Excuses."

"Is it my fault you always pick an inconvenient time?"

"Tomorrow morning."

"I'm sleeping in."

"Then lunch time."

"We'll see about that."

Jones knew very well who would win the next round: Everett, the most ornery person he had ever known. Years ago, Everett had decided that his father was cracked about the highways and the traffic lights and that he would have no part in it. He would not humor him, accompany him on excursions, read his letters to the DOT, mail them, check the car or truck for damage from what Clarence called criminally neglected roads, take film of potholes to be developed, pick up the pictures or participate for one second in any discussion of anything to do with highways or the DOT. When Clarence started to rant, Everett left. When Clarence sneakily began asking questions leading to the forbidden topic, Everett refused to answer. When Clarence sprang things on Everett, such as impromptu readings from his correspondence with the DOT, Everett would turn away and start a conversation with someone else. Unlike his younger brother, he gave his father not an inch, was unyielding in his thorough disapproval of this peculiar obsession and his refusal to be drawn into it.

Everett was stubborn in other ways as well. He would get an idea about something, some grievance or other, and never let it go. He tried to hide it, but he held grudges. He never forgot an insult. But by the same token, he had great loyalty to his friends and family. Once he decided you were part of his life, it was a permanent commitment. And if one of these elect injured him in some way, his dilemma would be obvious to all: loyalty versus the grudge. He would never be able to resolve it satisfactorily, because, to him, it was the clash of two absolutes, each with the same claim upon him. Hence his refusal to cater to paternal eccentricities. It was as if Clarence's oddities somehow insulted him. This was terrible, because the injury came from his father, and every time Clarence tried to wheedle Everett into some complicity, some acceptance, the conflict was too much, and Everett had to leave. He had moved out of the house before high school graduation, but he could not leave his family; his loyalty demanded that he atone for the fact that they drove him crazy, so he came home – a lot. He had an apartment, but at twenty three still ate most of his meals at home and slept there often.

He shared his father's political views and was close to the family that lived in West Virginia. This combination had led him to participate in a wildcat strike, which had radicalized him. He had a simmering hatred for the mine owners, for what they were doing to *his* family, the conditions they made his relatives work in, the dangers they exposed them to, the corners the owners constantly cut. Everett took it personally, but he also hated the mining companies abstractly, on theoretical grounds. He had begun to talk about moving there, working in the mines, joining the union, agitating for improvements. So far Clarence had succeeded in talking him out of it. Whenever Everett brought up the subject, Clarence's blue eyes would flash. "What do you think I left for?" He would demand. "So you can go commit suicide?"

"Rather a harsh view," Jessie often said.

"Look at your brother or my dead cousins and tell me my view's too harsh. I dare you."

Clarence's domain, his inviolable lair was the workshop in the basement. There he could tinker for hours, even if Everett and his buddies were howling at the tops of their lungs in the next room. His workshop had a door into the backyard, and on weekends, Clarence

could often be seen, shuttling between the workshop and the trim little
shed across the grass where he stored his lumber. He made and repaired
furniture. He replaced the siding on the house. He fixed the roof,
replaced the gutters, steam cleaned and sealed the back deck, which he
had built with help from a few friends and Everett. The one time Jessie
had suggested a handy man to replace the linoleum on the kitchen
floor, he had been shocked and accused her of not trusting him, of not
valuing his work, of underestimating him, and so forth. The list went
on. She never did that again. Of course, when he needed an extra hand,
he drafted one of his sons. There was no question of them evading such
a ukase. "Donny, put your book down and get the ladder," would come
the command, and his son's afternoon leisure would vanish. "Everett, get
up on the roof," and Everett would telephone his girlfriend to postpone
their matinee movie date.

No matter how much labor he put in, however, he always had time
to read before going to sleep. Clarence was a political news junkie and
had lassoed his younger son into the task of scouting the bookstores and
public libraries for volumes about the perfidy of Republicans, the greed
of big corporations, the corruption of elected officials and the history
of the labor movement. Clarence and Jessie's bedroom under the eaves
was lined with books. Every corner was crammed with tomes. At night,
after a long hard day, Jessie would lie on her side in her nightgown with a
pillow over her head, while next to her, Clarence sat up, tilting the pages
of the latest history of the Iran/Contra scandal or exposé of corporate
malfeasance into the little circle of light cast by the bedside lamp. He had
more energy than he knew what to do with and was a light sleeper who
always awoke after six hours. So he would sit, far into the night, reading
and fuming about the injustice in the world. He read massive quantities
and insisted that his children read his recommendations as well.

He was closest to Donny, who enjoyed spending time with him and
could even tolerate his harangues on the depredations of Maryland's
traffic planners. By the time Jones was fourteen, he knew a great deal
about being a handyman. But there was always more to learn, and not
just for him. Clarence would take on new projects, like paneling the
basement and teach himself, and at the same time his second son, how
to do it. They would pass long hours with scarcely a word, and given
Clarence' customary loquacity and tendency to lecture, this time spent
in silence, except for the occasional "pass that drill," or "hold this
steady," was precious to Jones. He believed that it had taught him more

about his father's essential nature than all of their discussions – about his patience, thoroughness, exactitude, attention to details and the occasional inspiration. This time working together formed the core of what he regarded as his childhood experience with his father. So it came as a surprise one weekend afternoon in the paternal workshop when Clarence dusted the sawdust off his hands and said, out of the blue: "I'd like you to go to college."

"I've thought about it. You know that."

"Not enough. And I don't mean community college. I mean the University of Maryland."

"What brings this up, if I may ask?"

"You've got the brains. You could be a professor. Or a trial lawyer. Something...you know...big."

"I've never heard a single good word from you about lawyers."

Clarence shrugged and looked away, almost evasively. "Some lawyers are okay. Like your friend Sherwin's brother. Not the corporate hotshot, the other one."

"How long have you been thinking about this?"

Clarence looked him in the eye. His blue eyes locked onto his son's. "Since you were four."

Jones was staggered.

"That," Clarence said, "was when you learned to read. I knew then you could do anything."

"Mom taught me."

"Yeah, but you learned. She taught Janie and Everett too, but they didn't catch on 'til first grade."

They continued working and said no more about the future, but the conversation that had just passed hung in the air like a secret between them. An hour or so later, as they went upstairs, his father clarified: "Just don't get greedy. You know what greed is for."

"Greed is for pigs," Jones quoted one of his father's favorite sayings, and Clarence chuckled.

Superficially Clarence's wife was his polar opposite – quiet, reserved, in no way garrulous or irascible – but every now and then she would come out with some unexpected opinion that revealed her to be as unforgiving as Everett and, in her view of the social and political world, to have a will of iron. When Jones, studying the French Revolution and the execution of aristocrats in his history class, had asked some question, she had replied simply: "They didn't go far enough."

"But they wiped out thousands of clerics and aristocrats," Jones said.

"They didn't wipe out them all," she criticized.

She rarely participated in the family's political discussions, but when she did, it was usually to wish some powerful conservative or corporate bigwig into an early grave. Once thus anathematized, this figure would thereafter only be mentioned in the family with the epitaph, "may he drop dead soon." No one dared cross her in these matters. Jones' friends regarded her with much respect, except for Chandra, whose respect bordered on alarm and whose royalism she considered a form of dementia and sought to cure.

Chandra had a most unfortunate effect on Clarence, in Jones' view, because Chandra actually encouraged the mania about the roads and traffic lights. Once he had gone so far as to bring a road map of the county over to the Jones.' He had marked the most offensive stoplights with little red x's and the most dangerous potholes with little blue circles.

"Now that," Clarence said, pointing at a little red x "is the slowest goddamn traffic light in the universe."

"Slower than the ones in the Alpha Centauri system?" Jones asked.

"I can't tell you how many times I've sat at that red light, watching the minutes of my life tick away and feeling my blood begin to boil. I can't tell you."

"Don't tell us," Jones said.

"About ten thousand times," Clarence went on.

"I wrote a letter about it," Chandra said.

Clarence rubbed his hands together in anticipation. "And what did the bastards say?"

"They never replied."

"I tell you, that department's like the Bermuda Triangle. You could bombard them with letters from now 'til kingdom come –"

"Like someone in this room," Jones said, "who shall remain nameless."

"And never hear a peep in reply. Your letters just vanish. I spent twenty-five years on the road, Chandra, drove through ever state in the USA I don't know how many times, and always, without fail, coming back into Maryland was like entering the twilight zone."

"I was thinking of a petition about that light," Chandra said.

Jones groaned and put his head in his hands.

"Excellent idea. Give a copy to me. I'll get Donny here to take it around the neighborhood."

"Whoa!" Jones exclaimed. "You'll get who, where, to do what?"

"You heard me."

"I heard you utter something so unlikely as to make me think you had lost your marbles."

"Then Everett."

"Your grip on reality is slipping, Dad."

"Then I'll do it myself," Clarence nearly yelled. "The only one who's got any sense about anything is Chandra!" He roared. "Chandra!"

"Not about politics he doesn't," Jessie said, clearing away the dirty glasses from the dining room table, around which they sat, the map spread out before them. "I heard him praising Ronald Reagan the other day. The world would be a much better place if Ronald Reagan had stuck to his chimpanzee and his acting career and not inflicted his nauseating political views on the rest of us."

A pall descended on the little group at the table. "I only said," Chandra meekly began.

"He *fired* the air traffic controllers," Jessie interrupted. "That was the first thing he did."

Chandra opened his mouth, but Clarence caught his eye and gestured silence by raising a finger to his lips.

"He went to Bitburg and put a wreath on an SS grave," Jessie went on. "He waged an illegal war, using the contras. He was contemptible." She departed with the glasses back to the kitchen. For a moment no one said a word.

Clarence leaned forward, put the tips of his fingers together, making a steeple with his hands. "About this map, Chandra. I think you missed a few lights." Clarence fetched a blue pen and a red one from the cup by the phone and made additions to the map.

"To think all these years I suffered on these roads, and I never thought to use a map like this. Wonders never cease."

"They better cease," Jones grumbled. "I don't think I could stand another wonder like this."

"It just goes to show," Clarence went on, using now the blue pen, now the red, "that two minds are better than one."

Jones rolled his eyes.

"Perhaps we should send the map to the transportation officials," Chandra suggested.

"Genius!" Clarence cried.

"I would have used a different word," Jones said.

"But then I'd have to part with this map," Clarence went on.

"God forbid," Jones said.

"And I intend to frame it and hang it on the dining room wall."

"What, so we can all get sick to our stomachs, listening to your lectures about it, every time we sit down for a meal?" Jones demanded.

"Maybe we should make a color Xerox copy and send that," Chandra went on.

"Well you're just full of great ideas today," Jones said sourly.

"Twice a genius!" Clarence cried.

"I don't think I can take any more genius," Jones said. "All these brilliant ideas are making suicide look very appealing."

"Donny here will get it copied."

"Very, *very* appealing."

"Your father isn't asking a lot," Chandra remonstrated. "After all, you don't have to get the signatures on the petition."

"You know Chandra, the Inquisition could have used you –"

"Everybody's a critic," Clarence said. "That's what happens, Chandra, you have children and then you're surrounded by critics."

"You see how effective criticism is," Jones said. "I could say I'll go jump off the Chesapeake Bay Bridge before I'll copy that map, but he won't even hear me."

"You'll get it copied when I'm done working on it," Clarence said. "Then we'll have one on the dining room wall and one for those numbskulls in the state government. I'll send it certified mail, return receipt requested."

"Why don't you just get two copies while you're at it – one to decorate the statehouse in Annapolis as well?" Jones rather acidly asked.

"There's a pothole you missed," Clarence continued, addressing Chandra and pointing to the map. "And another."

Needless to say, when Chandra showed up on the very Sunday morning Clarence intended to photograph the pothole near his house, Jones was less than thrilled.

"I'll just call you Benedict Arnold," Jones said to his friend, when Chandra responded enthusiastically to the proposed picture-taking project. But then, to Chandra, there was nothing more unusual about photographing potholes or firing off missives to the DOT than anything else about the Joneses, who were, in his view, quite exotic. Clarence's stories about the mines in West Virginia, union organizing, the Teamsters, Jessie's silence and political bloodthirstiness, their refusal to be dazzled by wealth, their cynicism about corporations and politicians, who they routinely referred to as bought and sold by various moneyed interests, everything about them was, as he said to Jones, "out of this world."

"Yeah, well as far as the DOT is concerned, we want to bring Clarence back *into* this world, not push him farther out of it. And you're not helping."

"Are we photographing that huge pit I just ran into, before I got to your driveway?" Chandra asked.

Clarence nodded. "We're going to nail those morons this time, with photographic evidence."

"Uh, Dad, haven't you been nailing them with photographic evidence for almost a decade?"

"You never know when you're going to get lucky, Donny. Today could be the day."

"Yeah and Chandra here could be a left-wing radical."

"That too may come to pass," Clarence beamed at his younger son and clapped him on the shoulder. "Quickly get you camera."

Looking quite disgusted and skeptical, Jones passed his Nikon to Clarence, who put the strap over his head. Thus girded, also armed with a tape measure, and ready to do battle with the pothole, he gave a signal to the two young men, and they all proceeded out to the street. "It's a doozy," Clarence said. "Donny, step in it, to show how deep it is."

"Like hell. You're not snapping any shots of me in this pothole and sending them to the highway officials."

Chandra obliged instead. From a distance the depth of the pothole concealed his feet.

"Now lay out the tape measure," Clarence instructed. Again Jones refused, and Chandra assisted. "I may adopt you," Clarence said to Chandra, as he photographed the tape measure. "You're much more agreeable than Donny."

Jones snorted in disgust.

"It may have never occurred to you," Clarence began, glancing accusingly at his son, "but I do not like my public spirited concern for the state of our roads, highways and traffic signals being regarded as some sort of a peculiarity."

"I don't regard it as a peculiarity," Jones said.

"Oh."

"I regard it as insanity, rank lunacy, and I'm worried some highway official is going to catch on and have you committed."

"You see the support I get," Clarence said to Chandra and snapped another picture of the pothole. "It's a miracle I keep at this."

"Miracle isn't the word I'd use," Jones said.

"It's just like my battle over the speed bumps."

"Good God spare us."

"Did I ever tell you about that?"

"More times than we can count."

"The neighborhood association wanted to put in speed bumps," Clarence said to Chandra, pointedly ignoring his son. "Nothing's more of a nuisance than speed bumps, and so of course our transportation officials like nothing better. But I got up a letter writing campaign, and we squashed that proposal," Clarence closed his hand into a fist and shook it for emphasis, "like a grape."

"A grape?" Jones asked.

"It was my finest moment," Clarence went on. "I saved copies of all the letters we sent,"

"I don't like where this is going."

"I'll read them to you, when we're done photographing. What about it Chandra?" And Clarence gave him a nudge, "eh?"

"I'm sure Chandra has better things to do with his Sunday than listen to readings from you letter writing campaign."

"No, no. I would be honored," Chandra said, regarding Clarence with a look of wonder, as if he were some spectacular specimen of a life form from another galaxy. "I'm sure I've never heard anything like it."

"Oh, you can bet on that," Jones said and snorted in disgust once again.

Clarence bent down and palpated the edge of the pothole. "Come here, Donny."

"No."

"Chandra then. Now, put your hand here so I can photograph it. So they can see exactly how deep it is." Chandra took all this in stride, after all, he was used to doing whatever his parents ordered. Since his father worked in the department of education in Baltimore and his mother as an art teacher in a parochial school outside of Annapolis, their commands usually pertained to homework, his parentally assigned reading list – he had just finished the plays of Tagore and had next been directed to Bertrand Russell's *History of Western Philosophy* – and parentally arranged educational projects, usually scientific experiments, or excursions, mostly to museums and galleries. Never had his parents ordered him to squat in the middle of the street and put his hand in a pothole. Never had they suggested, as Clarence Jones was now doing, that he should ride around the county with them in a pickup, scouting other potholes, measuring and photographing them and timing various traffic signals. Nor did they approach him as Clarence did, as an equal, almost a co-conspirator, the two of them in some rather shaky, officially disapproved of endeavor together. No, his parents were rather strict, formal and given to what he described to his friends as a "top down" style of child management. They told him what to do, and he did it. They did not hang on his every reaction, come alive when he expressed the slightest enthusiasm. No. In fact they seemed to have no interest in his reactions. They were merely concerned to make sure that he completed the tasks they gave him, and it was assumed by all that these were for his benefit. "I could do this all day," Chandra burbled.

Clarence beamed.

"Benedict Arnold," Jones repeated.

"Oh come on, Jones. It'll be fun going around on all the roads, looking for potholes."

"Some people have a strange idea of fun."

"And some people," Clarence said and looked his son in the eye, "are killjoys." Rubbing his hands and muttering to himself, "we're gonna get the bastards this time," Clarence returned to the house for the precious map. Then the trio piled into the cab of the pickup, Jones with the camera, Chandra with the tape measure, a stopwatch Clarence had fetched and the map, and they were off.

"It's time for the first coordinates," Clarence boomed.

"It's time for the straightjackets," Jones said.

Chandra read a street name, reeled off the cross streets, and the truck crashed into a pothole.

"Goddammit!" Clarence hollered.

"You go looking for trouble," Jones said sourly, "see what you get."

"How come this one's not on the map?" Clarence demanded.

"The map's not perfect," Chandra said.

"The map's a product of an obsessional neurosis," Jones commented.

"Lemme see that," Clarence took the map. "We'll fix it right now," he took out a pen. "Cause this baby's gonna be flawless."

Jones rolled his eyes. "Not a neurosis, a psychosis."

Clarence eased the truck out of the pothole and parked. They all trooped out to measure and photograph it. "It's an odd shape," Clarence remarked.

"It's not the only thing that's odd around here."

"Kind of like a person's rear end."

Jones' eyes bugged, then he said: "That's more than we wanted to know."

"Chandra make a note of that," Clarence, ignoring his son, handed Chandra a small notepad and a pen.

"Aren't you the lucky duck," Jones said. "Go on, I want to see you write this down."

Chandra, who could quite obviously scarcely believe what he was doing, began to write. Whereupon Clarence began to dictate: "We found this oddly shaped pothole," he intoned, "on Homestead Lane at one oh five p.m. on the afternoon of –"

"Now you're *dictating* these loony tunes?" Jones cried. "They're highway officials! They don't give a flying fuck what time you saw the pothole, and they're going to think it's damn peculiar that you compared it to a person's ass."

"A rather lumpy one."

"And they'll be right. And if you keep going like this, the men in the white coats will be coming, and they'll cart you away, and when they get a load of Mom's 'slaughter the plutocrats' line, they'll cart her away too."

"You're a worry wart. Keep writing Chandra. Said pothole," Clarence continued, "is about three feet wide and two feet long. There is litter in it."

Jones glared at his father and snatched the notepad away from Chandra.

"I hadn't gotten to the part about litter," Chandra said.

"You're encouraging him," Jones accused.

"It's about time somebody did," Clarence said and snatched the notepad back from his son. "All I get from you and Everett is criticism and mockery. This is a serious issue here, and we're going to get some attention."

"That's what I'm afraid of."

"Come on, Chandra," Clarence resumed calmly and handed him the pad, "keep writing."

The lecture about the pothole lasted nearly five minutes. Chandra transcribed every word and then read it back to Clarence, who made corrections. Jones sat on the curb with a look that combined profound disgust and irritation. Chandra, goggle-eyed, trailed Clarence back to the truck. "We've hit a new low today," Jones said, "the loony lecture circuit."

"C'mon Donny," his father smiled at him, full of cheer at his discovery of Chandra the stenographer, "hop in."

For Jones the afternoon was boring – he refused to participate, so he spent most of his time sullen in the cab. They traipsed from pothole to pothole. Standing by the truck, Clarence would ramble on about the hole in the road, where it was, what it reminded him of, how it had probably got there, the damage it had probably caused, etc. Chandra would jot it all down, this, of course, after measuring and photographing it. At traffic lights, Chandra would be instructed to set the stopwatch and make notations. They also ran a few red lights, when Clarence's frustration reached the breaking point. "This is way better than *The History of Western Philosophy*," Chandra exclaimed, as they sailed through a red light, Clarence cursing and ranting about broken timers.

"If you want to do it every Sunday, I'm sure it can be arranged," Jones said. "Just count me out. I'm sleeping in from now on and will be incommunicado after that."

"Incommunicado?" Clarence asked.

"If I hear or utter one syllable about roads or traffic signals, I cannot be responsible for my actions."

"You're another Everett," Clarence replied. "Just my luck."

By the time they finally arrived back home, it was dinnertime. Jessie and Janie reheated the vegetable casserole, spruced up the salad, cooked some potatoes, and there was a roast chicken.

"Roast chicken!" Jones exclaimed. "Not again."

"Be quiet," Jessie said. "Janie prepared that herself."

"Yeah, if you mean 'I got it out of the box I bought it in,' sure I prepared it."

"You didn't need to go into such detail," Jessie said.

"Cooking has been on the decline in America for many years now," Clarence began rather pompously, serving himself some salad.

"Oh, what would you know about it?" Jessie asked.

"I know the difference between these store-bought roast chickens you get and your homemade, breaded chicken cutlet."

"I've been buying the cutlet pre-made in the meat section for the past five years. All I do is heat it in the microwave."

"Could've fooled me."

"I guess we could have, but we didn't. Janie here tells you every time we have cutlet."

Chandra's cell phone beeped. He excused himself and retreated to Jones' room.

"I've been frantic. I've been calling you all afternoon," his mother said.

"I didn't know," Chandra lied. "I had my phone off."

"I wish you wouldn't do that."

"What? So you can call me every ten minutes?"

"Where have you been? I thought something terrible had happened. It's been all I could do to restrain myself from telephoning the police. Actually Rajit restrained me from telephoning the police."

"Well, thank Dad for me, will you, for preventing you from ruining my afternoon. And if you must know, I was riding around the county with the Joneses."

"Those odd people."

"Scouting for potholes."

"For what?"

"As a public service."

"Maybe you could get credit for this at school."

"Not likely."

"Come home, and we'll discuss it. I'll call your counselor about it this week."

"I'm eating dinner with them, and I hate to throw a wet blanket on your weekly communications with my guidance counselor –"

"Not weekly. Maybe bi-weekly."

"You'd think I was a discipline problem. I've *never* been kept for detention. Mr. Sanchez keeps Harry Sullivan for detention every week, but his mother doesn't call the counselor on a regular basis. I could understand if she did, but not you."

"This is hardly the time to discuss my conversations with your counselor," Sara Patel said. The truth was that Sara, who had radically Anglicized her name, loved phoning anyone in any position of authority with regard to her husband or son, since it gave her an opportunity to state her name and thus plant the doubt in her listener's mind about whether or not she was a native of India or the United States. She believed that this uncertainty enhanced her clout, something which, overall, she was convinced she did not have enough of. She especially disliked Chandra's counselor, an abrupt woman given to suspecting the worst. Every phone call from Mrs. Patel was presumed, in the beginning, to spring from trouble. She assumed Chandra had been sent to detention or suspended, when no such thing had occurred, then or ever. But Sara had beaten her down. She called so frequently, asked so many questions, made so many requests, took up so much time, that the counselor had learned to keep her nasty thoughts to herself and reply, as often as possible, in monosyllables. Sensing her victory and thrilled by it, Sara had doubled the number of calls, and the counselor, Madge Hawkins, told colleagues that this woman was going to cause her a nervous breakdown.

Sara was quiet, soft-spoken and tenacious. She and Rajit had high hopes for their only son, and did not fail to remind him of these, several times a day. In elementary school, they had compelled Chandra to do all of his homework assignments twice, once in English for the teacher and once in Hindi for them. This practice had been abolished in Chandra's seventh grade year, for the simple reason that he had rebelled, something which had shocked his parents beyond words and remained inexplicable to them, until Isabelle Lenthican had remarked in passing that "kids do that all the time." So it was an American custom. This knowledge sanctified Chandra's rebellion as something acceptable, though his parents still referred to it warily, as if mention of it might provoke another American outburst of independence and self-determination.

The Patels were great believers in education. Rajit even had a PhD in the field. His brothers were doctors and professors in India. His sister, to escape an arranged marriage, had never returned home after her education in the United States and worked as a pediatrician in Philadelphia. Sara had a double master's, in art and education. Theories of education, symposia, prominent journals and the lectures of various luminaries constituted most dinner conversation in the Patel household. Though a loving, obedient son, Chandra could not wait to leave home, even if it meant pursuing more education, in college.

As if subliminally aware that their incessant emphasis on education had finally begun to repel their son, Rajit and Sara flailed around for alternative ways to connect. A colleague of Rajit's at the department of education had a very fancy boat – would Chandra like to accompany his parents on a weekend's sail around the Chesapeake? Chandra's friends all went to the gym to work out regularly – he too could have a membership if he wanted. Colleagues of Sara at the parochial school camped regularly in Shenandoah State Park – perhaps Chandra (who shuddered at the thought of his absent-minded, intellectual father attempting to start a campfire) would like a week's camping trip during the summer? Or a trip to visit Rajit's sister's family in Philadelphia? Or a vacation at Bethany Beach in Delaware – Sara had found townhouses on the internet renting for cheap. Or a longer excursion to the Outer Banks? Or tennis lessons? Or a dog?

"They treat you like you're royalty," Harry goggled.

"Yeah. The little prince from Bengal," Chandra said, with more than a touch of irritation. To say that his parents bombarded him with offers of new activities, hobbies, gifts, would be an understatement. This new shtick, as Sherwin called it, was almost as bad as the old one on education. But nothing, nothing could compare to the annoyance of his mother, concerned about his whereabouts and armed with a cell phone.

"Wow," Jones exclaimed, when Chandra returned to the meal and placed his cell phone on the table. Jones picked the phone up. "She called you twenty-four times this afternoon."

"Shows she's a good mother," Clarence said, savagely chomping on a drumstick. "When was the last time anyone around here ever called me on the cell phone, no less twenty-four times?"

"If you want your mother to call you twenty-four times a day, I don't think I can arrange it," Jessie said. "She's been dead six years."

"Kevin might be able to arrange it," Jones said. "He's got a Ouija Board."

"Don't speak ill of the dead," Clarence admonished, waving the drumstick at Jones.

"Who's speaking *ill* of the dead? We could actually talk *to* her with the Ouija Board."

"I thought it was some kind of curse."

"Where do you get these ideas?" Jessie asked.

"Well, when you talk to her," Clarence resumed, "ask her why she doesn't call me twenty-four times a day."

"Because she's dead," Jessie said.

"Ask her why she never called me twenty-four times a day."

"Because she didn't know your cell phone number when she was in the nursing home, and besides she wouldn't have been able to remember it, because she couldn't even remember her own name," Jessie said in some exasperation. "You wouldn't have wanted her to call anyway, because she couldn't remember who you were. She thought you were Ronald Reagan and threw things at you every time you visited. She challenged you to just try to do to the mine workers what you had done to the air traffic controllers – remember?"

"Oh," Clarence said. "Yes. That was unpleasant."

"You come from a most unique family," Chandra said to Jones, who merely rolled his eyes.

"Too bad you never met my mother," Clarence spoke with his mouth full, waving another drumstick at his guest. "Now there's unique."

"One of a kind," Jessie agreed.

"Out of this world," Janie added.

"I'm so disappointed I never met her," Chandra said.

"Consider it a little bit of luck," Clarence went on. "In all probability she would have mistaken you for Mahatma Gandhi and lectured you on the futility of nonviolence. You got off easy."

"You don't know how easy," Jones added.

"When Reagan got elected the second time," Clarence said, "she predicted the end of civilization as we know it. When George Herbert Walker Bush got elected, she announced that the end had arrived. She was a pessimist."

"She had a dark streak," Jessie explained, eating the peppers and tomatoes from her casserole. "Kind of believed in doomsday."

"And didn't hesitate to tell you about it," Clarence added, "drove my poor father nuts. Straight into an early grave."

"That was black lung disease did that," Jessie clarified.

"Well, her carryings on didn't help. Can you imagine," he asked Chandra, "what it was like to grow up in a world under constant siege by reactionaries? That was her view."

"She was right," Jessie said.

"Yes she was," Clarence munched thoughtfully. "No denying it."

Over a dessert of butter pecan ice cream, Chandra's phone beeped again.

"Tell her she can call me, if you won't answer," Clarence said. "I would love to get calls."

"You have no idea what you'd be getting into," Chandra replied.

"No," Jones corrected, "*she* has no idea what she'd be getting into."

"Maybe she'd like to hear about the state of Maryland's traffic and highways," Clarence began.

"If you could link it to higher education and getting me into an Ivy League college, I'm sure she'd be all ears," Chandra answered.

Later, as he drove home, through the last of the day's light, Chandra felt oddly at peace. There was something about the darkness that was akin, he thought, to certain kinds of light. There was a kinship between supposed opposites that he had detected before, and now, the similarity in the thoughts and emotions they evoked washed over him. There were shadowed hedges, spots beneath a tree here or there, the step beneath the overhang of a front door; such shade suddenly evoked in him a feeling of peacefulness, reticence and caution, it was the darkness where only certain special souls felt at home, mirrored by the yellow light from certain old lamps, shining in isolated circles of illumination in the night, there also certain men and women dwelt, people with whom he felt a sudden bond, people who appreciated the silence and safety of shade or the lone lamp light in the evening. These thoughts flickered through his mind, and he strove to define them, to elucidate for himself what it was about these people that linked them to this darkness, to this light, why he had these suddenly powerful and strange feelings about them and how in the great vast world he could find them, quiet and retiring and careful as he believed they were.

When he arrived home, this distinct mood was still upon him, so he hurried to his room to be alone, to ponder it more. He switched on the lamp beside his bed, and the thoughts he had had in the car crowded back in on him. People of quiet, people of solitude, a man pausing on the step at the side entrance to a house at twilight, men and women who liked to watch fireflies at dusk, lighting the darkened, huddled forms of bushes and gardens, people who sat up far into the night reading by a lamp, as Jones said his father did, people who looked back on the journey of their lives and were overcome by the quiet, unobtrusive strangeness of it – images of all these men and women filled his mind, and he could not forget them. Indeed he had no desire to.

He opened *The History of Western Philosophy*, read about St. Augustine and wondered whether, at age seventeen, Augustine, his Manicheanism not yet in bloom, conversion and years as an African bishop far in the future, had felt the curiosity about others, the serenity that came from knowing there were some like him, there had to be, out in the vast wide world, or was he another sort, the churchman who ended his days burning Donatist heretics at the stake, the sort who branded people with his beliefs, yoked them to his doctrines, sought to force his will upon the bruised flesh and blood of his contemporaries. Chandra had already begun to suspect the latter and already felt his initial admiration for this

saint and theologian fading fast. Chandra liked to think of himself as
a conservative, but in the old sense of the word, as one who abhorred
violent change, who wanted to protect the fragile good that already
existed, who wished to conserve, not uproot and destroy. Oddly he saw
no incompatibility between his temperament and Clarence's, though
a gulf yawned between their beliefs, there was no denying that. Yet he
shared with Clarence an aversion to violence and cruelty, though they
ascribed it to different sources – Clarence to members of the owning
classes, Chandra to some defect in human nature itself. But there were
people without these flaws, people of whose existence had had become
so acutely aware on his ride home. Those were the ones he had to find
in his life, and, fortunately, many existed already, in good numbers in
his quiet, rather ordinary world, where he would graduate from high
school and go to college, probably the University of Maryland, since
he did not regard himself as Ivy League material, much to his mother's
chagrin. He would major in business, get an MBA and make his
uneventful way through the corporate world, at least that's how Chandra
saw it. He knew very well that Jones disagreed, had told him it was dog
eat dog in the corporate military industrial complex, but he dismissed
these objections, did not really believe them. Besides, he wanted to do
something his parents had not, namely, earn a lot of money. He was not
quite sure how this desire fit with that evening's vision of the decent,
unassuming people he wished to include in his life, but with youthful
optimism and innocence believed he could somehow make the two
mesh.

Perhaps, he thought, in some unanticipated way, the time he spent
with the Joneses had begun to rub off on him. Perhaps his inner self was
drifting or being pulled in a new direction. Perhaps that was the meaning
of his epiphany on the way home. Chandra did not have many such
experiences and was somewhat at a loss as to what he should ascribe it
to. "When a boss fires his secretary, he's taking food out of her children's
mouths," Jessie had said. "I hope you'll remember that Chandra, in your
climb to the top."

Sentiments such as these were new to him, for only recently had
Jessie become aware just how utterly Chandra was, in her words, "in
need of some guidance." Usually taciturn, she had nevertheless begun to
share her perspective with him. Subtly it had begun to affect this young
man, who had long attended lectures at a libertarian think tank, the
Cato Institute, in Washington D. C. Recently, when true conservatives

took the podium, he found himself disagreeing or mentally supplying Jessie's rebuttal. But all this had occurred on a rather intellectual level. Now suddenly, on his way home had come this sudden burst of emotion and insight into himself and what he wanted from the world. What could have caused it? Would he have more of these experiences? The idea that his very own soul contained surprises for him, that there was a subliminal mental life developing all along, undetected but which had suddenly swung into view, like a range of mountains and valleys from a highway that takes a sudden turn – this all had a novelty for him that he could not shake off. He liked to think of himself as a regular guy, but this mental event was, well, irregular. He sat in the darkened room by the little lamp and wondered.

"Thank God you're home. I just saw the car. If I hadn't, I would have called the police," Sara Patel said, upon bursting into his room.

"It wouldn't be the first time."

"You act as though it was a regular occurrence."

"It was, years back."

"That was poison control, not the police. And yes, I guess I did call them rather frequently."

"At the drop of a hat."

"You ingested many odd things. What are you doing sitting in the dark?"

"Thinking."

"What?"

"Private thoughts."

"Oh. Well, there shouldn't be secrets within a family."

"If there weren't, I would have gone insane years ago."

"Would you like something to eat?"

Chandra shook his head.

"How about a shower?"

He shook his head again.

"A game of scrabble?"

"No."

"Have something to eat."

"If you go through the list again, I'll scream."

"Why are you so standoffish?"

Chandra sighed, put his book down, rose and walked into the living room, where Rajit had already set up the card table and was laying out the scrabble board.

"Prepare to meet your match," Rajit chortled.

"Fat chance," Chandra replied.

"You are talking to last year's third place national scrabble championship tournament winner in Baltimore," Sara beamed proudly at her son. "You will never beat Chandra."

"No one will with you playing," Chandra said. "You go out of your way to give me openings. And you can't play tonight, unless you raise your hand and solemnly swear after me –"

Sara raised her hand.

"I solemnly swear," Chandra began, and his mother repeated the words, "never to forget my son's mantra, namely, I will play to win." Sara repeated this.

"I will *only* play to win," he reiterated, and so did she. Then they sat down to scrabble, all having vowed to play to win, but in Chandra's heart there lurked a new and disconcerting doubt as to whether or not that was really still the most important thing in life.

Five

"Today is your big day," Monica Dawn said, bustling around the little galley kitchen, as she cooked her son's breakfast. "Graduation at last."

"It feels like I already graduated. I've been working almost full time for Mr. Lirano for the past two weeks."

"Seniors always have lots of time off at the end," Monica said. "Now don't you look nice?"

Kevin wore a pair of tan, recently pressed pants, a white dress shirt and a tie. "I may look nice, but with that cap and gown on top of this getup, I'm liable to die of heat prostration. It's supposed to hit 90 degrees, and the air conditioning in that auditorium is rickety, to say the least. Look," he said, pointing to his brownish blond hair, plastered in the damp heat against his forehead, "I'm sweating already. Turn up the AC. No, on second thought, I'll do it. You're liable to set the thermostat at 60 and break the unit."

Monica served them both cantaloupe and orange juice, followed by scrambled eggs and buttered, whole wheat toast. They ate in the small dining area, right outside the kitchen. It was separated from the living room by the back of a long, beige couch that matched the room's pale yellow vases with dried eucalyptus, tan rug, off-white walls and beige armchairs. The living room couch faced glass sliding doors with a view past the grassy backyard straight into the woods. Upstairs Monica had the master bedroom, distinguished as such not by size but by having its own private bathroom. There was another bathroom in the hall and then Kevin's rather messy room, with its balcony looking out over the back and into the trees. The townhouse also came with a half bathroom off the front hall on the first floor and a fully fixed-up basement. They had lived there for over a decade, since Monica's divorce, a time in which, aside from Kevin, the only good thing, she often said, had been finding Whispering Woods, the little townhouse development with its many trees arching right over the buildings and its reasonable prices. On quiet evenings deer emerged from the thicket, rabbits were everywhere, raccoons attempted to rifle the well-sealed garbage over by the carport, bats circled high in the night air, and an occasional owl hooted in the trees. Without too much effort, Monica and Kevin, sitting on the little back deck beyond the sliding glass doors, drinking their red wine and beer, respectively, could imagine that they were in the country, the real, true, great deciduous forest of the northeastern United States, so much of which had vanished from Maryland generations ago. Kevin had read a great deal about that forest, had biked and camped in what remained of it up in New England and identified birds and other fauna for his mother. The fireflies would flash here and there, and he would describe what he had seen in New Hampshire and Vermont, the plant specimens he had gathered, the rocks, the different insects, the bears, wildcats, otters, beavers and moose he had sighted. When he was younger, she had urged him to become a botanist or zoologist, but now he no longer thought that practical, though he never said why. Nonetheless, he loved to sit out at twilight on the edge of the woods, as the stillness and darkness crept out with the lengthening shadows, and Monica felt the magic of it too, of this tiny corner of wildness, and would not have the silence broken for anything except Kevin's soft, soft whisper, "look there, a deer, a buck," and sure enough, its antlers aloft as it sniffed the air, the shy creature would step forth onto the edge of the lawn, while behind it others stirred in the leaves.

They had had more than ten good years here, and Monica saw no reason why it should end any time soon. There would eventually be college, of course, and marriage – but perhaps Kevin and his wife would live with his mother, while he got on his feet financially, perhaps even his future wife would want to live in a townhouse in Whispering Woods, and they would purchase one. There would be many advantages for them, so Monica reasoned. First, the prices were still moderate, the location was good, there was Monica to help out with grandchildren, and Kevin could still have his hour at dusk to sit at the edge of the woods and watch night casting its long, dark blanket of shadows over the trees and buildings.

"If it really is law school you want," she had said one evening, as they sat in the quiet and gathering shade, "perhaps environmental law would be good for you – given your interests in natural history."

"Great minds think alike," he replied. And so it had been settled – that was the eventual goal, but along the way he had to earn plenty of money, he said, to support her. Despite Monica's protests, Kevin held firm – as soon as he earned enough, his mother would retire from her back-breaking job. Perhaps she would find other, less onerous work, perhaps she would not work at all. But there would be no more trekking around the county from school to school, pushing heavy, metal cases filled with books hither and yon and arranging them for display at book

fairs. He would work for a year, then go to college, then take out loans
for law school.

"By then I'll be dead," Monica would laugh.

"Don't talk like that. Not even as a joke."

So he sat, that morning of his graduation, eating his scrambled eggs
and thinking that it was about ten years until his mother's retirement. It
seemed too long. "Couldn't you do something else for that company?"
He asked at last. "Or maybe get a different job altogether?"

"I've put in a lot of years with them. If I start over somewhere new, I
won't make nearly as much."

"In six months, it won't matter. The mortgage will be paid off. You'll
be able to afford a cut in salary. You could come work for Angelo. Who
knows..." They both laughed. Paul's father, Angelo Lirano, was also
single. It was a standing joke that Monica and Angelo would make a
great couple. Nothing ever came of it, both parties having been utterly
traumatized by ugly divorces. No matter that they had occurred in the
distant past, their tentacles reached into the present, always ready, so
it seemed, to wrap around their victims' neck and strangle them again.
No, Monica would never remarry. She had said so many times. Besides,
Angelo was a known workaholic, who did not even take Sundays off.
What could marriage to such a person possibly be like? She would have
more companionship if she stayed single, lived with her son and saw her
friends on the weekend.

"Have you got your cap and gown?"

Kevin nodded, his mouth full as he chewed his toast. He picked
up the Metro section of the newspaper and was soon mesmerized by
an article on the ecological destruction of the Chesapeake Bay. Blue
crabs were doing poorly, as indeed were all shellfish, and the fishermen
who depended on them complained bitterly about runoff from chicken
farms. "This factory farming is garbage," Kevin said, reaching for some
cherry Danish that his mother had just unloaded onto the table. "I think
Harry's mom's right. We should go organic."

"And go broke," Monica replied.

"How much worse could it be?"

"Try three dollars for an avocado."

Kevin, a lover of his mother's guacamole, grunted skeptically. "Maybe
non-organic for items like avocados. Says here runoff from those broiler
farms is turning the bay to green sludge. No wonder we can't find
any fossils anymore. They're hidden under the sludge." He paused to

demolish his Danish. "Even when Chandra and I were on that boat last weekend –"

"Oh yes. The friend of the Patels with the boat,"

"Out in the middle of the bay there was algae, there was litter. Everyone figures an estuary is just a gigantic toilet, that it flushes itself every day, but they're wrong –"

"Are they nice people?"

"No, people who think that are idiots."

"What did you say they think?"

"That they can just dump as much trash as they like in the bay."

"Did they do that?"

"Who?"

"The Patels' friends."

"I'm not talking about them."

"Oh. I'm confused."

"What else is new?"

"Who are you talking about?"

"Chicken farmers."

"Chicken farmers? How did we get on the subject of chicken farmers? I thought we were talking about the Patels' friends."

"You were talking about the Patels' friends. I was talking about chicken farmers."

"Why were we talking about different people? Why can't we have one conversation about one group of people?"

"Because we never do that. We always have at least two conversations going at once, until you say you're confused. Sometimes we have four or five discussions going at the same time. It's a miracle I'm not ADHD."

"So, were they nice?"

"Who?"

"The Patels' friends."

Kevin nodded, and his mother asked if they were Indian also. He did not reply at once, engrossed, yet again, in the article. "They say in ten years the bay could be virtually sterile."

"The Patels' friends?"

"No crabs, no oysters, no clams – nada, zip."

"Are they environmental experts too?"

"You don't have to be an expert. Just go out on a boat and look around."

"Like the ones the Patels' friends use, to, to gather information?"

Kevin glanced at his mother sharply. "I think you're lost again. At least I can say you're confusing me."

"How have I confused you?"

"Well, for starters, what, precisely, would the Patels' friends be gathering information on?"

"The sterility – not of themselves as I first thought you meant –"

Kevin put his head in his hands.

"But of the bay."

"And why would the Patels' friends be gathering information on the sterility of the Chesapeake? Because they co-authored this article?"

"Now that's a surprising development."

"No doubt it won't be the last."

"So they're journalists."

"Of course they're journalists. They wrote the article, and *no*, I'm not talking about the Patels' friends."

"Then who are we talking about?"

"That," Kevin slapped the paper on the table, "is the sixty-four thousand dollar question."

Fortunately the telephone rang. It was Edie Sullivan, making arrangements for a group photograph of the eight boys, right in front of the Millard E. Tydings High School, after their graduation.

"Then we can all go to lunch. Clarence Jones recommends Szechuan Palace. All the boys agree, but I," Edie said, "am skeptical. Ask Kevin if they have brown rice."

"We're going to Szechuan Palace. Edie wants to know do they serve brown rice?"

"Highly improbable, but a more exact answer would require a phone call."

"To whom?"

"To whom? Who do you think?"

"You tell me."

"The restaurant!" Kevin cried in exasperation.

"Kevin says call the restaurant."

"Well I don't need Kevin to tell me that."

"He's just trying to be helpful."

"I just bet they drench their food in MSG. Clarence is not exactly a paragon of healthy eating. Raw fat, salt, sugar and chemicals like MSG. That's what he goes for."

"How do you know?"

"I went over there once, and he offered me a tub of Kentucky Fried Chicken. Then his son Everett kicked up a horrible fuss. Something about Clarence gobbling up his precious chicken and offering it to anyone who crossed the threshold. You'd have thought it was something from a gourmet feast he was handing me, not some greasy old chicken, deep fried in enough fat to clog all your arteries. What a ruckus! I told them to come over to my house for some vegetable stir fry and James, he was with me, made some completely inappropriate remark about how then they could learn about starvation first hand."

"Men!" Monica clucked.

"Always thinking about their stomachs," Edie went on. "That and sports. Of course James had to pull up a chair, gorge himself on Kentucky Fried Chicken – it was a nineteen-piece bucket, if you can imagine – and indulge in this excruciatingly inane chit chat about college football. Just the sight of him devouring that chicken coagulated my blood. You can be sure there was no fat in his diet for months after that. He kept whining, 'what did I do to deserve this?' and I just said 'if you don't know, I'm not telling you,' and he said, 'it's better that way, it'll save me from falling on the floor and foaming at the mouth,' so I said, 'the initials are KFC.'"

"And did he?"

"Did he what?"

"Fall on the floor and foam at the mouth?"

"Yes. Well, on the couch. He kept pounding the wall and begging for an early death. Such drama. Then he snuck out to the nearest Kentucky Fried Chicken and stuffed himself silly."

"He told you?"

"No. He came home smelling like a drumstick boiled in lard. I accused him, and he caved in and confessed."

"Just like that."

"No. It took about six hours."

"Six hours of accusing?"

"Yes. I take his diet very seriously."

"Oh Edie, I'm not at all sure we should go to Szechuan Palace."

"Well, the die is cast. Arrangements are made. Who can say where it will all end up?"

"Szechuan Palace will be fine, Mom," Kevin said.

"Oh, but you have no idea of the gastronomical carryings on at the Sullivans.'"

"I think I do. Everybody does. Don't tell me: James Sullivan has begged someone, anyone, to put a bullet in his head. The last time it was Harry or me. We agreed that the meal was unsatisfying, but not worth a homicide rap. We refused –"

"He *asked* you to what?" Monica was shocked. "Edie, do you realize your husband asked my son to kill him, to –"

"Put him out of his misery were the words he used," Kevin clarified.

"To put him out of his misery?"

"Oh, he asks everyone to do that. I keep telling him, 'one of these days, James, someone's going to take you up on it, and then where will you be?' and he always answers, 'I don't know, but wherever it is I won't have to eat your tofu.' The only thing good about this Szechaun Gardens,"

"Palace."

"Palace, is that we won't have to listen to him talking about suicide. He'll be too busy stuffing himself on sesame chicken, which has more fat, more syrupy goo, more chemicals and calories than you can shake a stick at and therefore, naturally is his favorite dish. In all probability we won't hear from him at all, he'll be so busy loading the vittles into his mouth. Let's just hope Clarence Jones doesn't bring a bucket of Kentucky Fried Chicken to jazz things up, because if he does, I can't be held responsible for what I may do."

"Just a meal at a restaurant," Monica marveled. "I had no idea it could be so complicated."

"Oh, that's just the beginning," Edie went on dourly. "Be sure we don't let Clarence sit next to Stella Goodman. He's a sloppy eater, and if he gets a spot on one of her designer outfits, she'll be apoplectic. What a figure she has. Not like yours truly."

"Nonsense, Edie. You look fine."

"And if Sherwin's oldest brother, the corporate lawyer, comes, keep the sharp cutlery away from Jessie."

"Oh dear."

"Are you writing this down?"

"Should I be?"

"Yes. We'll need it at the meal," Edie said. Monica fetched paper and pencil and commenced writing.

"Above all, keep both Patels off the subject of higher education," Edie dictated.

"Won't that be hard? After all, it's a graduation, and higher education is usually what comes next."

"Not for most of our kids. Also, no one is to mention traffic congestion on the Beltway in the presence of Jacob Goodman. And no one, no one is to mention anything about traffic congestion, highways, the condition of the roads or cars, if Clarence Jones is in earshot. I think if I have to listen to his tirade on that subject ever again, I'll commit suicide. There is to be no discussion of dating or marriage, if the Lenthicans can hear, because Dorian and that Anna girl are having difficulties, and Isabelle, as we all know, had her heart set on grandchildren. The topic might make her burst into tears. With that fruitcake, Angelo Lirano, I don't even know where to begin. No one is to mention any culinary matters around my husband. That would set off an intolerably long and boring lament that will end with him demanding that someone in the group kill him. Harry's SAT scores are off the table."

"Why would they be on it?"

"I meant figuratively. Another topic that is verboten, this one in the presence of the Ignacios, is the military. There's some pretty sharp dissension in that family over Luis going into the air force, mostly from his sister Elena, and if she and the Joneses get together on that topic, there's liable to be a brawl. Lastly for myself: no one, not a soul, is to mention that lunatic Bradley from the army if I and my son can hear it."

"Maybe we should seat you and Harry apart?"

"No. I want to be next to him on his big day, but we have had a terrible dispute over inviting Bradley to this meal. I think I prevailed, and that nutcase isn't coming. I was afraid he'd be dressed up as a turkey or Ronald McDonald."

"How odd."

"Isn't it? Well, you've got your notes. Now you know what to do."

"Me?"

"Yes."

"What?"

"Make a seating plan. I'll bring little name cards, and that way no one will sit next to someone with whom one of these...these social time bombs could explode."

Monica hung up the phone in a dither. She explained her assignment to her son, who dubbed it "an exercise in futility," because no one, he said, would sit in an assigned seat. James Sullivan, he averred, desperate for a good meal, would grab the first seat, the first menu and order and eat everything before the entire party sat down. Clarence would sit next to Jacob, and in no time they would each be in a furious lather over commuting in Maryland. They would utterly drown out any other conversation at the table, and the entire meal's discussion would be devoted to the earth-shaking question of which was worse – the Beltway, I-95 or Route 50? Angelo Lirano would talk the ears off everyone in his vicinage with his numerous eccentric fixations. The graduates themselves would eat quickly, then decamp to one of their houses to play Doom, leaving the adults to talk about them behind their backs.

"So I shouldn't make a seating plan?" Monica asked.

"Don't waste time on it. Make any old plan. No one's going to stick to it."

"Edie will never forgive me."

"Edie will never remember. When she catches sight of Bradley in his blue and purple, cap-and-gown graduate get-up, she'll forget everything except heading for the hills. Which is a good thing. Light a fire under Mrs. Sullivan, and things happen, such as a quickly ordered meal and the timely arrival of the food."

Kevin returned to his article on the ecological degradation of the Chesapeake Bay.

"Poor Isabelle. She had her heart set on grandchildren."

"Sterile in five years," Kevin announced.

"Who – Dorian?"

"This runoff has wiped off life on the bottom. Algae blooms, toxic sludge, you name it. What a disaster."

"But what's this got to do with Isabelle's grandchildren?"

"Isabelle Lenthican?" Kevin looked surprised. "She has grandchildren?"

"Well if Dorian married Anna –"

"Ain't gonna happen," Kevin slurped his coffee. "He's not going to college, and she's taking it personally."

Kevin finished his coffee and tromped upstairs to his room in the back to get his cap and gown. Monica had decorated this room in blue – blue carpet, navy blue quilt, walls and ceiling painted sky blue. Originally two paintings of an aquamarine sea had adorned the walls; however, in middle school Kevin had disposed of them with the explanation that he liked posters. Monica had stored them in the basement along with those few remaining toys she had not gotten rid of – the expensive or particularly ingenious ones. She explained this salvage to him by saying that perhaps his children would like them, and, to her surprise, he agreed. Kevin's room contained a computer, a phone, many articles of clothing on the floor, his trombone, his football gear and a shelf of books, mostly on the environment but with a few classics – *Moby Dick, Crime and Punishment, The Divine Comedy* – interspersed. Whenever he needed to think, he came up there, shut the door, opened the glass sliding doors to the balcony facing the woods, and lay down in the coolest, most shadowed, breeziest room in the house. The calm and quiet always helped him order his thoughts, often so saturated his pensive mood that he would find himself drifting off, midday on a Saturday, dreaming about whatever dilemma had led him to seek refuge in his room in the first place.

Kevin liked his life in the townhouse with his mother. He was not particularly keen to live on campus when he went to the University of Maryland in Baltimore, for several reasons. First he worried about Monica, alone without him. She did not do well with solitude and regarded his eventual departure, he knew, with trepidation. He did not like the thought of her eating breakfast and dinner alone and going to sleep in an empty house. She would be bored, lonely. She would miss him. After all, he knew very well that her life had revolved around him for eighteen years – what would hold her steady, keep her from flying off into who knew what, if he was not around? He *was* her life. She had said so, more times than he could count.

The other consideration pulling on him to stay at home was that he did not like change. His father's abrupt departure when he was seven years old had been change enough for a lifetime. Kevin had cried, off and on, until he was nine, until somehow the thought sank into his child's mind that his father was gone for good, that he would never return, even for a visit, that all he had in the world was his mother. The horrible finality of this realization had somehow shut off his tears. The vacuum it left was filled by a desperate attachment to Monica, to their new home, to his routine. He wanted everything to stay the same; he wanted no more changes.

And he was happy to forget the last two years with his father – the screaming matches with Monica, the parade of girlfriends, the drinking, the withholding of essential money from his wife and young son. Those years had been so horrible that Monica did not even at first pursue child support. She wanted never to see her husband again and to owe him nothing. Edie and Isabelle had talked her out of that. "Why make it easy on him? You're alone, working full time, there's day care – make him pay his share. Stick it to him. He deserves it." But the child support always arrived erratically. The Dawns could not count on it. There were court orders, contempt citations, but very little cash. Kevin, by then a preteen, did not like this dunning of his father. He feared it might lead in some convoluted way to his return, to the undoing of all the arrangements, changes and adjustments Kevin had made in his absence. He had come to like his life with his mother and his friends. He did not want the nasty old blowhard and philanderer to reappear on their doorstep to explain his refusal to remit a measly few hundred bucks, or whatever the excuse might be. No, Kevin wanted things to stay exactly as they were. They were good. They were better than good. As he became a teenager he realized how happy he was with his life. He did not want more. He was content.

Looking back, he knew very well that he had adored his father until the age of five, when, as he told his grandmother, his father did bad things to his mother like make her cry, hit her, stay out late and not come home and yell at her. He also saw that his mother fought back, making peace even less likely. He was torn during this period, not knowing whose side he was on. Then his father vanished – no more games of catch in the yard, no more weekend trips to Annapolis, the aquarium in Baltimore or the National Zoo, no more snowmen in winter or snowball fights, no more candy treats at any old time, even right before dinner. His mother said he was gone. In the silence of his bed at night, Kevin had contemplated "gone" and found it unacceptable. He would come back. He had to. He wouldn't just leave Kevin, why, Kevin and his mother were too important – or were they? And with that thought the tears would come, hot, uncontrollable, welling up in his seven-year-old eyes no matter what he was doing, who he played with, where he was. Grownups started talking about him in hushed tones, dealt with him in a constrained, artificial manner – all except Monica, who wiped his eyes and promised, "I will never leave you. Never."

So Kevin learned to wait for his father, to look at the grown men in the supermarket or the mall to see if one of them was him. He searched for a head of blondish, brown hair, a medium build, a work-shirt. But even the strangers who fit this description were wrong. They looked back at him with alien faces, wondering what that kid was staring for. It was not until one Saturday in Toys R Us with his mother that he realized the finality, the immutability of the loss. He had run up to a stranger, yelling, "Dad! Dad!" The man turned, smiled awkwardly, and Monica, embarrassed, approached and led Kevin away. That wasn't Dad. And if it was, he would not want to see them.

"Let's get those Legos and forget it. You father doesn't want us," she said, "and we don't want him."

In that moment his father – the smell of him, the rasp of his voice, the touch of his shaved cheek, the sight of him – slipped over the horizon of Kevin's childhood and was gone. He did not cry that day or thereafter. The tears had vanished, along with their source.

Sometimes, when he needed to be alone, he would lie on his bed with the door shut, the curtains blowing out onto the balcony, nearly touching the branches of the trees and think back, but never farther back than age nine, than that day in the toy store, when the contours of his life shifted once and for all into their current configuration. Kevin, his mother, his friends, the townhouse, school. College threatened to alter all that. He was not ready for such change. As he rummaged in his closet for his cap and gown, he muttered, "I'll live at home and commute to class."

Now that he had finished, he could see that what he had considered his salad days in high school had in fact been the pinnacle of felicity for him. Already the somewhat numbing rhythm of work had made him appreciate what he was losing – seeing his friends in the hall, the pranks, football, some of the classes, his girlfriends. There had been two of those – Jessica in ninth grade and later on Jennifer, who had dumped him for Harry. He harbored no ill feelings toward his friend for this, rather he thought he had got off easily. After all, as he put it to Paul, "there's not a snowball's chance in hell I'm going to be an itinerant performance artist." And when he observed the gusto with which she went about organizing Harry's life, he realized that in fact she had approached him with the same attitude. He just had not seen it at the time. He was too busy looking at her long red hair and lovely face and figure. Once she had left him and set about "improving" Harry, he wondered how he had ever tolerated her. "You escaped," Luis said. "Our buddy Harry's at the National Gallery of Art on this gorgeous Saturday, and we are sitting here playing video games."

"Yes. But Harry gets to sit with her at the movies tonight."

"A small sacrifice for you," Luis concluded. "Besides, it'll doubtless be something very worthy and educational."

Over the months Kevin had come to agree with him, especially when Jennifer finally left Harry for a straight-A honors student, who did not play football but practiced yoga in his spare time and who, with Jennifer's encouragement, got up a petition for the drama department to offer classes in mime.

"I wonder if he wears a leotard in dance class," Harry said sourly.

"Probably," Kevin replied. "And maybe a tutu as well."

"A little pink frilly thing," Sherwin remarked. "Think, if you guys weren't so narrow-minded, you could be wearing it now and watching the love of your life doing pliés."

Harry and Kevin exchanged a glance. It was a hot summer afternoon at the swim club, and Sherwin was standing by the edge of the pool. Without a word, Kevin lunged, shoving Sherwin, glasses, T-shirt, flip-flops, a copy of *The New Republic*, and all, into the water.

Another aspect of these years, which he contemplated with considerable satisfaction, was his effort with the trombone. There was no denying that Kevin had a tin ear and that no amount of practice would make him a decent trombone player. But he had given it his all. He had practiced every day, producing squeaks and honks that led his mother to purchase earplugs. No one could say he hadn't tried. Mr. Walsh, his teacher, was a paragon of patience – at twenty dollars for every half hour, he could afford to be. He would stand, listen, occasionally smoothing his lank, thinning, gray hair and then attempt to join in on the French horn or saxophone. The music they thus made was uniformly abysmal, but Kevin, who could scarcely tell the good from the bad, was not perturbed. He played along, in blissful ignorance of the fact that he was hopelessly off key, unless a little frown began to twitch at Mr. Walsh's rather pallid lips. This usually happened when Monica sat, waiting in the next room. Mr. Walsh wished to impress her and was irked that Kevin's lack of musical ability prevented that. What he usually did under these circumstances was to say, "wait a minute," then pick up his own trombone and perform a lengthy and marvelous example of what the music should sound like. The reason for this bit of showing off was not fear that Monica would conclude she was throwing money down the drain, which she was, no. It was that Mr. Walsh, "call me Cecil, and I hope I may call you Monica," was rather smitten by Kevin's mother. At age 55, Cecil had pretty much given up on matrimony, and then he had met Monica, who had managed to keep in shape and who, a few years younger and with her hair darkly colored, looked very good to him.

When Cecil discovered that Monica, like him, was divorced, his hopes soared. He made inquiries about Kevin's home life that he thought were very discreet. He needn't have bothered. Kevin had no idea of the state of his trombone teacher's heart. Rather he thought that Mr. Walsh's mind wandered a bit, and the odd question at the unlikely moment only seemed to confirm this.

"We're in G, Kevin, not E. How long have you and your mother lived in the townhouse?"

"Uh, G not E. About ten years."

"You're not blowing right. Do it like this. I guess your mother has a very busy social life?"

"I guess," Kevin resumed squeaking on the trombone.

"Still not in G."

Squeak, squeak, honk.

"She goes out a lot in the evenings?"

"Nope," squeak, squeak.

"Perhaps you and she would like to attend a jazz performance that I'll be part of in Annapolis."

"Thanks, Mr. Walsh."

"She must consider a musical education very important, to keep you at it so faithfully," Mr. Walsh remarked, wincing as Kevin played *very* off key."

"It's mostly me," Kevin paused. "But she'd back me up, whatever I did."

"Good grief," Mr. Walsh murmured. But Kevin heard not a word. He was busy missing his high notes again. "Such faith in her only child is admirable," he blandly resumed. "You *are* the only child?"

"The one and only," squeak, honk,

"Yes, you could put it that way, I suppose."

An entire series of squeaks and screeches ensued, and Mr. Walsh grimaced in auricular pain. "You're sure you're practicing daily?"

Kevin nodded. "So much," he put the trombone down, "that my mom has bought earplugs. She says the music distracts her."

"No doubt it does," Cecil said with what Kevin took to be an unaccountably splenetic expression on his face. "Earplugs - now there's a thought. A very good way to keep the music, as you call it, from deafening you."

Again, Kevin heard not a word. His trombone was busy bellowing and honking again.

"G, Kevin, G."

"I appreciate your patience, Mr. Walsh."

Cecil turned away and rolled his eyes.

"I'll get it yet," squeak, honk.

"Not 'til kingdom come, would be my guess."

"What, Mr. Walsh?"

"Practice makes perfect. That's all I meant."

"You'll be happy to know I practice at least an hour a day."

"Unbelievable."

"Yep. Though sometimes I think I'll never make first chair in the school band," squeak, squeak.

"Probably not."

"Say what?"

"You never know."

"Would you, uh, write me a recommendation for my music teacher, urging him to reconsider putting me all the way in the back?"

"Perhaps your mother could assist me. She doubtless knows your talent better than anyone. The earplugs signify a woman of great practicality."

"Great," Kevin beamed.

Unfortunately for Mr. Walsh, Monica was not interested in the prospect of romance. The trauma of her divorce so many years back had never really vanished. She always had one excuse or another as to why some man was not acceptable. In Mr. Walsh's case, it was that he was not her type.

"What makes you think he's interested?" Kevin had asked, toward the end of his senior year.

"A woman can tell these things."

"I haven't seen or heard the slightest evidence of this."

"Well, at least he's discreet."

"He's loony is what he is. His mind wanders."

"Another strike against him."

"He's the only person I know who constantly interrupts himself. First he's telling me what to do with the trombone, the next second he's asking some utterly irrelevant question about who knows what."

"Well, I'm glad I stopped coming to the lessons. I believe he was on the verge of asking me to dinner."

"He was on the verge of asking you a thousand addle-pated questions about nothing in particular. That's what he was on the verge of."

"I wouldn't have liked that, either."

"Damned annoying is what it is. Guy can't concentrate for thirty seconds. He and Mr. Lirano ought to get together. Now there's a conversation that would wander." Kevin had observed this about his boss so many times that Monica had begun to picture a rather demented computer geek. She had only met Angelo Lirano once, and the encounter had not gone well, mainly because everyone in their acquaintance had been urging them to get together. This set up quite a resistance in both of them, so that when they finally parleyed, they were mutually terrified. It was as if a jolt of electricity propelled them away from each other. Each scampered away and vowed never to repeat the experience.

Angelo liked Kevin but had noticed right away that he was not particularly talented at computer repair. Kevin, on the other hand, thought he excelled in this field and did not discern that his boss consistently gave him the easy jobs, saving the more exacting ones for Paul – Pauli, as his father affectionately called him. But if Angelo thought little of Kevin's repair skills, that was nothing compared to his alarm at the sight of Harry, busting into a CPU.

"He's all thumbs," Angelo said to his son, shortly after hiring Harry to work part time in addition to his Best Buy job. "Don't mention why, but we're putting him on the cash register."

Mr. Lirano loved to hire Pauli's friends. He liked "the kids," as he called them, and saw their presence in his flagship computer repair store as a means of keeping Paul around. With his buddies right there, Paul had less of an incentive to ask for time off or to rush away at closing. But Mr. Lirano had to admit that he was disappointed in the quality of their work.

"Why don't you get your friend Animal to come work here? He's better with computers than all the others put together. Not to put too fine a point on it Pauli, but Harry and Kevin couldn't find their way out of a paper bag."

"Put them on pick-up and delivery. They can drive the computers back to the office buildings."

"If their driving skills resemble their computer repair skills, they might wind up in Kalamazoo. Then where would I be?"

"Right here, in Crofton Maryland."

"You know Harry's mother brought a home computer in for repair."

"Really. What happened to it?"

"I think Harry tried to log on. A most unusual lady, that Edie Sullivan. She had a lot to say about trans fats and partially hydrogenated vegetable oil. Do you know they're everywhere?"

Paul put down the screwdriver and glanced at his father in annoyance. They were in the back office of the computer store, fixing a particularly recalcitrant MacIntosh. "Let's keep the conversation on one topic, okay Dad?"

"Okay Pauli, anything you say. What's the topic?"

"The Sullivan's computer."

"It crashes all the time, not too surprisingly, since I think someone spilled coffee into the CPU."

"How can you tell?"

"Smell. You know I got the best nose on the East Coast."

Paul rolled his eyes.

"That unit reeks of coffee. Choc Full O Nuts, I'd say. Which is rather surprising. For someone so picky about her food and what her family eats, Edie Sullivan really skimps on the coffee. I'd have thought one of those special, imported whole bean coffees that you grind for yourself in the supermarket. Now there's a system they could improve on. Half the time you get someone else's coffee, cause they left the beans in. The other half the time, the machine doesn't grind to specification. Maybe I'll make a complaint."

"Maybe you'll fix the Sullivan's computer."

"You think I could use that as an excuse, to get out of dinner?"

"They invited us again?"

Angelo nodded. "I just can't take those bean sprouts, Pauli."

"But they don't have any hydrogenated oil."

"They don't have any anything. It's like eating air. Boy am I lucky I didn't marry Edie Sullivan. I'd have starved to death years ago."

"Her husband claims he's starving to death now."

"We gotta get out of this dinner invitation."

"It's one meal. Relax."

"But all those different kinds of mushrooms she serves, Shitaki, Portobello, this, that. I like to know what I'm eating, Pauli. I like steaks and burgers and mashed potatoes."

"You get those 364 nights a year. It's a miracle you haven't gone into cardiac arrest. One meal won't kill you."

"Don't be too sure."

"A little brown rice is good for you."

"Oh, the brown rice!" Angelo threw up his hands. "I hate the brown rice! If she serves that again, I don't know what I'll do, Pauli. I can't be held responsible for my actions. Anything may happen."

"I can see the headlines now. 'Middle-Aged Italian Man Goes on Rampage at Arby's, Eats Restaurant Out of Roast Beef,'" Paul resumed working on the computer. "If she serves it, you'll eat it."

"I may become bulimic."

"Good. You need to lose a little weight."

"I'm gonna say I'm busy, fixing their computer. I'll say it's got the most mysterious case of computeritis I've ever seen and that I don't feel right availing myself of their hospitality, when I haven't finished fixing it for them."

"That just postpones the day."

"I can live with that."

Kevin and Harry came in. "We're ready to help," they said in unison.

"God forbid," Angelo muttered under his breath.

"What are you," Paul demanded, "the Bobsy twins?"

"Hey Mr. Lirano, have you figured out what's wrong with our computer?" Harry asked.

"Everything's wrong with your computer."

"Can you fix it?"

"Buy a new one."

"Well, I know someone spilled a little coffee on it."

"Someone poured a pot of Chock Full O Nuts directly into the CPU."

"How'd you know we drink Chock Full O Nuts?"

"Don't ask," Paul said.

"I have a nose," Angelo began, "like no other." He paused, letting the silence fill with speculation, become pregnant with possibilities, as Harry and Kevin stared at his nose. Paul rolled his eyes and muttered, "I don't believe this."

"This nose can distinguish the flavor and brand of gum you're chewing at a distance of three feet," Angelo tapped his remarkable olfactory organ, as Paul put his head in his hands. "This nose can distinguish between wild and farmed salmon without being anywhere near the grill. This nose knows the difference between penne and rotini boiling in the pot. This nose can name the different countries of different bottles of wine."

"Oh," Paul said, "so now it's a talking nose."

His father ignored him. "This nose can tell if you're smoking a Marlboro or a Camel at a distance of fifteen yards. It can tell the difference between a Marlboro and a Marlboro Light at six yards."

Paul gave his father a look that said, "can it tell you to shut up?" as clearly as if he had spoken the words. But Angelo merely paused to let his fantastic nasal accomplishments sink into the minds of his young listeners. He rubbed his hands together and eagerly resumed. "Without seeing the box, this nose can tell what brand of sparkler you're using in your back yard on a summer night."

"I'm glad your nose didn't see the box," Paul said, "because that would be so remarkable I might not be able to stand it."

"This nose can tell that you, Harry, used Herbal Essence shampoo this morning."

"He's right!" Harry exclaimed.

"Stop encouraging him," Paul spoke with irritation.

"And this nose knows that Kevin hasn't taken a shower since yesterday morning."

"The nose may know that," Paul said, "but *we* didn't want to."

"This nose can tell that Harry had scrambled eggs and sausage for breakfast, that Kevin had pancakes with syrup and bacon on the side. This nose is getting hungry."

"That's right, Dad. Go feed your nose. And be sure to tell it to keep its secrets to itself."

"This nose knows that Paul," Angelo stopped. His son had looked at him very sharply. "Never mind," he rather lamely concluded.

"Exactly," Paul said. "Now take your nose out to the front, because while your nose was knowing who bathed and who didn't, who ate what where and when, these ears," Paul put both hands up and pushed his ears forward, "these ears detected the presence of a customer in the shop."

"Oh my goodness," Angelo exclaimed. "I was paying so much attention to my nose, I forget my ears." He hurried into the front of the store.

"Harry, you're on the cash register," Paul said.

"Aw geez. I'm sick of the cash register. I want to fix something."

Paul eyed him coolly. "We all *want* to do lots of things, Harry. That doesn't mean we can."

Failing to detect any double-entendre, Harry went on, "why don't I work on my family's computer?"

"Well, that would about finish it," Paul said.

"C'mon."

"Oh fine. Kevin, you take the cash register."

Kevin stepped out – Angelo stepped back in. "Are you nuts?" He demanded in a whisper. "You let Harry touch anything, and it's ruined for good."

"He's working on his family's computer," Paul whispered, jerking his head toward the back of the room, where Harry noisily rummaged around. "That thing's done for, what harm can he do?"

"Don't ask."

"Why not?"

"Something horrible might come to mind. Like me losing my excuse not to go to dinner at their house."

"I got news for you Dad: you're going to dinner."

"Well, I don't know who your sources are, but what they don't know could fill the Grand Canyon. I am not, I repeat not, eating that woman's food ever again."

"So now she's 'that woman.'"

"Any woman who serves food like that is 'that woman,'" Angelo hissed in a loud whisper.

"You would think the world revolves around your stomach."

"Yours does. Why can't mine?"

"Hey Harry, I know you just ate breakfast," Paul said loudly.

"Scrambled eggs and sausage," Angelo said and then tapped his nose.

"I know," Paul sighed, "the remarkable nose." He turned around to face Harry. "Why don't you run over to Subway and get me a twelve-inch veggie delight?"

"Throw in a twelve-inch meat ball marinara for me," Angelo said.

"Make that two," Kevin called from the cash register. "I know I just ate, but it never hurts to eat again."

"Right," Paul said, "you never know, starvation could be just around the corner."

"Like when we go to the Sullivans' for dinner," Angelo hissed to his son in a whisper.

"I shouldn't be hungry," Harry said. "After all, I had the best breakfast I've eaten in weeks. Usually my mom gives me this cereal called

Fiber Plus. It's like chewing hay. But today she had to leave early, so I got to cook for myself. But what the heck. I'll get a roast beef sub anyway."

"Maybe when we come to your house for dinner, you'll cook," Angelo said hopefully.

"Oh, you know I think my mom must have made a mistake."

"Praise the Lord," Angelo breathed.

"With graduation in two weeks, and all the stuff we have to do, I don't see how we can be having people over for dinner."

"Neither do I," Angelo said. "And Paul and I are very busy too. Very busy. You give your parents my apologies, tell them we completely understand how busy they are, and tell them we'll see them for lunch after graduation at a restaurant."

"Sounds good to me."

"Best news I heard all day," Angelo muttered under his breath.

Harry collected the money and made his way to Subway at 9:30 in the morning.

"That was a close call," Angelo said. "Too close for comfort. We're going to have to develop a plan, Pauli."

"What plan?"

"A permanent excuse, like that I developed diabetes and am on a restricted diet that I only prepare for myself at home."

"Diabetics still go out to dinner."

"Not when they're having their dialysis."

"At dinner time?"

"The plan may have some kinks. We'll work them out."

"Some kinks? Like being completely ineffective and a bald-faced lie to boot, one that's bound to be found out and embarrass us, *me*, horribly."

"Why can't we go to dinner at the Joneses instead. Clarence always has that big bucket of Kentucky Fried Chicken."

"Yeah, he and Everett are always fighting over it like cats and dogs. 'I bought it.' 'Who raised you?' 'That's no excuse for stealing.' What a joy that is, eating Everett's fried chicken. I don't know how Jones can stand it, going through that scene every night. It would drive me to homicide."

"It drives him to a lot of sarcastic remarks, I notice," Angelo said. "In which he more than a little resembles another person I know but won't name."

Paul pushed back his dark brown hair and looked at his father sharply. "It's not as if that other person has nothing to put up with," whereupon he began pointing at his nose: "My nose! My nose! My marvelous nose! Come one, come all. We're going to put it on stage! It'll tour the world. It can smell your popcorn at 300 feet."

"More like one hundred."

"And it can smell your feet at ten yards. Think of all the revolting things this nose can do."

"I was very impressed with your nose," Kevin said, ambling back in.

Angelo gave a half bow. "*Somebody* appreciates a wonder of nature when they see it."

Paul put down his screwdriver and glared at his father. "So now it's a wonder of nature?"

"True, you've told me about your nose before," Kevin went on.

"Really, when?" Angelo asked.

"Yesterday. And the day before."

"That often?"

"About twenty times," Paul growled. "It's a miracle we don't all go to sleep dreaming about your freakin' nose."

"There are worse things to dream about."

"Maybe we could have a moratorium on the nose," Paul suggested.

"I don't think that will work," Angelo said.

"Why not?" Paul demanded.

"Because this nose perceives so many wonderful things that no other nose knows about that it's simply impossible for me to keep quiet. It bombards me with information."

"So now it's throwing things."

"I told you it was remarkable."

Harry returned with the food and distributed it to everyone, seated around a worktable. Angelo held up his meatball marinara and melted cheese sub and admired it. "What a beautiful sight, and good for you too."

"If going into cardiac arrest is good for you, then I suppose you could say that," Paul commented.

"Don't act superior just because you got the veggie delight. It's got sauce."

"*Wine* dressing, Dad, Not a lot of fat in that."

"It says in the window, 'doctor approved.'"

"Yeah, a podiatrist."

"Nonsense," Angelo snapped and ferociously bit into his sub.

"You show me a cardiologist who approves of that sub for a fifty-year-old, overweight –"

"Mildly overweight."

"Mildly overweight, rather sedentary businessman, and I'll show you a quack."

"Quack, quack," Angelo snapped, marinara sauce appearing at the corners of his lips.

"Quack, quack yourself. Don't talk with your mouth full."

"I wasn't talking. I was quacking."

"Frankly, I don't care if it's bad for you," Kevin said, taking three huge chomps of his sub in rapid succession.

"You're eighteen," Paul said. "He's fifty."

"You sound like my mother," Harry remarked.

A look of terror came over Angelo's face. "God forbid."

"Well she would be right. He should skip all this red meat and stick to vegetables."

"That's what happens when you get old," Angelo said. "People start taking things away from you."

"My father says that's what happened when he got married."

"He would be right," Angelo said. "That's why I got divorced. One of the reasons. Screw the Catholic Church."

Kevin raised his shoulders and held out his hands as if to say, "Whaaaat?"

"My father's a Unitarian now," Paul explained. "He couldn't remain a Catholic and get divorced."

"It's a great religion," chomp, chomp on the meatball sub. "No rules, no regulations, no stupid rituals."

"No God," Paul said sarcastically.

"Oh there's God," Angelo was licking his fingers now. "But only if you want Him."

"Who could ask for better terms," Paul said.

"Pauli here stayed a Catholic. He refused to leave the Church. Only ten years old, and he was that stubborn. Can you imagine?"

"Only ten years old and the sight of those retarded hippies in your congregation tipped me off that here was one first-class phony religion."

"Quack, quack."

"Quack, quack yourself."

"I had no idea your family was so riven by religious dissension," Kevin smirked.

Paul glared at him. The look said, "now you've done it."

"We're not riven," Angelo said, still chomping. "We're at war. We disagree about everything to do with God. The state of affairs on this topic in our household makes the European wars of religion look like child's play. Pauli is a religious fanatic."

"Now I've heard everything," Paul said.

"He believes Catholic doctrine, every iota of that nonsensical, superstitious, backward –"

"Enough Dad. We get the picture."

"I just want it to be clear, Pauli."

"It's clear as a bell."

"Good. I, on the other hand, believe in one God, who works through the world, is what our minister calls immanent. But I don't believe in organized religion. Organized religion is, as Jessie Jones says, for fascists."

"So now I'm a fascist."

"I hate to have to break it to you, but if you believe and consider it good that billions of people are going to roast in Hell and suffer eternal torment for sins like getting divorced, or infants who die before they get baptized, then you do not have a very warm-hearted, humane or tolerant approach to humanity."

"Maybe a lot of humanity is bigoted, cruel, wicked, criminal, power-hungry and just as happy to inflict misery on their fellow man as anything else. Maybe a lot of people deserve to go to Hell."

"I rest my case," chomp, chomp on the meatball sub.

"Geez," Harry said. "Do you two have discussions like this every night at dinner?"

"Since I got divorced, every night without fail."

"It's a miracle you still talk to each other."

"We don't," Angelo and Paul said in unison.

"My family has no religion whatsoever," Harry went on. "I've never set foot in a church. My mother wouldn't allow it."

"That's surprisingly reasonable of her," Angelo said. "She's got more common sense than I thought."

"She's a terrible cook," Harry added, as if he were informing them of something they never would have guessed.

"No really?" Angelo rolled his eyes.

"You should try her steamed vegetables."

"I think I'm losing my appetite."

"First she burns them. All of them. She steams them too long, all the water evaporates, and they burn. Then she puts this lemon sauce on that tastes like pee."

"Aw shut up Harry. We're eating," Kevin exclaimed.

"Or we were," Paul said, regarding his vegetable sub with sudden distaste.

"I think I need to go lie down," Angelo remarked.

"That's what my father does every night after dinner," Harry went on. "Lies down on the couch and moans. After forty minutes of 'What did I do to deserve this?' 'Is there no God?' 'Just kill me now, Edith,' and so forth, he sneaks out to McDonalds or Wendy's or KFC and orders the biggest, fattiest, baddest meal he can get and wolfs it down with warnings like, 'If you tell your mother, I will personally murder you,' 'If Edie hears about this, I know where to find you,' 'Keep this to yourself or I will wring your neck,' and other such warm, loving bits of paternal advice. I usually just get a coke. You see, I'm used to my mom's cooking. It's a point of honor with me to eat every bite."

They all looked at him as if he had taken leave of his senses.

"I mean it," Harry went on. "Anything she can dish out, I can eat. And let me tell you, she has dished out some doozies."

When the big day for graduation came, Harry's father was in a state of shock.

"I can't believe it," he said, settling into an auditorium seat next to Edie, "he's really gonna graduate. Our long national nightmare is almost over."

"It's not over yet," Edie snapped. "He has to make it across the stage without tripping over his robe, high-fiving the principal, doing a break dance or otherwise making a spectacle of himself, get his diploma, then, without dropping or misplacing it, make his way back into his seat."

"Sounds like kind of a lot."

"Yes," she said glumly, "it is."

"Oh looky. There are the Joneses."

"Yes, I saw Everett's 'United Mine Workers: Striking For Our Brothers' T-shirt when they came in. He's dressed for the event, as usual. Couldn't be anybody else."

"Hi Luis! The Ignacios too."

"I do hope you're not going to name everyone in the whole goddamn school, because if you are, I'm moving."

The Goodmans sat down next to them.

"You wouldn't believe that Beltway last night," Jacob groaned.

"Don't try me," Edie said.

"So the big day finally arrived," Stella said. "I can scarcely believe it."

"None of us can," James said.

"It isn't over yet," Edie cautioned.

"I'm so excited I almost blew a gasket," Stella went on.

"Indeed," Edie said.

"You mean you almost blew a gasket on the Mercedes and got us stranded in Howard County," Jacob grumbled.

"Howard County?" Edie asked. "What were you doing way out there?"

"She got so excited, was so beside herself with disbelief, shock, suspense, wonder –"

"I get the picture," Edie said.

"That Sherwin was finally, after all these years –"

"And all these detentions," James put in. "My God, I can't even count them."

"And that too," Jacob continued, "that he was finally really going to graduate that she blew a gasket, floored the accelerator, missed the exit, missed the next two exits and before you know it, bingo! The car's got a rumble under the hood, and we're in freakin' Howard County." Jacob glared at his fashionably attired spouse. "Whereupon I said, give me the wheel. Me – who hates driving, is allergic to the goddamn Beltway, twenty years on that overrated, underpaved, congested, multi-lane superhighway filled with the rudest drivers and most obscene truckers in North America. Me – who never drives except under duress, namely, my daily commute, because I can't otherwise goddamn avoid it. I said, 'let me drive.' Boy, you know it's a cold day in Hell when I say to Stella, 'let me drive.'"

"Let's hope it's not a portent of things to come," Edie said dyspeptically.

Clarence Jones approached and leaned over the back of their seats. "How'd you like that backup on Route 50? Boy the morons in the DOT really outdid themselves with this weekday roadwork."

"I wouldn't know," Jacob said. "I was in Howard County."

"Now there's a county with some big pothole problems," Clarence said.

Edie rolled her eyes.

"But it's nothin' next to PG."

"What is this, the county by county road condition comparison chart?" Edie snapped.

"Shh, shh," Stella hissed. "It's starting."

"I can't believe it," James said.

"I can't either," Clarence agreed. "And I'll wait 'til Donny hands me that diploma, and I read all the fine print and make sure there are no last minute exceptions, then and then only will I believe he really pulled it off. Do you believe when he took Tech. Ed., I got weekly phone calls from that psycho Mr. Nagoogaram,"

"Nagoulsalaam," Edie corrected.

"Right, urging me to get Donald into psychotherapy? Me. What kind of money did he think I had? If I could have afforded psychotherapy, I would have spent it on Everett and Jessie years ago."

"They do entertain rather violent political fantasies," Edie remarked.

"And you haven't even heard the details."

"And I don't want to."

"Uh-oh, here comes Angelo. He's tapping his marvelous nose," Clarence said. "Excuse me, while I hide."

"I knew it!" James cried in despair. "He's not graduating. All the kids are in front. There's Stone, Sturm, no Sullivan. I knew it was too good to be true."

Edie leaned forward in alarm. "He's there," she said after a moment. "He was just crawling on the floor."

"Crawling on the floor? It's graduation, not day care. I'll break his neck. If Harry louses this up, I will personally see to it –"

"Shh!" Stella hissed again. "It's starting."

In moments members of the senior class were crossing the stage. Edie put her head in her hands as Harry, receiving his diploma, startled the principal by embracing him, then did a little jig the rest of the way across the stage.

"I don't believe it," James said. "He actually got the diploma." Then a moment later: "I don't believe it. He actually made it across the stage. True, he did a little dance, and it looks like he alarmed Mr. Johnson with that bear hug, but Edie – tell me I'm not dreaming."

Edie, her head still in her hands, said: "No, unfortunately you are not dreaming. Harry just made an absolute idiot of himself in front of the entire school."

"But they can't take the diploma back for that – or can they? I knew it was too good to be true."

Edie looked up, saw her son strolling up the aisle, high-fiving the seated seniors. "No," she said. "I don't know how it happened, but he really graduated."

"I got the evidence," Jacob said and tapped his video camera, which had been running when Sherwin and each of his seven friends made their appearances on the stage. "Frankly, I can't believe it either. The way things were going, I kind of thought Sherwin would be in high school 'til about 2010."

James Sullivan sat forward, his arms hanging limply at his side, and stared, rather slack-jawed, as Harry resumed his seat among the seniors. He looked as if lightening had struck him to the spot. "I still don't believe it."

"Me neither," Clarence hissed, leaning forward. "We gotta read the fine print."

Afterward, the eight young men gathered in front of the school, as their proud parents took pictures.

"Knock it off, Harry," James snapped. "I want one photograph where you don't look like a clown."

"Kevin, straighten your cap. It's crooked," Monica said. "And I'm certainly not photographing you with a tassel hanging between your eyes."

"Chandra, don't make me speak to you again."

"Sherwin, any more of that, and I'm taking back the car keys," Jacob hollered, "and you will have to *let me drive* it to the restaurant."

"Dorian, uncross your eyes. In every picture you look like you need eye surgery."

"Luis, the air force regalia stays out of the picture," Elena snapped. "I want *happy* memories."

"Donny, cut that out. You cut that out, or I'll get Mr. Nagoogaram out here and put *him* in the picture instead of you."

"Pauli, what do you think this is? America's worst home videos? You're supposedly an adult now."

When they arrived at Szechuan Palace, their party took up three long banquet tables in the center of the restaurant. Everybody ignored the nametags and, to Edie's dismay, sat wherever they wanted. James, rubbing his hands in anticipation, muttering, "oh boy, a Chinese meal, oh boy," and visibly salivating, sat next to Clarence and across from Jacob. Elena and Jessie sat next to each other, and there were a number of other such unfortunate matches.

"Why is Bertram sitting opposite Jessie?" Edie asked Monica in subdued tones. "I told you to keep them apart."

"Why, isn't this delightful," Jessie began, a glass of water in hand and one which Edie feared soon might be splashed in the face of the person seated opposite her. "I get to sit across from the lickspittle lawyer for corporate interests, conservative lobbyists and right-wing Republicans, Bertram Goodman."

"And proud of it," Bertram said.

"Well, there's no accounting for tastes."

"Speaking of which," Monica interrupted. "Let's look at the menu, shall we?"

"I want three of everything," James said.

"Three? You don't get three of everything," Edie replied.

"Why not? Three is my lucky number. We've got three kids."

"Are you going to eat them, too?"

"The servings here are humongous," Clarence enthused, and then called to the waiter: "Hey, Lin, when you going to get a proper union in this place?"

"You organize us, eh Mista Jones?"

"I smell Oil of Olay," Angelo said. Paul put his elbow on the table and his head in his hand.

"How remarkable," Stella responded. "I use Oil of Olay."

Angelo placed his index finger alongside his nose. "This, madam, is what is remarkable."

Stella's eyebrows went up. "The corner of your eye?"

"My nose. You are also wearing a Chanel perfume."

"Jacob, this is so unusual."

"Maybe you could sniff the menu and tell us what to order," Paul said.

"So I leave a message on their frickin' machine," Clarence was saying to Jacob, "pointing out that the state of the roads in Maryland is a goddamned disgrace, that traffic congestion is enough to cause a nervous breakdown and that the lights all have either broken timers or timers that were set by sadists."

"You should have mentioned the Beltway specifically," Jacob said, pouring a cup of tea. "They cannot get too many complaints about that so-called superhighway. What I wouldn't give to get my hands around the neck of the genius who designed those exits –"

"The exits!" Clarence exclaimed. "What about the entrance ramps? You gotta go from 30 to 70 in ten feet and be ready to stop or merge at any moment. The designers were homicidal maniacs and should all be electrocuted."

"Here we go," Jones muttered.

"Waiter, I'll start ordering," James said. "I would like the sesame chicken, the moo shoo pork and the shrimp with black bean sauce."

"Wait a minute," came the voice of Rajit Patel. "We need to get organized here."

"Great. He thinks we need an opinion poll and someone with a PhD to conduct it," Clarence muttered. "I'll have your triple delight."

"Oh, I didn't see that," James said.

"You're not getting it," Edie informed him.

"What are you getting?"

"I'm sharing with you."

"Harry, all good things come to an end."

"What, Dad?"

"You watch, Harry. I'm just going to get one mouthful."

"What you're just going to get is a very large bill," Edie snapped. "Now don't order anything else."

"She's cheap, too," James said to Harry.

Edie had opened her mouth to reply but shut it promptly upon catching sight of Bradley, a vision of royal colors, blue, red and purple, in his magnificent, feathered cap and gown.

"Oh dear," Monica said.

"He thinks this is the Renaissance Fair?" Edie asked. "It's a graduation lunch."

"The master of ceremonies has arrived," Bradley intoned and grandly swept his feathered chapeau off his head.

"The master of the loony bin, he means," Edie said. "Someone tell me I'm not seeing this."

But no one did, because everyone was busy telling one of the three waiters what they wanted to eat. Miqueas Ignacio, aged eight, complained because there was no grilled cheese, his brother Rafael, aged ten, mimicked him, Bertram held forth in his most pompous manner about the glories of the free enterprise system – "Yeah, black lung disease," Jessie riposted – while Elena regarded him with ill-concealed distaste, Kevin and Monica were lost in a rambling discourse on the various sections of the menu on her side and the state of affairs at work on his,

Sandy Lenthican told Billy Sullivan that his older brother and Anna were basically kaput – "keep your mouth shut," thus Animal – and no one except Edie, who was transfixed, appeared to notice Bradley, parading around the restaurant, flourishing his feathered cap, waving his ample gown, lecturing loudly on something to do with graduation and generally making an imbecile of himself. "I don't believe this," she said.

"It's a very complicated menu," James averred.

"It's a very complicated lunatic."

James looked up, saw Bradley. "Oh, the nutcase. Ignore him."

"Who is that person?" Stella demanded.

"The one in the medieval getup?" Jacob asked, peering over the tops of his glasses and the top of his menu. "I seem to have seen him before."

"Me too," James agreed. "But he was different."

"He was dressed as a chicken," Edie said.

"How unusual," Jacob replied. "Who let him in?"

Stella leaned over to her husband. "I think he's a friend of Sherwin's, dear."

Jacob started. "Now he's hanging out with mental patients?"

"He came to the house once, swam in the pool. But he looked normal then."

"He doesn't look normal now."

"Looks psychotic," Clarence put in, slurping his tea.

"Hey Bradley," Harry called out. "Sit down. You're alarming the geezers."

"Geezers?" James asked.

"I will speak with you later, young man," Edie said and would have gone on, but the food arrived, and she was distracted, much to her disgust, by her husband, scooping huge portions off each of his three platters onto his plate. "Do you think you've got enough?" She rather acidly asked.

"Never enough," James replied, slurping on his shrimp with black bean sauce.

"It isn't a competition, you know."

"That's what you think. All these people here will go home to lovely dinners, steaks, pasta in Alfredo sauce, grilled salmon with rosemary, salads with walnuts and gorgonzola, trout almondine –"

"Have you been reading the menu at Chez Michel again? You know we can't afford that food. Besides we had a moratorium on recitations of menus of local restaurants."

"How about from some that are further afield?"

"Those too."

"My point is, all these people have dinner to look forward to. I don't. All I've got are burnt vegetables, overcooked fish, some limp bean sprouts,"

"Oh, stop thinking about your stomach."

"I'm starving. How can I think about anything else?" And with that, James ceased talking and began the very serious business of eating.

After the meal, around the time it dawned on the young children that in addition to no burgers or spaghetti, this establishment also lacked any satisfactory desserts and they became vociferous about his, about the time that Angelo leaned back and exclaimed happily, "what a medley of aromas here!" Paul quickly stood up and announced that the eight high school graduates were decamping to Animal's abode to play video games and that it had been a wonderful meal, thank you, and all parents would be seen again later that evening. Edie was happy to note that "that nitwit," as she had taken to referring to Bradley, departed with them.

Six

They sat in the Toyota in silence for several moments, Harry and Kevin in front, Jones in back. The open windows let in a cool October breeze, and an occasional red or yellow leaf drifted in. Blue skies, cool air, flaming orange, purple, multi-colored trees, all signified yet another autumn afternoon like many before it and many to come.

"But today is different," Jones broke the angry silence, "because you two bozos actually are going to sign your life away."

"If you're so against this," Harry said, "why are you coming?"

"To talk you out of it, so you don't get killed in what is clearly going to be a holocaust in the Middle East."

"Stop exaggerating."

"Okay, not a holocaust. A disaster. Because we're gonna attack some country over there, you know that. And after we bomb, we'll send in ground troops, and guess who will be the lucky suckers to go?"

"Hey, after September 11 you thought about enlisting yourself."

"Until September 12."

"What happened in one day, Jones?"

"Everett happened. My parents happened. They all talked some sense back into me. But you two won't listen to your families. They're against it, why? Because they love you and don't want to see you get killed for something that clearly should be handled as a police operation, not a military one. You don't know what this administration will do, but one thing's for sure, once you're in the army, you won't have any say about whether you like it or not. You'll just have to go. Since when did you two become so bloodthirsty you've got to go shoot up a bunch of Muslims?"

"If they belong to Al Qaeda..."

"Forget Al Qaeda. If this government wanted to stop them, they would have done it after they blew up our embassies in Africa or after the USS Cole. You're not going to be hunting Al Qaeda. You're going to be 'pacifying' some God-forsaken country where the people hate your guts and rightly, because they'll see you as invaders."

"Sorry Jones, you still haven't convinced me," Harry said and started the engine. "You don't have to come if you don't want to."

"I'll come. You may change your mind."

"You gave us the same speech two days ago. Nothing's happened since then."

Edie appeared on the front porch. "Harry!" She hollered. Harry rolled down his window and looked up at the usually bustling form of his mother, now still, slimmer than he recalled – had she been losing weight? – her salt and pepper hair pulled back in a short ponytail.

"What, Ma?" He called back.

"Don't go."

"We've been through this."

"Let's go through it again."

Harry shook his head.

"Ask Donald what he thinks. Discuss it with him."

"I know what he thinks. So do you. I'm sorry." With that Harry rolled up the window part way, shifted into drive and pulled the car out of the parking space into the street. As he drove away, he glanced into his rearview mirror and saw his mother still standing there, up on the front porch, her shoulders slumped, a tissue to her face.

They drove in silence for a few moments, until Jones said: "It's not too late to turn back."

"Who's turning back?" Harry asked.

"I can see you throwing your life away and not caring, after all, your parents will still have Billy, Johnny and Benjie, but you, Kevin? You know darn well you're all your mother's got. What happens to her, if something happens to you?"

"I'm not explaining myself to anybody," Kevin replied. "And I'm not making excuses. I'm doing what needs to be done."

"You and John Wayne," Jones sighed in disgust. "You know it's bad enough Animal enlisted, and Luis had to report back to his base, but now Sherwin, Chandra and Paul are signing up too. It's mass insanity. You guys got each other so worked up, you won't know what you're doing 'til you wake up in the wilds of Afghanistan, getting shot at by Taliban fanatics."

"Those people are responsible for September 11th, too," Harry said.

"So send the FBI after them," Jones cried. "They're criminals. Police catch criminals. Are you a cop? A world policeman? You're a manager at Best Buy, who moonlights at Mr. Lirano's computer repair stores, picking up a few credits at community college. Since when do you put on a helmet, grab a machine gun and go chasing Islamist fanatics through the desert? What am I missing here?"

"The whole picture," Kevin said quietly.

"No, that's what you're going to be missing," Jones snapped, "when you're lying in your blood, giving up the ghost in some dusty hamlet in the middle of nowhere. You'll be missing college, marriage, kids, buying a home, middle age, retirement. You're the one who'll be missing the whole picture."

They rode in more silence, under a pall of disagreement and, undeniably, a nasty foreboding prompted by the many grim scenarios Jones had portrayed. For his part, Jones was seething at what he saw as the idiocy of his friends, every last one of whom would soon be in the military. He himself still had his go-nowhere, heavy-lifting job, but he was also enrolled in Anne Arundel Community College and intended to transfer into the state university system the next year or the year after. The worst part of the situation was that he understood the initial impulse behind this urge to enlist, because he too had felt it on September 11. The atrocity of three thousand people incinerated in two towers had made him want to do something, anything, but that was precisely the problem, as Everett had pointed out. If he was going to do anything, why not picket the government offices of the intelligence agencies that had failed to guard against this disaster? Why not get up a petition, or work for a congressman or lead a demonstration? Why on earth would he dream of enlisting – some revenge fantasy? Everett had gone on and on, so had Jessie and Clarence, even Janie, and Jones, as he saw it, had come back to his senses. But when he tried these same arguments on his friends, they fell on deaf ears. Chandra just guffawed. Sherwin and Kevin turned away in silence. Luis very nearly punched him. Animal, Harry and Paul listened, argued back, lost these debates in Jones' view, but stubbornly refused to budge. "What am I, the last sane man on earth here?" He had asked.

"The last coward," Luis had replied, setting off another shouting match.

To Harry, driving along the back roads of his hometown, it seemed that he was embarking on a distinctly new phase of his life, one that he approached as an adventure. He understood that to Kevin it was more of a chore, something that had to be done, an obligation that they had to shoulder and quickly. Of course Harry felt some of that, but he had a sudden bright notion of what it might be like to be a soldier, to visit a Middle Eastern country, to find the enemy who had committed this terrible crime and drag him back to justice. He did not mention these meditations to Jones, Jones would have torn them to shreds, and then where would he be? Back at Best Buy and community college, profoundly traumatized by the events of September 11 and unable to take action. He reached his hand in his pocket and touched the card of the army recruiter he had met the previous summer. At that time, down in the sultry depths of July, he had had no plan to join. So why, he pondered, had he kept the card? Had it been there all along, the seed of his fantasy, waiting to come to life? And what if those planes flying into those buildings had never happened? Then one day, six months hence, he would have found the card in a pocket, wondered what it was doing there and probably dropped it in the trash, and this new cosmos of possibilities, of becoming someone other than the one he seemed destined to be, would vanish into the back of a garbage truck. He knew his mother's response: "good riddance." And Jones would say the same, so would his whole family, Elena Ignacio, Monica Dawn and many others. But now he had no difficulty braving their disapproval. It was unfortunate but in no way daunting. He pulled the card out and glanced at it.

"Remember Gary?" He asked Kevin, who nodded. "That day in July, by the school? I kept his card and called him yesterday. I said I'd finally decided to join up and might bring a friend."

"Gary the geek. I remember him," Jones said.

"I asked him if he knew Bradley," Harry went on. "He just laughed and said it's a pretty big army."

"Filled with the likes of Bradley and Gary, who thinks the internet is really 'cool,' if I'm quoting him correctly. Wow, that's an organization of people I'd just hate to miss joining."

"As my mother would say, Jones: Don't be sour," Harry admonished and parked the car. Inside a small office they found Gary, waiting for them.

"Oh, you brought two friends," Gary beamed.

"I'm not joining," Jones said. "I'm here as a witness to an act of reckless insanity."

"Don't mind him," Harry said. "He's a pacifist."

"Save your pitch for these two. I'm just sitting here in the vain hope that they change their minds."

They did not. The trio exited the recruiter's office, got back in the car and drove to the sub shop. Jones ordered two, twelve-inch meatball subs. "When I get upset, I eat," he explained.

"But you're skin and bones," Kevin observed.

"So now you see what a rare and terrible thing you two have done to me."

"Hey, we're the ones going," Harry exclaimed.

"You're imbeciles, all right? You're not responsible for your actions. I, however, am in full possession of my faculties, know exactly what you're getting into, and I failed to stop you, failed utterly. You didn't even slow down the car on the way over."

Soon Harry was off to basic training. He expected to get sent to Afghanistan, but that did not happen. Time passed and before he knew it, it was spring 2003, and the United States was preparing to invade Iraq.

"Lucky you," Jones said one weekend, when Harry was home on leave. "You get to go half way across the world to invade and subjugate a country that had *absolutely nothing* to do with nine eleven."

"They expect it'll go pretty quickly," Harry replied rather lamely.

"What they don't know could fill the Sahara Desert."

Edie, hovering on the edge of this conversation and wringing her hands, finally spoke up: "Then it's definite? You're going to Iraq?"

Harry nodded.

"Where you should be going is a march against the war," Jones said. "This invasion is in violation of the Nuremberg Laws. It could very well be a war crime."

"They say Saddam had some contact with Al Qaeda," Harry ventured.

"What contact?" Jones answered. "Nope. These leaders of ours just want to show they're doing something, so they settle an old score and go off and attack Iraq. That's my charitable interpretation of events."

After Jones left, Edie came over and hugged her son. "I wish you weren't going," she said.

"It's not exactly what I signed on for," Harry said. "I kind of thought it would be Afghanistan, and I'd get to go after Al Qaeda and the Taliban. That would've been fine by me. But this – I just don't know. I mean Saddam's a monster, but there are lots of monsters in the world. We don't go overthrowing every tin-pot dictator we see. Jones is right about that."

Edie turned away, sniffled and wiped her nose on a Kleenex. "You could be a conscientious objector," she said hopefully.

"I'm against this invasion, Mom. But I'm not *that* against it. I still think the army was the right choice."

On this sojourn home, even James was somber, so somber he forgot about his gastronomical laments and was caught, several times by Harry, gazing at his oldest son in a rather melancholy reverie. "You know I did *not* volunteer for Vietnam," he said at one point. "I got a deferment."

"I know, Dad."

"I'm not ashamed of it, either. It was a rotten war. We had no business being there."

"Your point?"

James shrugged. "History repeats itself. That's all. But this time it's worse, because my son did *not* get a deferment, or keep himself out of harm's way. He went and signed up."

"It's very hard to get any support around here."

"The truth is, for all my misgivings and thoughts that going into Iraq is a mistake, I'm proud of your decision, Harry."

"You are?"

"Yes. I just wish you hadn't made it."

Harry's days at home were idle and lonely. All his friends except Jones were now in the military. Luis had been in the Persian Gulf for quite some time, and Bradley had fought and been wounded in Afghanistan. Jones was difficult to be with. He had become positively vitriolic in his rage against the military, the president and vice president, the Congress, everyone responsible for the coming invasion. But, even worse, he was very busy, between his job and community college, and could only get together at the sub shop occasionally. During the day, with Johnny, Benjie and Billy at school and his parents at work, Harry slept late and rose to a quiet, dream-filled house. He would lie in his bed, the late morning sun dappling the wall opposite, unsure of where he was, whether or not this room was an extension of the surreal landscapes of his dreams, most of which were about travel by train through strangely blasted and ruined countrysides, except for the one where the train went underground, away from the surface of the world, deeper and deeper into a realm of shadows he had never known existed, about which he queried the other passengers. But they did not answer, just sat in the semi-darkness of the downward moving train and remained silent. Harry did not know what to make of these vivid dreams about travel, except for one thing: he was sure that they were about wanderings through the land of the dead. That was all. Why he journeyed there, who the silent others were, what catastrophe had occurred in the destroyed panorama outside the train windows – he could not say. But he understood right off, in the very first of these many dreams, that he was not traversing the land of the living.

He would return from one of these mental excursions, and the mood of it, the atmosphere, the hold it had on him, would fill the room. Sometimes he would call out one of his brothers' names, but the house was empty and there came no reply. He lay still in bed, repeated the details of his dream in his mind and wondered about its similarity to the other dreams; always travel, always a train, always a pulverized landscape, everything in shadow, the silence of other passengers and the sense above all of the end of things, of spring and sunshine and days at the swim club, of Animal and Anna and Jennifer, of the tiger lilies his mother had planted by the front porch, of fireflies at dusk, of his entire, peaceful, suburban paradise. Then he would reach over, touch the pale blue wall, press his hand against it to feel it solidity, its thereness, its assurance that he was not in the land of shadow, but still, now at this moment at least, in a world of light.

He would lie thus, his hand pressed to the wall, for twenty minutes or a half an hour, filled with memories of the land he had traveled through, of night and death, separations and endings, the reality of all this, the doomed struggle to deny it, but his hand would remain in contact with the wall, its smoothness, coolness, its reality, its link to the world of the living holding him, his connection, his promise, his rope to life from which he dangled, by one hand, over an abyss of shadows.

He was almost relieved to return to duty, to abandon the loneliness, idleness, the emptiness of the house during the day, the sense of being out of place, of no longer fitting in anywhere, and above all, to have those disturbing but oddly placid dreams come to a stop. But they did not stop. They continued throughout all the preparations for departure to Iraq and even once he arrived. He considered telling his buddy from Prince Georges' County, Delante Guest, about these dreams, but he was antsy with that, feared exposing himself to ridicule. Not that Delante was contemptuous or insensitive, far from it. He, like Harry, had been working his way through community college. Like Harry, the events of September 11th had galvanized him, and he had left the security of his middle-class, African American suburb to join the army. Like Harry, he was dismayed by the prospect of invading Iraq and wondered what on earth Iraq had to do with Al Qaeda. They came from the same part of the country, they shared the same view of the world. But Harry hesitated to mention his dreams, fearing that that would somehow solidify them, endow them with a reality he could no longer dispel merely by reaching out his hand and touching the wall.

When he awoke from a catnap on the road to Kut, covered with dirt, longing so much for the shower in his house back in Maryland that he thought he could feel the smooth, clean, blue tile, the first thing Harry saw was Delante, clutching his gun, looking up at the edge of the ditch.

"I dreamt I was in the land of the dead," Harry blurted out.

"You are," Delante said, matter-of-factly.

"No, I mean the real one. A world of shadows, of people who don't talk because it's the end. I'm traveling there on a train. I dream it over and over."

"It doesn't sound like a good omen," Delante said. "Did you see those piles of bodies by the road on the way in?"

Harry nodded.

"Talk about the land of the dead," Delante paused to wipe the sand off his cheeks. "Welcome to Iraq."

"They say we won't be here long."

"They say all sorts of things."

They sat in the dirt and waited for their orders, Delante sucking on a candy, Harry sipping from a water bottle. "You know I didn't always live in beautiful Largo," Delante said after a while.

"You told me," Harry replied. "Your first 14 years alone with your mother just over the D.C. line in hideous Capital Heights. I know that area. I got lost there once. Wrong turn off the Beltway, then I was driving and driving down Central Avenue, and the neighborhood was getting sketchier and sketchier."

"Sketchy," Delante chuckled. "You could say that." He paused to peek over the top of the ditch. "We had this idiot principal at my elementary school there," he went on. "I mean the place had been built in 1932. It had rats. The puke green paint was peeling. Asbestos everywhere. Some parts always under repair. It had leaks all over the place that would splash down on you whenever it rained. And it seemed always to be raining. There were used condoms and syringes on the playground. And the smell of that cafeteria was enough to put you off food for a week. The whole place stank of sewage, but in the cafeteria it was the worst. Anyway," Delante paused to light a cigarette, "this principal liked to visit our classes, and she would come out with nonsense like, 'boys and girls, we have a wonderful surprise for you today. You're going to love it, and you're going to have some fun. You're going to run home and tell your

Mom and Dad all about it.' She would go on with this drivel for five, ten, fifteen minutes before she came to the punchline. The big surprise, the marvelous gift, was a state-mandated test – the MSPAP."

"Oh brother, I hated that MSPAP," Harry commiserated.

"Everyone did, but only a few educators were dumb enough to try to pass if off as a treat. My point being, if the principal said something, you knew the opposite was true. If she said 'up,' you knew it was 'down.' If she said 'out,' you knew it was 'in.' Just like our fearless leaders. They say we'll be greeted with flowers. Well, I don't see no flowers. I see bodies and I hear explosions. And just like our officers. They say we'll be outta here soon. Well Harry, I'll believe that when I see it."

Clouds parted and the sun scorched down on them. "You think Sarge'll let us have some of those sodas he's got in his truck? I'd like a Pepsi. What do you think?" Harry asked, wiping his mouth and swallowing thirstily.

Delante shook his head. "I tried while you were napping. Sanchez was already there asking, and Sarge said what do we think he is, a soda machine?"

"What are we supposed to be looking for?"

"The enemy, I think."

"But there hasn't been anything besides little kids in rags, old people and dead bodies for miles."

Delante shrugged and crouched lower, saying that he was going to try to sleep, so Harry had to keep watch, which was fine with Harry, who had no very great desire to return to the slumberous gloom, the pall of the underworld that stretched over his dreams. He had begun to regard them as visitations, and a drifting into his mind of the atmosphere of another realm, one that he had begun to believe actually existed and with which he would feel safer avoiding contact. Unfortunately, he was routinely sleep-deprived in the army and did not get the luxury of lying in bed for a half an hour to pull himself out of somnolent Hades. No, he had to leap up and get dressed at once, sometimes not even knowing where he was, thinking he was still on the train, passing through barren terrain of charred and twisted black trees, thinking the other members of his platoon were emissaries from that kingdom of silence and shadows. He would walk out, and not 'til much later, seated in the back of the Humvee with the machine gun cradled in his arms, surveying the occasional heap of corpses as they sped by, would he realize that he had awakened from one country of death to another.

Time passed, and Harry found himself living at a forward operating base near Baghdad and going on foot patrols in that brown, dusty megacity. He did not like it much and neither did Delante. They liked it less when, many months later, Sanchez and two others from their platoon hit an improvised explosive device. Harry tried to help, indeed called the Medevac, but the burns, blood and screams stayed with him a long time.

Then one excruciatingly hot dirty afternoon in 2004, he and Delante were on patrol on the outskirts of the city. They had finished at last and stood near the Humvee, Harry and four guys to one side, Delante a little ways away. Suddenly they heard a telltale sound, something sizzling through the air, and a grenade landed at Delante's feet.

In the split second it took Harry to yell "Run!" Delante screamed "No, you run," and threw himself on the grenade. Harry was screaming "No!" when it went off. The four other members of their crew escaped with minor burns and bruises. But for Harry and Delante, it was different. They did not escape at all. On that little street of shacks and raw sewage, they died. Harry had let go of the wall, the connection to the world of life and friends and hope and dreams, and he swung out and then down, into that abyss of shadows that had so long haunted him.

When Harry had left for basic training, Edie had wept. None of her children had ever moved away from home before, and it was quite difficult for her.

"Please stop sniffling," James said over breakfast. "You're upsetting the children."

"No she's not," Billy replied. "She's upsetting you."

"Quiet, smarty pants."

Edie's eyes continued to water, and she blew her nose.

"How come you never cried like this when I went on those Parks Department trips to Atlantic City?"

"You go into basic training, and I'll cry."

"Do you think the food's any better?"

Often, in the shower, she just broke down. She did not get out or turn off the water until the sobs that wracked her body had ended. Then she sat on the toilet, a towel wrapped around her and dried her face with a cloth. "Harry," she said aloud, "why did you have to do this?"

"Because he's a grown man," James hollered through the door once. "Because it was time for him to get away from home. Because he wanted to do what was right, even if he did it the wrong way."

"What are you talking about?"

"The military. In my view that's the wrong way to do what's right. But lots of people who want to help their country think it's the only way."

"Harry was confused," Edie shouted through the door.

"Nope. He knew exactly what he was getting into."

Edie opened the door. "Go away."

"You don't want to hear the truth."

"Your version of it, not particularly."

"I ran into Clarence Jones at the supermarket on Saturday. You want his version?"

"I can just imagine."

"He thinks our kids are just cannon fodder for a military industrial complex run by fascistic reactionaries."

"James!"

"I kid you not. Besides, he may have a point."

"So now Harry's cannon fodder?"

"Look Edie, he made a mistake. He doesn't think so, but you know so and I know so. Maybe something good will come of it. Maybe he'll realize he erred. Maybe he'll learn. Maybe he'll...pick up a skill, something mechanical."

"You know Harry," Edie sniffled again. "He's all thumbs."

At work Edie checked her email every half hour, and, happily for her, occasionally there were missives from Harry, complaining about some aspect of basic training, describing the people he had met, his dislike of some of the officers, asking for news of Jones, who didn't stay in touch enough. Jones, Edie reported back, spent much time going to marches and working for antiwar groups. He had even sat-in at a congressman's office.

"No way," Harry emailed back. "I've got to tell Animal and Paul and everybody about this."

Edie sent him long, detailed emails every day. She depicted Billy's, Johnny's and Benjie's doings in school. Johnny, in middle school, had the same math teacher, a Mr. Gargle, that Harry had had, with the same disastrous results. He understood nothing and was barely passing.

"That's because Mr. Gargle doesn't talk. He lives up to his name. He gargles out formulae and facts and equations, and it's all jumbled. You have no idea what goes where. My advice," Harry wrote, "is get Johnny a tutor before he flunks."

"Benjie is the one I'm really worried about, because you were so close to him," Edie wrote. "He really regards you as *his* older brother, his alone. Now that you've joined the army, he's terrified that bad guys are going to shoot you. After all, he's only in second grade, and his idea of what's going on all comes from cartoon shows. He was terrified after nine eleven. Remember how he would come into bed with James and me every night, afraid that terrorists were out to get him? He still does that, but now he says he's afraid they're out to get you. Once he falls asleep, if I try to carry him back to his bed, he wakes right up. So naturally we're all exhausted around here. James is a real grump, keeps threatening to go to the Holiday Inn to get a decent night's sleep. If you could write Benjie, send him an actual letter, with a picture maybe, it would help."

So Harry mailed Benjie a "Far Side" card he had somehow brought along with him and tucked a little photo of himself inside. Benjie was ecstatic and carried the card around in his backpack for a week and finally, after he nearly lost it, allowed Edie to tape the card and the photo to the wall in his room over the bed. Thereafter, to everyone's surprise, Benjie stayed in his bed at night, though often he was clearly awake, because he could be heard talking at great length. Once, when Edie looked in, she saw him facing the wall, with his little hand outstretched, pressed against it next to the photograph.

"So that's who you're talking to," she said, "the picture."

"I'm talking to Harry," Benjie replied. "He thinks he's going to die. He needs the X-men to help him."

Edie became alarmed for the small boy. "No, no, Benjie, he doesn't think that, because that's not going to happen."

Benjie turned and regarded her with serious eyes, but did not remove his hand from the wall.

"You understand?" Edie asked. "Harry's okay."

"No," Benjie said. "He's not."

Not too long after that, news of the impending invasion of Iraq gripped the country. Stories of chemical weapons, biological weapons, mushroom clouds filled the newspapers and the evening news. Troops moved into the Persian Gulf. Demonstrations against the scheduled war sprang up spontaneously all over the world. Jones dropped by one Saturday to enlist Edie's help in convincing Harry to speak at a march. The organizers wanted the words of military personnel, and Jones knew that Harry was skeptical of the hysteria and opposed a hasty assault.

"You know Harry can't do that," Edie said. "He'd get into all kinds of trouble."

"He's pretty against it, Mrs. Sullivan."

"He thought he'd be going to Afghanistan to hunt Al Qaeda. He hasn't the faintest idea why he'll be shipped to Iraq or why Saddam has to be toppled."

"No one does, except the geniuses in charge, to whom, presumably, God has delivered a personal communiqué: 'thou shalt smite Iraq.' If we could get soldiers like Harry to speak out, it might make a difference."

"If I persuade him, he might wind up in a military prison."

"Better that than Baghdad."

Edie wrung her hands. "Oh, I wish he had never joined."

"So does he."

"He came out and said that?"

Jones nodded. "Animal too and a few of the others, though not, of course, Luis. Most of them can't make sense of this – why Iraq? It's like somebody in power played pin the tail on the donkey and pinned it on Iraq. It's that random."

"I'll mention it," Edie said at length, "but I think it's unlikely. Harry's not the type to draw attention to himself, and he's not big on breaking the rules."

"There's a chance we could stop this."

"You think?" Edie was doubtful. "This administration doesn't seem filled with the sort of people who heed demonstrators."

After Jones' departure, Edie entered Benjie's and Billy's room and sat on Benjie's bed. She gazed at a picture that Harry had drawn for Benjie. Tears welled up in her eyes, and she found herself murmuring, "my child, my son," as she pressed her hand to the wall beside the picture and imagined that Harry was there and they touched, hand to hand.

"He'll be all right," James said, poking his head in the door, a soda in one hand, a ham sandwich in the other. "Harry can take care of himself."

"Harry's horrible at taking care of himself."

"I mean in a bad situation. He'll take care then."

"Have you ever seen Harry in a bad situation? Other people have the fright/flight reaction. He has the fright/freeze reaction. So the idea of him dealing with disaster is not very reassuring. If you want to calm me, you'll have to do better than that."

"Come out back after I finish this sandwich and watch me play badminton with the boys. They're creaming me."

Sensitive to anything related to Harry, Benjie became anxious. "Iraq," he asked at lunch. "Is that where the bad guys are?"

"What bad guys, dumbo?" Billy demanded.

"Billy!" Edie snapped. "Shut up."

"Do you mean the terrorists?" Johnny asked.

Benjie nodded.

"No, there are no terrorists in Iraq," Johnny said.

"How do you know that?" James demanded. "I read the newspapers, and they imply that there are. Television reporters just come out and announce it."

"And I read the internet, and it says there aren't."

"Why's he going if there are no bad guys?" Benjie asked.

"There are other bad guys," Johnny explained. "Though what they've got to do with us is a mystery."

"Will they shoot Harry?" Benjie asked, and a miserable silence descended upon the table.

"No, baby. Nobody's going to shoot Harry," Edie consoled him.

That night Benjie padded into their room in his Power Ranger pajamas, hand-me-downs from Johnny, and stood next to the bed, where James, on the other side, snored gently, and Edie lay with her eyes wide open. The little boy took her hand, and as they gazed at each other, tears filled her eyes. Benjie climbed in bed beside her and said: "Good, now I can dream about Harry and the happy people."

"You do that Benjie. Go to sleep," and she rubbed his back, the small shoulder blades poking up, the thin fabric worn from many washings, barely concealing the warmth of the skin below. Long after she heard the steady, quiet breathing that signified he had fallen asleep, Edie lay in the darkness, thinking about her oldest son.

His letters and emails began talking of a new person, his buddy Delante Guest, from Largo, Maryland. He depicted Delante's childhood in rough tough Capital Heights, the pit bulls, the bombed-out buildings, the high rate of gun ownership, the frequent sound of gunshots, the gangs, and then, he portrayed the middle-class splendor of Largo through Delante's eyes. He and Delante agreed that this invasion of Iraq was "for the birds," and both had given up any daydreams of a military career. From the moment he set foot in Iraq, Harry's missives related doings that involved Delante. They were very close, they were buddies, they were a team.

Harry's time in Iraq filled his mother with dread. She began noting
bumper stickers, on her drive to work, especially the one that said,
"One Day at a Time," and she would think, "just today. Just let him get
through today." His return kept getting delayed, so she kept hoping,
and as the American body count rose, she found herself scanning the
newspaper section entitled "Faces of the Fallen," with her fingers crossed,
at new altitudes of anxiety lest Harry or someone familiar turned up.

This boxing match between hope and fear, in which each would
punch at her head only to be followed by the other, had so befuddled
her, that the day the doorbell rang and a soldier stood on the threshold,
she did not put it together, not even as he started saying that the
president of the United States and the U. S. Army regretted to inform
her...Then came a lightning bolt of comprehension. There would be no
more hope and no more fear, only despair, only the memory of Harry
and the certainty that she would never set eyes on him again, even in a
casket. He had been blown to bits. Delante had tried to save his life, but
Harry either froze or wouldn't let him, wouldn't have his life saved on
those terms, she would never know which. She did not want to know.
She wanted it all to be a nightmare, and she wanted it to be over. But
she did not wake from it, and it did not end. As she sat on the couch,
too stunned to weep, she seemed to see him as a little boy, four years
old, lying right there, kicking his feet, as he refused to let her put on his
sneakers.

Days passed and nights of weeping. She took time off work, stayed
home, sat on the couch and remembered her son. It seemed vital to
catalogue every image of him that remained in her mind: his face in
the delivery room, in the hospital after he had his appendix out, his joy
when his third-grade soccer team finished first for the season. Sometimes
she would take out the photo albums and study the pictures of the little
boy she would never see in person again. She did this often. James called
it rubbing salt in the wounds, but she did not care. And it was thus that,
after a week, she was sitting, gazing at photographs, the doorbell rang
again. She opened it and there stood a tall, elegantly attired, middle-aged,
African American woman, who was wiping her face with a Kleenex and
who introduced herself as Charmaine Lear. "You know, Delante's Mom.
Delante from Largo, who –"

"I know," Edie replied and clasped her visitor's hands. They stood
thus for some time, in the strong, slanting, late morning sun that
glistened on the tears streaming down their faces.

When Kevin heard from his mother about Harry's death, he wrote to Edie. "This is terrible news, and I don't know how my condolences could help, but here they are. Harry and I were in touch quite a lot during this Iraq invasion, which we both had our doubts about. As you know, Harry had hoped to get sent to Afghanistan. Sometimes I think he personally wanted to capture the leaders of Al Qaeda, with his own bare hands. But there's no Al Qaeda here in Iraq, just a lot of sullen locals who consider us occupiers, and, frankly, I don't know what we're doing here. True, Saddam is a son of a bitch, but he had nothing to do with September 11, and isn't that what we're doing is supposed to be all about? Three thousand of our people are incinerated in towers, and these clowns leading our country send us to Iraq? Why not Qatar? Or Saudi Arabia? It's that nonsensical. Supposedly there were weapons of mass destruction here, but we haven't found any. So that was wrong. Or it was a lie. What really are we doing? Stealing Saddam's oil? Before he died Harry became convinced that was what it was all about, that we were some kind of elite bodyguard, janissaries for our oil companies. I told him that was too smart and devious for us. We're here because the people at the top don't know what they're doing. It's that simple. They're a bunch of dim bulbs, and a lot of twenty year olds are paying the price. We're in the wrong country, fighting the wrong war, for the wrong reasons. Harry thought we should have invaded Afghanistan, but I agree with Jones that even that should have been a police operation, handled by the FBI counter-terrorism unit. Everything has been bungled, that's what Harry thought. But he went into it with his eyes open. He wanted to help. He got cheated out of that, and he knew it. And now he got cheated out of his life as well. I'm sorry, Mrs. Sullivan, it makes me so angry when I think about it, I just can't see straight."

Kevin had been in and around Baghdad from the beginning. He called the locals sullen, but he was just as ill-humored. Life had become one unpleasant chore after another, all performed in blistering heat. He had viewed enlisting as an obligation, but now he believed his good intentions had been abused. He was cross and went through his days in a low, simmering rage. Unlike many other members of his platoon, he did not develop a prejudice against Iraqis, but he furiously resented being shot at. He was known by his friends as someone who never cursed except in a firefight, and then he hollered obscenities nonstop. On patrols, he gave children his candy and was cordial with adults, but whenever another soldier addressed him, all he had to say was, "I can't wait to get out of this country." He did not talk about his friends or his mother, or his beloved home in Crofton, until Harry's death. The morning he heard the news, he went back to his cot and lay down.

"Hey," said his closest friend in the platoon, Allan Singleton, "we're supposed to be moving, Kev."

"One of my best friends just got killed in Baghdad, in a southern suburb. He got blown up by a grenade."

"A friend from Maryland?"

"Knew him all my life, since kindergarten."

"That sucks."

"You're not kidding."

"But then everything in this God-forsaken country sucks."

"We enlisted together. We were gonna make the terrorists pay for nine eleven. What a joke! What idiocy! Now he's dead, and they don't even have a body to put in a casket, so his mother can look at him one last time."

"Tell Sergeant Baum you need some time to yourself today. He's been pretty understanding lately. And you've never asked for anything – anything that I can recall."

Baum appeared in the doorway. "Dawn, Singleton, what's the delay? Move it."

"Uh, Sarge, Kev just found out his best friend from way back got blown up by a grenade in Baghdad."

Baum looked at Kevin with concern. Kevin sat on the edge of the cot, his head in his hands, muttering, "Goddammit, we were such idiots."

"He's cursing, Sergeant Baum."

"I hear him."

"He only does that when we're getting shot at."

"I know." Baum came over to Kevin. "Are you ready for this patrol?"

Kevin nodded. "I got nothing else to do around here."

"You could stay back for a while. Use the laptop, email your friend's family."

"I'm not coherent enough yet for that."

"You let me know when you are. I'll give you some time for it. How long did you know him?"

"Harry? I met him in kindergarten. There were eight of us, a whole group of buddies. We all enlisted except one."

"He had the brains," Singleton yukked.

"Yeah," Kevin growled, angry again. "I guess he did."

Baum clapped him on the back. "C'mon, it'll do you good to do something else. The patrol will take your mind off it."

That day Kevin did not give out candy. After he wrote to Edie, he became quieter, angrier, even withdrawn. When it was announced that a reporter from the *Washington Times* would be embedded in their unit and that this reporter was a gung-ho supporter of the Iraq war, Kevin snorted in derision. "There are idiots everywhere."

"Dawn, I hope you'll keep your opinions to yourself. This is the press we're going to be living with," Baum said. "And we want to make a good impression."

R. L. Jackson, Louis for short, lived up to Kevin's description, and in a matter of days, all someone needed to say was, "watch it, here comes Louis," and eyes would start to roll. After the first week it was no longer, "watch it, here comes Louis," but "watch it, here comes the asshole," or "watch it, here comes the dumbest fuck ever to walk down the streets of Baghdad." Kevin avoided him.

He could not, however, stay away from him entirely. One afternoon, when a car bomb went off in a market, Kevin, Allan, Baum and the rest of their group were the first on the scene. Louis insisted on going with them. Baum was on the radio at once, calling for medics, while Kevin was using his rudimentary CPR skills to bandage an eight-year-old girl's arm, which was bleeding profusely and wouldn't stop. "This is what this war's all about," Louis said.

"Shut up and help," Kevin replied.

"It's about bringing it to the enemy. Fighting the Islamofascists in their lair."

Kevin turned away in disgust.

"It's about little kids getting blown up for no Goddamn reason," Singleton said, handing Kevin more gauze.

There was blood everywhere and several charred bodies. The wounded lay about, screaming in pain, as ambulances tore through traffic and medics hurried to the market. It was over one hundred degrees, and Kevin's uniform was drenched. He took off his Kevlar helmet and laid it next to the little girl, whose eyes suddenly sparkled. She picked it up and put it on.

"American soldier," she said and pointed to herself.

"You don't want to do that," Kevin said in a soft voice, wrapping yet another layer of gauze tightly on her arm. The bleeding seemed to have stopped, and she appeared to be no longer in pain.

She pointed an index finger at him and made a shooting gesture.

"She's seen a lot," Singleton remarked.

"Shoot bad guys," she went on.

Kevin looked into her dark eyes, pained and sparkling at the same time. "Yeah, shoot bad guys," he said.

She handed him back his helmet.

Bullets whistled through the air. Kevin shifted the little girl behind the protection of a parked car, and followed Allan, who had signaled him.

"Those shitheads," Kevin muttered, running up beside Singleton, "first they blow up the market, then they come back to shoot the medics and the wounded."

"Look on the bright side. Maybe they'll get Louis. I think they're down that alley, c'mon."

Kevin saw an Iraqi with a machine gun leap across the little lane, then turn and point his weapon at Allan. Kevin had him at point blank range and shot him. The man crumpled.

"I owe you one," Allan said. The bullets kept coming. They were pinned down in the market for almost an hour, before any reinforcements arrived. By some miracle, none of their team got shot, not even Louis, who found that the firefight exhilarated him, aroused his bloodlust.

"Somebody shut him up," Allan said, after the insurgents had fled.

Kevin was examining the bodies of the two men they had killed. He collected their weapons.

"Baathists?" Louis asked. "Al Qaeda in Iraq?"

Kevin gave him a sour look and said nothing. The medics had finally arrived and so had the ambulances. They loaded the wounded onto stretchers, but Kevin did not see the little eight-year-old girl among them. A sudden horror surged through him, and he sprinted over to where he had left her, behind the car.

She lay as she had died, bullet wounds in her chest. Her little, white, schoolgirl's blouse soaking red, steaming in the heat.

Kevin crouched down and put his head in his hands.

"There was nothing you could have done," Baum said, coming up alongside him. "You had to leave her here. You had to go fight." They stayed like that, in silence for a moment, until Baum spoke again. "What kind of person does that – murders a wounded eight-year-old girl?"

Kevin gently held her hand and said nothing.

Sometime later, after Louis had moved on to greater glories with another platoon, Kevin's squad had another guest. For a few days they were assigned to shuttle around a bigwig from a neoconservative think tank. "Actually, he's more like a big fish from a small pond," Baum explained. "But of course everyone will be on their best behavior."

Lawrence Wrash had written many papers on the need to confront terrorism in its home, the importance of doing so violently, the necessity of bringing about a sea-change in Islamic culture, a liberal, secular, democratic transformation that involved friendly feelings toward the West and, if this could not be brought about, the imperative of war against Islam in any of its radical forms. He was an expert on Turkey and was becoming one on Saudi Arabia. The Wahabbi strain of Islam he considered particularly virulent and had advocated, in a document widely disseminated in the administration, a policy of closing down *all* madrassahs in Pakistan. He had a PhD in political science, two master's degrees and tended to regard everyone around him as in desperate need of enlightenment, which, Kevin told Allan, was putting it kindly. In point of fact, Mr. Wrash had a stratospheric opinion of his own intelligence and a much lower one of everyone else's. He had learned from neoconservatives in government that the "reality-based" intellectual community was to be distrusted. The world was to be remade, as he and his colleagues saw fit, and the magnificent excuse for this mission was September 11. He knew no one who had died or lost a loved one on that day and did not care to. They were merely pawns in a grand game. To Kevin fell the thankless task of chauffeuring this luminary about.

"Aw geez, Sargeant. Why me?" He asked after the first day and three intolerable hours in a jeep with "that fathead," as he referred to Mr. Wrash. "What did I do to deserve this? How did I offend you?"

"You have better diplomatic skills than anyone else in this platoon. Remember the unfortunate events involving Louis."

"I didn't get along with Louis."

"But you did not punch him in the nose."

"I wanted to."

"Nor did you tell him his nickname was 'the asshole.'"

"I almost did."

"Nor did you salute him with phrases like, 'hey you stupid fuck get over here,' or 'watch out shit-for-brains, they're shooting at us.' I heard these things."

"I bawled him out."

"That was after he almost got you killed. It was excusable. What was not excusable was the behavior and language of this squad to a member of the press."

"It was water off a duck's back, Sergeant Baum. If you don't mind my saying so, it had no effect on him, did not even dent that enormous, steel-plated ego."

"I observed that. It was very fortunate that Louis believed his treatment was standard army behavior. Otherwise he might have filed a complaint, or, worse, written a negative story."

"Louis' stories were strictly from Oz."

"Luckily for us," Baum snapped. "Now you'll drive this Wrash or Wrat or whatever his name is and be polite, deferential, courteous. He thinks he is one of the great minds of the century. You are *not* to disabuse him. Get it?"

"Yes sir."

"The Pentagon likes this guy."

"Yes sir."

"No accounting for tastes."

So Kevin drove Wrash around Baghdad, showing him the sights and what army life was like. Wrash was a short, wiry, balding fellow, who wore suits even in the stifling Iraq heat. He always carried a briefcase stuffed with papers, which he would periodically remove and describe to Kevin in great detail. They had all been written by Wrash himself and delivered at various conservative think tanks and symposia in Washington D. C. Wrash loved to quote from his own work and bored Kevin nearly to tears with length recitations from his oeuvre. He also dropped names, mostly those of mucky mucks in the defense establishment, but more than once hinted that the president himself had perused his papers. Kevin merely rolled his eyes, which Wrash, fortunately, did not detect, as he was nearsighted and always busy peering through his thick glasses at his latest magnum opus: "The need to confront Islamofascism at its root by means of regime change in Syria and Iran."

"How would you feel about invading Syria?" He deigned to ask his driver.

Kevin squirmed, "well the, uh, invasion of Iraq doesn't seem to be going all that well or exactly according to plan."

"Nonsense. A few casualties, and the leftwing, radical terrorist sympathizers in the Democratic Party trumpet that the war is lost. You know very well we're winning the war on terror. Mind if I quote you in my lecture today in the Green Zone?"

"I'm just a lowly soldier. Really, I'd rather not be quoted."

"As you wish. I'm willing to give you a moment in the sun –"
Kevin grimaced.

"But you don't have to take it. What's that – up ahead?"

"I don't know, but I don't like it."

Traffic had become very thick, and they were separated from their convoy. Now a crowd formed in the street. Nervously, Kevin turned off the main road in the hopes of coming around through back streets to meet up with the army trucks again. But as he drove along through streets and alleys filled with trash and human excrement, he began to realize they were in trouble.

"The way these people live is inconceivable," Wrash averred.

"They're poor," Kevin said, gritting his teeth and trying to ignore the hatred in the dark, hostile eyes of the passers-by.

"Even poor people can pull themselves up by their bootstraps. Look at them. They don't seem to appreciate what we're doing for them in the least."

A bullet winged by the jeep.

"Nope," Kevin agreed. "They definitely don't appreciate it."

"That was gunfire."

"Correct Dr. Wrash."

"They're trying to kill me."

Another bullet whizzed by. Another one hit the fender.

"And me," Kevin said.

"Well, you're a soldier. You expect to wind up in these situations."

"Thank you, Dr. Wrash," Kevin rather acidly replied. He heard another bullet and felt a sharp sting under his shoulder. Up ahead was a little bridge over a small gully. If he could just make it across, fast enough, they might get out of range. He floored the accelerator, and the jeep shot forward, but just then he felt another sting, under the other shoulder, and he lost control of his arm. The jeep caromed out of control, shot over the side of the bridge and landed upside down on the boulders.

"Just my luck," Kevin thought. "I get to die with this pompous idiot." Kevin and Dr. Wrash, trapped in their seats, were crushed together.

That day her son died, Monica as usual struggled through work on too little sleep. Insomnia had plagued her from the very day he enlisted. She would lie awake at night, worrying about everything that could possibly happen to him and unable to stop. Sometimes she drifted off around three a.m. or four a.m. Sometimes she did not sleep at all. She thought of him in helicopters that got shot down, blown up in an army truck by an improvised explosive device, shot by an insurgent, burned and torn apart by a grenade. The one thing she never thought of was death by car crash.

Never heavy to begin with, she had lost ten pounds, had permanent dark circles under her eyes, and her hair, previously salt and pepper, had gone white. She was disorganized from lack of sleep, and her superiors noticed. In desperation she took Ambien. It worked for a while, then its effect wore off. She explained to her doctor that this was an absolute emergency, that she had to sleep or she would lose the job upon which her life depended. They tried different pills, which always gave her some rest for a while, then became useless. No matter what the doctor did, at three a.m. she would find herself staring at the shadows on the ceiling, at the rectangle of faint light cast by the streetlamp and wrestling with anxiety over how she would live if her son, her only child, were to perish. Eventually, reluctantly, her doctor prescribed barbiturates.

She had taken to visiting the Lenthicans on Friday evenings, to trade news of Kevin and Animal and their other six friends. They gossiped a good bit about Luis, who had gotten married and left a pregnant wife behind before shipping out to the Persian Gulf. How often he had advised everyone against that, citing the ruin of his older sister Nathalie's life by a precipitous marriage. But mostly they talked about their sons, their descriptions of the war, the bloodshed they incessantly witnessed, the deaths of friends, the maimings, the relentless threat of violence. Tom Lenthican did not like to participate in these discussions. As with Monica, the war and his son's role in it had visibly aged him. He seemed worried and absent-minded and would postpone decisions with the remark, "we'll wait 'til Dorian gets home." Isabelle, on the other hand, had put up a good front, kept busy and insisted on cheerfulness. It was this attitude Monica had come to depend on.

"Well," she remarked one evening, "Dorian did always want to see Mesopotamia, He got an A on that unit in history, on the civilization of the Tigris and Euphrates river valley."

"Kevin almost flunked it," Monica chuckled and then, a jolt of anxiety electrifying her, "God, that seems like eons ago. How I wish that textbook was the closest he ever came to Iraq. How I wish he'd never come up with that idea of enlisting."

"Actually it was Harry who started that."

"They were all headed in that direction, from the moment the World Trade Towers collapsed."

"It's too late now. We can't be worrying about it all the time."

"Can't we?"

"You'll make yourself sick, if you haven't already. Have a glass of wine."

"Not with my sleep medication. That's a bad idea."

"Have you spoken with Kevin recently?"

"Two days ago. He did a hilarious imitation of a *Washington Times* reporter, who had been embedded in his unit, a real armchair warrior who finally got a chance to look at things first hand and decided Kevin's platoon wasn't classy enough for him. Kevin thinks he might be home this summer. I'm just trying to keep my fingers crossed."

"Take it one day at a time, like Edie says."

Monica tried to take this advice to heart. She knew that deep down Isabelle was as alarmed as she, that she followed the war news compulsively and looked at the photographs in the newspapers of soldiers killed in action, thinking, "Thank God he's not there. Dear God, don't ever let him be there." But somehow she had an ability to blanket her worries, to cover them up like stains on a wooden floor beneath a rug, dark stains, that kept getting larger and darker, like the blood stains on that little girl's shirt, red flowering out over white, until there was no white left, as Kevin had told her. To see such murder, to experience such carnage – she wondered if he would ever be the same. And then he had had to kill people. True, all the men he had shot had shot at him first, but he said he was getting good at it and that that scared him, that they wanted him on a sniper detail, and what about when he started killing people who had not shot at him first, who just *might* do so? He did not want the sniper detail, did not want to relinquish another corner of his soul to this killing machine in which he found himself a cog. He wanted to come home.

He repeated that in every letter, every email message. "I want to come home." The first time she saw those words on the computer screen, she had a little shock, misreading it, as if he had asked to go to God, ready to die, but no, that was not possible, she realized her misinterpretation; her fears infected everything, were destroying her common sense. "I want to come home," meant to Monica, to Maryland, to life as it used to be. And she had written back: "I want you to come home too, back to Crofton. God speed the day."

But the day was not speeding. Each day seemed to drag out for weeks, each week months, each month years. Time passed so excruciatingly slowly, was suffused with so much emptiness, so many moments in which fear of his death or wounding could torment her, that when she lay down at night and took her pill, it was all she could do to say, "well that day is done, thank God."

When she heard Harry had been killed, she took the afternoon off work and hurried over to the Sullivan's house. The entire family was there. Benji sat alone in a corner, alternately gazing at and touching the wall. "The bad guys got Harry," he said to Monica, and Edie burst into tears. "Come sit over here, Benjie," Edie said after a moment. But the forlorn little boy just shook his head. He looked so lonesome and lost, Monica wanted to weep. "I brought you a casserole," she said.

James glanced up with sudden eagerness, but then the shadow of misery descended on his features again.

"So you don't have to cook," Monica went on. "That's probably the last thing you want to do. And since it's Thursday and I got tomorrow off work, I'll stay over. Johnny, you can show me where the sheets are for the roll-away in the basement. I'll stay the weekend and cook for you, and do the dishes. You know, stuff like that."

"They don't even have his body," Edie sobbed. "They just have parts."

"That's something," Monica said. "But the important thing is you have memories."

"And about fifty hours of videotape," James added helpfully, putting his hand over his wife's.

"How could they do this to him?" Edie demanded. "Send him to Iraq. Why Iraq? What was he doing there? What was the point?"

"You're torturing yourself with these thoughts," Monica snapped. "So stop it."

"Monica's right," James agreed. "Maybe you should try to calm down."

"I don't want to calm down. What good is that? Will it bring Harry back?"

Monica and James looked at each other. "Nothing will," he said after a moment. "You know that."

"You'll see him in the next life," Monica consoled her.

"I don't believe in the next life. I believe in this life, the only one we've got, the only one we'll ever have. Here and now. And Harry was cheated out of about sixty years of it. I don't believe I'll see him again."

"Well I do. So that will have to suffice."

"You do?" James asked.

Monica nodded.

"It will?" Edie asked.

Monica nodded again.

"Maybe you could move in," Edie almost laughed through her tears, "and remind me that that's what you're sure of, every day, that you're sure I'll see him again."

"That's why I'm staying the weekend."

"I was thinking more like thirty years," Edie said.

Monica sighed. "Do you ever consider going to church?"

Edie shook her head. "I don't notice it's done such wonders for you. You haven't slept since Kevin signed up."

"But it might do wonders for you."

"Antidepressants would do wonders for me. Lots of them."

Monica found that residing with the Sullivans and passing herself off as a pillar of strength not only helped them, it helped her. While she was there, she slept without pills. She read Kevin's email to Edie and for the first time allowed herself to hope that he would make it home in one piece. Although Edie did not eat, James and the boys gobbled up everything their visitor cooked. And at night, Benjie came down to the basement to talk. He was always sad.

"I don't want it to be over," he said the first night, and when Monica asked what, he replied: "all this fun, all these good things. Someday it's all going to be over. Like for Harry."

"Not everyone believes that. Some people think that there is life afterward."

"Do you think that?"

"Yes."

"How do you know? Did someone tell you?"

Monica straightened his Power Ranger pajamas and took his hand. "I know from God."

"Who is He?"

"He made the world."

Benjie's eyes widened. "And all the things in it?"

Monica nodded.

Sudden sadness and despair seemed to come over the small child. "Where does He live?" He asked wistfully.

"In heaven, where Harry is, living the life after death. I *know* it's true."

"I wish I knew it was true. I wish I could talk to God. I don't want it to end," and he started to cry. She calmed him and then he said: "Edie says there's nothing to be afraid of. That it'll just be like it was before I was born. But I can't remember before I was born. She says I can't because there was nothing. That after a long, long time, when I die there will be nothing again. I don't want nothing."

"You won't have it. You'll see Harry again. I promise."

After that Benjie came down every night to talk about Monica's beliefs about the afterlife. She was vague, but he wanted specifics. He wanted to know how he would see Harry again, when Harry was in many tiny pieces because he had been blown to bits. He wanted to know where he would live in the afterlife and what he would eat.

"She's filling that poor kid's brain with hogwash," James said.

"If it makes him feel better, leave it alone. I wish I could believe that hogwash."

"What? You're the one convinced me there's a God but no afterlife. Now you've changed your view?"

"I said I *wish* I could, not that I did."

"Frankly, if there's a God, I don't see how he could let this happen to Harry."

"Harry enlisted, remember? God didn't do it for him."

"Still."

"Still nothing."

When Monica returned home that Monday evening, her little townhouse seemed empty. She turned on the television in the living room and microwaved a Healthy Choice chicken dinner. She rifled through the accumulated mail and read a brief letter from Kevin with a pang. Suddenly he seemed so far away again. She put the mail aside and forced herself to eat. After her meal, it took thirty seconds to clean up, and then she found herself staring down the long, deserted corridor of the evening before her. She telephoned Edie and tried to cheer her. She telephoned Isabelle and vented all her anxieties about Kevin. Then she moved to the living room, removing her shoes, and switched on the news hour with Jim Lehrer. There were photographs of dead soldiers at the end, photographs that made her want to weep. Harry Sullivan was among them. After that, she no longer wanted to watch television. She sat, tired but wakeful, in the lonely silence of her living room, thinking how alien the house seemed, how little like home now that her son had gone.

In the weeks that followed, the house stayed empty. "Desolate" was the word that came to her mind. She communicated with Kevin regularly, but somehow her various epistles did not bring him closer. He mentioned that he had been selected to chauffeur a think tank pooh-bah, one Dr. Wrash, around the Iraqi capital. He called him a warmonger.

And then came the news of Kevin's death. She had dreamt of it the night before, feared it for so long, that it was no surprise. But nonetheless, the life went out of her. She turned away from the soldier at the door, and all the strength she had so magically summoned for the Sullivans drained away. With it went her faith, which she had expected, in her wildly anxious imaginings of this moment, to sustain her. It did not. It was not even a matter of details. She wondered if there was a god at all, and, if so, why He cared so little about her. But there could not be. "We come out of nothing and to nothing we return," she said aloud.

"What ma'am?" The soldier asked, concerned.

"Nothing," she said, closing the door. "There is nothing."

She sat in the empty living room and wept, as the shadows slowly darkened and filled the house, so quiet now and, she thought, forever. She did not get out the photo albums or videos of her son. She sat and waited until the house was completely dark and the hour very late. Then she walked up the stairs, paused to look into her son's room, to absorb his presence one last time and went and sat on her bed. She opened the bottle of sleeping pills on the nighttable next to it, swallowed a massive overdose, laid down and died.

Seven

Luis' wedding had been a mammoth affair. It had been held at
the local Catholic Church in June 2001, when he was home from the
air force on leave. All of his friends and their parents were invited.
Afterward there was a reception in the Ignacio's back yard, because
the bride's family lived in an apartment and rental of a hotel ballroom
was too expensive. Sandra Ignacio and the bride's family tried to keep
costs down, but it was difficult. "Maybe they could bring their own
champagne," she joked to Cesar.

"And maybe we could have it at Burger King," he snapped. "What is
this, the Wal-Mart wedding?"

"Yes, as a matter of fact. What's the matter with Wal-Mart?"

"My son comes home from the air force, is madly in love with
Graciela Morales, so madly that he breaks the rule he's been holding all
his life, namely don't get married young – it's his wedding for crying out
loud. His one and only wedding –"

"You hope."

"What's that supposed to mean?"

"Young people these days, raised in America –"

"I don't want to hear it. And I don't want to pinch pennies."

"Well we have to," Sandra hissed, "cause pennies is all we got. If we
don't pinch 'em, we won't make the mortgage."

At the ceremony Jones stood next to Sherwin and could not stop
talking. "This is the first time I ever set foot in a church," he said.

"I'm not too big on visiting houses of worship myself," Sherwin
replied. "This is quite a crowd."

"I didn't know Luis knew so many people."

"There's his family, her family, his friends, her friends –"

"Did you get a look at her? She's knock-out beautiful. How'd Luis get
a girl like that?"

"Maybe the same way you'll get Elena, if you really try."

"Knock it off," Jones spoke grumpily. It was a common joke among
his friends that he was sweet on Elena, to which, since her graduation,
there was more than a little truth.

"But you'll have to pick your way through a political minefield,"
Sherwin continued. "Elena has very strong opinions, and she's very pc."

"So? I'm not pc?"

"More than anyone I know."

"Thank you."

"It wasn't a compliment."

"I know, but I decided to ignore that."

The bride walked down the aisle. "She could be a model, for God's sake," Jones exclaimed.

"Don't take the name of the Lord in vain in a church."

'What do you know? You're not even Catholic. You're Jewish."

"But I'm also superstitious."

"And there's a strong vein of that, as we all know, in all religions."

"Could you two shut up?" Animal turned around and growled at them. "I'd like to hear the vows."

"That Graciela's a knock-out," said Harry, next to Animal.

"Just what I said," Jones put in.

"Where'd he meet her?" Harry demanded. "Because wherever it was, I'm going there."

"Right here," Kevin put in. "He met her in church."

"That Luis!" Jones said. "Picking up gorgeous girls in church. You know, I may become religious."

"You may become silent first, if you please," Animal hissed. "I can't hear a fucking word."

"Now you've done it," Sherwin said, groping around in his pockets. "You've gone and offended God in one of His houses of worship. Where's my yarmulke?"

"You brought one?" Jones asked. "I didn't even know you had one."

"I kept it since my bar mitzvah. I was kind of fuzzy on protocol – this being a Catholic Church and all. But I figured if there was any possibility of coming into the presence of the Almighty, I better have it."

"I liked your bar mitzvah," Jones said.

"So now we're going to reminisce about the goddamned bar mitzvah?" Animal whispered angrily.

"Somebody is rather foul-mouthed today," Jones said.

"Somebody won't *shut* his mouth today."

"Dorian," Isabelle said from the row in front of him, "keep it down."

"Me?" Animal cried. Heads turned.

"Now you've done it," Harry whispered.

"Who's that talking?" Came a harsh hiss from Clarence behind them, "is that you Donald?"

Jones winced.

"Don't you go getting us thrown out before the food," Clarence went on.

"I'm looking forward to that cake," James said, rubbing his hands and smacking his lips.

"And the champagne," Clarence went on in a whisper next to him. "You know, I never get champagne."

"And there may be hors d'oeuvres," James continued.

"Good God, can't you ever think about anything other than your stomach?" Edie snapped. "Luis is getting married today. He's going to spend the rest of his life with this woman."

"Let's hope she can cook," James said rather splenetically, "although you never know 'til it's too late."

"How come you never give me champagne?" Clarence asked Jessie.

"You like beer. Remember?"

"Oh, yeah. I wonder if there will be any beer at this reception."

"Probably," James said. "Cesar always keeps some in that fridge in the basement."

"Maybe a little beer," Clarence danced a step or two in place, "maybe a little KFC."

"You can forget the KFC," Edie told him.

"What? You're not my wife."

"She's right," Jessie put in. "You, Cesar and James are not kicking off your smelly shoes and settling in front of whatever sporting events are on TV with the beer and the tub of KFC."

"Why not?"

"This is a wedding."

"I certainly hope you never eat that chicken fried in grease," Edie said to her husband.

James pulled a long face and shook his head. "Wouldn't dream of it."

"Cause it'll clog your middle-aged arteries like that," and she snapped her fingers in front of his nose.

"Maybe I want my arteries clogged. Maybe that's better than one more night of tofu stirfry. Maybe those limp vegetables have robbed me of the will to live. Maybe you should just get out a gun and kill me now."

"I will," Harry hissed over his shoulder, "if you don't shut up."

"I want to see it," Chandra said. "I want to see Mr. Sullivan, Jones and Igancio enjoying themselves with beer and fried chicken."

"Don't forget Angelo," James said.

"He only comes if he promises to keep quiet about his remarkable nose," Clarence said. "I will not have him sniffing the air and telling the world what kind of fungus I got on my feet, when I take off my shoes."

"You're not taking off your shoes," Jessie said. "This is a wedding."

"We'll see about that," Clarence said and gave Chandra a wink.

"You know she's not El Salvadoran," James said, popping a mint into his mouth.

"Who?" Edie asked.

"The bride. She's Mexican," slurp, slurp on the mint.

"So what?"

"So, Luis always said he would only marry a girl form El Salvador. He's very conservative, culturally," slurp, slurp. "Luis, that is."

"Who else would we be talking about?"

"I thought she was from Guatemala," Clarence broke in. "Donald –"

Jones winced.

"Donald, didn't you say she came from some town with an unpronounceable name in Guatemala?"

"I said her cousin did."

"Her cousin? Who's talking about her cousin?"

"You were. You collided with him coming into the church."

"So now you're saying she's Mexican, Donald?"

Jones winced again. "Yes."

"Get your story straight."

"Get your brain straight. There's no problem with my story. She's Mexican. Her cousin's Guatemalan."

"Would you shut up?" Animal turned around and demanded.

"Tell him to shut up," Jones jerked his thumb back at his father. "I've been trying for twenty years. Clearly my methods are not effective."

"These kids got no respect anymore," Angelo broke in from the other side of Jessie. "They tell their parents to shut up, just like that. Last night Pauli called me an agnostic hedonist. Who's he think's been working sixty hours a week for the past two decades to support him in his life of luxury?"

"What luxury?" Paul demanded. "You won't even give me the remote. Not one night in the whole freakin' week."

"It's a good thing you said 'freakin' and not what you almost said."

"I didn't almost say what you think I almost said. We're in a church, a Catholic Church. I respect that. Not like some people I know."

"You're not responsible with the remote, anyway."

"What, because I don't watch the 'Sopranos'? I like the History Channel. What's not responsible about that?"

"Did either of you ever consider buying another TV?" Clarence demanded. "I mean, how often do I hafta hear this argument about the remote? They sell TVs. In stores. They don't cost that much. A little thirteen inch color, you could get for, Oh –"

"Shut up," Jessie said.

"My sentiments exactly," Jones muttered.

"They're married," Edie pointed at Luis and Graciela coming down the aisle. "Thank God. Can we go home?"

"No. There's Cesar's beer and TV and a bucket of fried chicken," James replied. Edie opened her mouth. "No matter what you say," he interrupted. "I'm celebrating today. In my own way, perhaps, but I'm celebrating."

"In the emergency room with a coronary bypass in all likelihood," Edie snapped.

"Always looking on the dark side."

"Your doctor says your cholesterol's too high."

"Phooey. I want a second opinion."

"He *was* the second opinion. Besides, you don't need an opinion to read the results of a blood test. I don't know how your cholesterol could still be so high on what I feed you. I see every bite you take."

Two rows up, Harry rolled his eyes.

Cesar, walking down the aisle to exit the church, paused to get a mint from James. "Thank God that's over," he said, mopping his forehead with a handkerchief. "It must be a thousand degrees in here."

"That's another thing I hate about church," Angelo said. "No AC."

"I don't like this priest, either," Cesar went on. "What a stuffed shirt. I been coming here Saturday and Sunday for I don't know how many years, he still calls me Mr. Ignacio. You'd think that just once, on the day of my son's wedding maybe, he'd call me Cesar. Just a little touch of warmth and friendliness. Not this bucket of ice."

"Speaking of buckets of ice, I guess there'll be champagne," Clarence said.

"Fountains of it," Cesar slurped on the mint.

"What about beer for the older generation that wants to relax, watch some sports, you know, whatever's on –"

"Tennis," slurp, slurp. "That's it. I already checked."

"Tennis?"

"You could do worse than tennis," James said.

"How?" Clarence asked.

"Cricket. Cricket would be worse."

"Okay," Clarence sighed. "It's tennis."

"You get the chicken," more slurping. "If I spend one more penny today, Sandra's going to kill me. Besides, I'll need some time to meet and greet. This girl's got relatives from all over Central America. We got half the United Nations in this church."

"Are they legal?" Clarence asked.

"You've got to be kidding," more slurps. "Half of them still thinks they're in Oaxa or Guadalajara or Mazatlan. Legal. That's a good one. Ha!"

"Not that I care," Clarence explained. "People need work, they come here any way they can. I'd do the same. I was just curious."

At the reception, Luis and Graciela were the center of attention. Miqueas and Rafael crowded around, and when he thought no one was looking, Miqueas touched the lace on her gown, thinking that perhaps it had magical powers, since it resembled the garment of a fairy godmother. Elena kept going on about their upcoming honeymoon in the Florida Keys.

"The Keys in early June?" Jones asked. "Isn't that kind of hot?"

"I like hot," Luis replied. "Besides it's off-season. It's economical."

"I researched it on the internet," Elena burbled. "There are undersea forests, coral reefs, barracudas, and you can take a tour in a glass-bottomed boat. You've got to take pictures Luis, for me."

"What's she saying?" Jones asked about Graciela, who chattered in Spanish to a cousin. "The Spanish I learned from one-of-a-kind Sanchez isn't helping me."

"That's because it isn't the kind of conversation the Bureau of Alcohol, Firearms and Tobacco would be interested in," Luis said.

"She's talking about Key West," Elena explained. " How lovely it's supposed to be and how it was one of Ernest Hemmingway's haunts."

"Well, you finally got hitched, captured, lassoed," it was Bradley, for once not in a costume.

"Yeah, I guess I did," Luis conceded

Elena, aside to her brother, inquired: "Who invited him? I don't remember his name on the guest list."

"An oversight."

"No oversight. I specifically left it off, after that performance last year at your graduation."

"He's harmless."

"Mrs. Sullivan thinks he's psycho."

"Nah."

"He may not be, but he upsets all the parents. They think he's going to do something unexpected, unpredictable –"

"Like show up as a chicken and lay an egg? Come on Laney, get him a piece of cake."

"I'll do it," Jones, who had hovered on the edge of this whispered dispute, volunteered. "So Bradley," he passed him a slice, "how's the military life?"

"Great, Donald. Still got that tic, I see. Well, I'm on the party circuit. All the army families invite me to entertain at their kids' birthday parties, like I did for the Sullivans a few years back."

"Oh yeah. I heard about that."

"It was a blast."

"So I gather."

"And let me tell you, now, I'm having the time of my life."

"I can imagine."

"I have all these different getups – a chicken, a bear, a turkey, a clown, a pig –"

"A pig?"

"Yup. The kids love it."

"What do you do?"

"I oink a lot. What do you think I do?"

Jacob Goodman approached, en route to the cake. "I just want seconds," he explained and then, recognizing Bradley, "oh, I remember you. You had that costume."

"He's still at it," Jones said.

"Not today, I hope. One bride and one groom is plenty."

"Apparently at the base, he entertains at kids' birthday parties," Jones explained. "Dresses up as a pig."

"Yep," Bradley said, wolfing down cake. "Also a chicken, a bear, a turkey, Santa Claus, a clown –"

"And a pig," Jacob repeated.

"Jones said that already," Bradley observed.

"It's just that it's…not kosher."

"Not kosher? No, I guess it's not."

"Well, ta, ta," Jacob edged away.

"Ta, ta."

"Stella," he bellowed and pushed his way through the crowd until he found his splendiferously attired wife. "Stella, that loon from graduation's back, and evidently we escaped, by the skin of our teeth, witnessing him perform as a pig this year."

"A pig?"

"Apparently he dresses up as one, regularly."

"Well, it's a good thing he didn't' today. Clarence and James would have roasted him and carved him up. Did you see the size of those tubs of fried chicken they snuck down to the basement? They could feed an army."

Down in the rec room, a ferocious argument was underway about how much chicken to save for Cesar. Clarence and Angelo voted for a bucket, James for five pieces.

"Seems pretty skimpy, five pieces, for the father of the groom," Clarence said.

"I could eat both buckets alone, in twenty minutes with an arm tied behind my back. Wanna see me?" James demanded.

"No, I don't think so," Angelo said.

"You're looking at a desperate man," James went on. "You don't know what I had for dinner last night."

"But I know you snuck out to McDonald's afterward," Angelo replied.

James looked astonished. Angelo tapped his nose knowingly.

"And you don't get any pieces," Clarence roared, "if you mention that nose. Now I'm taking off my shoes – gimme that remote – and drinking my beer, and I don't want to hear a word about tofu or strange smells or burnt vegetables."

After most of the guests had gone home, Luis left his bride for a moment and descended upon the basement to fetch his suitcase. "I don't believe it!" He cried when he saw the foursome, three on the couch, his father in the La-Z-Boy, all glaring at a tennis game on the TV, drinking beer and eating the remains of the fried chicken. "This is my wedding day. How could you, my own father –"

"I greeted everyone," Cesar replied, gnawing on a drumstick and then pointing it at his son. "Which is more than I can say for you."

"Who? Who didn't I greet?"

"The Lehtinens, her cousins from Cuba."

"Cuba? She doesn't have any cousins from Cuba."

"Ha! You see how much you know."

"They must've been crashers."

"No. They're in-laws on her mother's cousin's side. Flakes too. All these Cubans ever want to talk about is Fidel. Like I care. Like I'm ever going to set foot in Havana. Geez, I'm not ever setting foot in San Salvador again if I can help it, no less Havana."

"Graciela wants to see San Salvador."

"Graciela needs her head examined."

"Hey, where's your patriotism?"

"Right here, in the U.S. A."

"We come from San Salvador."

"Correction. The slums outside of San Salvador. And certain people who don't remember what it's like to live without running water and with one working light bulb have all sorts of idealistic dreams about going back to San Salvador," Cesar bit down savagely on his drumstick. "Certain people don't appreciate what they got here in Maryland. Like no death squads."

"The death squads are gone, Dad."

"But I don't see the people that were in them gone. I don't see them hanging from the trees by their broken necks, like they deserve. No. They're still big, important men, in government, business and finance. They run this, they're in charge of that. You tell Graciela, if she wants to see a Spanish country, go to Puerto Rico, where she won't have to rub shoulders with former butchers who murdered priests and peasants. San Salvador. You couldn't pay me to go back home."

"See, you called it home."

"A slip of the tongue."

"I still think, on my wedding day, you could have stayed out of the basement."

"This is my refuge."

"Refuge? From what?"

"From you, from Sandra, from my family, from life. Don't get me wrong. I love you all. But a man needs a little peace and quiet, where he can relax..."

"And belch and fart to his heart's content."

"That too."

"I'm disappointed."

"You haven't been married yet. That's all. Give it a few years. You'll be down here with me."

"I don't think so."

"Clarence pass me another drumstick," Cesar dropped the bone onto a paper plate, covered with grease and gristle and other bones.

"Graciela wanted to talk to you, to hear you reminisce about El Salvador."

Cesar looked at his son as if he had taken leave of his senses.

"So she talked to Mom instead."

Cesar rolled his eyes. "Did she tell her the truth or give her the sanitized version?"

"Mom has a different view than you."

"Oh, so it was the land of flowers and happy peasants routine, with the dead bodies omitted, the missing cousins, her entire uncle's family vanished –"

"Mom's uncle was a revolutionary."

"I don't care what he was. He didn't deserve to be 'disappeared.'" Cesar held up his fingers to make quote marks. "Aka murdered, along with his wife and six children. You're lucky they didn't decide to wipe out your grandfather's family too, because then neither you nor your mother would be here in Maryland enjoying a wedding party today." Cesar paused, demolished his drumstick and pointed it, this time at himself. "They might have killed me too. They killed our priest."

"Sounds like a great time in the good old fascist days of El Salvador," Clarence remarked, guzzling his beer.

"It's all different now," Luis explained.

"Yeah, they're not disemboweling people. They're just running the country," Cesar said sourly. "And you still can't get a clean glass of water."

"I came down to ask if you'd like to drive us to the airport."

Cesar sighed, looked like he was about to say something intemperate, then bethought himself and took a breath. "I'd love to," he lied. "But I've had too much beer. You'll have to let your mother."

"Actually Animal can drive us. I just thought it might be nice to have some time together in the car, especially seeing as I know how much you love tennis."

"Who can follow this ridiculous game?" James asked.

"Give me soccer any day," Cesar said.

Luis and his wife flew into Miami, where they were met by one of her
cousins, who lent them his car, as they were still too young to rent one.
Her cousin also thoughtfully provided a map. They followed the route in
a straight line south to Key Largo, where they spent four days in a clean,
pleasant efficiency, very near a fancy hotel with a restaurant on an upper
floor. Seated by the window, they looked directly out over the water, at
the boats, at the men fishing on a sandbar and, compared to Maryland,
this, Luis announced, was paradise. If only Cesar and Sandra could
see it. He snapped dozens of pictures for them and delivered breathless
bulletins over the cell phone.

"I'm calling from a glass-bottomed boat," he huzzahed at one point.
"We just got in it. It's fantastic. You can see all kinds of fish underneath."

"Like what?" Cesar demanded.

"A barracuda. No wait. A pod of barrcudas."

"I never saw a barracuda," Cesar said. "I probably never will."

"Don't say that. Graciela's taking pictures."

After the ride in the glass-bottomed boat, they swam in the pool
in their little apartment complex. It was near the water's edge, so they
wandered among the rocks, and Luis snorkeled. Graciela took pictures of
mangroves a short distance away and fretted about alligators and sharks.

"So when we have children, you'll be too afraid to let them go into
the water?" He asked.

She pointed to a story in the paper about a shark attack.

"We're much more likely to die in a car accident," he explained,
but that did not soothe her. After Key Largo, they traveled down to Key
West and spent three days there. "We could move to Florida," Graciela
suggested, as soon as she set eyes upon Key West. "I have lots of family
here. It's not as if we wouldn't know people."

"Maybe," Luis answered, but privately resolved against it, against
leaving his family and friends.

Before he knew it, however, he was leaving everybody. September
eleventh happened, and he deployed to a base in Saudi Arabia. He was
not ecstatic about military life, which surprised him. Had marriage
sapped all his eagerness for the air force? But he was impatient to engage
the enemy.

That did not happen right away. After months at one base in Saudi
Arabia, he moved to another. Then for a while he was on an aircraft
carrier. Then he got to go home on leave. Next he was back, here, there,

finally sent to invade Iraq. Luis stayed in Iraq a long time and never allowed himself to doubt the mission.

"But there are no weapons of mass destruction," Cesar said on one of Luis' visits home. "There's no reason to be there. You should get out of the military and come home, as soon as you can. I don't like this."

"It's fine, Dad. We're doing good work here. We got rid of a very bad guy."

"Maybe so. But you take my advice. Listen to your father, if you won't listen to your mother, sister or wife."

Luis did not listen. He stayed and before long found himself driving a Humvee along the airport road on a much more regular basis than he liked.

"I'm in the air force, for God's sake," he would complain to the others. "I'm not supposed to be driving a Humvee to the airport. I wanted to be a pilot."

"You'll be a pilot," his superior officer said. "Just be patient."

"Maybe I should've gone to the Air Force Academy. Hey what's that?"

"I don't know, but what's his rush?" The officer craned his neck to look in the rearview mirror.

"I think he just wants to pass," Luis watched the blue Honda with two Iraqi men come up alongside. Then it passed and sped ahead. He sighed in relief. But then a strange thing happened: the man in back turned around and looked up at him through the rear window. The Honda stopped. The Humvee plowed into it. The last thing Luis saw, before the Honda blew up was the man's dark-eyed gaze, smoldering with hatred. As Luis met those eyes, he seemed to see the large quiet, sunny room that was just for him, that he had dreamt of since childhood, vanishing forever. One soldier, in the back of the vehicle, survived, but even he was terribly wounded.

The news of Luis' death literally felled Elena. She collapsed on the couch in her father's arms and then later went out to her vegetable garden and collapsed there. She had nothing to say to pregnant Graciela, who lived with them and whose first response had been: "Who will take care of me and the baby?"

"Who indeed?" Elena asked loudly and rhetorically to the marigolds and tomato plants. "The same people who've taken care of you since he left – us. Oh Luis, Luis, how could you go and get yourself killed?"

She started ripping up weeds as tears streamed down her face. Then she would wipe the tears and smudge dirt on her cheeks. "Luis, Luis," she said, over and over.

"It won't bring him back," Cesar said from the back porch. "You can call and call. He won't come back."

"I don't accept it." She shouted in Spanish.

But Cesar, true to form, would not speak Spanish either. "Luis knew he could die. I just don't know what he thought he would be dying for. Some stupid war in some country where people blow themselves up. It's senseless. I never understood it. I never understood him. If I had understood him, if I had tried harder to understand him and if I had succeeded, I would have been able to talk him out of this, this reckless, fatal decision. The air force! Did I ever say I wanted him to join the air force?"

"But it was *you*," she almost shouted, "with your constant 'America is better,' 'the U.S.A. is the greatest,' it was all that that made him so proud, so determined to be an American soldier. It was you!"

"Elena!" Cesar snapped. "You will not talk to me like that. You don't know what you're saying."

Elena continued sobbing and weeding.

"I didn't try hard enough," Cesar continued. "He baffled me. And I let him do that. I should have insisted he go to college or come into contracting with me. That's where I failed. Not like you say. Not for saying this is the greatest country. I believe that. I still believe that, even though my oldest son just died for this country, and I don't know why."

Sandra exited the house, sobbing into a Kleenex. "Get her out of that garden," she ordered. "She's lost her mind."

Cesar suddenly looked at Elena in alarm. But aside from weeping and weeding, she did not look insane.

"Come, come," Sandra urged, as she and her husband approached the vegetable patch.

"I will not go back in there with her," Elena hissed.

"Graciela is a little self-centered," Cesar said. "We all know that. No one's perfect."

To Elena, it was immediately and undeniably clear that Luis was gone forever. Not so Sandra, who made mistakes when she heard the front door slam, such as "that must be Luis."

"No, Mom, it's not Luis," Elena would reply, as Sandra ran water in the kitchen sink to conceal the sound of her sobs.

A part-time student at the University of Maryland Baltimore campus, Elena found it difficult to concentrate and took the rest of the semester off. Instead, she worked full time at the campus library, something she had done irregularly until her brother's death. Jones saw her there one afternoon in summer.

"I'm enrolling here part-time in the fall," he explained.

"Me too," she said. "I just took the semester off. For obvious reasons."

"Harry, Kevin, Luis," Jones said, looking across the counter at her, scanning books and dropping them into a bin. The library was an oasis of air-conditioned cool and quiet and made him pensive. "Sometimes it's like I forget they're dead. I think, 'oh, that's a good one. I gotta tell it to Luis,' or 'Harry'll really get a kick out of that.' Then I remember, and there's nothing – just an ache."

"Don't forget Kevin's mother," Elena said.

"Who could forget that?"

"Luis's wife had a baby boy, Pablo."

"I heard."

"I think she wept once."

"Don't fret about that. She was just Luis' trophy wife. He was showing off. He could marry the most beautiful girl in Maryland."

Elena laughed.

"It was something like that," Jones continued. "He was quiet and reserved, but when Luis wanted to make a point, he really clobbered you over the head with it."

"Like joining the air force."

"Yes, that's an example of it, though I still haven't sorted out exactly what his point was, what he was saying to us."

"It was that this country meant more to him than anything, that it was the best, that he would risk his life for it and that was more than the rest of us would do. It was that he was a hero. That was his point." She paused to wipe away a tear.

"You shouldn't cry," Jones said. "You tried harder than anyone to stop him. Besides you've shed enough tears."

"What's enough?"

"I don't know really. It's just something people say. Well, I'm glad you're not sitting in your vegetable patch anymore. Last time I saw you I thought you were growing roots."

"Sometimes I wish I had just turned into a zucchini plant that didn't know when the other plants around it shriveled up and died."

They talked for some time, until Elena got her break. Then they walked out into the sweltering mid-Atlantic heat to go for a cup of coffee and ruminate more about the people they knew who had been killed in the war.

After hearing the news of Luis' death, Edie and James Sullivan visited. Edie had a large bowl of ratatouille for them, a dish, James confided to Benjie – who was the only one he could get to listen – that he would not touch with a ten-foot pole. They also brought a carrot cake with a cream-cheese-based frosting that James had sampled from the edges of the plate. "Not bad," he had murmured in astonishment several times. The day was unseasonably warm, and as the Sullivans stood on the front step, they could hear the hum of the air conditioning unit on the side of the little house. Sandra's calico cat crouched in a branch of the dogwood tree, salivating over a dozen drab sparrows, perched higher up. The sky was blue and careless: as if it did not matter who lived or who died, it would shine like a dazzling sapphire, only marred by the occasional mauve and white, silver-rimmed cloud. Edie rang again. Sandra opened the door, and they both burst into tears.

"I brought you this casserole," Edie sniffled with so much congestion that it sounded like, "I bought you dis cataro."

Cesar understood, however, and removed the offerings to the kitchen.

"The cake's pretty good," James called after him, "if you want to try it now." This idea appealed to Cesar, who brought forth this confection, plates, forks and a knife. The men chewed thoughtfully, with an appropriately somber slowness, as if to demonstrate that they were not inordinately enjoying the cake, as the women wept on the couch.

"I blame the leadership," James spoke quietly. "Clarence is right. These right-wing reactionaries have gone too far with this war."

"I can't even think about politics," Cesar replied. "I see red every time I do."

"But then, by the same token, our boys made mistakes. They didn't have to enlist. Donald Jones stayed out of it, and he'll live to a ripe old age. We tried to talk them out of it, but they would not listen. This generation's different. In my day, you could not have paid us to go to Vietnam. Now, they sign up. My own son, Harry. I still can't believe that he did this, no less got himself killed."

"I hear you met the mother of that kid, Delante."

"Delante was a hero."

"What's his mother like?"

"Just a normal, ordinary person. There's no clue as to how she raised a young man who would give his life, just like that."

Miqueas wandered in and wanted cake. Seeing his mother in tears on the couch, he said, "poor Luis."

"Poor nothing," Cesar corrected. "Luis died doing what he believed in." Then after Miqueas left the room: "whatever that was." He paused to eat more of the baked goods. "I have trouble sleeping," he said after a moment. "I like awake, imagining his last moments. What did he see? What did he think? And then I tell myself, at least it was quick. But that doesn't really help, because it was so violent. Then I think how I failed him, how I should have talked him out of this insane idea of the air force. I just can't sleep."

"The same thing happened to me at first. Then you get used to the emptiness."

"Not Monica."

"No, I guess she figured she'd never adjust to it. Or there was too much of it. Kevin was all she had, her whole world, I guess."

They ate in silence. James noticed that the many photographs of Luis that had decorated the mantelpiece had been removed. He understood. Many months would pass before he could look at pictures of Harry casually, or retain any semblance of composure. For his part, Cesar observed that his guest's usually thick dark hair had quite visibly grayed and that Edie had new lines at the corners of her mouth. He wondered if he too showed signs of grief and then recalled the haggard face that had greeted him in the bathroom mirror that morning, the beringed and somewhat bloodshot eyes, the unhealthy pallor. "How are we ever going to get through this?" He asked out loud.

No one answered. No one had any ideas.

The next day a malignant smog that smelled faintly of chemicals settled over the vicinity. Probably, Cesar explained to Sandra, it was the tractor-trailer loaded with hazmats that had overturned on Route 50. Residents had been assured that there was no danger, but the odor persisted.

"Benzene, if you ask me," Cesar said, sniffing the air as he got out of the minivan with Sandra and the two boys. They had just returned from church, where he had confessed to a crisis of faith. He had said that he expected he would get over it, but that the death of his son had really "knocked me off course." Absolved, he drove his family home with the windows shut and the air-conditioning on high, which did nothing to conceal the toxic perfume that pervaded the atmosphere.

A new, silver Mercedes was parked outside of their house, a car Cesar instantly tagged as the Goodman's. Stella was dressed to the nines, as always, in an Yves St. Laurent sundress, while Jacob wore shorts and a blue Lacoste shirt. Cesar was glad that he had just left church and was thus well attired. The Goodmans immediately offered condolences, and Sandra raised a tissue to her eyes.

"It seems like only yesterday we were here for the wedding reception," Stella murmured to her husband, as they entered the Ignacio's abode.

"That was some accident on Route 50," Cesar remarked.

"Well, if they paved the highways properly, these things wouldn't happen," Jacob answered, and a rather prolix debate on the deficiencies of the local roads ensued. Stella noted the mantelpiece, bare of all evidence of Luis, but said nothing.

"Luis gave us such faith in Sherwin," she said presently.

Sandra was so surprised, she forgot to weep. "He did?"

"Oh yes. He was a wonderful influence. He nearly talked Sherwin into applying to Johns Hopkins and majoring in biology. We were thrilled. We figured the next stop was medical school. Luis always radiated such confidence in our son. I can't describe its effect on him, on us."

"It made us believe there was hope," Jacob put in.

"Of course there's hope," Cesar said.

"But now he's in the army."

"Not everyone has Luis' rotten luck."

A silence descended upon the little conclave, a quiet in which the grief of one family and the worry of another palpably mingled. Miqueas and Rafael tumbled into the room, opened the door to let in the cat and demanded sweets. Sandra arranged a plate of chocolate chip cookies and placed it on the coffee table. The two boys munched happily.

"Well, that's my last kid that goes into the military," Cesar remarked. "After this, I just forbid it."

"Bang, bang," Rafael said. "I could be a soldier."

"You're going to be a carpenter, like me," Cesar replied. "Guns are for idiots."

"I never owned one," Jacob mused.

"I do. I got a twenty two," Cesar said. "Maybe I should get rid of it, to make the point to the boys."

"Maybe all we got to do is say 'remember what happened to Luis,'" Sandra snapped, and in odd contradiction to her harsh tone, tears dripped down her cheeks.

Stella clasped Sandra's hand. "I meant to tell you about Luis and Sherwin, how Luis was the only person other than an expert psychologist, years ago when Sherwin was a baby, Luis was the only one who perceived that Sherwin was different. Luis had astonishing powers of perception. He divined things about Sherwin that even Sherwin did not know. He saw that Sherwin would be good at biology, but that's just one example. It happened whenever he came over. There was always something he saw, that no one else had seen. It was like he had laser vision and could look into some people's souls. I always meant to tell you that you had this remarkable son with this irreplaceable gift, but somehow I never did, and now he's gone, and it's too late."

"It's not too late," Cesar spoke, visibly choked up. "I never knew that about Luis. I'm glad I know now."

Sherwin took the news of Luis' death very hard. He was in Iraq at the time and by a hair's breadth had missed getting sent to Falluja. Instead his platoon was in a backup position, waiting any day for orders to advance. When he heard about Luis, he told his new friend, Ubaldo Vasquez, who insisted he see the chaplain.

"But I'm Jewish," Sherwin weakly protested.

"Well, I don't see no rabbis out here. You'll have to make do."

Sherwin had not adapted well to the army. He tried to change his attitude, but he could not deny that he hated the military life. He hated not getting enough sleep. He hated constantly being ordered around. He hated being dirty. He hated the ready-to-eat meals. He hated getting shot at. He hated his friends getting killed. He hated the heat, the sand, the lukewarm water, and, worst of all, he missed home. The army made him decide that if he survived it, he would commute to college and not leave Crofton. He would live with his parents, who he liked better than anyone he had met in the military, and he would apply to Johns Hopkins. The memory of his home resembled a vision of paradise. He could scarcely believe that he had give up the safety, freedom and support of his parents' house for the blood, grit and grime of the desert. "What was I thinking?" He asked himself several times each day. "I must have been out of my mind." Then he would remember his mother's nephew Albert, trapped on the one hundred and first floor of the World Trade Towers and Albert's desperate last phone call to Stella's sister, to say good-bye.

Albert Brand had not even worked in the World Trade Center. He was a financier whose office was several blocks away. But that day, he had been particularly unlucky. He had had a meeting with a big investment banking firm in the doomed skyscraper. He had realized at once that there was no escape. He could not go down – that meant traversing a roaring inferno. He could not jump, for obvious reasons. So he telephoned his wife and mother, conveyed his last wishes and perished when the building collapsed. He was twenty-eight years old and had one young son.

"Don't you live like a lonely old widow," he had advised his sobbing wife. "Remember me. But remarry."

"Who thinks of things like that," Stella had later asked through tears. "Whose last word to his wife is remarry?"

"Maybe he was concerned about her welfare," Sherwin had suggested. "You always said she was a clinger."

"She is a clinger. But she's got nothing to cling to now."

"Maybe he knew that. Maybe that's why his last word was remarry."

"Not even 'I love you.'"

"He said that earlier. You always said he worried about her, about her...mental strength."

"The eeriest thing about it is that she has it on tape, because the message machine picked up. Everything, his description of the chaos, the smoke, the secretaries sobbing, the view out the windows of people jumping from the other tower. For some reason he didn't panic, I mean after the initial terror. He regained his calm. He knew he was going to die."

"He might have still hoped for a rescue."

"No, she has that on tape too. 'They'll never be able to rescue us.' Those were his words. Albert was always very clear-headed. No mush in that brain. That's how he made so much money. That's how he ran his family. He did the thinking for both of them. That's how he died."

Meditating upon the fate of his cousin Albert Brand, Sherwin recollected why he was in the army, though he still wondered why he was in Iraq. He said so to the chaplain, who had commenced their meeting with assurances that he had often visited synagogues in his hometown of Chicago and that he knew the rabbis there quite well.

"That doesn't matter," Sherwin explained. "The truth is, I'm not very religious."

"But you know there is a God."

"I don't know what I know. I just wish my best friend Luis Ignacio had not been blown to bits on the airport road."

"Everyone has to die."

"But not when they're twenty-one years old. Not when they've got a twenty-one-year-old wife and a baby."

"You said the same thing about your cousin Albert Brand."

"If there is a God, how could He let that happen?"

The chaplain sighed. Sherwin was not in a complacent mood. He made it quite clear that he held God personally responsible for both deaths. "And for my friends Harry and Kevin," he added.

"But you all knew the risks when you enlisted."

"We were all imbeciles. Jones was right."

Sherwin received a few hours off that afternoon. He spent it idly at the forward operating base. He jogged, read some more of *Crime and Punishment*, recommended by Animal as the only classic Anna had made him read that really stayed with him, napped and showered twice. The shower would have been an inconceivable luxury just a month ago, when his platoon had camped out in an abandoned government building, hot, filthy, surrounded by alleys that reeked of excrement. But now, with three hours to himself – to grieve, as the chaplain had explained to his commanding officer – he lingered in the shower, soaping himself twice each time. It felt wonderful.

"Hey Goodman," one of his friends joked, "you're gonna be the cleanest soldier in all of Iraq."

That evening Ubaldo entered their crowded little trailer. He was hot, sweaty, dirty and beaming. "Good news," he grinned. "We're too late for Falluja. They're sending us back to Baghdad. I know, some of you were dying to get into the fight, but not me."

"Me neither," added Sherwin, as Ubaldo sat across from him, and then spoke in an undertone: "Those two idiots, Johnson and Robertson, are complaining to the CO 'how come we don't get to go to Falluja. We want to be part of this fight.' They ought to have their heads examined."

"Half the army needs its head examined."

"This may be our first lucky break, Sherwin. The way I see it, up 'til now, everything has been shit. And I mean literally. I still got that diarrhea I picked up in Baghdad. I'm sick, I'm tired, but at least here I get a shower. And the food has improved, sort of. Best of all, they're not sending us into that hellhole. It's our lucky day. So far only two guys from our platoon have been injured. We go back to Baghdad, and we make it out of here in one piece."

Johnson and Robertson came in cursing. "They say we're too late," Johnson complained. "Fallujah's filled with insurgents, and we're too late?"

"I'm going back to the CO," Robertson said, "see if he'll be reasonable, one more time."

Ubaldo's eyes met Sherwin's. "I wouldn't do that," Ubaldo put in. "He's real sick and tired of people second-guessing his decisions, besides," he continued to ad-lib, "it's really out of his hands. So you'll just piss him off for nothing."

"It's something to think about," Johnson said.

"Yeah, if you had a brain, I guess you could," Ubaldo muttered under his breath.

"I want into this fight!" Robertson exclaimed.

"Don't worry," Ubaldo replied. "There are still plenty of insurgents, bullets and IEDs in Baghdad," he looked at Sherwin and muttered again, "into this fight! Into the loony bin is where he belongs. These guys could screw up everything."

"You better get a shower while you can," Sherwin said. "If we're returning to Baghdad, we'll all be stinking to high heaven in a few days."

"I smell that bad now?"

"You could use a little soap," Sherwin said.

"Not 'til I'm sure the Hardy Boys here don't go and louse things up," Ubaldo whispered. Robertson and Johnson still loudly argued the merits of another appeal to the powers above.

"I've got an idea," Ubaldo announced. "There's no way they're sending the whole platoon to Falluja. Give that idea up." The fearless duo looked profoundly disappointed. But Ubaldo continued: "However, you two could make the case that you should go, attached to another group."

"I like that plan," Robertson averred.

"And permanently stay linked to another group," Ubaldo muttered.

On the road back to Baghdad, Sherwin's convoy hit an IED. The Humvee directly in front of his was destroyed, and two people in his own vehicle were killed. Sherwin was lucky he survived, though he did not feel that way at the time, lying in the dirt by the side of the road, with two broken arms, a cracked rib, burns and a left leg that had no sensation.

"Sherwin!" Ubaldo screamed for the second time.

"I can't hear very well," Sherwin groaned.

"Medic!" Ubaldo hollered. "He's alive."

"I'm wet," Sherwin complained.

"Yeah, a little blood. But they didn't get you, not this time."

Sherwin said nothing. He had lost consciousness. When he came to, he was on a stretcher, in a helicopter, with the cool stream of an IV dripping into his arm. A medic was working on him. "A few broken bones," the doctor shouted. "And you may be a little deaf for a while," Sherwin was aware of excruciating pain in his arms, chest, leg and on the side of his face.

"My face," he said.

"A little burn. Not too bad. It hurts now, but it'll heal. That's the least of your worries. What's more, you got off without any brain trauma."

"Yeah, but I got every other kind of trauma."

"Don't talk." The medic was busy with his leg. "He's going to lose that leg," the medic said more quietly to another. "Give him more morphine. The doctor will amputate as soon as we get down."

For the next day or two, Sherwin was as high as a kite. He did not even know what painkillers they gave him. At one point, he realized Ubaldo sat next to him.

"You're awake, Sherwin? Can you hear me?" He shouted.

Sherwin nodded.

"You're going to Germany. You're out of this shithole, once and for all."

"I suppose I should look on the bright side. My arm, my leg –"

"Don't think about that. Remember Smithson, next to you in the back of the truck? He got a head trauma. It's horrible. At least you still got your brain."

"I don't know about that. I'm so high, I'm not even sure I'm me. What am I on?"

"Morphine, last time I checked. I hear the nurses are beautiful at the hospital in Germany. The food is supposed to be first class too."

"Ubaldo, I can't raise my head."

"Why should you?"

"I want to see if I still have my leg."

"What do you want to see that for? You just take it easy and heal. You're lucky to be alive."

"You call this luck?"

"Well then, I'm lucky you're alive, because I don't know what I'd have done if you snapped your neck when you shot out of the back of that truck."

"You saw it?"

"With my own horrified eyes. I was sure you were dead. And then there were all the others, killed and wounded. You've never seen blood like that. Lucky for you, you were unconscious. Boy, am I glad that's over."

When the Goodmans heard Sherwin was wounded and on his way to a hospital in Germany, they booked a flight there for the next day.

"If my father knew I was going to Germany," Jacob said, "he'd roll over in his grave."

Stella's eyes flashed. "If your father knew what had happened to Sherwin and that you considered for one instant not going, he'd jump out of his grave and strangle you."

"You're right, of course," Jacob was contrite. "I didn't think before I spoke."

From the moment Stella heard what had befallen her son, her life was remade, refocused on the sole aim of caring for him, of repaying the God who had not killed him, for the gift of his life. She planned Sherwin's future. He would have a wheelchair, live at home, and she would wait on him hand and foot. He would commute to college, major in biology and, if he wanted, become a doctor. It would be difficult, but she would be there to make things easier. At least he was not dead, like Luis, Kevin or Harry. At least he was not burned beyond recognition. At least he still had an uninjured brain. Since Sherwin had departed for Iraq, his mother had taken to reading all the news about the war. She even spent an hour on the internet every day, reading everything about attacks on American soldiers. She watched the TV news and hollered at the commentators who supported the war. She had a "Bring Them Home" bumper sticker and had wanted to put a "War Is Not The Answer" sign on the front lawn. Jacob dissuaded her, said it did not show sufficient support for Sherwin. "The best support would be for him to get out of that country and come back to us," she replied.

"Some soldiers don't appreciate pacifist signs."

"Sherwin's not one of them."

Jacob sported a "Support Our Troops" emblem on the back of his Mercedes. Once he heard that Sherwin had almost been killed and had sustained terrible wounds, he changed his mind. He took the "War Is Not The Answer" sign out and planted it on the front lawn. Then he came back into the house and packed for Germany.

Stella had never liked flying. It made her claustrophobic: "I feel like a sardine, crammed into a tin can with lots of other sardines, and the tin can is shooting over the earth at thirty-five thousand feet, and there's no good reason why it shouldn't just plummet to the ground and smash all the sardines to bits." So she rarely flew. When she did, she took Ativan. On their last trip to the Bahamas, she had been so woozy that she thought they were in Cancun when they landed. For this trip, however, she did not take any pills. Her mind was full of thoughts and anxieties about Sherwin, and she wanted to keep it clear. Foremost among her worries was what would happen to him if she and Jacob were killed in a plane crash on the way over.

"You know," she said to her husband, "maybe we should take separate flights."

Jacob glanced at her over the tops of his glasses. "So that if one of the planes crashes, one parent still survives?"

"I didn't say that."

"Not in so many words. No, I don't think we should. Did it ever occur to you that by this logic, we're increasing the chances of one of us being in a crash?"

"But there still would be one left over."

"Your brain's left over, at that therapist's, who never cured you of your peculiar little fears of this and that. Take a pill."

Harvey entered. "Mom, Dad. It's terrible about Sherwin."

"It could have been worse," Stella said.

"Your youngest son lost his leg and his hearing, and it could have been worse?"

"They say he'll get his hearing back," Stella explained. "Besides he can still understand you if you shout."

"So nothing's changed in that department," Jacob said.

"You're so nonchalant."

"We're heartbroken, all right?" Stella asked in exasperation. "But he didn't die, thank God, and we've got to pack to go over and see him."

"You're flying? You hate flying."

"My youngest son just lost his leg and his hearing, to quote someone. Hello? Am I his mother? Am I going to just leave him alone in a hospital in Germany? Of course I'm flying. I'm not going to swim."

Harvey helped them pack. "I don't believe it," he exclaimed when finished. "The luggage queen got everything in one suitcase."

"This trip isn't about me," Stella said.

The phone rang. It was Bertram, calling to commiserate and say he was too busy to come by. "I'm handling a big telecommunications merger. Gotta wrap it up."

"Well I certainly hope you're not going to use that lame excuse when Sherwin gets home, because if you try it, even once, forget about visiting," Stella said. "You'll be banned from the premises."

"Mom, hundreds of millions are involved here."

"I don't care if hundreds of billions are involved. Your brother lost his leg and his hearing –"

"I thought Dad said he'll get his hearing back."

"He won't get his leg back."

Bertram was silent.

"How much is his leg worth, Bertie?"

"Please don't be like that. I suppose he'll live with you."

"Where do you think he'll live? Walter Reed Hospital?"

"Well, he's lucky we live outside D.C. He'll get superb medical treatment, with the army hospital here and whatnot."

"Whatnot is his mother. I'm going to be taking care of him for the rest of his life."

"You could hire someone, a nurse or a home aide."

"Where is your heart, Bertram?"

"I'm just thinking of ways to make it easier on you."

"Think of ways to make it easier on him."

"They can do wonders these days with prosthetics."

"I haven't heard one word about a commitment to see him, to spend time with him, to visit regularly."

"You know I'm busy."

Stella put her hand over the receiver and said, "I know you've got your head up your ass."

"What's that?" Bertram asked.

"Make yourself less busy. Make time for Sherwin."

"He doesn't even like me."

Harvey, who heard the little voice in the receiver said: "Nobody does."

"Harvey, I heard that," Bertram shouted.

"Not so loud," Stella said.

"What I make in a day, you make in six months," Bertram shouted again.

"But I don't have to live with you," Harvey snatched the phone away from his mother. "I get to live with me, not some icy son-of-a-bitch who couldn't care less when his own brother gets a leg blown off in Iraq."

Stella took back the phone. "Sherwin will live here and commute to college. I'll take care of him. I would like it if you picked a night, once a week, to set aside to come see him."

"What am I, his therapist?" Bertram asked.

"Wake up Bertie. Your whole life is going by. All you can think is 'money, money, money.' But there are a few other things happening too."

Grumbling, Bertie got off the phone.

"His head up his ass? Mom, I've never heard you talk like that," Harvey said.

"One of my children never lost a leg before," Stella replied.

"So now we get profanity," Jacob asked, hefting the suitcase and placing it in the hall. "Is this the new Stella?"

"Things are different now," Stella said. "Everything has changed for us, forever."

For Stella, in her Versace outfit with her Luis Vuitton carry-on, the flight was an ordeal. Every time the airplane trembled, she was convinced they were all going to die. The worst part was takeoff. There was a wind.

"All summer and fall it's as hot as a sauna, and you would die for just the slightest breeze," she said. "But the day we take off, there's a wind at the airport. Do they have wind machines here? There was no wind at home when we left." The plane bounced violently. "Dear God, if we die, please make Harvey live up to his promise to go to Germany for Sherwin."

"Have an Ativan," Jacob said.

Stella shook her blown-dry blond head. "I'm going into this with my eyes open. I called Johns Hopkins before we left this morning and requested an application. There's a lot I've got to do, Jacob."

He nodded.

"I've basically got to do it all."

"Don't forget me, and Harv."

"And Bertie, the louse."

"Don't count on him. He's fixated on his bank account. He has no time for anybody or anything else. That's why he's not married. He's afraid of a divorce, of some woman getting a chunk of his money. He told me."

"What did I do wrong?"

"Everything apparently. I don't want to make you feel guilty, because I'm to blame too. I'm convinced it was that bar mitzvah. We probably should have raised him a Buddhist."

"But he didn't have to go to Temple after age thirteen. We let them all stop."

"It warped his mind. Angelo Lirano is right. Organized religion's for the birds."

"Angelo Lirano's a fruitcake."

"He has done very well with that chain of his."

"And Bertie's done very well in the law, but he's still a heel. My point is that people can make a lot of money and still be out of it in one major way or another." The plane lurched, and Stella let out a little scream. Heads turned.

"Stop that. You'll have the marshal bothering you."

"Is there a marshal on the plane?"

"Over there. The beefy guy trying to look inconspicuous. I heard him talking to the stewardess on my way to the bathroom."

"Well, at least we won't get hijacked."

"I suppose there's an up side to everything."

It was all Stella could do to keep the tears out of her eyes when they entered the hospital. The sight of doctors, nurses, patients, young men in wheelchairs, young men with IVs, made the tragedy of what had happened to her son suddenly overwhelming. "Stop a minute," she said to her husband. "Before we get in the elevator, I've got to get myself under control. I don't want him to see me crying."

"He'd think it pretty odd if you didn't cry, after what happened to him."

"I'm not going to make things worse. I'm going to be upbeat and focus on the good news."

"What good news? He lost his leg and didn't die of gangrene? Oh, his hearing will come back? The burn's only second degree?"

"That he's alive."

"That'll make him feel great. 'You're burnt, broken, deaf and crippled,' but you're alive. Ain't life great?"

"Jacob!" Stella snapped. "You better not be saying he'd be better off dead."

"I did *not* say that. I just think it's pointless to try to sugarcoat what is a perfectly dreadful calamity. Good. You're not crying anymore."

Sherwin lay in his bed, staring at the television, both arms in casts, with a bandage on the side of his face. "Don't talk about me," he said, "because I can hear now."

Stella hugged him gently. "We brought kreplach," she said.

"I hate kreplach."

"I know. I wanted you to feel at home."

Sherwin chuckled. "Harvey called, but that was before I could hear well. One of the nurses had to act as a go-between. Bertie called too. He's setting up some kind of trust for me. Did you ask him to do that?"

His parents shook their heads.

"What came over him?"

"You mother told him he had his head up his ass."

"It takes an earth-shaking catastrophe for someone in this family to tell someone else the truth," Sherwin said.

"I wouldn't say that," Stella corrected. "We've been telling Bertie the truth one way or another for twenty years. Your father here blames Bertie's astronomical selfishness on his bar mitzvah."

"Definitely a trauma," Sherwin said. "But still no excuse." He paused, then spoke quietly. "I really like the doctors here and the ones back in Iraq. I've decided to go to college and medical school. Do you think you could request an application from Johns Hopkins?"

"Consider it done," Stella said.

Eight

In the fall of 2000, Chandra and Paul entered the University of Maryland at College Park. They roomed together in a large, crowded dorm, site of numerous parties and far-into-the-night bashes. They enjoyed the social life, but did not let it overwhelm their academic purpose. Within weeks Paul had a girlfriend, Megan, and so was away from the room a bit. For both of them that cubicle they shared was an anchor into their old life, a reminder that their friendship dated to elementary school and was rooted in a larger agglomeration that numbered eight.

They did not find the campus particularly endearing. Traveling around on foot was tiresome, due to its vast quads and mammoth buildings. But moving one's car from its precious parking space was not worth it. They returned home often on weekends, and the drive back on Sunday, down Route 1, left a sour aftertaste, because it was what Route 1 is anywhere, ticky tacky and hideous – cheap motels, fast food restaurants, with the occasional quaint car dealership tucked in between run-down strip malls. Traffic clotted up on Route 1 and even late Sunday was bumper to bumper. The one time Clarence Jones drove down there to pick up his son, he became so frazzled he nearly had apoplexy. With vehicles at a full stop, stretched out as far as the eye could see like a titanic parking lot, the traffic lights going through their mismatched cycles and not a car budging, he started screaming: "Somebody just get out your gun and shoot out that light. It's goddamned useless." He arrived at the dorm nearly foaming at the mouth, avowing an intention to make the numbskulls at the DOT suffer renewed assaults in the form of numerous, furious epistles.

"That traffic was backed up for miles," he hollered.

"Well, I guess I better be going now," Jones sighed to Chandra and Paul.

"They don't have light timers in Maryland. They have astrologers."

"Astrologers?" Chandra asked.

"The lights are on an astrological system," Clarence fumed. "Is that Route 1 like this all the time?"

"Every day of the week, ever hour of the day," Paul enlightened him.

"Then excuse me, but I'm never coming here again. Donald, you'll have to take the bus."

"What bus? There is no bus."

"Then you'll have to be creative, because those knuckleheads at the DOT who can't answer one lousy goddamned letter or phone call are not getting the satisfaction of me having a seizure and expiring in traffic that their incompetence, stupidity, idiocy and all around laziness has made the worst on the East Coast. They're not getting that satisfaction, Donny!"

"The thought of spending my last minutes on earth on Route 1 is appalling," Chandra averred.

"I tell you, when that tractor trailer ahead of me came to a dead halt, my life passed before my eyes. And I was stuck in traffic so long," Clarence embellished, "it passed before my eyes twice."

Chandra and Paul admitted a mild fascination for the ugliness of Route 1. Occasionally they would patronize a McDonald's there and always marvel at the misbegotten, dusty, dirty conglomeration of strip malls. They explored Prince George's county where the university was located and found much of it equally unlovely.

"It's just one big sprawling Jiffy Lube, Pep Boys, KFC, check cashing joint and pawn shop after another," Paul said. "Every part of the county seems designed for maximum ugliness."

"Maximum profit, you mean," Chandra replied. "Somebody had to make money off this. They got their zoning, put up their strip mall, took the easy cash and ran, leaving behind boarded-up shops, sprawling car dealerships, the occasional strip joint and big abandoned buildings, like a pile of turds."

The campus, though not gorgeous, was far more tolerable than the environs. They especially liked the main library, where they passed many hours studying. The stacks were quiet and endless and a cool refuge in September. On days that were not beastly hot, students lay about on the main quadrangle, like college students everywhere, reading, talking, eating and playing Frisbee. It was thus one afternoon, when birds chirped in the trees, the rare butterfly fluttered about and the sun beamed down through bright cool air from its spot in a cerulean heaven that rolled out dazzlingly in all directions, dotted here and there by a little fluff of white or silver.

Megan, a business major like Chandra, had decided to focus on accounting. She was a most practical young woman, whose grade point average and very high SAT scores had got her a full scholarship and entrance to the honors program. She lived in the honors dorm with, as she put it, the other nerds. She considered Paul's major in engineering sensible, but worried about the jobs going to foreigners on temporary visas who could be paid less, and so urged him to double major in economics. That way, if he could not get an engineering position, he could work for a large investment banking firm and make pots of money.

"Pots?" Paul asked, sipping his coffee and doodling on the paper where he was supposed to be solving an equation.

"I have a friend whose older brother graduated in econ and went to work for J.P. Morgan in Manhattan. You wouldn't believe how much he makes."

"Paul here could always take over his father's business," Chandra put in. "It's a very successful chain."

"That's a good fall back," Magan said. "But the real money is with the firms I mentioned."

"Well, it's still only freshman year," Paul began, hemming and hawing a bit, more than a little bedizened by Megan's long blond hair gleaming gold in the sun and how pretty she looked in her capris and tank top.

"It's never too early to plan for the job market," Megan corrected him.

Chandra stretched out on the grass, an open textbook over his face. "The job market," he groaned. "I don't want to think about it."

"You'll have nothing to worry about, with an MBA," Megan said. "I just hope I can get into a big accounting firm."

"Of course you will," Paul encouraged, unable to conceive of anyone who, under any circumstances, would turn such a one as Megan down, and thinking that if it was up to him, he would hire her in an instant and then musing that that was probably why it was not up to him. Big accounting firms doubtless had sound criteria other than pretty blue eyes and a breathtaking smile. As he lay in the fragrance of the fresh-mown grass, gazing into the azure empyrean, however, he suddenly did not want to do anything, not economics, not engineering, not even helping his father run his business. It all seemed remote and unimportant. He wanted to get in his car and drive north and west into the densely forested Catoctin Mountains. There was a lake up there, surrounded by a thin strip of beach, overhung by the dark green of trees, and paths through the woods full of deer, raccoons and, some said, bears. He suddenly longed for the cool stillness and peace that could, he believed, only be found in the great deciduous forest, or what was left of it in the Northeast. He and Kevin had hiked the Appalachian

Trail, they had climbed the White Mountains in New Hampshire and the Green Mountains in Vermont; they had wandered wooded tracks to the Canadian border. There was a solace in that wilderness that existed nowhere else, balm for the injury of deformed strip malls and endless traffic. He thought of the shadows in the forest by that sparkling lake in the Catoctins, of the sun dappling the leaves and piercing the wild gloom here and there, of the sounds that emerged, like an orchestra tuning up, when one stood still and silent long enough, the sounds of life, other life, not human, and he longed to hear it. He turned his head into the grass, inhaled, then gazed up through the treetops, the shifting net of green leaves, sapphire sky and golden sunlight and decided to go into the mountains with Kevin that weekend. He wanted to lose himself in the forest. "Only two more days," he murmured.

"Two more days 'til what?" Megan asked.

"'Til I go to the Catoctins."

"What for?"

He rolled on his side and looked at her, something slightly harsh and critical lurking beneath his conscious thought. Then he ripped up some grass and, laughing, threw it at her. "What for? What do you think?"

"To escape, perchance, this beautiful metro area?" She asked.

"You can come too."

"Not if I want to ace my test on Monday."

Paul took out his cell phone, called Kevin at work. "Let's bring Harry and Animal too," Kevin suggested. "I already said I'd get together with them this weekend."

"Me too," Chandra said.

"You?" Paul laughed. "I've never heard the slightest interest in nature from you."

"That trip over to Route 1 yesterday got under my skin. I could use some green, lots of green."

The afternoon drifted on. Studying on the quadrangle was followed by class, and despite daydreams about the glories of foliage and fauna in the Catoctins, Paul somehow managed to concentrate on the lecture. He turned in his homework, took notes, even asked a few questions, but all the while he seemed to see the silver sheen of the lake, surrounded by woods, isolated in the lonely mountains. It glimmered between the trees, beckoned with serene hints of quiet and solitude.

That evening, after studying with Chandra in their room, Paul closed his book and went out to ramble around the campus. It was dark, and the area had the reputation of being a bit dangerous, but he did not mind. He tramped past the huge, darkened, muffled forms of classroom buildings, over to the library, in whose entrance, a little island of light, students still came and went. He ambled in the shadows under the trees and gazed up into the night sky, black but spangled with the luminous white of stars and thought that he would like to live like a hermit, deep within a dark forest, where the clamor of civilization was only a memory.

Again he smelled the fresh-cut grass, the damp earth, the mulch in the occasional plantings. He wandered slowly back to his dorm, musing idly about transferring to the University of Vermont and wondering if that plan would appeal to Megan, who was not completely immune to the charms of nature. Unfortunately for her, they were a distant second, third or fourth to other more practical matters.

On Saturday morning at six thirty a.m., Animal, Kevin and Harry arrived at the dorm in Isabelle's minivan. It took a while to get going, but finally Paul and Chandra sleepily tossed Sandy's soccer gear off the back seat and settled in for the ride up Route 270 past Frederick. Even at that hour on an early weekend morning, the highway was filled to capacity.

"Where are they all going at this hour?" Harry asked. He sat in the front passenger seat, drinking a bottled ice tea and frowning at the vehicles around him. Animal drove and softly cursed the congestion. "They're going north?" Harry asked. "What's north? Nothing. If we get stuck in a traffic jam, I may lose it."

"You sound like Jones' father," Paul said. "Maybe you'll write a letter to the DOT."

"No I won't," Harry snapped. "Because they'll just use it as an excuse to build the Inter-County Connector. That's all we need – another eight-lane superhighway, tearing across the middle of the state, more cars, more pollution, more development – as if there's an inch left to develop – and within five years it'll be so crowded you'll be lucky if you can do twenty miles an hour at rush hour. Then they'll talk about toll lanes. As if tollbooths ever speeded anything up. All they do is congest traffic. No. What this region needs is massive expansion of the D.C. Metro. Everybody loves the metro. Every chance I get, I drive down to New Carrollton, park the car and ride it around the city. It's clean, it's quiet, everybody pretty much behaves, and it takes thousands upon thousands of cars off the road."

"Quit Best Buy," Animal said. "You have a career in traffic planning."

"I've read about this on the internet," Harry went on, smoothing back his light brown hair. "There are proposals to expand the metro in several directions, in Virginia, in Maryland. Why not just extend it so far north that it goes past where they want to put the ICC?"

"Money would be the answer to that, I bet," Animal replied.

They drove on, well below the speed limit, with Harry and Animal discussing mass transit and the other three napping. Up past Germantown, traffic picked up. They flew past Frederick, and soon the low, rolling deep green of the foothills was visible. Animal woke everyone by shouting that it was time to hear their very simple agenda: hiking, eating the sandwiches in the cooler, then swimming in the lake to refresh themselves. As they had decided not to camp overnight, they had considerably less gear than on other excursions.

Soon they turned off the highway and followed a winding road uphill through the forest. Fortunately Animal drove slowly enough that he was able to stop for three deer, meandering across the road. The sky, where visible from the black ribbon of road, was silver gray, with big patches of blue. The trees had not yet begun to change color, so everywhere lay a dense blanket of green.

"Not a car dealership in sight," Paul said.

They drove to a small parking lot deep in the woods, left the minivan in the shade, locked it and walked down to inspect the lake, deserted at this hour, with a snapping turtle clambering on some rocks. The cries of birds echoed over the water. Somewhere an animal rustled in the woods, while a faint breeze tossed the treetops. Over the entire place hung the solitary atmosphere of the prehistoric. As they turned to begin their hike, no one said a word.

They traveled through forest for an hour and a half, until they reached a river. There they stopped, as always, and looked at the frogs under the logs and watched for fish in the water. A raccoon ambled down the riverbank to drink, and Animal was convinced he found a bear track. They sat on the rocks, dangling their feet in the pools, as Harry complained about the paucity of fossils in the mountains.

"If we had an expert, like Bradley, he'd know where to look," Animal said.

They stretched out on the rocks and stared up at the strip of blue between two green rows of treetops, lining the river. A slight breeze

cooled their sweaty faces and made the daisies on the bank sway
gracefully.

"We should have brought our fishing gear," Chandra lamented.

"Not today," Animal replied. "We're not going to be here long
enough."

"I could *live* here," Paul averred. Kevin agreed. They had discussed
the house-in-the-forest fantasy before.

Upstream the raccoon had lumbered back into the woods, replaced
by an opossum, gray and ugly. It too soon vanished in the foliage.
Chandra watched it. "Think," he said, "two hundred years ago, there
were bears here, bobcats, moose, otter and wolves."

"Up in New England, in the forest that borders Canada, some say the
wolves are coming back," Paul said. "But all they have to do is kill one
cow, and that's that. People will hunt them right out of the region."

"Think about it," Chandra went on. "A vast wilderness in which
there were wolves, the animal with the strongest parental instincts on the
planet. Those creatures are marvels. Did you know –"

"We all saw the same nature program," Paul said. "Look, I think
they're fantastic. But they're not coming back. A certain two-legged
species with guns rules the world now and probably won't stop eating up
space 'til there's nothing but McDonald's and Wal-Mart left everywhere
on the globe. The wolves are doomed."

They lay for a while in melancholy meditation on the extinction of
large, magnificent predators in particular and nature in general.

"At least there are some places left," Chandra murmured, as they rose
to leave. "Places like this."

"It's a state park," Paul said. "And you better believe somebody had to
fight for every inch of it."

They returned by the same route, through dense forest, until the
undergrowth thinned, and they entered a grove of tall pines, the gloom
pierced here and there by shafts of sunlight with dust sifting through
the yellow beams. In the distance, a flash of silver revealed the proximity
of the lake. But they stopped at the car first, took out the cooler and
then settled at a picnic table in the shadows amid the pines. It was only
a little past eleven, but the walk had made them hungry. They ate their
ham, chicken or turkey sandwiches ravenously and slurped down whole
containers of Gatorade. All wore swim trunks under their clothes,
so they stripped down to those and hurried over to the beach. A few

families sat in chairs, watching small children gambol in the sand. It still looked like a small lake, left by a glacier, in a primeval forest.

"Maybe there could be wolves again," Chandra said. "I hope so."

For a long time, vague thoughts about wolves mingled in his mind with his impressions of the forest. He recalled images from the television special he had watched, of armed men in helicopters hunting down wolves over white, snow-covered, shelterless expanses in Canada and Alaska, and some of this found its way into his dreams. He would awaken with a start in his little dorm room, to hear Paul snoring in the bunk below and would slowly come to realize that he was not standing in the woods, watching the silhouettes of wolves as they crossed a moonlit ridge. "They belong to another world now," someone had been saying to him in the dream. "Another reality." And he woke with that phrase in his mouth. If only they did belong to another reality, he thought, and not just to oblivion.

After September 11, 2001, Chandra did not delay. He enlisted the next morning. Luckily his father had taken out tuition insurance, so his less than wealthy family was able to get his fall semester tuition refunded.

"But your education!" Sara exclaimed. "Your education!"

"It can wait," Chandra replied. "Sometimes you have to stop what you're doing because something else, something so important comes first, over everything. I'll be in the army a couple of years."

"But then you won't get your PhD until you're in your late twenties."

"I won't get it ever. I'm going for an MBA, remember? People with MBAs go and work for corporations. They don't stay in academe."

Sara wrung her hands. "Some people with PhDs work outside the academy. Look at your father."

"He works for the state department of education. That's hardly big business."

Chandra was soon off to basic training. Like his friends, he expected to go to Afghanistan to fight Al Qaeda. But he was surprised. In the spring of 2003, he was on the way to Iraq. Shortly after that, he found himself cooped up in a Bradley, rolling through the suburbs of Baghdad, with rocket fire all around.

"Out," Sergeant Delany shouted. "Everyone out the back now."

They all literally rolled out onto the ground. So did Chandra, who discovered he was being fired on from a little row of trees along a drainage ditch. He shot back and so did his buddies. They fired so many rounds, the saplings just fell over. After a little while, there was no more gunfire. In the distance came the occasional explosion of a rocket-launched grenade.

"Patel, you're with me," Sergeant Delany began advancing to the trees, taking cover where he could. Nothing moved. Chandra dashed from behind a car to the safety of a wall. Still not even a shot. They were close now and could see right into the trees. A few lifeless forms lay sprawled on the ground. They got closer. There was no one left alive, just three dead Iraqis with AK-47s and three young, unarmed Iraqi women.

"We killed those girls," Chandra said.

"They fired on us," Delany replied. "What were we supposed to do? It's called self-defense."

Nonetheless Chandra discerned that Delany felt as he did – very bad about it. They returned to the Bradley. The rest of the squad had spread out in the other direction and was taking fire. "Did you get them?" One soldier asked Chandra.

"Yeah, and a bunch of teenage girls," Chandra said. "I just killed three 15 year olds."

"And three adults with machine guns," Delany put in, "who were doing their best to kill you."

That night, as he slept on his cot, Chandra dreamt he flew in a helicopter, shooting at wolves as they fled across the frozen tundra. He awoke with a start, ran a hand over his sweating face and murmured, "I didn't sign on for this, not for shooting young women and girls." The room was full of the sound of snoring. Nobody heard him. Nobody ever did. Night after night, for quite a while, he flew in the helicopter, shooting the magnificent and terrified wolves. Night after night, he awoke with words about those young women on his lips. Then, for no reason that he could see, it all passed.

Delany also planned to get an MBA when he left the army. He and Chandra had much in common and became friends. Chandra never mentioned the three dead girls again, because Delany made it abundantly clear that he never wanted to talk about it or hear about it. Instead they concentrated on their mission, which was fighting their way through the suburbs of Baghdad.

One morning they pursued gunmen into a warren of little streets. Chandra and his platoon mates kicked down the door of a house they thought a sniper had fled into. The house was empty, but inside on the floor of the main room lay a heap of weaponry – machine guns, rocket launchers, grenades, small firearms. They heard noise above and gave

chase. On the stairs, however, the soldier in front of Chandra, a twenty
year old from Delaware, collapsed in a pool of blood, shot twice in the
chest. "Medic!" Chandra screamed, bending over the wounded man.
Somebody passed him some gauze, with which he tried to stop the
bleeding. He heard someone else calling for backup, calling for medics.
Delany and the rest pursued the gunman to the roof, where they shot
him.

The eyes of the wounded soldier filmed over. "Tell Marianne," he
started to say, then passed out. Chandra sat there, with the dying man
in his arms, soaked in his blood. By the time the medics arrived, he
was holding a corpse. He staggered away, down the stairs, back into the
main room where now a group of officers clucked triumphantly over the
weapons cache. He lurched out into the street and nearly tripped over
the crumpled body of the sniper, who had fallen off the roof. The man
lay on his side, his stare riveted forever on the dust of the street.

"You look terrible," Delany said, approaching.

"That kid Matthew from Delaware just died in my arms."

Delany poked a toe at the corpse. "That's the last American he'll ever
kill."

"Matthew said something about his girlfriend. Those were his last
words."

Delany shook his head in sorrow and lit a cigarette.

"He looked like chalk," Chandra went on, "so pale and so white.
And he didn't even fight it. He just...gave up." He paused and gazed
down the empty street. "My mother," he began, "had a great dream for
me. She wanted me to get a PhD and be a professor at an Ivy League
college. This MBA means nothing to her. If I go like Matthew, I'd like
you to convey a white lie – that I had decided she was right and was
planning to get a PhD."

"Wouldn't that make her feel worse?"

"I don't think so. She would take it as proof of love."

"And if you come out of this, which you will, what then? A PhD?"

"Are you kidding? I'll get the MBA and go work for Exxon."

They laughed, and Delany smoked and for a long time afterward the
disjunction of it – the corpse at his feet, his body soaked in Matthew's
blood and the laughter and the cigarette – haunted him, came into his
mind at odd moments, when he walked through suburban Baghdad,
his gun in his hands, or riding in the Bradley, or dining on a ready-to-
eat meal. He would think of death and laughter so close to each other,

and an unaccountable despair would wash over him, a feeling that what
he had become here, as a soldier, would be inalterable, immutable,
something he really would not have chosen had he known, something he
would always regard with regret. Then he would shake it off and go joke
with Delany. But in the back of his mind, the question nagged, "What's
wrong with me? What am I worried about? And what am I worried about
if I don't worry?"

It seemed that he lost either way. He tried to express this to Delany,
but botched it. Somehow though, his sergeant got the idea. "You're
worried about killing people. Then you do it more and more, and you
stop worrying. Then you're afraid you've become some kind of killing
machine. Am I right?"

Chandra nodded.

"Welcome to the army. Welcome to war."

Chandra kept hoping that the actual fighting would abate. It did not.
It seemed that every day he was shot at and shot back." Sometimes it
seems like I kill someone every day," he said to Delany.

"Better them than you," his sergeant and good friend replied.

After a while he became numb to it. Unlike some of the other
soldiers, who found a kind of romance in the military, who only truly felt
alive when bombs were bursting around them and they were exchanging
gunfire with the enemy, Chandra saw it all as a sorry, miserable war,
whose point eluded him. His duty, however, remained clear, and he was
a sharp, efficient soldier.

One morning, his back to the Bradley, with no other cover available,
he killed three men before they got a shot at anyone in his platoon. His
buddies cheered him but then the shooting began again, and he gave
chase. Delany and three others sprinted ahead of him and pursued the
shooters into a building and up on to a roof. Chandra was pinned in
a doorway, exchanging fire with a man down the street, who he finally
managed to kill. When the man fell over, Chandra lowered his gun, took
off his helmet and wiped his sopping forehead. "Thank God that's over,"
he said.

He heard more gunfire from above. A body fell off the top of the
building and landed face up at his feet. It was Delany, shot many times in
the chest and the abdomen, his dead, blue eyes gazing up and reflecting
the gorgeous but indifferent azure of the heavens, a color, Chandra
knew, he would never forget as long as he lived.

Chandra made only the barest mention of his friend's death in an email to his mother: "Sergeant Delany died today. It was awful." This worried Sara, who gathered from her son's communications and from news reports that a lot of Americans were being killed and that Chandra had seen his fair share of it. He was in constant danger, about which she could do nothing. She felt helpless, powerless and frantic. So did Rajit, who retreated into silence and his newspaper.

"There's news from Chandra," she said, turning away from the computer to regard her husband, seated in a large, comfortable armchair, his legs on a footstool, the newspaper open before him. Rajit folded up his paper, rose and came to look.

"Delany," he said. "That was pretty much his closest friend in Iraq."

` Sara nodded.

"To this day," Rajit went on, "I will never understand why he enlisted. He thought he was going to fight Al Qaeda. Well, hasn't he had a lesson in the absurdity of politics? Iraq had nothing to do with September 11, but there he is, knee-deep in carnage, risking his life, for what? We came to the United States for this?" He stalked back to his armchair, as if this sudden, uncharacteristic outburst had surprised him as much as his wife, reopened his newspaper and resumed reading.

Quite by design, Chandra had not discussed his plan to enlist with his parents. He presented them with a fait accompli. When he did, his mother went to pieces. "How could you?" Sara demanded. "You don't know where you'll be sent. You could be killed." She had tried vainly at first to see if there was any way to undo this decision. Chandra assured her it was impossible. Then she had launched the most useless argument of all, that he was delaying his education by years. If he did decide to get a PhD – "I won't," Chandra assured her – he would be old by the time he finished. She harped on her various objections until he left for basic training, at which point she became so anxious, she could no longer sleep and so started seeing a therapist in Annapolis, Dr. Greta Wayland, who sought to convince her that there was little she could do and to accept it.

"You tell me I'm useless, powerless to make any difference?"

"He's a grown man."

"He's not even twenty. And he has the mental age of a fifteen year old."

"Are you sure about that?"

"No. But he doesn't seem very mature to me."

"On the bright side, this military experience may mature him."

"It may kill him."

Dr. Wayland nodded. "That's your biggest fear," she rather obviously said.

"Of course it is. And my second biggest is that he'll be maimed. And next that he will see and do horrible things that will alter him forever."

"There are therapies for Post Traumatic Stress Disorder. But not all soldiers suffer from it by any means. Some are, strangely, immune."

"That is not reassuring. For Chandra to be immune to the horrors of war, well, he would have to be some kind of moral cipher. That would almost be worse than traumatic stress. There's no way around it: I lost on September 12, when he signed up."

Dr. Wayland prescribed sleep medication, antidepressants and tranquillizers, only if the anxiety became acute. She also suggested that Sara immerse herself in her art, that she should resume painting in her small studio at home. And so, high on her little cocktail of medicines, Sara would stand at the easel, producing paintings, sometimes two a day.

"What's that?" Rajit demanded late one afternoon after work.

"Chandra, of course."

"It looks like an insect eating a flower. It looks nothing like Chandra."

"It's abstract art."

"Hmmph." And he stalked off to read his newspaper.

"Don't pretend to be a philistine," she called after him. "You know very well what abstract art is."

"I know what Chandra looks like," he called back. "And it's not that painting."

Despite such criticism, Sara labored on and found some relief in the activity. Then, one day, she saw a news report on television about young, wounded soldiers returning home. "I've decided to volunteer at Walter Reed Hospital," she told her husband.

He put down his newspaper. "You honestly think that will help you stop worrying?"

"It may. But more importantly it may do some good for people who have gone through what Chandra's going through. Not a lot. Just on the weekends."

She volunteered for two months. Though the work was valuable and her help greatly appreciated, the dreadful wounds she saw, the lives broken by war, renewed her fears for her son. She quit upon the news of his imminent return. Intuitively she understood that she would need all her energy now for him.

That insight could not have proved more correct. Chandra was a different person. He slept on the floor on a sleeping bag, drank beer, lost his temper over the most unaccountable things. He planned to delay his return to college.

"Not too long, I hope," Sara remarked.

"Maybe forever," was his curt reply.

Mostly he lay on the living room couch all day and watched television. He yelled at the commentators when they reported on the Iraq war. On the weekends he spent time with Jones, who advised him to see a therapist. Then came the news of Luis' death.

Chandra was either silent or drunk after that. All he would mumble was the chant, "Harry, Kevin, Delany, Luis. What the fuck for?" He did manage to sober up to visit the Ignacios with Jones, but afterward he disappeared for two days. The Patels were frantic. When he finally turned up, haggard and unshaven on the front doorstep, his first words were: "Mom, I think I'll take you up on that Dr. Wayland offer."

So he started therapy, the first session setting the tone: he found himself shouting at a rather retiring but excessively understanding, middle-aged woman. The he would apologize. Then she would ignore his apology with the words, "that's what I'm here for." Dr. Wayland also tried to get him psychiatric help through the military, through Walter Reed Hospital. But for some arcane reason, the red tape was insurmountable.

"PTSD is really one of the dirty little secrets of war," she told Chandra. "The army does not like to acknowledge it. At the rate we're going, we'll have psychiatric help for you from the military in time for your sixtieth birthday." Chandra stayed in therapy for a year before he re-entered college, and he continued it throughout his entire undergraduate career. It helped him get through the day, but nothing helped with the nights.

Over and over he woke up in the deep of the night, at two thirty or three a.m., sweating and screaming about Delany, dead in front of him, or Matthew, bleeding to death in his arms. Sara would hear his yells and pad out in her slippers and bathrobe to the living room.

"Shh, shh, you're home," she would say. "You're not in Baghdad. Delany and Matthew have been gone a long time." And she would gently grasp her son's arm and shake him a bit, to try to jog him back to reality.

"Did you see his eyes?" Chandra asked.

"He is not here, Chandra. He is dead. He died in Baghdad. There was nothing you could do."

"And those young women behind the trees."

"They were with armed men who tried to kill you. You had to shoot back."

"I was at Harry's the other day, just to chat with Mrs. Sullivan. We reminisced. A friend was over, with her teenage daughter – I couldn't stop thinking about her and the Iraqi girls behind the trees. Whenever I see teenage girls that age, I think about them, lying still on the blood-soaked ground."

Sara would soothe him, bring him a glass of water and a sleeping pill. Then, as he drifted off, he would hear her words, full of unreality yet strangely calming: "Forget about Iraq. Think about your life before it. There are things you did that it can never touch. Go back, to high school, when you were so happy with your friends. Remember that. We only have what we remember. Don't let the worst blot out the best. Remember your days with your friends..."

Sara drove home from work every day with the same hopeful image before her mind's eye: a note from Chandra on the kitchen table that said he had gone over to the University of Maryland, to register for classes next semester. Instead, every day, she found her son lying on the couch, watching television, the day's detritus – dirty dishes, juice bottles, the newspaper – scattered on the coffee table. Often he was still in his boxers. She could only guess what time he woke up. When she asked, he always replied: "Oh, sometime around noon."

When she inquired about anything, she got the same reply: "My life just dissolved. Unless you've got a magic wand, I don't know how we're going to get it back." Dr. Wayland prescribed antidepressants.

After months of what Rajit called "destructive loafing," Chandra began to read books again. At first he read war novels, and he read slowly, sometimes just a few pages a day. But soon he picked up speed and branched out. Sometimes Sara came home to find a note to the effect that Chandra was at the library. Sometimes she arrived home to find him sprawled on the couch, reading, with a stack of shiny, mylar-covered library books nearby.

One thing he never let lapse – his email communications with Animal, Sherwin and Paul, still in Iraq. His parents heard him tapping on the computer keyboard, far into the night, when the house lay in shadow except for the computer corner with its little desk lamp; while the neighborhood slept in darkness, Rajit and Sara drifted off to the sound of clicking, faint lonely noises in the vast ocean of night. Sometimes it stopped for a while, and the sudden silence woke Sara, who wandered into the living room in her long, white nightgown, just in time to hear the soft, musical ring of an instant message, a notice that across the world a friend was still at war, but had a moment to himself; above all it was a tiny signal through the immensity of space, the sea of oblivion in which the world hung suspended, that he, that old friend, that very young soldier, was still alive.

That little sound always stopped her. She would pause, loath to interrupt something so distant and tenuous but momentous, would turn instead and drift, the white of her nightgown somehow luminous in the shaded house, back to bed.

Like clockwork, Jones appeared every Saturday. He arrived at eleven a.m., while Chandra still snored on the floor on top of the sleeping bag and shook him 'til he woke. Cursing, Chandra always turned on his side, his back to the room, and pulled the beach towel he used as a blanket over his head.

"Rise and shine, Chandra Patel. You have an appointment today," Jones said after several months.

"Appointment?" Chandra snapped. "What goddamned appointment?"

"A meeting of Iraq veterans against the war, over in Montgomery County at one thirty p.m."

"Who said I'm against the war?"

"Every molecule of your being except your mouth says it."

"Hogwash."

"I don't see you signing up for another tour."

"You don't see me foaming at the mouth like a demented psychopath either."

"I couldn't have said it better."

"Just because I don't relish the thought of going back to a dusty, dirty, sewage-filled megacity, where religious fanatics try day and night to kill me, doesn't mean I'm a pacifist."

"Who said these guys are pacifists? They know some wars have to be fought. Just not this war."

Chandra flipped over to his other side angrily. "You name me a war, any war, that you believe had to be fought. I don't think, in all honesty, you can do it."

"Wrong. World War II – the global war against fascism. I would have enlisted then."

"You would have been drafted and if not, I doubt you'd have enlisted."

Jones sighed. "You're too ornery to be believed. So I'm not going to argue. If you don't get dressed, I'll take you to this confab as you are."

Grumbling, cursing and glowering at his best friend, Chandra staggered off to the bathroom to wash. Later, groomed and dressed, he went out to Jones' father's pickup. "Just this once," he warned, but in fact, after that first time, he attended regularly. He emailed Paul about it, but Paul replied simply, "I just can't see it."

Paul had not volunteered at once. Unlike Chandra, he and his father had not taken out tuition insurance, and Paul did not feel right throwing the money away. So he finished the fall semester in 2001. By then everyone expected the war in Afghanistan to be the main front against terrorism. So, the tuition had not been wasted, and he was free to enlist. He had his doubts about Megan, though. They were engaged. She said she would wait for him, but somehow he did not believe it. Then he would chastise himself for his lack of faith in her, wondering what she had done to deserve this doubt. "Nothing," he said to himself. "It's just me, me and my tedious, cynical view of human nature. She says she'll wait. I'll take her at her word."

Paul spent the weekend before he deployed to Iraq in the house he had grown up in, with Megan and Angelo. Megan had visited their comfortable Cape Cod before, but had never viewed the entire domicile. Angelo gave her the tour. "This is Pauli's room," he explained, opening one of the two doors on the second floor, "you can tell by the mess." Clothing and books covered the floor. The bed looked like a tornado had hit it.

"I never knew you were such a slob," she giggled.

"Thanks for the help, Dad."

"I just want Megan to know what she's getting into, marrying you. I expect her to slap you into shape."

"Now show her your room."

"You see," Angelo said, opening the other door, "slovenliness runs in the family."

Angelo then showed her the living, dining and family rooms, and kitchen downstairs, and the rec room, bedroom and storage area in the basement.

"Geez Dad, she's not here to buy the place," Paul said. "And besides, she saw the main floor before."

"This is where Pauli has lived since he was born," Angelo explained. "And if you two want to live here when you get married, it's fine. You can see there's plenty of room."

Enlightened now as to his father's motive behind the grand tour, Paul directed everyone back to the family room. Golf was on the TV. Megan averred that she liked golf, so Paul made sure she was comfortable and then dragged his loquacious parent into the kitchen.

"What are you, crazy?" He demanded of his father. "Every two minutes you mention getting married."

"It's a big deal. I can hardly believe it."

"Well you won't have to at this rate. You'll scare her off."

"I've said it before Pauli, she looks like a model. Lots of guys will be after her. You should have gotten married before you deployed."

"Thanks for the faith in us."

"You're worried about it, too," Angelo pointed an index finger at the edge of each eye. "These eyes see everything."

"Just don't mention the nose."

"Have I said one word about that? Even though she uses Dove soap and is wearing Tea Rose perfume."

"Keep it to yourself."

"I notice she's wearing the ring."

"You made a good choice, Dad. She really likes it."

"Don't underestimate your father. I have another good idea."

Paul tried not to look too skeptical.

"We arrange today for me to meet her parents, Mr. and Mrs. Crutcher, while you're away, to kind of, of," Angelo made a rotating motion with his hands, "strengthen the bonds."

Paul had to admit, the idea was not half bad. He of course had met Megan's parents many times and was sure they regarded him favorably. Bringing his father into things would make their commitment more official. It was another way to strengthen the memory of Paul in her mind, while he was away. "Not bad," he said aloud, as he poured a glass of ice tea for Megan. He added a good bit of sugar.

"See," Angelo said, twirling an index finger in the air around his ear. "The wheels have been turning."

"Don't make that gesture," Paul said, "or people will think something else is turning."

"What else?"

"Your sanity. It looks like you're indicating you're psycho."

"Who's going to see? It's just us. And you know I'm perfectly normal."

Rolling his eyes, Paul brought the beverage into the family room. Megan lounged on the two-seater sofa, in impeccable jeans, designer heels and a University of Maryland sweatshirt, her casual weekend wear, as she had explained to Paul that morning.

"My Dad," Paul began, sitting next to her and handing her the overly sweetened potation, "would like to know if he could meet your parents sometime soon."

Megan considered this a "fantastic" idea, so Paul continued by requesting that she arange it, since he would be away.

"What about in two weekends?" She asked Angelo, who had entered the room at the tail end of this discussion. "We'll go to a restaurant."

Paul became a little nervous at the thought of all the aromas in an eatery, but decided to give his father a stern talking-to on the matter of behavior and which subjects were verboten before he left.

They passed the remainder of the day watching various sporting events on television and chatting about the future. After Paul and Megan went out to dinner, he returned home to find Angelo, glumly eating take-out ravioli from Luigi's, by himself in the kitchen.

"I meant what I said," Angelo began at once, without a greeting. "You and Megan can live here, have children here, if you want. I won't be in your way."

"I appreciate that."

Angelo dropped his fork on his plate and pushed his chair back. "Tell me what did I do wrong? What did I do to make you volunteer to join the army? Did I *ever* say I wanted anything like that?"

"It had nothing to do with you, Dad. It was September 11. This is just something I have to do."

"What? Because all your friends go like lemmings, plunging over the cliff, you've got to jump too? What about Jones? He's not going."

"You know very well Jones and I don't see eye to eye on many issues."

"Oh yes, because he's an atheist. He's also rational. He uses his common sense. He knows better than to go signing his life away to a military that could get him killed in no time and not think twice about it."

"Dad, it's over. We've had this discussion twenty times. I leave tomorrow. Let's try to keep it pleasant."

When they parted the next afternoon, Angelo said: "I'm proud of you, Pauli. But I'm worried too." He smiled and clapped his son on the back, but there was a tear in his eye.

Paul saw action from the moment he set foot in Iraq. He rode in a tank that took repeated rocket fire. He was shot at and shot back, pursuing snipers into buildings and onto roofs. He saw comrades gunned down next to him. In Baqubah, he, his buddy Greg Angelli from Virginia and a third soldier from New York were trapped behind a retaining wall, as bullets zinged overhead. One by one, shooting at the snipers, they crossed an open street into the safety of a group of low, brown houses. But they were still taking fire and could not determine where it came from. At last Paul spotted a figure on a nearby roof, armed with an AK-47. He shot him, but not before a bullet from the sniper killed the kid from New York, standing right next to him. One moment the soldier was there, the next he had slumped down, with a bullet hole in his forehead.

Paul liked the discipline of the military, the esprit de corps, the routines, the chaplain, everything. It reminded him in some impalpable way of the Catholic Church. Maybe, he thought, his father was right, and he had never met a large authoritarian institution he disliked. But he did not like seeing his friends killed and wounded. And he did not particularly enjoy killing the enemy, like many of the soldiers he got to know. Some of them went absolutely wild when they slaughtered insurgents, with war whoops, dancing around, pumping the air with their fists. But not Paul. He would wonder about the person he had just killed, if he had a family, whether he had always been a "bad guy," by which he vaguely meant one of Saddam Hussein's own. He never hesitated to kill the enemy, and he never ran from a fight. On the contrary, he was often out in front, but every day, when he was done killing, he would sit by himself and think of God's injunction not to kill and would pray silently, and completely unobtrusively, for forgiveness. Only Greg knew he did this.

He took part in the assault on Falluja, an attack that convinced him that no matter how good he was at the business of soldiering, he was not cut out for war. He and Greg and several other infantry advanced into the town behind the cover of a tank. They had heard that some Americans had been killed and their bodies desecrated. Everyone was horrified and furious. Everyone wanted revenge, especially the officer in the tank. Paul saw the bodies hanging from a bridge and so, evidently, did the officer. An operation to retrieve the corpses was under way, but those soldiers were being fired upon from the rooftop of a low, small, nearby building. In a very short time, fire from the tank's main gun destroyed the house. It blasted out the first floor, then, when it hit the second, it also obviously detonated a weapons cache, because the explosion was tremendous. Bodies flew out in the blast. In Falluja Paul lost count of how many people he had killed in Iraq, and Greg died in his arms, bleeding to death from wounds in his abdomen and legs. "You pray for me," Greg said, as his face turned ashen and the blood poured out of the tourniquet Paul had applied to his leg.

"Stop that, you're going to live," Paul said.

"No, you stop. Listen. God likes you."

"What?"

"You're first into every fight, you never get hit. I've watched it over and over. And you talk to Him every night. So I want you to pray for me." The effort of all this speech had exhausted Greg, and he was losing consciousness from loss of blood. "Put in a good word," he said and died.

Paul put in that good word, many times, and every time he did, he saw Greg's face again, pale and silent and gone from this world.

After that, Paul wanted to be out of the army. He put up with the grime, the bad food, the heavy loads, the heat, the hatred of many Iraqis – all of it without complaining. But he counted the days. The deaths of Kevin, Harry and Luis ground him down, just as the news of Monica's suicide filled him with misery but no surprise. She had approached him to try to talk Kevin out of volunteering, and at that time, he had had a keen premonition that if Kevin did not make it, she would not either. Recalling the clarity of the feeling, it seemed to have been more than a warning; it had been a prophecy.

When he heard of Sherwin's wounds, he promised himself that the first thing he would do upon returning would be to visit him. He approved of Sherwin's application to Johns Hopkins and his new ambition to go to medical school. For some reason he could not pinpoint, it came to him repeatedly that if their friend Luis had known of this, he would have been pleased. He also resolved to live up to his role as godfather to Luis' son, to visit the boy regularly, to take him out to the Chesapeake when he got older and show him the little beaches that used to hold such marvelous troves of fossils, that held some still. He would show him how to take apart a computer and put it back together, and he would take him and Harry's younger brothers and Benjie to Six Flags to ride the roller coasters on Saturdays. He had many plans.

On a late autumn afternoon, he rang the doorbell of the Goodmans' large, attractive but not showy house.

"The hero returns," Stella cried, and threw her arms around him.

"Hardly a hero."

"What do *you* know?" She asked and then, as she wiped away tears, "at least you're alive, and in one piece. Oh, it's terrible about Harry and Kevin and Luis. Those poor boys. And their families. Only God can fathom how they survive."

"Not all of them did."

"No. There was Monica," Stella dried her eyes. "But I don't want to depress you. You're here. You made it. And that's great."

"How's Sherwin?"

"Pretty good." She walked with Paul into the dining room, and they looked through the picture window out to the pool, where Sherwin sat in a wheelchair, reading. "He keeps his spirits up," she said. "But the truth is, it's a little lonely."

"That's why I'm here," Paul said. "And while I'll keep being here often. Forever."

He ambled out back by the pool. It was early November, but it was unseasonably warm. Leaves – red, yellow, orange – covered the grass. A few still hung on the stark branches that poked sharply at the sky like skeletons. The pool had not been completely drained. Leaves clotted the bit of water that remained. Though it was warm, Sherwin sat with a light blanket over his legs and was so absorbed in his book that he did not at first notice his friend's approach.

"Nice to be able to do that without some sergeant telling you to get up and risk your neck to go chase some sniper," Paul said.

Sherwin chuckled as they shook hands. Paul inquired about his book and learned it was a history of World War II, that Sherwin had read everything he could find on any war – Vietnam, Korea, World War I or II, the Civil War, even the Napoleonic Wars. "Morbid curiosity, I guess,"

Sherwin explained, "trying to comprehend the disease that injured me and killed three of my friends. You know, the other day, I went with my mother to Whole Foods. While she shopped, I got a coffee and waited, in my wheelchair, in that little restaurant area they have. I watched the people hurrying this way and that, trying not to look at me, and I didn't know what to make of them. I must have looked bewildered, because, get this, there was another veteran in a wheelchair and he rolled up to me and said 'welcome home from Iraq, dude.' We exchanged information about our platoons and experiences and he told me he had been home for eight months – 'and I still keep expecting my legs to grow back.' Just like that, he said the unsayable, the thing I wake up every morning thinking, with the idea that 'oh, I'll just walk over to the dresser.' I'm not asking for pity. I went into this with my eyes open. But it's still kind of a shock to realize, I'll never just hang out in a place like that, like Whole Foods or Starbucks again, because I don't like being a living reminder of another war this country got into by mistake."

"That's why all the books, I guess."

"Mostly Vietnam, the first big mistake, and World War II, which we should have got into sooner."

"I made a really good friend in Iraq," Paul said. "He was Italian, like me. He got shot right next to me, and I tried to bandage his wounds, but it was no good, he died asking me to pray for him, as if I was somebody unique, as if my requests would be granted, I don't know, special attention. I guess he was wandering in his mind, but I did what he asked. I don't know if it helped him, but it helped me. After he died, I said 'I have got to get out of this war.' I was counting the days. And you know what – they let us go when our tour was over, no extensions."

"So you're thinking maybe up in heaven He intervened for you."

"It had crossed my mind."

"You haven't changed a bit. All that bloodshed and still as religious as the day you signed up. I bet the first thing you did when you got home was hurry over to your Catholic Church and confess to having shot God knows how many Iraqis."

"You may mock –"

"Geez Paul, I'd have thought seeing all those people dead and wounded – look at me – would have convinced you that if God is somewhere, anywhere, he could care less what happens to us."

"This war was our own doing. A human creation. Another human error. God is where He's supposed to be, doing exactly what He's supposed to do. You can't blame this war on Him, or use it to discredit Him. Your argument won't hold water."

"Whoa Pauli," Sherwin laughed. "It's me, Sherwin, remember? I'm the one who only knows that he doesn't know. You're not debating some dogmatic atheist like Jones. I just wondered if your faith had wavered."

"Not one iota."

"You still talk to God?"

Paul smiled. Sherwin had caught him once, at the Lirano's house, asking for divine guidance. "From time to time."

"What's He say?"

"He says we're a sorry lot, Sherwin. And we need a lot of help."

"C'mon, you don't need God to tell you that. One trip to Southeast D.C. or Iraq or Baltimore would do the trick. I was up in the neighborhood by Johns Hopkins the other day. It's not exactly a garden spot. I'm going to live at home and commute, starting in January. Say, how's Megan?"

Things had not lasted with Megan. Paul had been gone a mere matter of months, but that apparently had been too much for her, as he had accurately feared. She had met a player on the Maryland basketball team, a Terp, a star on campus and a business major like her. She had told herself that she had not intended this to happen, that Keith had pursued her, not the other way around, that she could not be held responsible for falling head over heels in love. She had also found Paul's outpourings in his letters to her a little inappropriate, embarrassing almost, and his vivid descriptions of death and dying made her uncomfortable. Who was this Greg Agnelli, after all? Yes it was terrible that he had been killed, that Paul had been unable to save him, but wasn't that what happened in war? Why, after all, had Paul signed up? Didn't he know it would be like this? What had he been thinking? Such questions rotated through her mind, adding to a sense first of irritation, later of injury, a feeling that masked the unhappy truth that was the only thing that mattered, namely, that she no longer loved him.

She had mentioned none of this in her regular and frequent letters. She had, instead, kept up a cheerful patter about the weather, her classes, her friends, family and her workouts. Megan was a firm believer in much physical exercise and went to the gym religiously. From her letters Paul learned how many crunches she did, how long she jogged on the treadmill, how much weight she could lift. After a while he formed the impression that he was engaged to a minor league athlete, who spent her days warming up and showering down, whose goal in life was to attend a high-impact aerobics class every day and to burn more calories than she consumed. Amid the chaos, heat, work, sweat and carnage of Iraq, it was rather perplexing. But he was glad she wrote regularly and would have accepted descriptions of navel gazing happily – anything just to know she thought of him, that, if only in some corner of her mind, he was still a part of her life.

When he arrived home and called her, however, he got a most ominous reception.

"We have to talk," Megan had said, almost at once.

So they met in an Italian restaurant that he liked just off campus. The owner knew him and loved to greet him in Italian, then announced, "It's Paolo Lirano," to whomever happened to be standing nearby.

Actually, on the warm November afternoon of their meeting, Megan was twenty minutes late, another inauspicious sign. As he sat at the table, looking at his watch, Paul began to think of the future without her – he was just testing the emotional waters, he told himself. He found it a loss, but one that he would survive.

Such reason flew right out of his head when he saw her, however. She entered in a flurry of light, white cotton summer clothes, blond hair and perfume. She avoided kissing him on the mouth, instead bestowing a peck on the cheek. She was not, he noticed, wearing his engagement ring.

"So you're back," she said, sitting opposite. "It was more than a little nerve wracking, having you over there, in a war."

"Believe me, it was nerve wracking being there."

Megan burst into tears. Paul took her hands, comforting with "Shh, shh, it's over. I'm back. I'll be back in school in January."

"It's not that, or not all that," she sniffled. "I didn't hold up too well."

"What – you're on prozac?"

They both laughed. Then Megan dried her eyes. "Paul, I have to break off our engagement."

Paul sat quietly and sipped his Pellegrino. At the other end of the restaurant, the owner said to a waiter in Italian: "He comes home from the war, a hero for Christsakes, and there she is, dumping him, first thing."

"How can you tell?"

"Take a look."

There was a surprised, sad, worried expression on Paul's even features. "Why?" He asked, after a moment.

"I realized it when we were exchanging letters. We're not right for each other."

"You found somebody else."

The truth of his observation was evident on her face. Flushing pink, Megan took the little box her engagement ring had come in, out of her purse. "I have to return this," she said.

"You've absolutely made up your mind," he neither said it nor asked it. She looked at him wonderingly.

"Of course, Paul. Do you think I would subject you to this, if I hadn't? I feel terrible."

"You feel terrible."

"I know you're entitled to feel worse, but I still feel awful."

"Then why are you doing this?"

"Paul, if I couldn't last a few months while you were in a war...what's it worth? What kind of wife am I going to be for you?"

"This really isn't about what kind of wife you'll be for me. It's what kind of wife you'll be for him."

"Who says I'll marry him?"

"I do."

"You may be right."

Paul opened the box and looked at the ring.

"When did this happen?" He asked.

"It started in May."

"And you never mentioned it in your letters. While I was getting shot at in Falluja and waiting, holding my breath for every communication from you, you were falling in love with somebody else?"

"I know it sounds horrible."

"You're darn right about that."

"The important thing is you survived."

Paul ran his fingers through his dark brown hair, then pushed his chair back and surveyed her. Whoever she had fallen for was lucky, he started to think. "Not that lucky," said a voice inside him, and, as he thought it over, considered the flimsiness of her love for him, he began to feel that she was a rather foolish person, shallow, superficial – she was silly, and she could not help it. He laughed, which offended her.

"Don't get upset," he said, his hand closing over the little box with the ring. "I guess we were both idiots." He pocketed the box, rose and approached the cash register to pay. As he walked to the exit, she turned to watch him. She looked surprised, uncomprehending and miffed. He waved and left the restaurant.

"You forget about that floozy," Angelo said that night after dinner. "I knew when I met her parents it would never work out. Two lamebrains, the both of them. Besides they both use Ivory soap, and everybody knows that's bad for your skin."

Paul raised his shoulders and held out his hands, palms up. "My fiancé drops me like a hot potato, and all you can think about is Ivory soap?"

"It was an important detail, Pauli," Angelo rose and cleared their dishes. "Life is in the details. Myself," he continued, returning from the kitchen sink, "I thank God you're back. I've been on pins and needles for eighteen months. Mostly pins."

"I'm not even going to ask," Paul began.

"I couldn't sleep. I took medicine. I kept imagining you blown up by some IED or shot by some insurgent. I had a hard time concentrating on the business. Fortunately your friend Jones has been working part-time, and he seemed to understand what I was going through. He kept me focused. But when he wasn't there, I'd just sit in the back room and look at all the computer parts and think, 'What is this worth? It's worth nothing next to my son.' And then I'd start to worry again." Angelo came over and hugged his son. Suddenly there were tears in his eyes. "Don't you dare, ever, ever, do something like that again. I'm proud that you're a hero, that you got honors and medals. But don't you dare...ever."

That evening Paul stayed up late, writing a long email to Animal, his last friend still in the war. He had resolved to email him every day, and when he paused in the midst of his writing and pictured his friend, hot, dirty, his thatch of blond hair damp with sweat, his tall frame a little stooped from his heavy load, far away, half way across the globe, in a country where people were trying to kill him, in a city he could not wait to leave, he said to himself, "No, make that two emails every day."

Animal had come to depend on these missives. He and Edgar had the privilege of using one of the officer's laptops in the evenings. He also sent many letters by mail. Aside from his family, Paul was his most faithful correspondent.

"You're better off without someone like Megan," he wrote back. "If she couldn't stand a little separation, how long would it have lasted? Better to find out before you got married." He also wrote Paul about

how excited he had initially been finally to be in Mesopotamia. They had
had history together, and Paul well remembered Animal's report on the
topic. Yes, Animal depended on Paul, as did Sherwin, Angelo, Chandra
and even Jones, on his loyalty, on the sense he conveyed that there was
something special about them. "You have your doubts," he had written
to Animal, months back, informing him of Luis' death. "But I don't. At
the very least, long after we are gone, God will remember us, every single
one of us, everything about us, and everything we cared about. He will
never forget. And I believe Luis is with him now."

Animal had contemplated the news of Luis' death. Then he looked
up and said to Edgar: "Three of my seven friends are dead in Iraq. Harry,
Kevin and Luis. I guess I'm next."

About the Author

Eve Ottenberg has published three novels, *The Unblemished Darlings*, a comedy about a group of bumblers with a get-rich-quick scheme, *Glum and Mighty Pagans*, a comedy about real estate in New York City and *The Widow's Opera*, a dark novel about murder and betrayal set in Manhattan in the 1950s. She has given a reading from *Glum and Mighty Pagans* at the invitation of PEN. She has written another two novels, as yet unpublished and a book-length collection of short stories. She has written a weekly column, "Hard Times" for *The Village Voice*, about the politics of housing in Manhattan. She also covered the criminal courts for *The Village Voice*. Her book reviews have appeared in *The New York Times*, *Vanity Fair*, *The Baltimore Sun*, *The Philadelphia Inquirer*, *USA Today*, *The Cleveland Plain Dealer*, *The Nation*, *The New Yorker's* "In Brief" section, *The Washington Post*, *The Washington City Paper* and many other venues. She has published articles in *The New York Times Magazine*, *Vogue*, *Elle*, *Working Mother* and other magazines and newspapers and has worked as an editor at several publications. She has a bachelor's and a master's degree from the University of Chicago and an M.L.S. from the University of Maryland. She is married, has three children and resides in Maryland, where she is a school library media specialist.